A CANDLE

TO LIGHT THE SUN

A CANDLE
TO LIGHT THE SUN

a novel by

PATRICIA BLONDAL

McClelland and Stewart Limited

DESIGN : Keith Scott, MTDC

PRINTED AND BOUND BY
HAZELL WATSON AND VINEY LTD
AYLESBURY AND SLOUGH, ENGLAND

TO MY CHILDREN

Stephanie and John

A CANDLE

TO LIGHT THE SUN

·

A CANDLE TO LIGHT THE SUN

The horses slept in the stables, the dogs in the yard, the pigeons on the housetop, and the flies on the walls. Even the fire on the hearth left off blazing and went to sleep. Everything stood still.

That's the way it was. The long open-eyed sleep.

Although more than twenty years dead, it lives still in the remembering twilight behind our eyes. There's thirst a man can't slake.

1936. Mouse Bluffs hesitated and slowly drew up the out-rolled hope, paused and called in the future so that it might not be scorched by the incessant sun, its eyes destroyed by the drifting sifting soil, called in the future to hide behind the wet rags hung against the door frame so that it might not be blown to nowhere with the dry brown tumbleweeds.

Wait. The quality of waiting was virtue in plain men. God made no promises. The land must be thought upon, not watched. Men whose fathers had followed the slow feet of Sir Richard

Rashleigh's oxen knew that Mouse Bluffs was not expected to prevail; none of the quick hot dreams of wealth had ever come to Mouse Bluffs; God expected only that it endure.

The town does not grow. Or diminish. It is a bare seventy-five years old, yet there is a permanence about it.

The river bends wide to the bluffs. Below Crescent Avenue the valley spears a cleft of green for perhaps a mile through the prairie. When the wind blows and the dust heaves and twists with maniacal persistence, when the women wet rags and sheets to cover doors and windows, sit listening to the wind tearing the topsoil from the farms, forking it against the town, when the sky is pasty-grim with lost farms, the eyes gritted and rimmed with lost farms, and famine is the wind's brother, even then you can cross Crescent to the rim of the valley, go down the one hundred and eight wooden steps, cross the meadow and stand beneath the great oaks, smell the air sweet and green, hear the wind only distantly, its monotonous hunger eased by the tremble of the creek as it joins the river. Officially the valley is called Alexandra Park but the town calls it only the valley or park; a named park connotes care, lawnmowers. God made the valley, the oaks, and on the other side of the river the bluffs where the trees are smaller, bared to the wind but strong and knobbed with holding the low cliff against the prairie, the wind, the river.

1936. The wind blows the promises thin, the fears in. Against the time the oaks stand. When fall comes and crops are bad, the acorns under the oaks are so thick walking there is difficult. The leaves turn to blood and gold, go down to cover and nurture the acorns for the year to come. The town knows there is a harvest.

In winter the valley is rich with snow. Children toboggan down from Crescent Avenue to play in the white bells and banks, away from the wind that howls along the Crescent, down the ribs of Main Street and across the prairie, as if struggling to wrench away the snow and begin its feeding on the land again.

How thin we were upon the land. 1936. How untouching we were, with all the miles between us, the thin fine soil in the air between us. How thin the land made us, parching our lips, stretching fine the bones to unmuscled waiting. How it paid us out, whose fathers had made the land thin. Our sins stood thick upon the thinness of our worth, thick between us and the low red sun.

BOOK I

CHAPTER **I**

"Boy! Here," the old man called and waited. "The King is dead."

For a moment the hand sleigh made sharp whistling noises against the sheath of snow on the sidewalk. Snow, salt-fine, precursor of a storm, sifted a pale bloom against the street lamp at the mouth of the swinging bridge. The boy looked up at the man standing on the steps of the old house. The first house in the town. Old and big and solid as the old man. The door moved gently in the cold wind. The light from the hall cast a thin wash of white over the veranda, glinted on the snow that was already piling behind the screens.

"Boy?"

"Yes, sir." David's voice stumbled, afraid the old man might say it again.

Gavin Ross sat slowly on the steps. "Come here."

David drew his sleigh up the footpath and stopped at the foot of the steps. Beyond the angle of Gavin Ross's shoulder he could see the tapestries in the hall behind the open door, a door normally never open longer than the fraction of time it took the visitor or messenger to scurry through, couriers over a barricade in the winter-long war against drafts.

The open door, the swaying tapestries collecting the cold air and the silence. Silence and the hot wonderful knowledge that at last Gavin Ross had singled him out—they came over the boy's mind simultaneously, like fire and ice. He had imagined this moment often but never like this, these terrible words. The whistle on the power station down Main Street cried plaintively into the night.

"The King is dead."

A boy stands in a bucket of syrup, waiting for someone to free him, reach out and touch his hand and release him, waits and waits, watches with apprehension the adults, not wanting to go, yet aching for someone to show him how, free his way, afraid to leave for the larger place, afraid of the night, the bleak unhappy old faces. The King is dead and it is done. In his mind he had a sense of things falling away, the entire town peeling off into the black prairie wastes, leaving him and the doctor alone, still looking at each other but not seeing old man and boy, familiar parts of the town's body, not seeing as before, parts of the King now.

Tears swelled into David's eyes. The King was dead. They were depleted together.

"You're Arthur Newman's boy."

"What will happen to us?"

Ross, his hands hanging limply between his knees, did not answer at once. He reached into his coat pocket.

"What I wanted . . . Take this—David?—and go to the Prince Albert, tell Charlie Jaques to give it to my brother."

David pulled off his mitt, took the note. Pleasure rolled up through his chest so strongly he could not stay his smile.

To curb his joy against the disaster, he said again, "What'll happen?" and, as he said it, the loss and loneliness returned like the cry of the power-station whistle, plaintive but inarticulate. Without questioning it, he knew he felt exactly as the doctor felt. It was his first shared adult emotion and he wanted to stay, prolong the sharing, while at the same time his feet ached to carry the enormous news to the whole town, to run from door to door and shout the shock into each ear.

"The Prince of Wales is king."

"Already?"

"Takes getting used to. Go along now."

"Can I leave my sleigh here?"

The doctor looked down at the sleigh. The *Family Herald* and the *Illustrated London News* wrapped in a sack already covered with snow.

"Dad's papers."

14

"Best take it along. You'll want to cut along home straight away. Your father . . ." has no radio ". . . will want to know."

"I can go faster to the hotel."

"Leave it, then."

He did not know whether to run with the King dead. It seemed irreverent, so he walked very quickly, straining against the speed in his legs. When he got to the corner of Main, he bolted up the street, puffing an urgent stream of white into the snow.

From the window of his store at the other end of town Jacob Herson watched the beginning of the storm. January and night and snow in the end of the world. The stubby red brick outline of the railway station slid away. The thin line of lights that trimmed the tracks leading to the roundhouse puffed helplessly into the black wind.

"A blizzard," he said.

One of the men behind him grunted.

Brace Harvey, Herb Henderson, Lippy Jones were sitting on the wire chairs by the Quebec heater, sharing a bottle of stone ginger back and forth, in their overalls, mackinaws unbuttoned, caps pushed back. It was an accolade that they came at all, for Jacob had been only six months in town, one of a long line of Jews who had held the grocery store back of the depot. He would not stay, would never join the town or be asked to do the impossible. He had come to make a stake. The town was willing enough to provide this, for his was the first store in Mouse Bluffs to offer competitive prices. Before Jacob there'd been five grocery stores, the prices the same in each; Jacob had refused to join the club. And though these men accepted the other merchants at church, lodge, socials, where Jacob would not and could not go, they would not have felt comfortable sharing the fire of people they knew were cheating them.

Jacob touched the pipe in his pocket, looked at the clock. He wondered if he should light up, lean over the meat-block as he sometimes did, talk to the men. He did not like them but he was lonely; his dislike, hatreds of the past months fingered through his mind in an unreal fashion. It was always like this. His hate was only big when he was alone, an ulcer bred of loneliness and silence.

He touched the switch on the radio.

Brace Harvey said, "A little music, Jacob?" and the men looked at one another with sly smiles.

It was considered quite eccentric, that radio of Jacob's, a city trick.

"Mark, he's got plenty of money, that one," Julia Harvey had said when she heard of the radio. "He's just here to get every nickel he can."

"He lives there," Brace had reasoned mildly. "Open fourteen hours a day. He lives there."

"Every cent. A radio!"

"Maybe you'd market up at Seldon's again?"

"Every stray in town'll be sitting there listening to it, watching when I go for my order."

"Phone."

It was six months past. The radio remained. The joke remained. The strange wantonness in Jacob's placing a radio in his store still gave pleasure.

"Know what?" Lippy asked. "My dog can't stand it. Any time he hears a radio he just goes stark crazy."

"Funny," Herb Henderson murmured.

Each time the radio went on Lippy told them.

The radio warmed; the news came, the broadcaster in Winnipeg quite overcome. For a long moment the men remained transfixed. Then Brace Harvey got to his feet, buttoned his jacket, nodded to Jacob without meeting his eyes, went out. Herb Henderson rose.

"Terrible," Jacob said. "I didn't know he was so old."

The men paused in the doorway. Lippy hesitated.

"What a terrible night to die," he said.

Herb looked back at Jacob as if to speak, shrugged up his coat collar and went out. As the door fanned the night, Jacob heard the way-freight cry frostily of cruel loss and sudden loneliness. He switched the radio off, looked at the clock, began to put on the cheese covers.

He spoke aloud as he often did alone in the store. "Such a terrible thing! Why?" Vaguely he remembered hearing that Brace Harvey had been decorated or had met the King or something. "So why?"

Hatred sprang moist and bitter in his throat for his own loneliness and for these others who accepted, who made the world. He ached for his people in Winnipeg, for the forms and symbols he understood, for the old moral indignations against those who hated everything that was different, for the time before hatred had begun to leak into his own mind.

Is it more just to hate a great number than it is to hate a small number? Has hatred justice?

He smacked the cat off the counter. "No ambition! Nothing. No idea of anything better than this hell-hole." The idea plucked at his brain that they had no ambition because they had arrived. For them, to be as they were, to live in Mouse Bluffs, was quite enough of destiny; they did not hate.

"It's not enough," he said grimly and went to lock the door.

There would be no late customers.

There was a big clock, bigger than the one in the hall at the low school, an astonishingly big plant growing out of a brass-bound bucket, at least a dozen chairs, two chesterfields, several fine cuspidors. David had passed the white brick hotel many times. It had never occurred to him that one day he might go inside. Surprisingly the shades were only half drawn. The night and the storm glistened against the tall thin windows. The lobby was very warm and it smelled of cigar smoke, the faint pungent odor of beer. He had not been prepared for its elegance.

Charlie Jaques behind the high desk was doing a crossword puzzle in an old paper. He looked up as the door opened, stopped thinking about printers' measures, bristled as the boy crossed towards him. It was a scene he hated, the kids coming to get the men.

"What is it, boy?"

"A message."

It was always a message. "What message?" Always urgent. The result never nice.

"For Mr. Ross."

The boy passed him the note. A thin shabby snot-nosed kid. Jaques had seen him around. A leather aviator helmet, hand-me-down-looking jacket, breeches, moccasins. This one at least had proper mitts. Jaques unfolded the note.

"From Dr. Ross. It's for Mr. Ross!"

Jaques ignored him, read the note. He looked up.

"Wait here," he said, not seeing or caring about the boy's indignation.

To the left of the desk a swinging door opened into the beer parlor. Jaques looked through the glass, spotted Ian Ross, pushed open the door. Very quickly David glanced through the deserted lobby, went after him. He pushed the door open a few inches. A small room, not as big as the lobby. A bar ran across the far end. No more than a dozen men sat drinking at the tables, most of them in their coats, talking moderately, yet David was aware of a feeling almost of silence, as if the things said here were of a different pitch from the things heard elsewhere. He saw Jaques go to the bar, speak to the man with his hand on the tap, then turn and walk to Ian Ross.

The bartender went slowly down the counter, collecting empty glasses and shaking his head. Change enveloped the room like a sigh going up. The silence vanished. Ian Ross held the note in his long waxy fingers and, as he read, raised a hand to Jaques. The latter took the back bar of the wheel-chair and began to steer it out, threading through the tables just as the word fell over them and the men began to stir and button their coats.

The boy was standing at the desk looking guilty. Jaques's eyes raked the counter suspiciously.

"David?"

Ian Ross beckoned to him as Jaques pushed the chair through the lobby. David held the door while Ian pushed the storm door and Jaques lowered the chair down the steps, bumped it heavily to the street.

"It's easier the other way, Charlie."

"Lazy man takes the lazy way, not the easy way." The door slammed, cutting off Jacques's g'night.

It was snowing heavily. The single bulb on its iron question mark above George Lee's restaurant gave the only indication of life on Main Street. At the hotel hitching-rail a team of horses stood dismally, the buckboard creased and dusted with snow. Ian Ross sniffed, pulled the lugs of his tweed cap over his ears.

David rubbed his nose with his mitts. The rise to the corner of the Crescent was not steep, scarcely a hill at all, but Ross didn't push his own chair if he could help it. Generally he waited on the street outside the hotel till someone came by. Men could scarcely pass without offering. Boys he asked, gave a nickel to, spoke strangely to. Women never walked past the hotel.

"Will you push us up the hill, David?"

As David pushed, Ian began to sing in Gaelic, a harrowing drift of strange words in minor key, and the boy knew he was very drunk, felt a bit sorry, a bit fearful, as everyone did about Ian Ross.

Suddenly Ross cried softly into the wind, "Will ye no come back again?" and was quiet.

"There's the Prince," David said.

Ross exploded, flung up a storm of words against the night, a passion of articulation for the indifferent town. "Can you hear it, lad, rolling over the town? An era is dying, dying, rolling off the silver screen at the Wonderland and oh yes there's the Prince, always the Prince. Rarely in a man's life. Hear? Sublime moments? Three times? Loss and gaining. A pooling of many—millions of minds in loss, thought of loss. Y'see. Break. Break in common spirit. Till yes—yes, tonight there's not a soul alive in all Mouse Bluffs, tonight we all live in Empire. Hear the wind blow, boy, hear the wind blow. The great break. Cessation of personification. Oh the words! Cessation of . . . Hear the words, thunder in . . . A paradox, David, death of the symbol emphasizes the meaning of the symbol."

David shivered as the wind sliced through his jacket. From the corner he could see along the Crescent and rested a moment. No one. Back down the little hill the men, dark bundles in the tormented white wastes, were emerging by ones and twos from the hotel, moving down the street, across the street, carrying the news to their homes.

Ross watched the men and talked while the boy caught his breath.

David knew his father would be wondering what kept him so long. In his throat came murmuring, "Don't let him be mad." He realized that Ross still talked but he could make no sense of it, so turned left to where the doctor's house gloomed beside the mouth of the bridge.

". . . fed a man to an abstraction, peeled away his flesh and made him more than flesh. Long live King. There's theory. In fact . . . in fact! . . . a great break and a remembering and a knowing that all these millions can come together in such loss, be sad for wondering how we made him yes better than a man in his abstraction, a man incidentally if he chose but we . . . we never chose to see him a man; expected more and secretly knew, yes knew each of us that here in this muck-hole, this survival world, he was the cream, finest and best, grade A rust-proof heap-topper and his seed forever. As we made him so he made us. Whatever he was we were better through him. Oneness. Something else. Ay, always something else! Coming together in loss we change. War?" He cried contempt to the wind. "There's always war. God? There's always God. A King dies only once. Let the small print thunder. Hark to Mouse Bluffs. We are the kingdom and the King is dead. All we have is the best the world has ever seen; he was the best of the best. Mourn. Shared. Were subjects. Better than any of us and the best in all of us, a man . . . hear? . . . we never cared much about that because he was our King . . ."

David pushed the chair up the walk to the doctor's house. His arms trembled. Another hour, he knew, and the doctor would have had to send his driver, Billy Treleven, with the horse and sleigh. His hand sleigh was where he had left it; the increasing wind had blown the snow from the sack.

"You hear me, David? Tomorrow a republican. Dear brother come home my boy your dear old monarch's gone. Drape the manor in crepe. Purple and black. What a sobering damned night this is."

The boy knew he could not push the chair up the ramp at the side of the porch. Don't let him be mad. He ran up the steps and pulled the bell. The doctor came out and went directly to the chair without looking into his brother's upturned face. The snow blew against his hair, caught in the lapels of his coat.

"Gavin, good evening, a sad bad night."

David picked up the cord on his sleigh.

"Newman, you'd better come in and warm up before you cross town," the doctor said.

Newman. A word to a man. "No, sir, I'll have to get right home." Don't let him be mad.

Something in his voice came through to the doctor. "I'll make it up to you."

Ian said, "Give him two bits. Four bits. Appreciate in concrete." He fumbled in his coat pocket.

David drew back. "No."

"Delicacy? You win, David. This is not an occasion to surrender the favor."

The wind moaned through the timbers under the bridge. David was watching Gavin Ross. How strange his face looked, all shadows and hollows in the false light of the snow. Silently the boy waited. There must be more, he knew. The face smiled suddenly, briefly.

"Come and see me, David," the doctor said.

He took the chair and rolled it up the ramp as the boy began to run, pulling his sleigh with frantic haste through the storm.

"I shall speak to Dr. Ross. It's too bad of him to send an eleven-year-old boy into that place," Muriel Newman shouted at her husband in a voice not meant for shouting.

Rather tall, her dark blond hair well filled with gray, her smooth features classically English, the nose a trifle large, the cheeks overlaid with a bright flush, she had large light blue eyes that gave her the appearance of staring, as if she were in a constant state of stunned surprise. She was thin. She did not eat enough. There was not enough to eat. Sometimes she thought of her stomach with a kind of vague pleasure and fancied it about the size of a lemon, shrunken, doing the same job as larger stomachs, extracting every single atom of nourishment from what she gave it, no waste, the most efficient stomach in Mouse Bluffs.

"It's all right," Arthur said. He sat at the kitchen table, his papers before him on the pocked oilcloth.

"It is not all right!"

Arthur cupped his hand behind his ear, as he always did when it was her turn to talk. David ate his bread and milk in silence, wanted more sugar but feared drawing attention to himself. Arthur's hand on the oilcloth made little scratching motions. He often made noises, queer annoying little sounds that he himself could not hear.

"He could have gone himself!" his mother cried.

"No. It wouldn't be right."

"Why not? When it was so important. But to send a boy!"

Arthur thundered, "He's a gentleman."

"A gentleman." His mother sighed, turned away. "Yes, Ian Ross is a gentleman too. A fine gentleman that." How cruelly Arthur restricted ladies and gentlemen. She smoothed her hair with damp hands and the old muddle of thoughts congregated: home, where a gentleman might enter a public house, Arthur, who was not a gentleman but a good man anyway, hard but good, how she had lost some nebulous place in marrying him, yet gained another place, all the things which daily, hourly, tumbled through her head and which were never sifted, never examined, just came and lumped in her mind with a life of their own. "I shall speak to him," she said in a normal voice, knowing Arthur could not hear.

"Please," David said, joining her in the little world they could sometimes make under Arthur's deafness. "He was waiting for me. He was, Mother. And he said . . ."

"I've no doubt," she said, missing his meaning as she missed so many meanings, almost as if, he sometimes thought, she wanted to miss them. Needed to.

"They'll be standing outside the palace," Arthur said and looked at David significantly, propounding a lesson.

"Why?"

"Why!" Arthur's fingers drummed.

"Finish up and go along to bed, David."

"Bring me my box," Arthur ordered.

Muriel motioned David to sit still, went herself to the cold parlor and returned with the box, gravely placed it on the table. She took David's plate and glass to the sink, pumped water over them. David watched Arthur take out his key and unlock the box. Behind him the brown cupboards, their glass doors lined with intricately patterned oiled paper. The lamp flickered. The boy looked apprehensively at the amount of oil in it.

"You want wood?" he asked his mother.

"She got it herself," Arthur said sternly.

David colored. How much did Arthur hear? Often he did this, caught some commonplace from the world of David and his mother.

Now the pincushion Arthur had made from remnants of an old uniform while a prisoner of the Boers, a regimental button stitched to the top, the scarlet wool long faded to a dull plum shade; a plate Arthur's great grandfather had carried at Waterloo, a mess tin, pay book, black pocket-sized New Testament. Tonight they would all come out, right down to the chevrons and crown. All the weary musty treasures, perhaps even the medals, bright in their little boxes, the ribbons getting a bit soiled. And at length the stories, the blood, the glory, the disease, the brave, brave men of long ago. David cupped his chin on his palm and steadied to listen. His mother watched, her surprised eyes sad.

"The boy should be in bed."

Arthur did not answer, so she nodded to David. He got his candle and lit it at the lamp, went to the little door between the cabinets.

"Good night, sir. Mother."

"Good night, son," she replied, but Arthur, his bald head bent over the box, the skin of his face and head stretched brown and tight by remembered foreign suns, did not speak.

David's room was very cold. A cupboard of a room. The entire cottage was heated by the kitchen stove. In the parlor there was a small heater, never lighted except when his mother had ladies or the minister to call, hardly ever. He put the candle on the dresser beside his bed, pulled the blind, took his pyjamas from under the pillow, unlaced his moccasins and blew out the candle, got into bed to undress. The wrapped bricks his mother had put there were no longer warm. He wondered if school would close. It seemed likely. The wind howled. He knew the snow would be coming in around his window, that his mother would look at it in the morning and say, "I must get Arthur to calk that window," but she never did and David puzzled always about how one cocked a window. He could hear them talking in the kitchen, the loud rumbling voice, the high clear patient one. ". . . Prentice . . ." Private Dennis Prentice had been flogged for stealing bread from the officers' mess long long ago when history was being made.

Barker-Johns, corporal, had been lashed to a gun carriage for insubordination nearly twenty long long years ago. Who runs the British army? Sergeant Majors. Who made this Empire? Sergeant Majors. The brave hard Sergeant Majors. The glorious Sergeant Majors. Sitting in the quiet kitchen with the wind shrilling a counterpoint, the Sergeant Major ran his fingers over artefacts of glory and talked away the night, wasting coal-oil, wasting wood.

David thought again of the tapestries stirring gently against the wall of the big house and a powerful regret overcame him that he had not gone to warm his hands against their strange luxury. The hotel with its incredible amount of furniture, lights, the big staircase leading to an untold number of fine rooms. He lay with his eyes closed and watched all these things in the sliding ball of light against his eyelids. It grew smaller. He opened his eyes, tried to focus, capture it. If he looked a bit above it, the globe caught a moment, then began to slide again. He felt very sad, wanting to cry, to smile. He thought of the dead King, of bursting through the door, late, the papers clutched in his arms, and seeing, as he did so, Arthur's expected hand reach for the dog-whip lying on the table before him. "The King is dead!" and Arthur's hand fell away. There would have been time to go into the big house. His news had erased his crime. A Sergeant Major does not dog-whip a boy while a King lies dead. He almost wept. He had waited for this so long and had missed it. Next time, though. He saw again, enclosed in light against his eyelids, the doctor's strong old shadowed face. Come and see me, David. Next time he would go in, straight in, and Gavin Ross would say . . . He could not make the doctor's words but there would be words, words David had wanted for a long time.

He reached into the shallow bowl of his past and drew it out. Memory not quite memory. More like a shiny well-fingered ribbon now. They were walking together, his mother and he. It might have been their first walk in Mouse Bluffs; he wasn't sure. Fall and the whisper of scuffed leaves, his mother's hand. And his mother's voice talking, talking, talking. She talked more then, more fully, perhaps not less vaguely, though; it seemed to him that even then she had always been trying to keep things from being said. She was talking about the Old Country in a ripple of words of loneliness. She held it in her heart and he must hold it too, against the lone wind of the prairie sweeping the cottage, against Mouse Bluffs, against—yes, against the dog-whip of the Sergeant Major. That, he was sure, was the thing she was trying not to say. "He's a good man, David; yes, hard but good, a good father to you—it's just . . ." Then more about the Old Country and the house where she had lived with her family, and back again to Arthur who was such a good man, it was just that his ways were a little ... She didn't want to diminish him, but David must remember that there were other ... And all the while David's hand smarting in her hand and the tears just salty dry on his cheeks. They came to the big house, which was somewhat, she told him, like an Old Country house. Not, of course, quite. Not old enough. But it had been built by a man who had wanted to bring the old ways, old places. David looked up at its grandeur, its proud stance above the valley, but his hand hurt so and he was so full of hate for Arthur Newman, who was not, he knew, however often she said it, his father, that he could scarcely hear the gentle drift of words. He was to think of the house, she said, think of its being here, keep it as a secret, a promise of other... And then the door of the great house flung open, the tapestries in the hall swung and swelled in a gust of wind, and a tall old man sprang down the steps. Greeted his mother. Stopped to speak. "This is my boy David," his mother said as she'd said it so recently on another street to another man. And David knew. Knew what the secret was, what she'd been telling him without words.

He'd sometimes wondered if the doctor knew or if it were secret too from him. He needn't wonder now. I'll make it up to you, he'd said.

David pushed his clothes out of bed with his feet, stretched his toes towards the lukewarm bricks. How wildly Ian Ross talked, great proud words knifing into the storm. Death of the symbol emphasizes the meaning of the symbol. Rarely in a man's life. A king dies only once. Would he ever grow to understand such words?

Gavin. What a strong name the old man had. No one else had that name. It had a big sound, like a great bell that only speaks once on important days. He will call me soon, David thought happily as sleep clutched him, and I will go with him into my own house.

CHAPTER 2

During the summer months Arthur often had work of one kind or another but in winter he and David hunted almost every Saturday morning. David didn't like hunting but he had never formulated the dislike. Like cutting kindling or feeding the hens, it wasn't a matter of like or not. They needed the meat and Arthur couldn't hunt alone. Towards the end of February and into March, as long as the ammunition held out, need forced them out every Saturday. Sometimes it was very cold.

"I'm tired of hare," Muriel said and David wondered why she called it hare when it was rabbit, plain rabbit—jack if they were lucky.

He finished lacing his moccasins as she got out the cotton pyjama tops, dyed red, that they wore over their jackets. Arthur inspected the rifles, David's .22, his .30-30. The boy had cleaned and oiled them early that morning, crouched beside the stove waiting for the kitchen to warm. Arthur ran a finger over the stock of his old rifle. He had big hands for his size, hard work-blackened hands, astonishingly dexterous.

"Mrs. Andrews said she would take one," his mother shouted. "I need sugar."

"Hmm," Arthur said by way of a promise.

Mrs. Andrews would give fifty cents for a jack, twenty-five for bush, quantity being all. It was always a struggle for Muriel to decide which they needed most, the meat or some item from the store. Arthur's pension was trifling, went to taxes, wood, paint and other necessities.

"Hen food too," she cried, despairing.

"Next week," Arthur promised, referring to the small monthly sum he got from Al Blake for some cabinetwork he'd done the spring before.

"He'll be ten years," Muriel said.

"Move, boy." Arthur shrugged into the pyjama top.

"It's a bitter day."

Muriel's surprised eyes slid over their clothing. With lightning touch the clothing switch was tripped: David needs a new coat, breeches, the knees are gone, warmer sweater; Arthur's coat is worn out, he could be almost perished and not complain, poor man; the mitts, I need wool, good red botany and black for socks, of course we all need . . . and then there's the tablecloths. Her eyes, examining the breakfast cloth, came to rest on the guns; her face drew up into a smile of parting.

"Good hunting," she said brightly, the oil of their needs filming her eyes, her brain. "Get us a good fat buck, son."

She watched them from the low window over the sink. They were going straight north towards the Iron Bluffs. It was handy living right on the edge of town. They were over the tracks and hadn't water or lights but then it was almost a farm. One didn't expect luxuries on a farm. "From my kitchen window I see north and west, it is impossible to describe the beauty of the sunsets I have to myself each day. Although it is bitter cold, each evening the sun goes down in such a dazzle of reds and saffrons that I simply stand and gaze." That was a long time ago, to her mother in England. Now her mother was dead and only occasionally did Muriel really notice the sunsets. Too often now, in summer at least, the sun pressed low and red against the dust-dark air, an unhealthy bloated clot of fire that transformed the world into some freakish Martian landscape in which there was no ocean, no distant England, only Manitoba, before the plows freed it to the air called Manitou's land, reeling beneath the constant gray night, the voracious wind. She no longer wrote her interminable letters to everyone at home who would write in return. I'll write today to Cousin Argyle, she thought, as soon as I finish the washing-up. But when she had finished washing the dishes, she noticed again the kitchen tablecloth, so thin with laundering the pattern of the oilcloth showed through it. Of course there were women in the Bluffs . . . She would rather not eat than eat without linen. I must mend that straightaway or I shall forget and it will be worse tomorrow. David is rough without meaning to be. He should have a dog. It looks more like sport when they have a dog with them. But dogs do eat so much. Still it would be nice. There was something about a dog, a dependent animal. Raised one above mere grubbing. Not having a dog seemed redolent of city living, tradespeople. The Hendersons always have pups. I'll speak to them. Perhaps when the weather breaks. No pups in winter, thank you. A late spring. Well into March and no sign of a let-up. Of course there had been one or two lamblike days and David had walked the tracks. She had seen him while she was hanging the clothes and, as she watched him, slow on the cinder trail, she had been aware for the first time of a softening in the wind. The wet clothes stretched rigidly into the winter air but it was there, spring and the boy. With her mind she knew what he was feeling. With her heart she yearned towards it through him but she could not smell it or see it properly for herself. She wondered sadly what people did who had no child to transmit the messages, to bring them the scents and sounds, the amorphous lusts to go, go, go into the changing wind, all the joys that time stole. And time will come and steal my love away. Time. Love was not all time stole. Love was the least of what time took.

And gave. She straightened her shoulders. There was much to be grateful for.

"I'll take care of you," Arthur had said, and he had. He was such a good man but things had gone so against him.

"The boy is mine," he had said and she agreed; he could not convey ideas as others did but she saw his purpose and knew he didn't want it mentioned.

The boy was his. It had worked out. He'd been better than most fathers, certainly better than the father nature gave. God had given David Arthur and God was wise as well as merciful. Arthur had been in her father's regiment. One couldn't go far enough. She had known that when her family sent her to Canada to build a new life. It was not far enough. She'd been walking along Osborne Street one day with the boy and there was Arthur.

He had flushed with pleasure. "Miss Heatherington!" he said, smiled at the boy. "Mrs., now. I never knew you'd come to Canada. How's the colonel?"

Dead, she said. And out of her loneliness with the boarding house, the unfriendly world, she'd said without even thinking of it, "It's still Miss Heatherington, Arthur, and this is my boy, David," seen him flush, growl thickly, "Oh Miss, that took courage."

"I've bought a little place outside a village, Mouse Bluffs," he said later. "I'll do a bit of carpentering and with my pension should manage fairly well. Maybe I shouldn't have come here to retire; it's a young man's country but I always wanted to come. I managed to keep the doctors from finding out about my hearing for a long time but they were going to send us out to India again and it wouldn't have been right if there'd been action. I lived back in Hammersmith for a while but it was too long ago and I kept thinking about this."

She was lonely and he brought back the good days, the men with their straight backs, their fastidious attention to dress, their deference. He saw how it was, how badly she managed, alone, who had never been alone, without the help, the deference, and he had offered his home, his powerful sense of responsibility, without really expecting her to accept. She came. It hadn't been easy. At first especially. She had clung to the past, tried in loneliness to share it with the boy, tried through him to withdraw from a present in which she had felt increasingly distraught and lost, said or almost said some things she shouldn't have said. Disloyal things. But David was so small then, not quite four; he wouldn't, she was sure, remember. He'd settled in nicely, stopped his questioning. The pebble of doubt had plunged through his child's clear unremembering mind and left no trace. Time gave. He was Arthur's son, heir to Arthur's life and values, a good life, good values. It had worked out. She hadn't found forgetfulness or peace for herself or expected these, but with Arthur she'd shaped new ranks, built a home for the boy. It counted, she was sure. It really counted.

I must get out a bit, she thought; a reflex, an old habit learned in a gentler climate. Often she threw on her things and went walking at odd hours in incredible weather. The neighbors thought her slightly cracked on the subject of walking. "I can't breathe!" would flash over her mind and out she would go. It was her sanity.

She stood in the doorway in her thick old seal coat, the coat Arthur had bought for her when they came to Mouse Bluffs. Worn but a comfort. Pulled her fur cap down over her ears and gazed about her, looking as always startled, as if the blinding snowshine were unexpected.

She smiled as she closed the door, pushed her hands deep into her pockets, breathed deeply. If I really put my mind to it I could take a trip home in three years. There are fourteen dollars in the tea-can. A quarter here, a dime there. Yes, another three years. 1939. It would go quickly if she . . . Perhaps even David, too! Time gave.

"Fine day, Mrs. Newman!"

She waved back. "Good morning, Mr. Kendall."

"Ride?"

How pleasant the snow looked over the fields, all white, so vast. No one at home would believe it. She must take snapshots. She stepped along the path and had climbed on to the box sled beside Ty Kendall before she realized that she didn't want a ride at all.

"A grand day, Mrs. Newman. On my way to Kitchens'. That all right?"

"Yes, yes. I shall just go along and see if there's mail from home."

"Hear about the ruckus up at Hendersons'?"

She smiled vaguely. A female gossip was bad enough. Of course Tyrone was Irish and couldn't be expected . . .

"Arthur and David have gone hunting."

"Somebody tried to steal one of Herb and Matt's hens and old Matt let 'em have it. Buckshot. Found blood on the snow around the henhouse this morning. Now Matt's sitting outside Doc Ross's office waiting for the patient." Kendall's big laugh rocketed across the crisp morning.

"Really?" Muriel glanced about distractedly. "I see Grace Talmadge, do let me down, Mr. Kendall; I must speak to her." You offend me, now really.

She climbed from the seat and thanked him with cool civility.

Kendall chuckled. "Bet I know who got it and he won't be in to no doctor. Won't be the first time his old lady's picked buckshot out of his butt."

She felt her spine snap like a corset steel. Never again. You've proferred your last ride, Tyrone Kendall.

"Thank you," faintly.

Grace was sweeping her steps. She looked quite disgraceful in an old curling sweater and duster cap but then she always did. I shall tell Arthur, Muriel vowed. He'll horsewhip that blackguard. Butt indeed. She nodded pleasantly to Grace and passed on towards Main Street.

In the woods Arthur spoke little, except to give brief commands. "Hold." "Keep that rifle down, you know better." He always hoped they might get a deer but they rarely saw one. The plains had been stripped so badly that few deer roamed in the tiny clumps of brush and bluff; they stayed north in Wasagaming or south at Turtle Mountain, where law and nature gave protection.

The boy and the man moved slowly through the bush, eyes always on the move, and the bush moved slowly around them. Now a tuft of snow fluttering from a branch, now the creak of a tree shrinking in the cold, often the tops of the bare trees stirring faintly against the blue-white sky and occasionally the clutch, the stillness, long indescribable moments of quiet, the woods under snow.

Something moved to David's left. He turned his head carefully. A big jack sitting on a stump not twenty feet off, looking straight at him, its nose twitching delicately.

He raised the ·22 and sighted. The rabbit looked at him, raised its paws in a washing motion to its face.

His stomach contracted. He pulled the trigger.

The scream, queer, human, rammed through the air and struck him. He was sweating with excitement and tension.

The body stirred. The animal pulled itself up, tried to move over the snow but its powerful rear legs would not function. The bullet had gone through it. Through the belly and out its back. Blood poured out on the snow in spurts.

"Get on with it," Arthur said.

David raised the gun again. His back itched with sweat.

"I've told you not to waste bullets," Arthur said savagely and moved forward just as the boy's finger tightened on the trigger.

David fired. A miss. He reeled. Arthur gave him a startled glance, then went straight to the rabbit, which was still dragging its body over the snow, its legs sprawled behind in great pocks of blood. Taking it by the throat, he snapped the head back over the hard ridge of his other hand.

"Bring the bag," he ordered.

The animal tumbled bonelessly into the sack. David sat down.

"You . . . I nearly shot you," he shouted, his mouth trembling.

Arthur gave him an intent look. "Be careful next time. And for God's sake don't snivel." He laughed. "I didn't come through two wars to die by a ·22 bullet shot by an eleven-year-old."

David rubbed his sleeve against his eyes.

"Just a minute," he said.

He sat on the snow until his seat was cold and the shaking stopped. He couldn't remember Arthur's ever laughing at anything really funny; he always laughed in that harsh way at terrible things and to himself.

They shot one more rabbit for Mrs. Andrews and David shot a prairie chicken. Arthur was pleased.

"You're my ears," he told David on the way home as he always told him. "Deaf man can't. Not rightly. Funny about the Fritzes getting my ears, in a manner of speaking. When the regiment was positioned near the Pats in '17 they had a full-blooded Indian, Treetop they called him. Maybe it was his name. He had a bag, little bag, leather, guarded it like the crown jewels. Carried it with him all the time. Well sir, every night at the front Treetop would disappear, against orders but no one could stop him. Every night. The men got onto him about that bag, cutting up about scalps and so on, and one night they put him down, laughing and carrying on. Treetop glowered black death at 'em. They found out all right. A whole bag full of ears. I don't feel so bad about my hearing because of that. Good fighters, Indians, good troopers."

David had heard the story often. He was inured to it. Tuned out.

"Muriel! Shot a prairie chicken," Arthur shouted as they came into the cottage. In good spirits, a full bag. "Out. Damn. Well, boy, you boil up a bit of water and we'll clean these animals. I'll have to get over to Mrs. Andrews this afternoon if I'm to get that sugar from Herson's." He always spoke a great deal after a good hunt, as if the provisioning re-established something in his spirit from week to week, something that began to fade by Monday and by Friday had almost ceased to exist. "And clean the guns."

It was almost one o'clock before David got away to meet Lilja and Jon on the corner of First and Main. All over town the children, big and small, were making their way to the Wonderland, up the hill to Crescent, down Main, across Townsend's lots, through caragana breaks.

Lilja, Jon and David went slowly, kept their voices down to a whisper, for Ally James walked in front of them and, like most of the children in Mouse Bluffs, they were afraid of Ally. Every Saturday afternoon she stumped stolidly, without paying, past Mr. Lovat and went to sit in the front row left. No one sat beside her. Mr. Lovat pretended she wasn't there. Yet he saw her pass, saw her cunning pig eyes flickering a challenge at him. Mr. Lovat had passed through the fire of Ally James when the Wonderland first opened to bring Tarzan and Tom Mix to Mouse Bluffs and had never, after that once when, thwarted, Ally chose to have an epileptic seizure, tried to interrupt her passage through the portals of culture.

No children spoke to Ally. No teacher, after the first attempt, asked her a question in class. There was a conspiracy in town to pretend Ally did not exist. So she clumped along alone and she carried a very large club.

"How much did Mr. Herson give you?" Lilja asked.

David showed her. A quarter.

Jacob Herson had said, "Ten cents the half hour or any portion thereof," which of course didn't make sense. But he had smiled and left David alone to stack the wood and, when the boy went into the store an hour later, Jake had looked at the clock and given him a quarter from the cash register, explaining that he hadn't change, which seemed foolish for a store.

"Gee," Lilja admired for, although she had twenty-five cents each Saturday morning, twenty-five cents earned from a stranger had properties twenty-five cents from mother had not.

Ally slowed. They slowed. Looked at one another. Jon, eight, drew back.

"Come on," Lilja said and, very stiffly, single file, they passed Ally. "Let's run."

"Last one is a pig's backside!"

As they turned the corner by the Wonderland, David saw Dr. Ross driving past in his new blue Ford. He halted and sauntered slowly towards the theater. Afraid to wave, he waited for Gavin Ross to notice him, perhaps stop. "Come and see me," Gavin Ross had said. But a boy can't just go and say here I am. He needs a signal. When Lilja spoke to him, he did not answer but looked at the marquee.

"What's wrong?"

The car turned the corner.

"Nothing."

She said in an injured tone, "I like black better."

Jon bounded up. They got out their money, found Jon had lost his dime and had to go back along the street, searching frantically through the cracks in the boards.

Gavin Ross saw Ally James running awkwardly along the street and shook his head. Needed a good spank, that one. The mother couldn't do it, afraid of the fits. Pretty soon be too big to spank. Almost twelve. Menace. How many times had the mother brought her in and he couldn't examine her? Not that it mattered much. Very little to be done for any of these built-in things. The incurables. God how he hated them. Or psychogenic. Devil with them. Had a way of spreading out the evil too. Alice James had been a pretty girl when he first came to Mouse Bluffs. Wreck now. Eyes set deep, so dark in the pockets of worry she looked as if she wore circus make-up. Must be congenital. Of course. Joe James? Neither would admit any of it in the family. Nevertheless . . .

The new car was a gem. Couldn't beat a Ford. Snow perhaps. But he kept the team for that. Couldn't be counted a luxury.

"Cash, Dr. Ross? Wish I had more customers like you," Joe James had said in that peculiar tone of respectful envy.

"Cash." Gavin preferred his debts to lie between himself and the Bank of Montreal, found the growing practice of credit-buying noxious. "How's business?"

"Good," Joe lied. "Things are perking up. Sold Brace Harvey last week. Of course selling Fords is a sure-fire proposition. Like bread or aspirin. People can't do without." The sales manager had been up from Winnipeg the week before and transmitted the latest enthusiasms. "Say, Doc, about this insomnia of mine . . ."

Gavin bristled. "Come into the office, Joe." It served him right. How's business, indeed.

"But like last night, maybe half an hour at the most. A man just can't go on that way. And that medicine makes me dopey."

"The office, Joe."

He had driven away angry. Damned people. Would have him walking up and down the streets distributing advice, free, if they could get away with it. Incorrigible. Joe wanted paying for a grease job or for gasoline. Oh hell!

Something in the wind spoke of spring today. A gentle touch, something faint, elusive. Soon, the river.

The piles of snow along Main Street still resisted the warmth in the sun but one day, any day now, the wind would come full and warm, smelling of the waking earth in the south, and the snow would begin to go.

Christine did not speak as he came into the dining room. She rose and went to the kitchen and brought his lunch, hot on a plate from the oven. Rissoles. He didn't like rissoles. Cassie had a trick of slipping rice or breadcrumbs into them. Too much. Meat kept a man fit.

"The kettle's boiling."

She sat opposite him, her square face bright, tuned to the coming spring as she watched the river through the bay window. She was taller than most women of her generation though not tall by the standards of the lanky young ones the prairie was breeding, a bit thick in the legs and hips, full-breasted, an unfashionable figure. Her fair hair was just beginning to look fine and healthy after all the sun-bleaching of the summer before. It never gets a chance from year to year, he thought. He studied her as she went to make the tea, wondering if she had been as solid before all the swimming. He couldn't remember. It was hard to remember anything before the swimming. When time moved. He ate his rissoles while she dreamed towards the river. Her eyes never ceased to fascinate him. Whatever he was thinking or saying, a portion of his mind was always incredulous about those green green eyes. How rare really green eyes are, how disturbingly cold.

"Ian?" He raised his brows in a question.

She bent her head to the north to indicate the hotel.

"Cassie?"

"Market."

"You reminded her?"

"Yes."

33

Each Saturday the farm wives held a market in a vacant store on the western end of the Crescent. In winter root vegetables, preserves, eggs, butter, chicken; in summer fresh vegetables as they grew, fruit, saskatoons or blueberries or raspberries. Cassie went each week to buy a sealer of preserved jellied chicken from old Mrs. Wright, who brought only one pint to market, that for the doctor. He had tried through Cassie to get a quantity. "Ambrosia! What does the woman do with plain ordinary chicken?" Christine had explained laconically, "Spice. No one in Mouse Bluffs uses anything but salt and pepper." "Get the recipe." "Ha. You could draw out these women's fingernails and not get their recipes." But Mrs. Wright would not sell bulk. It seemed degrading, like business. Besides, fifty cents a week was better than ten dollars, which her old man would probably get, anyway; it was an ace in the hole, a tease for the doctor, a way of working off medical bills if she ever needed him.

Christine said as she poured his tea, "The ice will go soon."

She did not meet his glance. The windows reflected perfect little squares in her green eyes.

"Why don't you go up to Winnipeg for a few days?"

"Why?"

He hurt. He hurt all over, a dry aching hurt without real focus. Another summer then, like all the others for so long. He sighed.

"Paint the town?" Get drunk. Start a riot. Buy up all the shops. Not another summer. "Buy a new spring outfit."

"Ha!"

"Visit Mary."

"Your sister is hardly an inducement—for me."

He flung his napkin down. "Is there more tea?"

While she poured, he controlled himself. "I wish you would, Christine."

"I'll think about it."

That buried it for good. Communication died there.

At the office he found Mrs. Reeves, Mrs. Clawson, farmers' wives near confinement, Mrs. Daly, Mrs. Spruce, early pre-natal. At first the women had made it a practice to come to him late, just before confinement, and too often he had been confronted with a breech-birth or a nerve-racking decision about a Caesarian. He had lost a couple of patients through this apparent stupidity before he realized they were saving money and changed his fee to twenty-five dollars with or without pre-natals. It packed the office badly because now some of the farmers' wives came each Saturday. If they were unhappy or worried usually: they came and talked about indigestion and pains in the back and spotting, never about

34

bad husbands, overwork, hunger. Mrs. Daly would say primly, "I wonder if you could drop by and speak to John, doctor?" and he would nod the subject out, then have to stop by, five miles out of town, and tell John that his thrice-daily assaults were out of order, "Ease up on the wife, John. She's not too strong just now, needs her reserves." John would shrug, head for the house as Ross drove away, then leave her till well after confinement. Jane Daly had six children. She enjoyed her pregnancies. Gavin didn't like it. The body had a way of building hazards to what the mind found repugnant.

There was the Crane child to have his burn dressing changed. And one of the Hendersons sitting in a corner chair with his arms folded. Gavin raised his brows. Saturday rarely found townspeople in the office.

His surgery was at the rear of the drug store on Crescent. When he was first married he had used Sir Richard's office in the big house, but it was too much—the telephone, the door, people tramping up the hall. Here he shared the telephone with the drug store. It stood on a hinged trough between his office and the store and the operator staggered the rings. It saved money. And the phone seldom rang for Deacon, the druggist. Deacon was forever threatening to have Ross pay more than he did but he couldn't force the issue. The patients brought their prescriptions straight around the corner. There was old Drake down the way. It would be too easy for Ross to drop a hint to the patients. Ross wouldn't. Deacon could never be sure. Never push a Scotsman about money.

The patients filed through in the order in which they had arrived. The honor system. The telephone rang twice. Two more house calls. At last there remained only Henderson, Matt or Herb; no one could tell the big dark old-young men apart.

Gavin spoke from the office door. "Yes, Herb?"

Matt didn't move from his chair in the corner. "Matt. You closing?"

"Yes."

"Okay."

Ross folded his sphygmomanometer.

"I shot somebody last night," Matt announced. Ross froze. Matt added, "Buckshot. Some bugger in my henhouse. Saw blood on the snow this morning. Figured he'd be in here to get himself seeded out."

Ross laughed. He put on his coat and went through the waiting room, opened the door and ushered Matt out.

"Any gunshot wounds I see I report to the Mountie. I advise you to see him."

"Mountie! God, Doc, I can't afford court."

"Then fill your gun with rock salt or stop penning your dogs or don't shoot. How much is a chicken worth?"

"I'll find out who it is. You wait." Matt was evidently disturbed by Ross's suggestion. "Mountie!" he muttered.

"Perhaps it was an animal, Matt. Fox?"

"Two-legged, you bet." Matt hurried away.

Gavin Ross went to his car. There would be no call about a gunshot wound, he knew.

CHAPTER 3

There is no slum in the Bluffs. Across the track there is no sewerage, water, lights, and the houses are scarcely more than shacks, but each stands on a respectably large piece of land: vegetables growing, a few chickens, flowers, hedges. The people there are poor but a lot of people in Mouse Bluffs are poor. No one criticizes poverty; it blows too near all; only dirty poverty is frowned upon. The trash do not live over the tracks; they live right in town, squatting on various scraps of vacant property. The Yeates family went further, moved into an old abandoned store on Center Street, a weathered sagging mass of siding, the roof slumped in an alarming fashion. It was a coup. The town murmured but no one did anything. The property had been inherited by a man in Winnipeg who, when informed of the situation, said, "So what?" and stopped paying the taxes. He had seen the place. The store was on a corner; the only close neighbors were the Pike sisters.

"You!" Jack Yeates advised his children. "Keep away from that goddamned hedge, that garden, even that little mess of garbage, and them two old ladies'll never open their yaps. Hear? They's a line out there and you mind or you'll get the buckle-end."

There was a tap in the place, cold water, but the water had been turned off at the main long ago.

Jack fetched water from the pump-house for weeks on a hand wagon and cudgeled his brains about the tap, how to get that tap flowing. At length he went to Reese Todd, the town clerk, asked if he could mow lawns, run messages, although he knew there was no town job unfilled, and finally, after a devious and to Yeates scarcely intelligible conversation, it was agreed that the water would go on if Phoebe Yeates would oblige about Reese Todd's house one morning a week, Sunday. The town clerk was an old widower. He lived alone, his one son having been disowned years past.

Jack said to Phoebe, "Y'see, Phoeb, the Chink's is closed Sunday and old Todd likes a good breakfast and him with no hired girl, see?"

He had used her when they were first married and he had the horse. He had had money then too and they had lived in the red brick cottage on Front. He was a gambler and had raced the horse at fairs. When the money was in, she had everything. When it was out, he bet her and the payoff was made in the red brick cottage. She hadn't minded until the kids started coming but then he'd lost the horse and stopped being in the money and the men about town preferred something a little fresher. He was still a gambler; a calling and a profession. If he saw two raindrops on a window he would bet his pants on which one would reach the bottom first. Phoebe didn't ponder the nature of Sunday breakfast. She had ceased to be curious about anything a long time ago.

"No girl would go there," she said mildly.

"Well, you ain't a girl. Now, Phoeb."

She went and the ritual began; a queer world, she told herself, queer Todd's house.

The first morning old Todd opened the door for her, his grey-whiskered face puckered with sleep, his grizzled hair jutting like a shelf behind his large domed head.

"Make tea, Mrs. Yeates." He rubbed his cheeks with his fists and his eyes watered against the dayshine. "Then come along and wake me."

He floundered sleepily upstairs, the faded checkered dressing gown flapping against his shining shanks. Phoebe looked through the house, lifted a cushion from the sofa, twitched the carpet-edge. A gleam of relief flickered briefly in her dull eyes. She made tea and carried it up on an old-fashioned teakwood tray, inlaid with bits of yellowed ivory, and was already beginning to work as she rapped on the bedroom door, wondering if there was a way to bleach up ivory.

"Can you get those on?" Todd asked. A pair of old-fashioned pumps with French heels, long pointed toes. Phoebe was proud of her legs and feet, still good, not a vein or a callous. She unlaced her oxfords and put the shoes on. The old man sighed. "Now, Mrs. Yeates, that mirror. Stand there and undress. As if you meant it." She undressed slowly, hanging her housedress and corsets and bloomers over a straight-backed chair. "No. Leave the stockings and shoes." Across her slack abdomen the striae of four pregnancies. Her big breasts sagged nearly to her waist. "Now walk around." She walked. "Now you may dress and get my breakfast. Ham and four eggs, not too well done. Lots of toast." She dressed and went downstairs. As he sat down to breakfast, he said, "Have some tea and toast, Mrs. Yeates. We need not stand on ceremony."

The water went on that night. Each week something was added until the ritual took almost an hour. Todd bought a pair of fine silk stockings, then blue satin garters, a pearl-inlaid comb with which he asked her to comb her hair. "Not that hair, Mrs. Yeates." He didn't touch her, the breakfasts were good, the water ran in the old store. When she saw him on the street, he nodded his big head kindly, as he did to everyone. Jack never asked. It was not Jack's nature to bring such things out, yet she sometimes wanted to tell him. It was certainly different, you could say that much. Because of the breakfasts she rather looked forward to Sunday mornings. "You have fine legs," he said each time it was over for him. She often thought of that after the kids were off in Sunday School. It was nice to have someone notice, even old man Todd.

Todd was safe. Jack had his price. Besides, she knew no one, not even Jack, would likely believe a word of it, even if she brought the stockings and the soft old shoes to show them. The water was on and that was all that mattered.

She was given at times to vague worry about the older children. Elsie, fourteen, and Bruce, fifteen. They were restless and nothing to do. No work for Brucie when he got out of school. It wasn't right. The two young ones were all right, still a long way to go. Yet the fifteen years since she'd had Brucie had gone so fast there was no seeing them. Maybe, she thought, I'll speak to old Todd about it, he's pretty smart. But she never did.

One day in Todd's office the town engineer said, "What's about that water Jack Yeates is using?"

Todd looked reflective.

"What I can't figure is how he got it turned on. That's him. Slick fingers."

The engineer wouldn't say outright that Yeates was a thief.

The prevailing morality in Mouse Bluffs was a belief in good intentions. In the face of gory hands and a dead body anyone in town would hesitate to cry murder; it was always felt that any man given a fair shake could be found to mean well; this cushioned the effect of many things, made much acceptable that, though not morally irreproachable, was not practically eradicable; they lived too close to cry murderer, whore, thief.

Todd said, "Take the long view."

"Long view? God, Mr. Todd, you're too big-hearted, that's your trouble. Now, council will . . ."

"The Yeates make out. How I don't know but one or two dollars' water a month on the town helps. My opinion is that it's better to have Jack Yeates there, squatting, helping himself to a bit of water, than on relief. All those kids. On relief we'd have to find some other accommodation. This is the town's responsibility and I reckon we're getting off cheaply."

"I don't like it. The mayor comes to me getting all sweated up over everything."

"You tell him to see me. I'll make a note of it now so you'll be covered. I can assure you though that the mayor will feel the same as I do. No alternative. It isn't just laziness. There's no work for these men. You and I know that no matter what they say in the city papers. There's no work. So let's not push the families around."

"You make a note then."

The engineer fumed but said no more. He was afraid for his own job. Go along with Todd; mayors come and go but old Todd goes on forever.

Todd smiled wryly in his wake. A simple little water-tap. There was no reason, he assured himself, why it couldn't go on for a long, long time. Yet a small uneasiness grew in the back of his mind. He knew the town better than that. Still, for a while, anyway. . . In the end Jack Yeates would be blamed and no one could hold Jack Yeates accountable. Something to being dirt poor.

However rich a man got in Mouse Bluffs, particularly a man on the town payroll, he lived modestly. Of course there were rich men. Some said Gavin Ross had plenty but Todd doubted it. The brother drank too much, the wife was a snappy dresser, the old Rashleigh house a bottomless pit, and until the kid died they'd wasted a lot of money tripping around, even back and forth to the Old Country. Unless of course Ross had inherited money. He was pretty close-mouthed. Sir Richard hadn't left Christine a red cent. But there was old Macdonald, who'd made a packet in grain marketing. And Charlie Jaques. Brace Harvey, who Todd knew got big quarterly cheques from the Old Country. You'd never think any of them had two nickels to rub together. He smiled. You always knew by how loud they screamed whenever council talked improvements; every new sidewalk brought them out to sing like robins in a shower. And Reese Todd, of course, but that was the biggest secret of all. He wished rather sadly he could buy a new car but he didn't dare. Anyway, a new garage, he thought. I'll catch Arthur Newman and get him onto it. The new cars were longer. The old garage built for a model T would never close on a new car. Maybe he should have kept the stables. Damned silly the way everybody went and yanked down their stables a few years back. He must make it a point to start going into Joe James's service station, let Joe talk him into a new Ford by next spring.

"The trouble with Arthur Newman is that it is quite impossible to speak to him," said the Reverend Daniel Backhouse, pronounced Backhouse by choice against the somewhat subtler Bacchus.

Bacchus had, he felt, connotations quite unsuitable to his cloth. That the name of the wine god lay outside the lexicon of Mouse Bluffs he was unwilling to admit; he was simply not going to be call Reverend Bacchus, which after all was a contradiction in terms. With the advent of plumbing for the millions, he foresaw the day when the crude implications of Backhouse would filter away. Perhaps in two generations. Meanwhile it was a cross. Particularly for the children. But for that very reason he felt God had chosen wisely in sending him to Mouse Bluffs. It taught the children at an early age that nothing, not even the family name, had dignity unless one strove to earn it.

Solveg sighed. "I know. Nevertheless Lilja has her heart set . . . In any case, it's only April. Perhaps when you make your call there. The boy needs a holiday and I don't suppose he's ever been to . . ."

"You know what they're like. One suggestion, hint, the merest breath of charity, and they run for cover."

"If you explain about my brother?"

"This town is going to wonder about your brother one day."

"I know."

She wondered why they had considered all this subterfuge necessary in the first place. What if they had just said, "Solveg has money of her own"? Might it not have been easier than all these hints about gifts, now the two weeks at Clear Lake, from her

40

brother? It was almost lying. Almost. Of course Carl did manage things, collected the rents for her, but he carped. He had run his own inheritance up now to near the half million mark, while she still sat with one apartment block in Fort Rouge, not daring openly to claim that. "Take a chance," Carl pleaded. "It's good for a fat mortgage. I'll do it all for you. Get you five or six per cent on your investment. That's safe enough. Look, it breaks my bloody heart to see you out there wearing stuff five years old. What's wrong with Dan, I'd like to know? Christ, he knew you had dough when he married you. Never fear, he knew. It beats me." "You don't understand the people in Mouse . . . I don't want to be worried! And Carl, it is good to use it for . . . So many people helped by . . . Then there's no worry when Lilja and Jon are ready for college." While Daniel said, "A priest should not be fat in the midst of poverty," and of course he was right. "What I've never had, I cannot miss," he declared.

Though he'd never got really close to these people, he had a shrewd understanding of them and their motives that Solveg could not fathom. She was always an outsider. There wasn't a woman in town, she knew, who didn't feel superior to her because she was the daughter of an Icelandic immigrant. "The Scandinavians, now, they're not really what you might call foreigners." "This foreign cooking is surely interesting. Would you show me how to make that—what did you call it?" *Rulla pylsa.* A dozen times. *Rulla pylsa.* Condescension always. It didn't bother her too much. She knew that in some obscure way it helped Daniel. The town felt he stood alone, unfamilied, that he was in league with them in a way impossible for her. He was a good man, jealous but good, and he struggled fiercely against his jealousies; she knew they too were rooted in her foreignness, as if he felt that the differences in their backgrounds had equipped her with a set of motives unintelligible to him. Yet this was what had brought him to her in the beginning, the strangeness: her gnarled little mother, who wore the old country costume and still, after forty years in Canada, spoke no English, the different foods, the excitable hard-drinking big blond men, the intensity of the family relationships, the broad lines of her face, the eyes set out, slanted in a Slavic fashion, tawny, topaz streaked with brown like her hair; he had even, in those first days, spoken a bit of Icelandic. It was as near to Bohemia as he had ever come. Now he called the children Lily and John after the English. She kept the soft j in spite of him, knowing that, much as it bothered him, he would never make an issue of it. Having taken so much from her, he could not take this.

41

She suggested, "Just put it on the basis of . . . That the children are keen for it. Should I?"

"It ought to come from me. I'll be making a call there soon. Of course the mother will see it but I don't expect she has the say. Perhaps you could. No. I'll do it. I'll speak to her."

Solveg thought, I hate poor people, and began to clear away the tea things. Daniel would sleep now as he always did after tea.

"It's the railroad," she said.

"What?"

"If only the railroad would hire some of the men."

"They would if they needed them. Good Lord, half the town, more than half, is on the C.P.R. now."

"They could."

"It's more complex than that."

"Carl says hard times are a frame of mind."

"I'm sure he does. Have you seen Christine lately?"

"But I told you . . . at the library Monday night. That's why I was a little longer . . . Why?"

"Nothing."

He closed his eyes and leaned back against the sofa pillows. She stood with the heavy tea tray in her hands, looking down at him, then moved away.

He was satisfied on two counts. He knew she would go to see Christine. She was very quick to see any disquiet in him and act. Christine. If only the doctor were an Anglican or even a church-goer one could speak to him, Daniel thought drowsily, get the roots of it aired away. Not only was it too early for swimming, the river too cold but . . . That wasn't it. It was wrong of Christine. The town talked. Oh very quietly because she was Christine. A Rashleigh. They thought she was mad. Of course she wasn't. But still, it kept the wound open, didn't it? However, the doctor was a Presbyterian of sorts and one couldn't interfere even through the Reverend Mr. Scott in what he chose to call the United Church. And Christine? He pushed the uncomfortable thought away. Back-slid. Recalcitrant. But there was a cheque every Christmas and Easter. "Mind your own business," she had advised bluntly when he made the effort that once. It was his business. She would come to him one day. If only the child's body had been found. How different . . .

Matt Henderson slammed into the yard, put the brakes to Henry and came to a shuddering halt. He could see Herb working on the side of the house. It was a new idea. They were using broken glass in the stucco and already, with the east side done, the place shone like a harvest of jewels in the sun; it looked good. Of course anyone that leaned against it would suffer lacerations but no one came to lean against the Henderson house. They had lived alone since the family died in '19, had spent all their spare time improving the house. "What'll happen if one of them twins marries?" the town liked to speculate. "Who'll get the manor?" To which the reply was always "Don't be loony, they'd all live there. No woman'd know the diff anyway."

"Herb! I found him."

Herb looked down from the ladder.

"Jack Yeates. I'm going to kill the sod."

Herb shook his head, rubbed his palms on his overalls, climbed down.

"How'd you find out?"

He had know about Jack Yeates for a long time. He sat on the bottom rung and looked thoughtful.

"One of his kids let it slip. I was standing down at the power-house and that Brucie comes along. Old Lippy starts on about shooting, smart ass, and anyway Brucie says his old man accidentally got some buckshot in his legs out hunting last winter. That shit-livered thief! My chickens. No eggs for weeks."

Herb took a plug from his pocket and began to pare a chew. "Figure he was hungry. Kids hungry."

Matt exploded, "They're our chickens. I work. I pay for every damned thing I get."

"Yeh. Wait. You'll get your chance." He put the tobacco deftly in his cheek. "Simmer a bit."

Matt thought a moment, looked cunning. "You help me?"

"When the time comes."

"Time! Ten years maybe."

"Maybe. Better that way. Don't like a thief much. We'll wait.

"What I can't figure is why I didn't think of him right off. Jack Yeates! By God, he's a stray. I'll break his back I catch him here again."

"The dogs."

"Sure, sure."

It had been a mistake selling all the grown dogs after the bitch died; should have kept one even if it meant reneging and losing the money, instead of waiting on the pups and the pups twice as hard to train without a leader. Never again. They kept two now. A Springer and a Labrador bitch. Nobody came to Hendersons' without invitation. The twins trained dogs better than any kennel-owners in the province, maybe the country. Men had been known to come from a hundred miles or more to get a Henderson hunting dog, even from Winnipeg. Hunting dogs best but Matt could train a dog to any purpose. Probably, he bragged, even a circus dog if he ever got an order. He was not sentimental about the dogs any more than Herb was. They were simply working animals that must learn their trades before leaving the kennels. If an animal proved refractory it was despatched by a hose from the exhaust of Henry to a snug little box; any animal-trainer knows that some dogs can learn nothing and are a source of disquiet to the others.

"Matt, you need a phone."

He hadn't heard the car. Now he looked up to see Christine leaning from its window.

"Dogs in?" she asked.

Herb got to his feet, took his work cap in his hand. Christine got out of her car.

"Yes." Herb flushed. She sure was a looker, all in white today, white blouse, white sweater, skirt, even white shoes with brown toes. "If it's about that dog, he's not ready yet."

"That's all right. I want him. You two take more trouble over those dogs than a knitting granny."

"Well . . ."

Matt said, "Doc Spence says if we get him fixed he should stay an extra week."

"Well, I want him fixed and I'm sick of waiting."

"You want a watchdog it takes time."

She had brought articles of clothing from the house—hers, Gavin's, Ian's, Cassie's, Billy's.

"I don't want a dog that will bite all comers, just one that will raise the dickens if someone comes sneaking around."

"Know what you mean but I feel sort of like a mother about . . . I mean . . ."

Matt flushed painfully. Herb looked away over the garden.

Christine laughed harshly. "Let me see him. Let's see if he knows me from those old tennis shoes."

Matt said quickly, "Oh, he's your dog all right. Other day I took a stick to them shoes and he took on fierce. Making up his mind to go for me. Me!"

"I know, his mother."

They walked away to the kennels and the dog-run behind the house. Herb watched her, his eyes narrowed to fine slits. Some hips. Some walk. Gavin was too old for the job. Everybody said that when he married her. Woman happy at home doesn't wiggle. He wondered if there was some way to delay her leaving, just see her for a minute alone, but there was no way, he knew. He had schooled it out, into the far future. He spat. Damned shame, that kid of hers. Might have made all the difference. Some things money couldn't buy.

Without conviction he told himself grimly him and Matt were lucky. Bad luck, hard times, meant little to them. Hungry kids, dead kids, wiggling wives. None of that.

"Sure you can take him only he won't be neutered," he heard Matt telling her as they came back, she with the Labrador rubbing her thighs and bouncing against her as if he'd come home at last. Herb smiled faintly. They had done a good job.

"Prince? Crown Prince?" She smiled and said, "I'll take him now. Come on, fellow." As she drove away, the dog beside her in the car, she called, "Send the bill to the doctor, Matt. 'Bye Herb."

The twins watched the car turn onto the highway.

"That's a packet of woman," Matt decided.

"Cold potatoes."

"Think so?"

"Yep."

"Never saw a woman wear white before summer."

"She's done a lot of things other women never did. Some of them are like that. Got to be first. Different. Don't mean they enjoy it."

"It's a good deal, you reckon Doc'd ante up fifty?"

"Uh uh, seventy-five. Scotchmen. Got to have the best. Let'm row us a bit about it. Makes him feel better." Herb aimed a shot at the wheelbarrow-handle, missed. "Neutered."

"I'm glad too. What d'you figure she wanted him done for? No dogs around town neutered, only bitches."

"Wants to keep him home, I guess. Like Doc."

"Think so?"

"You bet. Let's drive over to Nellie's."

"She get you, Herb?" Matt smiled slyly, caught the thunder in Herb's eyes and backed up quickly. "All right."

"I'll wash up."

Matt looked at his overalls. "I'm fine, I guess. Should I take some gin?"

"We pay her."

"It just seems nicer."

"Nothing nice about it. Remember what Daddy said."

"I know. I know. Once a week and no amateurs. But it seems nicer. I like to take a jug."

"Your jug."

CHAPTER 4

The farms and the town.

On the farms memory of the good days is kept. The older men
know, they declare, that the land will come back; drought does
not last; the rich times, winter vacations, new equipment will
come again; but all the while they see through the younger eyes
the stripped places where greed worked the damage, places a man
passed daily with the thought, should've kept that stand of maples,
maybe hedgerows, too late now, twenty years before they retain.
On the farm, too, there is trouble with the young. No men with
even small substance for the girls to marry, no work in town, only
housework at three or four dollars a month. The children of
landowners should not have to go into service. The sons in despair.
Drought at fifteen never ends; it gets into the young heart and
wastes it old. From Winnipeg the experts sent pamphlets, sent
free films, college-bred farmers to talk about erosion, but everything they advised cost money. But they came and their coming
was more important than all the advice in the world. Officialdom
declared it was doing everything possible. Semi-starvation worked
because these men, four thousand miles and an era out of Ply-
mouth or Liverpool, would suffer greatly before giving up land.
They stayed.

In the town two societies, the lines of demarcation rigid. The
ordinary townsfolk and the railroaders. The original railroad in-
truders had been section hands, men culled from every hopeless
corner of Europe to build the roadbeds, lay the ties, become
brutalized by a brutal master; the stigma lingered; a railroad man
had never been mayor. But whatever the class differences, developed in the good times, the young are learning now. They know
that the children of the C.P.R. have a stability in their homes
found nowhere else. The sons of farmers, carpenters, shop-owners
are busy in 1936 learning the lesson of the twentieth century,
respect for the wage. The sons of sons of men who dared and suf-

fered much to escape servitude, boss, get property and be free of wages, are watching now the blessed wage, the possible pension, that special benefit, the travel pass, with greedy eyes. No matter what they are told of mountains to climb, fortunes to be made, before their eyes runs desirable reality, the railroad.

Within the railroad are special tensions engendered by the seniority principle that decrees that certain men are kept steadily on the job while others war over the leavings; but even so there is a kind of unity among them, a unity of needs, the union, a brotherhood that has a special abstract quality that goes beyond mere bargaining with the overlords.

Men of the railroad have, as well, a special form of communication with the nation. They knew its sicknesses, its sorrows, in those days as no other men in the west did. How many cars of wheat moved out of or through the area; how many trainloads of relief came in from the east, how much of that relief was clothing, how much seed or actual food; how many cars of animals went to Winnipeg to the stockyards; how much scrap iron and nickel was on its way to Vancouver, earmarked for Japan; the men did not talk a great deal about these things or develop their implications, but they saw and were disturbed; they had long ago stopped counting the hoboes that rode the rods in search of that impossible grail, work. Once, twice, a train of horses went through Mouse Bluffs on its way to Belgium, for meat, it was said. The idea seemed too grotesque; nevertheless, there were the old horses, certainly cheaper than beef, and it didn't make sense to take them all that way unless for meat. It was agreed in the bunkhouses that a man would have to be pretty bloody hungry, that it beat everything the way foreigners had to live.

The railroad was the rock of the town. As the west made the C.P.R., so the C.P.R. made the west. Gavin Ross knew, as did all the business men in Mouse Bluffs, that these were the only accounts really collectable. Along with the butcher, the baker, the power-station office, he waited for the C.P.R. cheques; when the C.P.R. payroll went out, the town was paid. But he knew too, as doctor to the town, that the railroad was not an easy master. In hard times it worked its men harder than men should work; even an old established union does not argue with a depression.

"Remember, the aristocrats of labor," Brace Harvey told Al Blake when Al was going to Winnipeg to write his engineer's papers.

In sight of that great goal Blake laughed, "And then some!" The aristocrats of labor—this was one of the few messages from the city union that had ever made sense to country-bred Al.

47

Brace sometimes made nearly four hundred dollars a month. He worked for it, more hours than any other man in town. But there were others, on the land, who worked as hard for little or nothing.

"Look, Al, me and the missus talked this over and never fear, it's a loan. You got four little ones. Forget it."

Brace and Julia, all dressed up, had walked purposefully through the quiet summer's night to Blake's where Al, sitting at the kitchen table, nursing the arm broken the week before, was wondering and worrying and conceding he was for it. Men who didn't work didn't get paid. No miles in, no money. Looking at the cheque, Brace's company cheque, signed over, plain and simple, he could scarcely speak. That bastard Brace Harvey who'd bumped him on the Crookston run.

"Can't say no, Brace." With horror he realized he had tears in his eyes.

Brace looked away. "Well, we'd best just get along."

"Tea." Al stumbled to his feet and called Gladys. "Brace, I owe Doc Ross and Herson and even Arthur Newman for some cupboards he put in. You never figure on this. Never."

Julia stared intently at the crocheted potholders behind the stove, as if she were scarcely present, let alone interested.

Brace cleared his throat. "Aw hell, Al. Look, don't you ever tell anybody about this."

"Never fear."

"You get a move on and get better that's all. No thanks, Al. I know I'll get it back. Evening, Glad."

Gladys came through the doorway, looked at Brace and Julia, mustered a smile. She was a grim bone of a woman, quite without shape, but her face was flushed, ruddy in the manner generally associated with the stout. She pushed back her faded red curls.

"My goodness, Julia, Brace, what a mess you found us in. Them kids won't settle."

"Just telling Al, good thing it wasn't his leg or we might have to shoot him. Heard of a case last week."

Brace exploded with forced guffaws. Gladys smiled faintly and Julia resumed her scrutiny of the potholders.

Al watched his wife. Not smiling, he pushed the cheque across the table. She picked it up, knew the color and meaning before reading it. Hope twisted her face to near smile, then she sat down heavily on a kitchen chair, put her head on her arms and wept.

Julia moved forward into the torrent and Brace rose clumsily and went outside. When Al came to fetch him for tea, he was sitting on the step dejectedly.

"Brace?"

"Al, I look at it this way, I give you my bank number and you deposit what you can when you can. I don't care if it's five years but I don't want to ever hear about this again. Not one word, understand? Now you go in there and tell Gladys. Not thank you or balls to you or I'm going to cut for the hills. Some day you help some other man, remember then, that's how it goes."

Al Blake paid the grocer, paid Gavin Ross, who applied the money to the cost of Christine's dog, and lastly paid Arthur Newman.

"Arthur, I should've paid you right off. I had the money then but it seemed like a good idea. Now we both know. Next time you work for a man don't let him pay you on time. Get the bird in the hand, Arthur, he might break his arm."

Arthur looked impassively at the forty-two dollars. "Blake, you ought to have Jimmy Gates look at that chimney of yours. I had a look at it when I put the side cupboards on. You need a new chimney."

Al grinned. "It'll do. Never any fires in Mouse Bluffs."

"Could be."

"I plan a new one next spring."

As he left, Arthur sat down and counted the money again. Muriel came in and stared at the pile of bills. She placed the pan of chicken feed on the sink tray and went to the table.

"It's all there, then?"

She eased herself into a chair. She had an odd sparse way of moving, as if unexpected movement might give her pain.

"Arthur?"

He looked at her lips, raised his hand to his ear. As she talked, his brown eyes followed the precise movements of her mouth. Her color, always high, was brilliant.

"The Backhouses want to take David to Clear Lake."

He nodded.

"Mrs. Backhouse's brother is wealthy, as you know, and he has taken a cottage for them. They would like to share their good fortune. They'll have sufficient accommodation for the boy. I said I would ask you but . . . Now he could have the things he would need in order to go, a new swim suit, a jacket."

"Fare?"

"They plan to drive."

"Why our boy?" he asked, and she knew his thought; two

weeks without the boy to shelter them from the shadows; two weeks without an object; also, would it be charity? What would the town say? Of course the town would say why not this one or that one.

"It's difficult to say. I don't know why children choose as they do but he and the girl are playmates. School, Sunday School. They're together all the time. The Backhouse children are nice children."

"Who asked?"

She knew if it had been Solveg he would refuse out of hand. "The vicar."

"Hmm."

He got up without another word, leaving the money for her to put away. She knew it might be days before he plumbed the depths of this, arrived at a decision. In the night and the cool morning he would consider the possibilities, the motives, what he knew of the Backhouses, watching the boy with furtive attention. She would not speak of it to David unless Arthur decided in favor of it. Before going outside, he went to the door of David's room and looked in, saw the bed as neat as a soldier's, the Sunday boots polished and placed neatly on the rack, the hat and jacket properly hung, the chamber pot precisely in the center of the floor under the bed, the almost-new scout uniform on the back of the door. He nodded as if mildly disappointed.

She began to plan the campaign she must slowly and painfully conduct. She had no resentment about this; as he was a Sergeant Major, so she was a soldier diplomat, exercising subtleties quite foreign to his understanding; if life required of her that she sacrifice overt pride in order to accomplish small things, she did not hesitate to comply. She bought raisins and other dried fruits out of her "home" money to make up a Lancashire loaf, scoured the shed and entry as a soldier should, took sand and rubbed the pump till it gleamed as a soldier's should, went to church only every other Sunday as if God were the Reverend Daniel Backhouse and she had never cared greatly for Him, and when she passed Solveg Backhouse on the church steps merely nodded, allowed no words or meaningful glances which might rouse suspicion of complicity.

Arthur was aware of the waves of persuasion all about him yet he could not detect the point at which they commenced. All these things had been done before. But not all at once. His obsessive sense of responsibility remained unsoftened. He resisted, watched the boy, studied loyalties and duties, and found nothing amiss except an annoying cough. Though this angered Arthur to the point of madness, sickness having no part in his scheme of a well-ordered life, it argued in favor of the holiday.

Muriel listened to the boy's cough at night as she buried her own in the pillow. Finally she took the boy to Gavin Ross, a further inroad into her "home" money, but there seemed no alternative.

"He's underweight," the doctor told her.

David, his face flushed, suspenders hanging and shirt open, climbed off the scales, waiting in agony for the signal to button up.

"He coughs a good deal at night, Dr. Ross, and his appetite is poor."

"Put your things on, David."

David buttoned his shirt, pulled on his jacket, surreptitiously watching the two. Would it be now, the moment he had been waiting for? He could feel the color on his face so hot the air against it seemed chilly.

"Would you wait a moment outside, son?"

The doctor opened the door. David's heart pounded the air from his throat. Son. They would talk about him. He glanced about the waiting room feverishly. He could not sit in this confined place, wondering, not quite hearing what they said. Outside in the alley he hunched on the running board of the doctor's car.

"Is his color always so high?"

Muriel smiled. "He's embarrassed."

Ross studied her intently. Her own color was high. Of course she had that particular English complexion. Still . . . In any case, he couldn't ask to examine her. One step over the mark and she'd glide away never to be seen again.

"Everyone should see a doctor at least once a year."

She chose to misunderstand. "I've been remiss, I know. I shall bring him in sooner next time."

Ross retired. "I wonder if I could give you a sample I have here? Tonic. One of the pharmaceutical agents left it with me for trial. Would you try it on the boy and let me know how it works?"

Muriel paused briefly, said graciously, "Of course. I shall write you a note."

"Couldn't be better, a written report. Now, I shouldn't worry about the boy too much. He's at that stage children get to, all legs and eyes and never still. As long as he gets plenty of eggs, milk and meat he'll be all right. Fruit."

"Of course."

Milk. Milk was the hard one. She placed the bottle of tonic in her handbag. It bulged but of course one did not come from the doctor's office bearing a package or a bottle. From her change purse she took a dollar and placed it on the doctor's desk. Without a word he wrote a receipt.

"Good day, Mr. Ross."

It pleased him in an obscure way, the Old Country address she often used. Not quite accurately. He was both surgeon and doctor to Mouse Bluffs. Everything about her pleased him, even the way she bore her circumstances. A lesser lady, he knew, could make it clear that she was superior to her present. It was a kind of monumental dignity with Muriel Newman that she should not. The wind as she blows. They put iron in those women. Where she is there are no savages. It's in her eyes, home. She thinks she'll leave all this one day; she hasn't yet faced it that now for her there is no home. If she can't make Mouse Bluffs home, then there is no home, only a myth, a song heard long ago and far away, a qualification of childhood. He understood too well. She always affected him powerfully, for, however shabby, however much a part of the town she looked, she carried with her the old places. The second generation survives. They shake away the learned nuances, the inhibiting sensitivities, adapt and survive. Carries herself like a duchess. Iron forged and iron bound, he mused. The old fellow too. He wondered how they had come together. But of course he would never know. Theirs was a different world, he knew, and dying, an era almost finished. Only a few of the old families that had come out with Richard Rashleigh were even capable of understanding them. A few dying limbs. Soon dead.

As he drove homewards down treeless Crescent Avenue, he thought of the Old Country, his Old Country, and wished he wouldn't. He was glad when he reached the elms at the corner of Main.

Ian was at the south windows in the drawing room, a book open on his lap, his eyes drifting to the river from time to time.

"Home?" Gavin asked and the faint sarcasm brought a bitter smile to his brother's lips.

"This man," Ian closed the book, "is quite out of our world, Gavin lad. If I read till my eyeballs ache I shall eventually get a hint. It's like a mystery story, but the mystery is inside the reader waiting to be unraveled."

"I've no time for mysteries." Gavin glanced at the cover. "I see enough Waste Land on my calls without reading about it." He glanced at the window. A cold hand clutched his groin. The dog was on the river bank. "I thought she was going to Solveg's today."

"She did. Just a dip before dinner, you know."

"It's cold."

"Cool."

"I wish you wouldn't watch her," Gavin said, unaware till he spoke that he would say it. He had had the thought so often that it had seemed by nature a silent dark thing, not suitable for voicing.

"She likes me to. It pleases her to think that if it happened, here I would be, helpless and watching."

"Has it ever occurred to you that the more she swims the better swimmer she becomes and the more unlikely it is? Like living, the more you do it the less you feel like dying."

"No one feels like dying, in spite of all this death-wish talk. It's just a question of feeling less like living than dying. There's when the alternative appears."

Gavin turned to go. "Keep watching. It keeps you out of the hotel."

"Always the last word. There's a letter from Mary in the hall under all those drug things. Maybe she's going to send the little swine down again this summer."

Gavin went quickly to get his sister's letter, annoyed to find the advertising circulars childishly heaped on top of it. As he opened it, he felt the familiar surge of pleasure.

. . . and I'm taking you at your word and sending Darcy to you in July. With his father away so much I feel it does him the world of good to be near you. He can stay till school starts if he's a good boy and not a burden to Christine. And Gavin dear I want you to *speak* to Darcy. You know how he adores you and I think it would be best coming from you. It's only natural that you should know much better than Charles or me how these things are done so I leave it to you. I pray pray pray I shall get down in August while Charles is away in the States and of course any of you are welcome here, any time. Do write. All love, Mary. p.s. Charles wants to send Ian a gift is it all right?

Whiskey for Ian and the facts of life for Darcy. He folded the letter and smiled wryly. Darcy was a scamp. Gavin was fond of the boy, too fond. He knew Christine didn't like it but, damn it, his own flesh and blood. Thirteen now, big and dark, the Fraser strain. He remembered the way David Newman's rib cage had looked and shook his head. Good stuff had gone into that boy; he'd be all right. He was overly thin, but he didn't look like a nervous child. Gavin found himself wishing it hadn't been so near dinner, that he'd taken more time with his examination. But there were always the human personal things that he could not alter. Old Newman was hard. Not that hard. Children were a prize in the west, a tradition. In the very early days a single woman with children had been considered a catch, the young hands already there and ready to work, the assurance of fertility plain, and though times had changed and the sexual taboos were now clearly defined, children were still a prize, in hard times a promise and an investment. Yet it was said Newman conducted meals with his dog-whip over his knee. It might stunt a boy's appetite. At any rate there was no way to Newman. In a sudden blaze of memory he recalled another boy whose father had kept a strap at the table. Now how had he forgotten that! Before Ian, but Mary would surely remember. He smiled. Boys needed discipline, the strong hand. Darcy could do with a bit of it. Charles was too easy. But it would be hard to whip Darcy. He had a way with him.

"And is the pride of the family to honor us?" Ian asked at dinner.

"Charles has a case of whiskey for you."

"Ah, Charles! He give me just what I want without all this moralizing everyone else goes in for."

Christine said, "Who does?" and Ian had no answer so she said, "He does the same thing with Darcy." She caught Gavin's eye. "Darcy's coming?"

He nodded. "Had the Newman boy in today," he said for want of anything better to change the subject. "Run-down. I hate to see the kids like this. Reminds me of the clinics in Glasgow."

Ian said, "By the way, did you ever repay him for that little favor he did us last January?"

"What favor?"

Ian nodded. "Gavin, you're a hard man."

"I must write Darcy and tell him not to bring his cat," Christine said. "I'm sure the Crown Prince wouldn't like it."

Slow fire started in Gavin's stomach. Crown Prince. There was no subtlety in her. All her ironies were a blow in the solar plexus.

"Do let Darcy bring his cat," Ian murmured. "I should like very much this year for Darcy to bring his cat."

"Cassie doesn't like that dog," Gavin offered.

"No one likes him. In fact he's the only unlovable dog I've ever met. That, of course is why we have him, isn't it, Christine?"

"I like him."

"It's so very obvious that he does not like you. You confine him too much, you know. He came here all glad and now he sits dully in his place quite bereft of gladness."

She whitened.

Gavin said, "It is not only foolish but unscientific to attribute human emotions to animals. Whatever they experience has no absolute parallel in human feeling."

"Again," Ian sighed, "the last word. Whatever gave you the idea that I ever tried or even thought it might be laudable to try for the scientific approach?"

CHAPTER 5

Wild roses blossomed in the second growth behind the high and low schools, whitish blooms fluttering a false fragility to the wind. Children from over the tracks stopped on their way to school to break off armfuls for their teachers. Adolph Hitler, following hard upon a resounding triumph at the polls, celebrated his forty-seventh birthday with resounding military parades; Addis Ababa fell to a proud Italian army and the Abyssinian royal family fled to Jerusalem; Edward VIII was proving as popular a bachelor king as he had been a bachelor Prince of Wales and plans were made for him to unveil the Canadian war memorial at Vimy Ridge; doom-mongers in Britain warned the populace of the dangers of gas warfare and found a slim audience. The doings of a world remote and trifling did not disturb Mouse Bluffs: Mouse Bluffs had larger problems at hand. Famine fed in the granary of the world, slowed the wheels of its railroad. The year was called 1936 but, happening, it hardly seemed a segment of passing time at all. It stood heavy on the prairie, meaningless in the silo, stretched to rest in the shallow valley of the Mouse.

Saturday nights during the summer the young people danced in the pavilion in the valley below Crescent Avenue. Matt Henderson always brought his truck as close to the back of the pavilion as he dared, backing it up through the long grass, so he'd be ready to bound away up the road on the western lip, although no one, certainly not the Mountie, who like Reese Todd took the long view, was going to interfere with Matt's selling home-made beer to minors at five cents a glass. They were very small glasses: the young had very few five-cent pieces. And as long as no one was blinded or poisoned or burned down the town hall, Matt's selling activities were felt by those in authority to be something of a safety valve. The valley was very dark on a summer's night. Behind the pavilion the least of sins was five-cent beer.

Watching the young people, Matt often ached for his lost youth. He would sit on the truck-gate and drum his fists against the boards, rack his brain to find out why he had worked so hard and missed so much. He always went to work the park; it was a job he liked. Herb, of course, was downtown drinking in the hotel —it was an alibi; not a soul in town could really tell them apart. Some of the men could see a difference talking to them, but talk didn't hold in court.

He wasn't jealous of the young couples. He liked to watch them, felt there was a certain health in the way they took their pleasures. Times sure had changed. When he tried to tell this to Herb, his brother always told him he had been with the dogs too much. Nevertheless he sometimes wondered if him and Herb might not have married if in their time the decent young ladies had stepped out into the long grass as willingly as the young ones today seemed to. The Talmadge girls now, five of 'em, and already two rush-up weddings. The little one was too young yet but the middle two were cutting it pretty wide and would probably end up the same; not that they were bad, just wild and raring to find out; out of his own cupidity he wondered if Steve and Grace didn't encourage them; sure cut down the cost of marrying off girls to have the job done quick and quiet. Not bad girls. Not by Daddy's definition. Like Elsie Yeates, a real looker. See her swinging her chassis down Crescent to the post office and half the loafers in town having trouble with their buttons. And didn't she just know it. No reason for a Yeates to go to the post office. Sometimes the old man sent her down for beer. Herb told him he mustn't think of her. As Daddy said, no amateurs, no trouble. No wife, no kids either. He'd always half hoped he'd get in trouble but he never had the chance; there was always somebody like Nellie. But trouble was the only way he'd ever have gotten away from Herb and the house and the dogs. Sometimes he wondered what him and Herb were saving for or why they were forever improving the house but he always assured himself Herb must have some plan, you could trust Herb. Too late now for trouble to get him a wife. Nobody his age left except three or four school-marms and they could run naked through the park and nobody give chase. Anyway they wouldn't have him or Herb, house or no house.

Back over the hill and down in the grove by the creek the bums slept and made a small camp. They never came near the pavilion. The Mountie was tough; all Mounties were tough on hoboes. Couldn't blame them. One man to police a whole town. Mackenzie took them to the cell back of the firehall and beat the bejesus out of them if they got smart in his town; it worked; the boes had a way of passing the word along.

From where he sat on the truck, waiting for the dance to end and the new batch to come out, Matt could see the trail down the western lip of the valley and, to the east up the hill on the river side, Doc's place, always full of lights as if they planned a party and nobody ever came. He thought he saw movement on the path to the west and nodded. Phoebe Yeates on her way to the boes. That sure was a stray. Trash. Twenty-five cents. He wondered if the Mountie knew. Jack sure did. Matt had seen him go down the first time, one Saturday night back in June, to get the lie of the land and Phoebe come along later. Week nights Jack went down and played craps with the boes. Never won. Jack had run out of winning years ago. Phoebe had to get the dough back Saturdays. Funny about Jack. His wife and all. Then he looked at things different. Part Indian. You could see it in Elsie; not much, just a dash.

"Watch it," Herb had warned. "That's a real amateur. Jack Yeates hears you been around he'll come after you with one hand out and a knife in the other."

"Yeates, ha!"

"The ones with daddies are no good."

Nor the ones with brothers and cousins and all the way till it left old Nellie and cripes he was sick of that trek, could hardly work her any more.

The kids were pouring out of the pavilion.

"Matt, prettiest girl in Mouse Bluffs wants a glass of poison. First time, kiddo?"

"I'm first at everything," the girl giggled. Matt handed her a glass: "Don't forget you give me that glass back when you drink up."

Somebody chuckled in the dark. "Come up and see me some-time, babe."

"Matt, I hear you make good gin. Why don't you bring us some gin, Matt, hey?"

"One drink of my gin and you'd float right up to Crescent is why."

"Ugh, it's awful."

"Girlie, they got cream soda inside."

"You got to acquire a taste for it. Come on, drink up and we'll take a walk out of these mosquitoes."

"Leave them glasses," Matt snapped.

Two for a nickel they cost in Eaton's mail order. Five cents was five cents. Work with the head, Herb said. One thing really riled Herb, Matt doing something without talking it over. Like the vacuum cleaner. But later Herb saw it was just like the salesman said; it don't do to have a house full of expensive rugs and not spend the few dollars might save them from the moth. Now he was starting to talk about getting one of them electric refrigerators. It was a lot of money. Herb had to figure it out on the basis of how much they earned, how many hours they worked, how much time it took to fill the icehouse, empty the pans under the ice-box; he had already written to the General Electric to find out how much power they used up. By the time Herb added it all up, they'd either make a profit or do without. If he decided, then would come the long debate about whether to have it shipped or go to Brandon with the truck, the disadvantage of having the neighbors know being weighed against straight cost. When Herb wasn't reading to improve himself—he'd read all the books in Daddy's bookcase maybe twice: Gibbon, Haggard, Dickens—then he was reading Eaton's catalogue and studying to improve their standard of living. He was a smart one. Matt didn't know what he'd do without Herb when it got right down to it.

In the beer parlor at the hotel Herb sat sipping his glass of beer, feeling the heat, wishing he were at home. Trial and error had proved he was in the coolest spot in the room, a small table near the back, beside the screened windows. Because the table was out of the way, he had to make it a point to talk to people so they would remember him; he wished he could go to the picture-show but they had talked it over and decided that as an alibi it wasn't good enough. He liked the picture-show, any show, especially the free ones sent out by the government. However, no one in a picture-house could say you were there continuously. He even made it a point not to go to the can, but that wasn't any trial because he didn't take on much beer. The men called him camel. "I'm very strong in the kidneys," he always explained. As a reputation it worked. Not that they would ever need it. But only a dummy neglected any possibility.

"Ah Henderson! Matt or Herb? No matter." Ian pushed his chair over.

"Hot, Mr. Ross."

"You said that last week."

Ian was well away, Herb realized. Funny, summer he didn't drink so much at the hotel. Stayed home more. Hot in the hotel. You'd wonder why a man living in a fine house like that, getting his liquor by the case from Winnipeg, they said, would come to the hotel at all. Doc wasn't home much. But she was.

"You always sit here, Henderson. You know, I just realized that from this angle you can look down the lane and see Gavin's place."

"Cool in this corner."

"It's cool at Gavin's. Very cool."

Herb studied his glass. He wondered if he could get Ian to talk about her but he wasn't much good at getting people to talk and he was afraid of Ian's tongue, the strange almost wild speed of it in pursuit of anything a man said.

"I was there once," he said.

"It looks like a castle doesn't it? From here. Bloody monstrosity."

"Daddy took me there when I was a nipper. Went to see Sir Richard."

"There's scarcely a point in this town from which one can't see it."

"Not from my place."

"We can't all be as fortunate as you, Henderson."

"A dollar a day he paid the workmen he brought from the Old Country to do the masonry. Sir Richard used to ring the yard bell for fire or river accident then run up a flag on the tower, red for fire, yellow for the river, so the men knew where to go— to the boats or the fire wagon. White too, then they had to go to find out, accident on some road or farm. My daddy told me. And when Guy was born a pale blue flag with the crest."

"Sir Richard, the one-man museum."

Herb bristled. "My daddy came out here a boy with Sir Richard in 1874."

"A fine old heritage." Ian watched with bright eyes the corner of the alley, the big old house. "I wish, I earnestly wish people wouldn't spring that date on me."

"It's a fact."

59

"It's yesterday. I should like to forget that it was only yesterday it all began."

"Can't argue with facts."

"That's my career, arguing with facts. For me it began only sixteen, no seventeen years ago."

Herb considered it gravely, didn't answer. Ian Ross talked like a half-wit sometimes, though there was always grain of sense if a man wanted to look. It puzzled him that Ian talked like an Englishman. Everybody knew the Rosses came from Glasgow. Maybe he put it on like la-di-da Spence. Although that wasn't likely. Should slip if he put it on, drinking as much as he did. Sure didn't talk like Jimmy Macdonald.

"We're brothers, Henderson, you and I. Fine old families and no progeny. Have you ever noticed how all the fine old families out here are being eradicated? Consider the Rosses, the Hendersons. Consider, if you will, the Rashleighs. All from different parts of the small old world but going. Going. Too raw for us. We must face it. The equipment we have is wrong. The Harveys and the Joneses and the Blakes and the Hoyts have what the Bluffs wants."

"There's reasons."

Herb felt his heart quicken; he might be getting to where he could edge Ian onto the subject of Christine. After a moment's deliberation he signaled Doug Wright with two fingers.

"Reasons? Of course, I've just given them. Don't be obtuse."

"But you . . . You were in the war and Doc, he lost his kid."

"That's it, a pattern, you see."

"Mighty hard on him, the girl drowning."

Ian slopped the fresh beer on his shirt front. "I suffer, you suffer, she suffers, he suffered."

"Makes a big hole in a house."

Herb laced his fingers together. She suffers. His breath expanded hotly through his teeth.

"Makes a house one big hole, Henderson." Almost visibly he clutched the idea: he shouldn't be talking of this here. "What of you, your brother? There's another pattern. Fine old stock, self-sufficing yourselves out of existence."

It's not too late, for me, Herb thought slowly.

"I'm thirty-eight."

Ian stared. "And I'm a hundred and thirty-eight. Got a cigarette?"

They were almost of an age. He'd imagined the Hendersons nearer Gavin's age. God, it was incredible. He wondered what he looked like to them, spread his bony fingers in a white knotted fan against the wooden table-top. Like a goner. Like a man who'd got a bullet in his spine and mustard gas in his gullet. He began to curse in a low steady voice.

Henderson glanced around in alarm. He beckoned to Wright and said quickly, "Bring Mr. Ross a package of cigarettes. A ten-cent package."

Ross started to laugh. He wiped his eyes. "Consuls, Doug. You can have the picture premium, Henderson. It's too good of you."

"That's all right, Mr. Ross." He totted up the account. She suffers. The beer and the cigarettes, twenty cents. It was worth it.

Herb walked home alone through the long black tunnels, the heavily treed side streets, not waiting as he sometimes did to give Ian a push to the corner. It was a nice time of night. Most of the houses dark, here and there people sitting on their porches to catch the faint breeze. The thought of rain everywhere. He sniffed the dark breeze. They needed it. Even the potatoes look bad this year. The grasshoppers were fierce. Everything came at once. Rain would ease it off. Potato bugs like measles over the sides of the houses in the daylight. He took off his cap and let the air thumb his short kinky hair. Across the street he saw Al Blake's older girl walking home with the Kendall boy. That wouldn't work. Kendall being a dogan. He'd raise hell when he found out. Everybody in town was waiting. But they were nice kids. The girl was a pretty thing. Nice girl too. Didn't catch Blake's kids fooling around. They surely wore their skirts short though, the young ones. Pert. He smiled. All girls, fifteen, were pretty.

He remembered Christine when she came back from that school in Winnipeg and old Sir Richard down at the depot, only sixteen she was and Guy, her daddy, dead in Flanders, her mother gone to the Old Country with the Red Cross never to come back. She wore a plaid cloak and a fur hat and she was prettier than any girl he'd ever seen. Too old the doc was but he had a profession and a good Old Country family.

Herb knew to the minute when it had started. Often in his mind he went back and back over that time and wondered how he could have stopped it or changed it.

She had been on that crazy bay of her daddy's when Bill Hoyt's dog, missing for days, came raring down Crescent, foaming at the mouth. Hoyt screaming, "Jaques! Get your gun, Jaques!" and before Jaques could get his gun Bunky Langdon came out of his barber shop with his Winchester and pumped two neat shots into the dog. By that time the bay was plunging and rearing like a rodeo horse with burrs under its saddle, eyes rolling white, but she sat him. Her hat was tramped and the pins all shaken from her hair; it fell down her back like a batch of warm honey. Herb on the corner, debating whether to go and try for the reins, wanting to but knowing how proud she was about handling that horse. She gave it the spurs cruelly and off it belted up Crescent, thundering like crazy past the dead dog. Then Herb saw Doc standing in his rig, his eyes shining like he'd seen Joan of Arc. She got the horse turned up at Maitland's and came galloping back to curse down Bunky or Bill Hoyt or anyone foolish enough to wait for her, sat on the horse, barely in control of his fear, and looked at the spot where the dead dog had been. "Bunky!" she yelled at the silent barber shop. "Next time you shoot you damned well call fire!" Doc got down from his rig and went to the bay, took the reins. "I had heard there were women out here who could ride like that." She laughed then, looked down into the handsome moustached face and they smiled at each other for just that one long minute, all that's needed. While Herb still stood on the corner.

Still, it was early on and the doc was even older now. Life took a mountain of planning and waiting. But it would work out. No matter how old he got, Doc was still fifteen years older and her four years younger. It was a fine night. He saw the truck in the yard and hurried homewards, anxious to learn from Matt what the take had been.

Ian Ross watched Henderson leave the hotel and drew deeply on the gift cigarette. As usual, it provoked a fit of coughing. No blood. He smiled to himself. Gavin never objected to cigarettes, whiskey. He would like me dead, Ian thought slowly, without rancor; he had wished it for himself so often it seemed almost altruistic of Gavin to want it for him too. Gavin knows it's a matter of time! Cigarettes and whiskey aren't going to alter that but without them I'd be a proper bastard. Funny, old Rainwell— old? he'd been thirty-six—had been gassed with the Pats. He died five years ago. And Rainwell took such good care of himself.

Henderson always put his back up. Why? He couldn't quite hit it. Stolid? Maybe that was it. Stupid? But stupidity was the common denominator in Mouse Bluffs. One's back would be constantly in an uproar if stupidity irked.

Gavin, he thought. Henderson always brings up Gavin in that doltish sheeplike way. Mass delusion. Everyone in town tried to see him as he was not. Saw him in Sir Richard's house, married to Sir Richard's granddaughter, pristine Christine. More to it

62

than that. Something to do with the profession. Blood and guts and you better be God; they're my blood and guts, oh holy one. He must talk about it when Basil came to save him next. Now why, dear Basil, do all these people pretend to love Gavin when it is quite obvious they do not even much like him? Let Basil rattle his gourds and prate about father images and breasts and all the other pap. Basil Waterman, brain excised in Vienna; here lies the brain of Basil Waterman, former sod.

"Maybe I should go," he said and Jack Yeates, lounging expectantly against the wall, caught his eye. "I said perhaps I should go, Jack!"

"Maybe."

"Jack!" Jack moved forward on cue. "Push me home. I've got a twenty-six of bonded overproof in the summerhouse."

Yeates hesitated.

Ian said disagreeably, "Don't expect me to coax you each time. The summerhouse is mine."

"I'm with you."

"Over the top!" Ian cried as they sailed out. In his eagerness Yeates almost tipped the chair on the hotel steps. "I shouldn't have felt a thing," Ian said.

They laughed.

The garden stretched down the hill into the valley and was bounded on the street side by a high wooden fence. They went rapidly down the street and Ian took out his key, opened a door in the fence that let directly into the summerhouse.

"There's a candle on the table."

Yeates hung back. "We don't need light."

Ian slammed the door. "Find it. You can see in the dark, Jacko. Here's a match. Gavin doesn't care how I go to Hell just so long as I do it quickly. Light it." He gave his guest the water tumbler, drank from the bottle. "How're you getting on, Jack. Let's talk of sin and destiny."

"A buck here, a buck there, we get by." Jack passed the glass back for refill. "My old lady goes on Sunday to Reese Todd, makes his breakfast, tidies the house. Young Brucie delivers the *Tribune*. Elsie cleans house for the Jew once a week. Dig in everybody. Get by."

"Admirable. A fine family show in time of adversity. But you are not alone, Jack. A hundred doing the same. Oh the decency of you, the steadiness! By God, have another. You do scoff it up don't you? Lower middle class, you know. There is no sin. We shall talk then of destiny. Or perhaps this is destiny, no sin. Or conversely, there may be no destiny in the welter, morass of no sin. Are you listening, old boy?" he cried over his shoulder.

Yeates looked in the same direction, twitched his shoulders uneasily.

"Forgive me, I sometimes talk to Gavin when Gavin is not there. For you. For me he is. Gavin is everywhere and there is no sin. Where do we go from there? Perhaps I should go to church tomorrow. The only good fights I ever get now are from Tim Scott."

"You fight with Reverend Scott!"

"We debate." Ian's chin sagged, his head nodded. "But two former Presbyterians arguing isn't really much of a—a war. Perhaps I should cultivate Backhouse. Would ye say mass at my lug! Would ye! No. No. Inconceivable, arguing with someone called Backhouse. Always one up. Unfair . . . hardly sporting." His eyes closed. "Eh!" he murmured.

Methodically Jack finished the Scotch before he wheeled the chair up through the garden to the kitchen door of the big house. Cassie Treleven gave him a hard look, didn't speak, took the chair and closed the door. He waited. In a few minutes the door slatted open. She passed out a quarter, slammed the door. Jack pocketed it, went whistling out through the front way, unsteadily down the Crescent; he thought of the dog at Ross's and laughed aloud, touched the knife in his belt. No cur bothered Jack Yeates. Nowhere in town he couldn't go. The town was an extension of his body in a way none of the others understood; he owned nothing and everything; born here, he had never gone farther than the fairgrounds of the surrounding towns; the Bluffs was his; he walked up the street as other men walked through their parlors. At the rear of Watkins's he found a gallon vinegar bottle, the top broken, and went to fetch Elsie to take it over to Matt to be filled for the quarter. Matt wouldn't ordinarily sell beer at the house and he wouldn't sell to Jack but he couldn't refuse Elsie. Twice as much as the hotel gave, more. The hotel was a sucker's game, wouldn't let a man in without a shirt, ten cents a glass. Still that silly bloody Ross was generally there and it was worth getting the shirt on to do him in a bit.

CHAPTER 6

"David?"

Reluctantly, "Yes."

"Come here, son," his mother said. "I wish to speak to you."
Her voice was very grave. Now! he thought. It had been a long
time. A month. He wondered how much she would tell him, what
they had decided, she and the doctor talking together that May
afternoon.

"Sit properly. Don't hump your legs like that."

He waited. In the quiet kitchen he could hear the thud of his
own heart as he had heard it often at night while he lay wondering, waiting for what she must tell him.

"How would you like to go to Clear Lake for two weeks?"

His gray eyes clouded with bewilderment, seeking to fit this in.
At length he said, "I'd like it fine."

She nodded. "The Backhouses want you to go with them on
Monday."

His breath came out in a long sigh. Not yet.

"Your father will speak to you this afternoon. It's very good
of him to allow you to go. Hear me, son? It's not every boy in
town has the opportunity to go to the lake. You show your father
you're grateful. Understand?" Her words poured out in a breathy
torrent as if she collected them in a gentle lump in her mouth
and blew them out all together. He nodded. "But no fuss, mind!"
He wouldn't have fussed but he was glad she put it that way. "All
right, now I want you to go to Dr. Ross's office with this. There's
no need to give it to him personally. Slip it under the door if he's
not there."

He took the note and his heart caught in a blast of wonder. It
said Mr. Gavin Ross, which was her habit; she had probably
known him before he was a doctor, and in the corner: By hand.
He wished it read: By David's hand. He put it inside his shirt so
no one would see it.

He went slowly through the town. The doctor usually dropped

in at his office on Saturdays, on his way home from the hospital for lunch. If David went slowly enough he might meet him. The letter creaked against his chest, secret document, message to Garcia. He lunged behind a telephone pole, peered out, continued stealthily through the jungle. Beneath his feet the grasshoppers cracked and crunched, grass on the veldt, the road out of Darjeeling to the mountains, stalking, being stalked alternately all the dusty sun-bleached way to town. He went past the Chink's and down the alley, very slowly. As he passed Center Street he saw the car pull up in the lane beside the surgery and began to run.

No one in the waiting room. The doctor was hanging his Panama hat on the rack behind his desk in the inner office.

"Boy, that's no way to come into a room."

David went back and closed the waiting room door. "I'm sorry. I've got a letter from my mother."

"Close the office door, too."

Gavin read the note, his face impassive. He folded it and smiled, met the waiting expression in the boy's eyes.

"Step on the scale, David."

The enormity of it, the absolute strangeness of being here in the office with him without her, having to unbutton his shirt without her, left him stunned. The cold mouth of the stethoscope moved slowly over his chest. The doctor murmured something. His head was so close the boy felt his fingers moving of their own volition to touch the beautiful iron-gray hair. From far off David heard the outer door. A patient. He almost wept.

"You eat a lot of eggs, milk, David?"

"Sure."

"How much?"

"I don't know. Lots of eggs."

"Meat?"

"Lots of meat."

"Cod liver oil?"

"No."

"Oranges?"

"Sometimes."

Ross went round his desk.

"I'm going to the lake with the Backhouses next week!" David said.

"Fine." Yes, that was good of Solveg. "Listen, David, I want you to take this dollar for spending money at the lake. For a favor you once did. Now, it's between you and me. No need to tell your father or your mother. Fill up on ice cream and sunshine." And Solveg's cooking. He saw the wasting disappointment in the boy's eyes. "And another thing, when you get back I want you to come up to my house—the first day you're home. I've got my nephew coming to visit. He's only ever been here a few days at a time before and he's a bit older than you are but perhaps you could show him the ropes. I'd certainly like you to meet him."

It worked. Something bright and hot fled across the dark gray eyes.

Politely, "What's his name, sir?"

"Darcy Rushforth. I'm sure you two will hit it off. Now, son, thank your mother for the note, I appreciate it. Remember, first day back."

The boy bounded away. Later that afternoon Gavin saw him with Arthur Newman going into the dry goods store and raised his hand in greeting. The boy saluted, two fingers. Newman, ramrod straight, his brown moustache gleaming with wax, turned quickly, nodded. Ross smiled.

Dear Mister Ross: re David Newman. I administered the tonic, one teaspoon twice a day beginning May 23rd and finishing June 22nd. Almost immediately there was a marked improvement in his appetite. However, I wonder if this was not inspired as much by your admonition as by the medicine. In any case, whatever the contributing factors, the boy's appetite improved. He appears to have gained weight slightly and is coughing less. We are hoping to send him to the lake this summer. I expect the change will encourage good health. Thanking you, I remain, yours sincerely, Muriel Heatherington Newman.

Ross stopped at the corner. A gang of boys was collected at the steps of the post office and Brucie Yeates stood on the concrete abutment.

"What the common people need!" he shouted and the boys cheered. "What the common people need," he yelled and Gavin remembered the C.C.F. organizer standing in just that spot the week before, using nearly the same words. "What the common people need . . ."

Gordon Kendall was chanting in the background, "Dominoes forever! Dominoes forever!" in the exact rhythm of the blessing.

There was a beat to it as if they had rehearsed the whole parody. Gavin grinned. The young of Mouse Bluffs could laugh still.

The chant grew, "What the common people need . . ." until the entire crew shouted in answer, "is bindertwine!" and burst into a jubilant chorus of "C.C.F., 'ray! C.C.F., 'ray! Bigger gopher bounties! 'Ray!"

A group of farmers watched, did not smile.

Ross shook his head. A people robbed of security was a people robbed of laughter, a people capable of any weird and wicked seriousness. Germany. He thrust the thought away; he had no time or desire for ideas. His life was a steady progression of deeds and days; ideas were a pack of hounds snapping at a man's backside; people, his duties to people, were all that he permitted to count.

He thought, I'll have to remember to catch that boy when Darcy comes, otherwise he might not come to the house. No one came to the big house; it was a tradition; at one time they used to have a party or two each year and everyone came but otherwise it was *the* house and old Richard had laid the cornerstone of their not coming. To come implied a petition.

Gavin passed the wall and, as he drove up the semi-circular driveway, saw, deep in the garden, Billy Treleven clearing bottles from the summerhouse, filling a wheelbarrow. He thought bleakly, I have even a Grace and Favor House. Why then am I not the laird?

You need a holiday, he told himself firmly. But collections were poor during the summer months with everyone trying to scrape up a bit of a holiday or send the children to scout or church camp. Summer? They were poor at any time. So Solveg was going to the lake. The vicar was a lucky man. But of course the vicar knew that, too well. He came with her when she visited the doctor. Daniel Backhouse, doctor of obsession. Well, there were plenty of them, none quite as bad as Backh— Dan. What made them do it? He couldn't recall ever being jealous of anyone. There were one or two others like Daniel in town but they generally hid it fairly well, knew it was a shameful business; women were worse than men. He remembered a colleague in Hamilton who'd told in utter despair of catching his wife on a stepladder, peeking over the transom while he examined a patient in the surgery. Gavin laughed gently as he went into the big cool hallway. How quiet it was. Dark. Too big. He wondered what it had been like in years past when Guy was small and there were ponies in the stables, lots of dogs, four or five servants. Long ago. Too big. He and Christine had vowed they would fill it up with kids, the only excuse for such a huge house. But the house had worked its destiny of decline against them. I'm getting maudlin, he scolded himself, riffled through the mail on the service tray. Nothing from Mary. Lord, he hoped she would come. A transfusion of sunshine.

Once long ago, a Frenchman (weren't they nearly always, those first intrepid men?) had come out of the lone and level leagues of the plains to this hill, seen the green-gray light hazing the river, the film of light in morning where the creek tumbled out spraying tiny rainbows into the pale air, the green valley where colors glinted more brightly than on the sun-sucked prairie, the oaks catching the sun on flickering oily rich leaves, the whole drawing the light into a froth, a cornucopia of gentle beauty, and had declared it *la rivière mousseuse*: inevitably the English map-readers had made it Mouse River. It was *la rivière mousseuse* when Mary came; she too effervesced like the champagne air above the tumble of the creek, turned the world bright again; they were all better through her. Especially me, he thought heavily, especially me.

We all need a holiday. Mary will be my holiday.

"You look happy." The dog was beside Christine on the veranda.

He said, "I thought he wasn't to be a house dog." She didn't answer. "What are you reading?"

"What everyone is reading. It isn't that it's such a good book, it's just that the title hits the situation everywhere so well. Gone indeed with the wind."

"I was thinking of you. A holiday?" He eased himself into the wicker chair beside her. She wore beach pyjamas and under them, he knew, her swim suit. "I could manage a couple of weeks at the Chalet at Clear Lake for you."

"I don't think so."

He knew they could not go together, go and let leisure find them looking at one another, hearing the past come creeping back on crooked feet. A holiday together was out of the question now. Still, he rather wished she would suggest it, even as a formality or as a remembrance of old times, old voyages.

"Call Cassie and tell her I'd like my tea, will you?" He took the matter in his teeth fiercely. "You should get away. The swimming is better up there. The river isn't much at this time of year and this year it's foul. It's already beginning to smell." The damp dank smell of a river without enough water draining into it, a place of slimy overgrowth and little current. "I'd like to put up a health order against the swimming. Polio's already started in Winnipeg. But where else would the kids go? All winter the rink; all summer the river."

Her green eyes passed indifferently over his. She went to speak to Cassie.

When she returned she seated herself politely. "Yes?"

"Solveg is going to the lake." She was barefoot. She had pretty feet. So few women had. He smiled. "You've got red on your toenails!"

She warmed. "Does it shock you?"

He shook his head to indicate that none of the many vagaries of women could shock him.

She said, "Clear Lake?" flatly and it was an affirmation of the door closed long ago.

She would not go, leave the river. His eyes shuttered against the brightness of it flickering through the trees.

Cassie brought tea and they sat drinking from the steaming cups, talking little, idle indifferent talk.

I do love her, he thought, and the monotony of this silent litany was a heavy cloth over his brain, without the texture in memory of what love's many faces had been. He watched her hands over the tea things, fine hands, long slim fingers, something sensual in all her movements, and over the harsh weight in his chest he wondered why they could not speak directly, when they had begun this oblique stabbing at subjects. Like going after a fresh oyster with a pickle fork. When? She's dead, Christine. Our Tina's dead long ago, drowned in that river eight long years ago. And I love you, must, but there is no way to give evidence of it when the witnesses within us both suffer their separate agony and will not speak. For me there is no way back. Once that other love is gone, like Tina it doesn't return. Filled a dozen men in the Bluffs with tonics and mild aphrodisiacs with great success but it's gone out of me and won't come back. Tina took my manhood to the river as you take your womanhood; keep it; it's too good for the river, love. Unmanned, I cannot even recall the words, nor how the sweet heat of it went.

"I'll swim before dinner."

"You shouldn't after tea."

He watched her go, the crown of gold hair glistening through the trees. Proud. The head proud. And we cannot speak. He closed his eyes. Distantly he heard Ian's chair on the ramp at the front door, the squeal of the ropes as he pulled himself into the house. The not-speaking is her sanity. One word and there's nothing left. Yet he wished he could make her smile, just once as she used to when she was a girl cutting up through the district like a healthy animal, laughing at everyone and everything. But how, with the barrier of sanity a thin bright shell holding off smiles as well as grief? He wondered if this were love's end always, the ultimate, to know there was no giving of happiness, that it grew always within, solitary and incommunicable, and that, having none himself, he could not spark it from her. His love was worthless, like Sir Richard's boxes of old gold mine stocks.

Ian wheeled straight through to the kitchen.

"Cassie! That husband of yours is in my place. If he lays a finger on my whiskey I'll—I'll stab him with a large dull knife."

"What whiskey?"

"You very well know what whiskey. The case my brother-in-law sent me from civilization, from Winnipeg, the Athens of the prairies, the font of whiskey. A Scot without whiskey is a ship without a—a galley. Hear!"

"Dr. Ross manages without it. I'm sure I don't know what you're talking about. I wouldn't go near your *place* and I'm certain Billy doesn't discuss it with me. There's no drink in this house, I'm sure."

"Cassie! Have you always been like this or did you learn it? Christine taught you."

"Mind your tongue!"

"Oh damn." He spun the chair about.

As he started out, she said, "Dr. Ross keeps his Scotch outside."

He wheeled towards the veranda. Christine was swimming. His eyes glistened as he saw the white cap on the opaque green water moving towards the bridge. He licked his lips.

"I told you not to bate your breath," Gavin said.

Ian kept his eyes on the river. "It's my breath and generally damned strong."

"Have a cup of tea. It's still hot."

"Billy's down at my place. Probably stealing my booze."

"Billy wouldn't touch your booze."

"Oh no, but his Christian conscience might make him tote it off in the wheelbarrow and dispose of it."

"Someone has to clean the place up. It's a sty."

"How do you know it's a sty?"

Gavin's mouth tightened. "I can smell it."

"To hell with you."

"Have some tea."

"I'm the only sinner in town; you should prize me, not thwart me. What would Mouse Bluffs do without me? Mothers would have no bad example for their sons. The women couldn't be sorry for you, the crosses you have to bear and a sinner on top of it all."

Gavin poured tea for him. "How childish you are."

"Shut up!"

"You will kindly lower your voice and remember yourself," Gavin said softly, anger turning out his r's thickly. "Now stop it. If you snivel I'll knock you out of that chair."

Ian took the cup. His fingers shook. He hugged it against his palms.

71

"I apologize," he said at length faintly.

"So you should. Now. It's a matter of food y'know. Regardless of how much y'drink y'must eat. Saves the liver. And we made an agreement. It's not been kept for a long while. Sundown. You've been drinking before sundown."

"Gavin, do you know how late the sun goes down these nights?"

After a moment Gavin laughed. "Eight o'clock then. But remember, winter and summer. No starting at four in December."

"That's fair." Both knew he could not do it. He gulped the tepid tea, looked away through the trees, the muscles on his taut white face working. "It's not that, not really."

"I know."

"It's Mary coming. Mary! And the sad sad time of it, Gavin, and all gone. And the road from Bridge of Weir. And the fogs and the good hot voices out of the hills. Mary and it all coming back and no good, no good."

He began to weep brokenly, as a man weeps who has forgotten how to weep, with breathy groans and knotted hands.

Gavin sat motionless, looking out over the garden, and presently said, "Christine's coming."

Ian put his arm to his face and rubbed his eyes before he wheeled slowly away.

Gavin did not turn to watch the white hands plucking the wheels, the gaunt shoulders stooped to the job. He remembered those shoulders. He thought once more of the proud back of Arthur Newman. The regiment's back; unbroken; the boy, straight as Ian had been. He studied Christine's fine round legs as she climbed the path, shaking her hair in the sun. His mind closed around Darcy's coming and a wisp of a smile twisted his mouth. Mary's gift. Time moved, the past a little tunnel of light travelling in a straight line to the future. Without such small glimpses a man was a heap of bones, his life one perpetual cheerless day.

CHAPTER 7

David's mother walked beside him as he carried his small suitcase to the Backhouses' that morning, talking steadily in her soft voice all the way along the path through the tall grass, across the cindered rise of the C.P.R. and down through the stirring town.

"The only reason . . ." her heavy breathing robbed even her vowels of depth, ". . . only—was because you brought home an excellent report."

Part of him believed her. She made it all so serious.

"Miss Campbell spoke to your father on closing day. He's proud of you although he doesn't say a great deal. We're both proud. You have your money? Your stamps? When you write—well, you know how to write us."

He knew how to write; it was what he did best. The delicate waiting look of the small writing tablet, the secret exciting open lines of the scribbler. Though to them a letter would be only a report.

Arthur had not said good-bye, just be good, be civil, be prompt, be clean, so David had asked him what he must ask; it was beyond him, "What shall I call him?"

Arthur smiled faintly, "You can't Reverend him all day, every day; give him my respects," thinking perhaps he answered.

"Just remember that the vicar on holiday is not the vicar in his parish," his mother said. "You'll see him perhaps swimming or—playing tennis. He may even do other things."

"Like what?"

The image of the minister in a swim suit was too much for his imagination.

Muriel wanted to say, dance, but refrained. Oh Mouse Bluffs! How it stunted them.

"Simply remember that he is a fine man and a man as well as a clergyman. Don't be rude or remark on anything—and when you write—and when you get back— You know?"

"Yes, Mother."

"It's a privilege to be invited into anyone's family circle and particularly a privilege in this case. It is a trust."

"Yes, Mother."

The first shock was the Reverend Mr. Backhouse in a suit, shirt and tie like an ordinary man, so transformed David could not help but stare.

"I was on my way to town," his mother said, although it was only eight o'clock, but Mr. Backhouse nodded.

Mrs. Backhouse was rushing about with sweaters, scarves, rags, cartons; at length, after a long worried look at the car, then a shrug, she locked the house. As they got into the car, David wished desperately that his mother had not come to stand looking so sad, so run-down, as if she were a toy unwound and would tumble to the grass as soon as the car moved.

Mrs. Backhouse took her hand and said, "My dear," and his mother said, "He's a good boy."

"Of course he is and we'll return him in fine . . . So good of you to let him come with us. I'd never have felt it safe to let Jon go to the lake with just Lilja, and David has his proficiency badge. Can't thank you enough."

"I'll tell Arthur."

She leaned towards the car. For one ghastly moment David thought she expected a kiss.

"Good-bye Mrs. Newman," Lilja cried, her blue eyes shining with excitement.

"Good-bye!" Jon echoed.

"David?"

"Yes, Mother."

"Mind."

The minister took her hand. "I'll drop a line, Mrs. Newman." He lowered his voice. "I wanted to ask you something. I should have spoken to Arthur but in the rush, you know. Would you ask him to have a look at the house a few times. You know, just to make sure, all these—men about." He removed the house key from his key ring. "I know it's an inconvenience."

A great sigh shook her. She smiled radiantly. "He'll be pleased to, I know. Don't worry. Arthur will take care of things."

As they drove away, David looked back. She was going homewards, hurrying.

Daniel Backhouse expelled his breath, loosened his tie as they passed the road-grader on the highway. As a last-minute inspiration, he thought, it was good. Something about the woman, a dread of obligation. It was endemic. Kept the entire town a group of solitary unobligated souls. If only he had enough keys to go

74

around. The thought of his study, all his papers, brought him a brief qualm. No. Not Arthur Newman. Honor before God, wife, life; it was old-fashioned but it had its merits. In any case, what was there to worry about? Nothing that couldn't be printed on the women's pages of the *Free Press*, not really. His diary was a monument to the man he longed to be. He wrote with posterity in view and Lord Chesterfield as example. He relaxed at the wheel, kept the car at a steady twenty-five. It would be a long drive.

"Children, calm down," Solveg said for the twentieth time, her oddly husky voice lacking command. "Jon, don't get excited. Jon, stop that. Jon, have you got your lemons?"

David giggled. Lilja pinched him. He seized one of her curls, gave it a sharp twist. She jumped on him.

"Daddy! Stop the car!"

Too late. Jon had missed the bag, missed the window. Daniel groaned as the odor reached him.

"Blast!" he said and David, shocked beyond words, retired to the clean corner with Lilja.

Solveg was prepared, dug the rags and sealer of water from the luggage rack, changed Jon's shirt, sprinkled sawdust over the seat and door and went to work with a whisk. With a towel under him, a paper bag in one hand, a lemon in the other, Jon was considerably calmer; he began to suck the lemon, casting white reproachful glances at the other two. David and Lilja, somewhat offended by his weakness, the smell, watched him silently, their mouths working over the lemon; Lilja ferreted a humbug from her pocket and gave it to David.

"Now," Solveg asked the patient Daniel, "may I drive?"

David braced his feet in utter astonishment. He had never seen any woman drive, except Mrs. Ross and she was different. If a woman drove a car through Mouse Bluffs the entire town would dash from their houses to marvel, just as they did when an airplane passed over. As Solveg drove, the minister leaned back against the seat and began to snore gently. David kept glancing at Lilja but she seemed to find nothing unusual. Even she was different, he realized suddenly. Mrs. Backhouse pushed vigorously on the horn and a hay-rick scooted to the side of the road. They looked through the rear window and saw the old man swearing, pulling on the reins. They stuck their tongues out and laughed, while Solveg, looking in the mirror, laughed with them before she spun deftly back to the right. David stared out the rear window at the vanishing farmlands. It was a big world.

There were four bedrooms, a kitchen, a living room with a small stone fireplace, and they sat at the fireside the first evening,

Mrs. Backhouse in her dressing gown, and made popcorn while the Reverend Mr. Backhouse read *Nicholas Nickleby*. From the street the cottage had appeared small but David found it strangely large inside, the windows enormous. The street was called Dogwood and Daniel told them this was a flowering tree generally associated with the Passion, at which David blushed. Nothing was what it seemed.

Compared to the river at Mouse Bluffs, the lake was astonishingly clear, the beach approaches shallow. In the cool of early morning David and Jon and Lilja ran down before breakfast, while the older people walked slowly behind in their beach robes, towels trailing. At that hour they were usually alone on the beach. Solveg did not swim later when the sun climbed high across the hot blue sky.

"My skin is fair. Well, of course I know people nowadays prefer a leatherlike complexion but it's the after-effects. Do you see? Moles and freckles stay."

"Quite. Nothing ages a woman like the elements."

David frequently had the impression that they talked of one thing and meant another, for she often washed her hair in the soft sudsy rainwater from the barrel at the back door and sat on the canvas chair in the bright afternoon sun to dry it, bleaching up the golden lights till her hair glittered with life. Then she would brush it or allow the children to brush it over the back of her chair. David never tired of the silky mobility of it under his hands, flying to meet the brush as if alive, smelling like warm flowers. Her skin turned the color of apricots and, although he often looked, he could not detect a mole or a freckle.

They came home one day for lunch with dewberries they had picked in the cool still woods and found her brushing in a desultory fashion, wearing, David saw, a halter. Nothing surprised him now.

Jon said, "Who's that?" and they glanced at one another uneasily.

Someone was moving into the cottage next door.

"Don't stare," Solveg murmured.

"Oh heck." Lilja plumped herself on the grass at Solveg's feet. "I bet they've got no kids."

A big dark man without a shirt, his chest a tangle of black hair, crossed the other yard, raised his hand in greeting without a word. Casual, but in his place. After all, David thought, we were here first.

"Solveg!"

Daniel came through the gate, the mail clutched against his

side. His lips were white, almost invisible. Slowly, a dreamlike quality in her movements, Solveg picked up her towel and brushes and went into the cottage; he followed directly behind her as if to protect her bare back from the stranger's sight.

"What's wrong?"

Lilja sucked a piece of grass, shrugged, her eyes cloudy.

"Is your dad mad at us?"

"Dunno."

Jon went to the fence. "Hello."

Lilja said, "Jon!"

The big man set down the bag he was carrying from the car and grinned. "Hi blondie."

David went to Jon's side; Lilja followed reluctantly. He had a lot of luggage, golf clubs even.

Jon asked, "Have you any kids?"

"I don't think so," the man laughed.

The children looked at one another aghast.

A woman with gray hair appeared in the doorway of the tiny cottage. "For heaven's sake, Leo, behave yourself."

He laughed again and said, "That's my mother, Curly."

Lilja pondered, "Mrs. Curly?"

"Curly Frank. I'm Leo Frank."

"Leo! Get on with the job."

"What's your name?"

"I'm Lilja. And that's my brother Jon and that's . . ."

"David Newman, sir."

"How do you do Lilja and Jon and Mr. Newman."

"Leo! I'm dying of hunger already."

"See you later, kids."

Lilja decided, "He's nice."

"Yeh."

She screamed, "Jon! Elephant. You can pick up those berries."

But she and David helped Jon pick up the scattered fruit.

"Full of grass."

"That's good for you. Remember Cabot."

Lilja said, "Columbus."

"Cabot."

"Columbus."

"Cabot."

She laughed it away. "Columbus. Now King David, here's your royal dinner, fried grass."

Jon stopped laughing when King David appointed him food taster.

In the house Daniel was saying, "Of course, if she's here, she's here and we'll do the right thing."

Lilja asked, "Who?"

"My . . . your great-Aunt Asta." Solveg turned to Daniel. "If she has no car as Carl says, then we must . . ."

She continued chopping the celery; she had dressed her long hair and now wore a blouse. Daniel was reading a letter.

"Do you know where the cottage is?"

"Of course, only a few streets over."

"Let's go this afternoon, get it over with." Daniel looked out the kitchen window. "They look like foreigners."

"Dan!"

"I mean those—next door."

Lilja said pleadingly, "They're not. He's Leo Frank and it's his mother, Mrs. Curly, and he doesn't know whether he has any children."

The adults exchanged a glance.

Solveg said weakly, "I've told you not to talk to strangers," and Daniel went to the living room where he could see the cottage next door more fully.

He was to stand there often in the days to follow.

"Solveg, *elskun*!" Aunt Asta was a stout red-faced woman with red hair, wearing red beach pyjamas and smoking a cigarette in a long black holder. She wore a great amount of lipstick. David had never seen anyone with so much absolute color. "Oh Daniel! And all the lovelies."

She kissed everyone, embraced the children all together, drew them to a large opened box of chocolates on the sofa.

"Aunt Asta!" Solveg cried happily. "This . . .'

"Aunt Asta knows what you like, Lilja *min*. Solveg, she looks exactly like Gudrun did at this age, a beautiful child. Come, *caffey. Mola caffey, eh elskun.* Solveg . . ."

"The dark boy is a visitor, David Newman. David, this is my aunt, Mrs. Bjornson."

"Sit, sit. Barney is at the store."

David had never seen a place so opulent. There was even a piano, much more beautiful than the one in the Sunday School, made of light wood; innumerable embroidered Chinese pictures, woven mats in eye-shaking greens, reds, yellows; pale furniture made of bamboo, upholstered a resounding red.

"Make yourselfs at home, please. Oh, it's good to find you, now Solveg tell me."

The children sat on a long bench beside the fireplace, Lilja with the chocolates in her lap, Jon and David on each side. The minister, looking somewhat stiff and lost, went to the piano, ran one hand gently over the keys.

Aunt Asta cried, "Oh Danny boy, I remember you playing, yes I do, keep on."

It seemed rude, David thought, Daniel playing gravely as if he were in a far place and, ruder still, Solveg chattering to her aunt, sometimes in a foreign language, their voices rising over the silvery music.

"I know, I know, but there is a woman here, a doctor, you understand, not real—a quack? *Laeknir*. She's got the cure for my rheumatism. A wonderful doctor, *elskun*. You stay, she comes this afternoon soon."

"Medicine?"

"No, it's like . . . It's all in the hands and the spirits, you know."

Solveg's eyebrows shot up; she laughed. "Asta!"

Barney came in, a burly man with immense shoulders. He embraced the children, kissed Solveg, told David he looked like Uncle Tedder and asked Daniel to have a glass of beer.

"No thanks, really."

"Oh Danny, I remember, come. A holiday?"

So the Reverend Mr. Backhouse took and sipped the pale drink while the women talked and Barney looked on with beaming pleasure, occasionally extolling the virtues of the *laeknir*, who cured every ill known to man. Daniel's lips relaxed and he scoffed gently, returned to playing the piano. After he had accepted a second glass, Aunt Asta brought two big trays of rich food to the coffee table, a pitcher of lemonade, and she and Solveg drank many cups of thick black coffee with sugar lumps held in the front of their mouths. David thought he had never seen Mrs. Backhouse look so pretty. From the piano came "O Star of E'en" and Aunt Asta wiped away a tear. Jon ate too much *vinarterta* and was obliged to dash hastily outside. No one noticed. David and Lilja went out together to the "earth closet," as his mother had taught him to call it. It was a magnificent two-seater so they shared the moment, she sitting beside him pensively and telling him shyly she hated her name, that he was the only one who had never teased her about it. When they went inside, holding hands, Jon was sitting rather palely on a hassock, barely holding his own. The doctor was there.

Very tall, iron-gray hair, a loud humorless voice, she held up two very large thumbs and said, "It's here. I was born with it. Some of us got it. Prayer and thumbs on the spinal cord. Never lost a patient yet."

Solveg smiled uncertainly, did not introduce the children, and Mr. Backhouse contrived to give the impression that the doctor in her tie, brogues, cropped hair, was not there at all.

As she led Aunt Asta into one of the bedrooms, he said gravely, "It is my duty to see the best in everyone."

Barney looked puzzled.

"Intentions," Daniel explained.

"Yah, shoor."

Daniel played "Onward Christian Soldiers" with great dash and Barney brought him another glass of beer. From the bedroom came groans and a chanting voice. Lilja and David exchanged a glance and went slyly to investigate. Aunt Asta, a great heap of naked flesh partly covered with a towel, lay face down on the bed, while the doctor pounded and slapped and pummelled with those extraordinary banana-like thumbs.

Call on Peter; call on Paul;
Call on Jesus, best of all.
Rheumatism go! Rheumatism go!
Call on Peter; call on John.
Rheumatism, rheumatism,
Gone! Gone! Gone!

Solveg caught them by the backs of their necks and drew them back, thumped them on the bench. "Behave!"

The doctor returned, her face wet with her efforts, took a glass of beer and pulled a chair to the coffee table to plow sturdily through the food; her brown eyes, set at a peculiar angle on her face like those of an alert horse, shifted cunningly between the two men as she ate.

"Where did you train, Dr. Laeknir?" Daniel asked.

"Dr. Gumm."

Solveg explained, "It means doctor."

"I didn't," Dr. Gumm announced. "I got the call."

"Oh dear," Solveg murmured.

"People don't relax, that's the nub of it, they wind themselves up, up, up. All they need is a bit of help. Think about the Lord and He drives out the pains and aches, the Lord is the Great Relaxer. See, the body is like a watch-spring, like I was telling Mr. Bjornson only the other day. Wind. Wind. Worry. And snap!"

"Dear lady, the streets are filled with people waiting for the word, I'm sure."

"You're not kidding. It's in the thumbs. Relax and pray, I tell them. Sickness isn't bugs or sin or any of them things, it's plain worry and the Lord knows how to deal with it, He just takes over your troubles if you let Him. Give Him a chance and bingo! Out she goes."

Daniel meditated as he took a fresh glass of beer from Barney. "It's there—the truth, I expect, but I cannot comprehend the translation."

"Play it by ear, I always say. Instinct. When I talk to the Lord I never know what I'm going to say ahead but it always comes out poetry."

"Remarkable!"

"It's a call, you either got it or you ain't as they say. Now I better go, got three more patients to see today."

Barney rose and took out his pocket-book, gave her five dollars.

She strode out, saying, "A good rich diet, lots of sweets, it's good for her."

"She's got a horse!" Lilja cried and indeed, looking through the screened window was a horse, a rather sad-looking horse, but large.

"Save it!" Dr. Gumm unlatched the gate and led her horse through. "Few weeks in this sun and it's perfect for the fireplace."

Barney scratched his head as she mounted up. "What?"

"The dung! The dung, of course," and with a negligent wave of her hand towards the lawn she was gone.

Solveg said into the silence, "Uncle Barney?"

Daniel signaled her with his eyes.

She said, "Gavin Ross gets three dollars for a house call. Would you believe it?"

Barney chuckled. "But he can't cure rheumatism, him."

Aunt Asta, rather pale, came from the bedroom in a violently flowered wrapper, her hair shaking out a storm of pins across the floor.

"How do you feel?"

"Like a million dollars, *elskun*, like a million dollars." She sank into a chair, heaved a mighty sigh. "Lilja *min*, there's another box of chocolates in the corner of the ice-box, fetch it for your old auntie."

When they left, Daniel was smoking one of Barney's cigars and promising the Bjornsons a ride up through the park the following day. Solveg took the wheel. Jon hung his head out the window looking rather green, and Daniel hummed "Rock of Ages" and said, "It takes all kinds," at least three times in the short drive.

As he stepped from the car he said, "I do believe I have a touch of dyspepsia," belched and without another word went to bed.

Solveg put Jon to bed and smiled at Lilja and David as if they shared a secret. The three put on their swim suits stealthily and went to the lake. All the way down the twilit road they heard the snores from the screened window behind which the Reverend Mr. Backhouse slept off his dyspepsia.

The lake was as smooth as brushed black silk. Dusk thickened along the lonely creamy sand. Solveg left them and swam to the raft; a dark figure on the raft rose to a sitting position as she pulled herself from the water.

"Mother's talking to a stranger," Lilja said.

"It's Mr. Frank."

"How can you tell?"

"Can't you see how black he is?"

"Black?"

"On his chest."

"Let's see who can bottom it farthest. David? You won't say anything about what I told you, will you? About the . . . earth closet? Spit on your finger."

They spat and linked fingers.

As they walked back along Dogwood, the stones biting their feet, Leo Frank said, "Would you come in for a coke?" and while Lilja was still begging, "Please," her mother turned in at the Franks' gate.

The following morning early David heard her saying in the kitchen, "No more, Dan. Why can't you just forget about it, all this—this guilt?"

"But I can't remember!"

"You know it does that to you. You remember promising to take them for a drive, don't you? I'll stay with the children; it's no pleasure with Jon in the car."

"Tell me the truth."

"The truth is you never played 'Twelfth Street Rag' so well."

She smiled to herself. It was good for a week.

Wearing the halter that afternoon after Daniel left, she washed her hair and sat in the garden, while the three children played in the cottage. Whatever they were up to, it was a riot. She smiled languidly and pretended to read and at length Leo Frank came and sat beside her and talked in a low deep voice, while the cottage rang with raucous laughter and cries of "Peter! Paul! Rheumatism!"

How happy they were, David thought. They talked so much. He hadn't realized how much silence there was in his home.

"Don't forget to write home, now."

Dear Mother, It is lovely here, all green and the lake like well water. The Backhouses are good to me and I look after Jon in the water. Next door there is a man named Mr. Frank and his mother. They are nice and he is an architect in Winnipeg. We help him cut the grass and he gives us a nickel. The Chalet is nice. It is not as big as the hotel in Mouse Bluffs but it has vines. I have never been inside. Your loving son, David.

They often saw Dr. Gumm riding about the village on her horse and once or twice, with sure instinct, teased her overtly, skipping along behind the horse, singing nonsense rhymes about Peter, Paul, John.

"Girl!" Dr. Gumm cried and Lilja froze. This was not part of the game. Lilja clutched David's hand. A long bony finger, the massive thumb at right angles to it, found her. "The hand of God is on you!"

Dr. Gumm rode away up the street. A cloud crossed the sun. Uneasily they looked at one another.

"What did she mean?"

"Crazy."

But the doubt was there. The big clouds always meant something. They dragged up the hill to Aunt Asta's as they often did, ate large quantities of sweets and forgot the coldness.

One day the three walked to the souvenir store and David bought an ashtray with Wasagaming on it for his mother with part of the dollar Dr. Ross had given him and a pocket knife for Solveg, too beautiful to pass up.

"She can use it in the kitchen," Lilja assured him.

"Or keep it in her purse," Jon urged.

They bought cones and still had six cents left, so they filled their pockets with blackballs at the corner store and found blackballs and vanilla ice cream made a tasty combination.

That night clouds piled up in the mountains and the long roll of thunder blackened the air. By nine it was storming badly. Daniel lit the fireplace and they toasted marshmallows.

"Friday," Solveg said sadly. "I can't believe we have to go back tomorrow."

"Seems like a million miles, doesn't it? Still I'll be glad to get home."

"Read to us, sir?"

"What will it be?"

"*Rhymes Of A Rolling Stone.*"

"*Tale Of Two Cities.*"

Solveg shivered. "Listen to that thunder. Should I turn out the lights?"

"I've told you the lights have nothing to do with . . ."

Someone was rapping imperatively at the door.

Daniel gave Solveg a sharp look. "Now really! This is too much." He stamped to the door, opened it meagerly, then swung it wide. "Christine! Come in, come in."

Solveg blenched. "Something's wrong."

Christine pulled off her jacket. "Yes."

Daniel took her things. He raised his brows, indicating the children. David got to his feet, his face white. It's the doctor, he thought. I shouldn't have spent the dollar.

"Carl phoned. It's your mother, Solveg. No, no: she's had a heart attack. That was at five o'clock this afternoon. I drove like hell. We had no other way to get you except through the police and Carl was afraid they'd get it—garbled. He asked me—I was closer and he couldn't leave anyway."

Solveg put her palms to her cheeks. "I must go."

"Carl is . . ." Daniel met her glance, swallowed. "Yes, of course. But how?"

Christine shook her head. "Solveg, I'm sorry. Gavin must have the car back. Can you hire a car?"

"On a night like this?"

Daniel pondered. "The next bus doesn't leave till tomorrow night and the train is worse."

Solveg turned to David. "Fetch Mr. Frank. Hurry. Take off your shoes."

David ran.

"You wouldn't, Solveg!"

"I must. You can't take me. You have to be back at the church on Sunday morning and I may be gone a week or more. Besides I don't want the children—Jon—on the road in this. There's David, I can't very well drag him off to the city. Good heavens, it's all there is to do."

Leo Frank in a black raincoat thrust open the door. Bare-legged and without shoes. Rain ran off his short black hair and down his dark face.

"Leo, will you drive me to Winnipeg? My mother is dying."

"Sure. Now?"

"Right now."

Within twenty minutes they were gone, with Daniel shouting into the raging night, "I say, Frank, this is good of you."

Christine made coffee and Daniel paced, said to the children, "Go along to bed now, it's late."

Jon asked, "Is Omma dead?"

"She's very sick."

"Will she get to Heaven?"

"I expect so."

"Does God speak Icelandic?"

"Go along."

Christine brushed back wet strands of her blonde hair. "Who is he?"

"A neighbor."

She raised her brows. "Sugar? Dan, can I help you here before I go back? I must start as soon as it lets up."

Daniel glared at the children and they left quietly, listened intently over the partitions for further news of the tragedy.

Daniel stirred and stirred his coffee, the spoon clinking nervously in the battened cottage. "I forgot to tell him not to wait to drive her back."

"He won't. He'll be back tomorrow."

"I should have made it clear. I hate being obligated to a fellow like that."

"Isn't it letting up a bit?"

"Please, Christine, sit down."

"Sit down yourself! What's wrong with you? Do you think he's going to pull over to the side of the road and make love to her on a night like this with her mother dying?"

"Really," Daniel said.

"You *do*! God damn it, Dan, you're a prize."

"I won't have this, do you hear? I'm worried about the roads. You're a fine one to go on like this."

"Say it!"

"Very well, you have to go back, rain or no rain, don't you? You've never left the river for eight years. Till now. Does it hurt? Is it not just guilty . . . Christine, how you bruise your own heart!"

"That's right. I can't. I'd never have come now if Solveg wasn't my only friend. I came. It disturbs—no, it hurts all right. But it hasn't anything to do with some perverse idea of yours about sin. By God, adultery is the least of sins. You'd think I'd lain with every buck in the west. I didn't. Swallow it, go ahead, you asked for it. Three boys before Gavin. Oh, I was a wild one! You make me sick. Wallow in it. Is that what you wanted to hear? God didn't kill my baby because of that. I came, I left it, it hurts and it has nothing to do with sin. Nothing in this world bores me quite as much as sex, the idea of it, the doing of it. Satisfied?"

"Yes, say it, talk about it, you'll feel better."

"Talk, talk, talk, that's your life, Dan. Let me rest. I can't talk. Certainly not to you. I'm going now."

He said softly, "She's dead, Christine."

"She's in the river, there's a difference. Get my jacket. As a father confessor you run a good Sunday School. Stop trying to hurt me just because you're blind jealous of some six-foot Adonis."

"If only I could reach you."

"You can't because you have no respect for me. Nor I for you. Where's that coat? I need air. Bring the kids to my house."

"Let's part friends."

"We are in our way but that doesn't prevent my understanding you."

The door slammed. Rain scattered fury over the cottage. Late, Lilja came and scrambled into bed between the two boys and they bundled together till morning chased the rain, left the air heavy and gray, the roads shining wet and the fertile sweet smell of ripe woods and blossoms everywhere. Mrs. Frank came to ask Daniel if she could help him but he said no thank you coldly, and they ate cornflakes for breakfast, toast and more cornflakes for lunch and late that afternoon packed and drove through the wet hours back to Mouse Bluffs. Mr. Frank had not returned.

CHAPTER 8

It was Saturday morning and Elsie Yeates had not come to the store to clean. Jacob wondered. In three years she had not missed a Saturday. Punctual. And clean. Even her ankles, a private test he had evolved for Mouse Bluffs girls. Of course, he knew that cleanliness was not next to godliness in Mouse Bluffs; cleanliness was equated with godliness. The town accepted almost any strange behavior of a clean woman, a fastidious housekeeper. When the tongues clacked over some misdeed, if it could be said, "She's such a good housekeeper," or "Her mother keeps a good house," then the scales were balanced. It explained much of the local toleration of Phoebe, for trollop, amoral, whatever she was, she remained extraordinarily clean; although she had very little to work with, her children always wore clean rags, she wore clean rags and the windows of the old store fairly sparkled from the energy of her only virtue. Perhaps, Jacob thought, it is equal to godliness. Elsie had a technique with the two and a half rooms: first the Morris chair, the cigar stand, the lamp, the sofa, banged into the middle of the floor, then the smell of turpentine, more banging and crashing as she attacked the place, an enemy to be subdued by hard work, frightened by loud no-nonsense noises. He was always surprised by her vigor. There was Indian there, obviously, and they were not noted for their aversion to dirt.

Only last week he'd thought, looking at her, I'd better get rid of her. Now she hadn't come and he missed her. The disquiet engendered by her not coming was a riot of half-imagined scenes, conjured vividly from his small knowledge of her life aside from Saturday mornings. The decay in Jack Yeates's eyes. The stolid unending unvicious vice in the mother. Last year—was it '38 or the year before?—the boy had died, the brother. Peritonitis. Growing pains, Yeates had scoffed, and by the time Elsie ran for the doctor Brucie was dead. Last year. How could he have forgotten? It just seemed longer. Last Christmas, the Friday before Christmas it had happened, and when she came Saturday morning, she told him, but he already knew; the men at his fire the night before had stood, disdained the chairs.

"That goddamned Yeates." The men generally waited for Brace Harvey, steady and generous, to give the talk its approved line, as if recognizing some kind of moral strength they required without being aware of their need; when Brace was not with them, they frequently drifted into gossip of a low order or talked of the townswomen and old sins with hearty viciousness. Now he had said unequivocally, "That goddamned Yeates," and the torch was up.

"You figure it's murder?" Jones asked.

"Manslaughter. Kid slaughter!"

Matt Henderson spat at the stove. It sizzled. "Think the law'll step in?"

"Doc came apart."

Jacob looked a question at Lippy.

"It was Elsie went for him, not the old lady or Jack, but Brucie was dead by then, dead when the doc got there. Appendix burst. Al Blake heard him carrying on, couldn't believe it was Ross at first, shouting half the people had things he couldn't help and when something easy came along in a kid the son of a bitch let him lie and die. Doc'll send him to the penitentiary, I figure."

"No," Brace Harvey said. The others stirred uneasily. "Doc won't. Can't. Reckon it up, Christmas and the other kids and the old woman. And proof. I don't figure a court would swallow it. Some smart lawyer comes along and puts Yeates in front of that assize judge and everyone can see he's a half-witted son who doesn't know his ass from a hole in the ground; he cries a bit, the lawyer talks about the depression, away it goes, the judge talks to him like a daddy."

Matt Henderson said grimly, "I got tar."

Harvey shook his head again. After a long silence he said, "Guess all we can do is show him."

As they filed out into the cold, Jacob asked Lippy, "What're you going to do?"

"Beat the shit out of him," Lippy replied and, without really thinking, Jacob said, "Give him one for me."

Alone, he locked up and felt a queasiness deep in his gut, for Yeates, for the doctor, the men who had gone, and a nasty shock of wonder at the extent to which he was joining Mouse Bluffs. Give him one for me. In Mouse Bluffs order was abstract. In emergency there was no authority as he understood it, defined in books and carried out with dispassionate thoroughness by trained paid men; justice fell to the moral giants and was administered

88

by lesser men with passionate will: the men around Jacob's fire.

Elsie had been punctual even on that next awful morning. She wore a red crepe blouse and a black skirt and under her black eyes the dark circles were like patches.

"My brother is dead," she said after she finished her work.

"I know," he said helplessly. "Make yourself some tea and lie down here for a while. I don't mind. You're done in."

"The doctor says Daddy killed him."

He didn't answer.

"He didn't. He's no good but he didn't say to himself I'm going to kill Brucie."

"No, the doctor was upset."

"It's the drinking, you see, he's no good at it. And Christmas and that. Last night the men came and beat Daddy up."

"Yes."

She began to cry. Jacob glanced apprehensively through the doorway into the store and went out to put up the lunch sign. He bolted the door and returned to her. He started out pretty well, put the kettle on, told her to lie down, that it wasn't her fault. At length she stopped crying, so he smiled and told her his mother had sent him some spiced sausage and a fruitcake and they would have a little feast, yet all the while alarm bells were ringing all over his brain. Elsie knew only one sort of comfort, prestige restoration, and he was aware of this, knew that fruitcake and salami would never be enough. Nevertheless he was so self-conditioned to no-trouble that he pranced about like a schoolboy and told himself he was doing the right and only thing.

She said, "Daddy made an enemy," and cried again. "He told Dr. Ross—Oh God!—he told him he no more killed Brucie than Doc had killed Tina."

"Jesus!" Jacob breathed.

"That's when the doctor hit him."

"Hit him!"

"Daddy thinks it was the doctor sent the men around. That's the way he is, see, he doesn't think it's because of what he did, he thinks it's because of what he said to Dr. Ross."

"He wouldn't—Ross wouldn't."

"Criminal neglect, he called it. Oh, Mr. Herson, will he go to the penitentiary?" He took her hands. She stopped crying, opened the big black eyes slowly. "Hold me tight."

All at once, only that once. A special occasion. She had never mentioned it and the next Saturday appeared as usual. There was nothing between them. He said tentatively, "Elsie, Christmas is a very hard time for me . . ." and she smiled wistfully. "It was a hard time for me too. You want me to try solvent on that spot on the sofa?"

That's all, a spot on the sofa. So let it be. Never again. Although he had thought of it. Now she had not appeared. Maybe she was sick. Couldn't be. She had put on weight, looked better than she ever had. The morning was slow, so he went back to his rooms and started to sweep and empty ashtrays. He felt dismal.

Am I not a man? He scoffed at himself. He wanted no part of the town, only its money. A man. At twenty-nine. He knew he looked older. He was heavy-set and had put on a lot of weight in Mouse Bluffs. There wasn't, after all, much else to do but eat. A man. Sometimes on a hot summer's night he would sit on one of the wire chairs outside the store and dream of lifting, flying out over Mouse Bluffs on the dead dry wind all the way to Winnipeg. Only once in almost four years. The girls walked the quiet streets to town, followed the trail to the pavilion in the valley. They were damned free with their favors with every pimply-faced buck in town or the leather-faced farm boys. But he was different. Well, you want to be different, don't you? he asked himself sourly. Tail is tail. Everywhere except in Mouse Bluffs. Even this has to be different.

A charity outfit I'm running. Quit giving jobs to the Newman kid, kick Elsie out, call in the accounts. Everybody needs money. I need money. Let 'em rot. God, how he had learned to hate poverty. Just once let a Cadillac go by, a woman in furs. Just once see a man or a woman without the stink of poverty coming into his nose. Even the rich ones hid it. Or like old Ross didn't give a damn. He wondered for the thousandth time what that house was like. Dark and full of junk a hundred years old probably. Sometimes at night passing by, you could hear her—or was it the cripple?—playing the piano. That at least was good. It sounded like a grand. He'd asked Cassie Treleven about it once when she came into the store for their order and she had glared, hadn't come back for over a week.

Maybe Elsie's gone, he thought suddenly. But it wasn't September yet and she'd promised to wait.

"Mr. Herson." She had paused, her eyes bright, her cheeks flushed. "I've been thinking of going to Winnipeg. Lally Talmadge went and got a job. They say there's jobs there."

There's bound to be. He watched her with hooded eyes. They're getting up a war. The King and Queen had come to quicken the tempo, get the people into the right spirit.

"Elsie, I just don't know."

"You know what it's like here?"

90

He knew what it was like. He wanted just on principle to tell her to go, get clear of Mouse Bluffs, but there were too many other things. No education, no talents other than the obvious. He knew she would wind up at a counter or on the streets, that life on that level could be far drearier in the city than in the Bluffs. She was so intent, so deeply disturbed, that he fought the conviction that there was something more than just the bare words she gave him, felt keenly all over again the insuperable difficulties he always knew when he tried to communicate with any of them.

"It needs a lot of thinking about."

"I've done a lot of thinking till I'm sick of thinking. I guess I just want to go but I'm afraid. . . . He might make me come back."

"There's that." Jack Yeates had behaved oddly after the boy died. He might force her back. Too, she contributed to the household, more than Jack did probably. Nevertheless, Jacob knew it would always be there, the promised land, the city. Maybe it was better to have it always in the distance, always something to look forward to, no disillusion, "Think about it some more, Elsie."

"You don't think I should go." Her lip came out. "I've got to go."

"I didn't say that. Promise me you'll think—at least till September. September is the best time to look for a job, all the folks come back from their holidays and settle down for the winter. You know things can be pretty hard for a young girl in a big place."

Fear spurted across her eyes and she grudgingly gave her promise.

He was committed. September. He saw she expected a decision from him and fell into silent self-cursing. Here, ten dollars, take it and go and never come back, go to my aunt, she'll give you a job as a housemaid; I'll drive you up myself on Labor Day. The town bleached the heart out of a man; the threat of scandal constricted any expansion of the heart. He watched her leave then, walking down the leaf-thick street, the sun on her black hair, clean black hair. She washed it in his kitchen sink once a week, for there was no warm water in the rat-hole Jack Yeates provided. In his kitchen sink. Even that, he knew, was enough to start an avalanche if she ever let it slip. The only flying I do. Often when he heard the water, he padded back to watch her, the smooth brown back, her blouse off, the quick silky motion of her arms as she bent over the sink, the round firm breasts as smooth and supple as all her warm brown body. To offset the surge of scalding weakness, he always told her afterwards, "Elsie, you sound like a water buffalo when you wash your hair," and she always blushed, her black eyes kindling with indignation.

He had let it be known that he was engaged to a girl in Winnipeg and that he was indifferent to anything in Mouse Bluffs; it was insurance of a fairly good order. The men in the store didn't rib him about it as he had half expected and at length he saw he was scarcely human in their eyes; he had a fiancée, one of his own kind; it was inconceivable that he should betray her, even to the extent of talking about her.

He thought too much about women, he knew. But it was a crazy life, his; no relaxation, no company. Like a monk. Nothing in his past prepared him for it. Thoughts of marriage were always washed cold by the conviction that he could not ask any Jewish girl to live in Mouse Bluffs, the life he had. If war comes, he thought, I'll clear out. There'll be plenty of money in the city with a war. I can get my sanity back. Have a roll in the hay without bringing down doomsday. He knew there must be professionals in town or around the area but he didn't know how to get hold of them and, worse, he could imagine what they were like. Save it. In quart sealers. Almost over, almost. The war. He wanted a war very much, to free him. There was one coming; even in Mouse Bluffs there was a feeling.

The bell over the door rang and Mrs. Newman came in. She sat on the apple-boxes by the door, her breath raking clear across the store. He went into the back to get her a glass of water. Her eyes were closed. Jesus, she's dead and doesn't know it, he thought, put the glass to her lips.

"You're sick, Mrs. Newman?"

"Quite all . . ." After a long moment, "Thank you."

Without warning, bubbles of sweat broke out on his brow. "Look, look, Mrs. Newman. There's nobody here now but you and me and I'm going to tell you right off you better get the doctor to have a look at you, you're not well."

It scarcely got through to her. She bent forward suddenly. "I'm quite all right, it's the walk, you see."

"Walk!" He rubbed his forehead, went back to the counter, muttered, "It's your funeral."

She bought some raisins and a tin of lard and walked out very slowly, her wide blue eyes glazed.

"Die! Go ahead and die. Just stop tottering in here always on the brink. God damn it, you die in my store and I'll throw you out in the street." He hammered the counter with his palms. Who cares? He'd told the kid, "Your mother needs a doctor." "She won't go." "Why?" A shrug. And he'd said to Arthur four or five

92

times, as much as he dared say to Arthur, "Mrs. Newman doesn't look good," got a glare that told him to mind his own business. Money? They always paid cash in the store. Maybe they didn't believe in doctors. Maybe she was sick of living. So die. I resign, give up. Die. But somewhere else.

He went out into the street again to see if Elsie was coming.

"How're you feeling, Mother?"

"Splendid." She looked all right. She had a fine color. She wasn't pale. "I went for a little walk this afternoon and crossed back by the cemetery. It looked so nice. Of course not well tended as they are at home but the cowslips are growing all along the fence."

David was silent.

"You used to pick them for me."

"Aw, I was a little kid."

"I used to see you walk there, all the way along the tracks to the cemetery." She looked into the dreamy distance. "How uneasy the dead are here, the trains racketing past not a hundred yards away."

"I think they like it."

She cocked a bemused eye at him. Memory trickled like mist between them. She had a curious way of making the present or the immediate past seem far off, as if scenes and acts had no clear definition in her mind. He thought of the poplars flickering their coin leaves against the sun, speaking low to him and to the dead; then the distant thunder of the train, the long urgent cry and the ground trembling as the big ones went by. At his feet the dead. And close by, moving as no man or animal could, the giants they had lived on and from and for. Death was stillness; life was the enduring song in iron; men died but the things they built remained, taking new life in others. The dead used his eyes. Sometimes he would put his ear to the steel veins, catch the melody of train-coming long before the cry went up. The dead used his ears.

"Perhaps you're right."

Aimlessly she began to straighten the shelf above the sink.

"What're you making?"

She turned, saw the bowl on the table and her brow cleared. "A pie."

She got the water she had gone to the sink to get.

"Darcy asked me to dinner tonight."

"Not the doctor? Not Mrs. Ross?"

"No."

"Well then, of course you can't. Darcy is not the master there, regardless of what Darcy chooses to think."

He wished he had lied. "May I go over to Herson's and phone to see if he had permission?"

She diced the fat into the flour slowly, as she did everything these days.

"Go along."

Her face sagged. Negative decisions were too much. She could not bear the feel of his resistance in her heart. His "Thank you" curled around the door as he went out.

She sat down, although, sitting, she could not see through the window, only the swathe of lilacs. She loved the window, long hours at the familiar view, the big sweep of prairie, the far-off cemetery. At the foot of the garden the apple tree she had planted was small and stunted. She knew now, in spite of all her hopes against the laughter of her neighbors, that it would never bear fruit. Still there were sometimes blossoms and a blossoming tree was a prize even without fruit and even though late frost invariably killed the blossoms. Arthur had built a high board fence on the other side of the henhouse to give it a corner of shelter. But the prairie had won. The prairie was best. She had been a long while coming to it. This year she had not even planted flowers, which needed such a lot of watering and attention. No flowers. The prairie bred the only flowers it needed, pale hardy blossoms in the sweet-smelling grass. And it wasn't that her arms were so tired or that her chest ached so. It was a wedding, a final meeting with the land. They shouldn't even set the plow to it, she thought dreamily. It wants no plow, no pansies or nasturtiums or anything else we give. It wants the wandering feet and the quick gun and the lone blanket against the wind of night. The bright green of home stirred in a quiet corner of her brain. Never enough. Old Gussie Macdonald crying over the tiny bluebells in memory of her Highland home. I wouldn't. There is nothing here to stir the memories. They are not the same bluebells, a different species entirely. "They're thrushes, not robins, son. The real robin's breast is red, not this rusty shade." Why? The prairie sucked the colors out. Of course they were robins; the children, chanting of little robin redbreast out of songs given them by foreigners, achieved a new red, new robin.

She smiled. No longer a foreigner. When I came everyone else was a foreigner, then slowly it was I, but now there are no foreigners. When I go home I shall explain all this to them.

She rose and went to the tea-can. Eighteen-fifty. By next spring.

Surely. I should not take from it without thinking. After lunch she had taken a dollar to go to Herson's for something and forgotten the change. It was in her pocket. She put it in the can. Although . . . The King was coming. It would be a pity not to see the King. Like a trip home, almost. And David. Certainly David should see them. There was talk of sending a bus-load of children to Brandon. But a bus-load had gone, David among them. How could that be? The King had not come yet.

The King. Everything quickens with the thought of his coming.

I must lie down, she thought, and it seemed such a long way to the bedroom. Perhaps I should have an eggnog. They build one up. She went to the pantry, saw the empty bowl, remembered she had not collected the eggs. She sagged against the door. So much to do always. Very carefully she lowered herself to the floor. Just for a moment. To rest. Perhaps, she thought, I should go to Mr. Ross. Tomorrow. She might simply ask for some of those vitamins that worked such miracles. It might prove that simple. But no. Not with Mr. Ross. He would insist upon an examination and medicine did cost such a lot. Tomorrow. Or perhaps next week when Arthur got paid by the school-board for the new racks in the cloakrooms.

Arthur would agree about the King. David must go. They'd talked about it only a few days ago and he had got out his box and together they had gone through it. Even David had expressed fresh interest in Arthur's treasures, Arthur's wonderful story of meeting the King in Portsmouth. Albert—Prince Albert he had been then. Perhaps she should tell the boy she had been presented. No, it wouldn't do. She had decided all that long ago. It wouldn't be fair to Arthur to . . . It would be nice to tell him before . . . Of course, there was plenty of time. When he was older and less impressionable. Of all, she still had her white kid gloves. She smiled gently. How cool the linoleum was. She had been fortunate.

She heard David whistle as he came past the gate and pulled herself up painfully. It was all in the chest somehow. She must get more fresh air. She was in her chair beside the table when he came in.

"It's all right, Mother, Mrs. Ross says yes. What's the matter?"

"Matter?"

"You haven't done it." He pointed to the bowl.

"Oh, I . . . I thought I'd wait a moment and see if you would be here."

"Darcy asked and Mrs. Ross says it's fine. Lilja's there too. Her mother went to the city with Jon."

"That's nice." She looked at the bowl. I'll throw it out. Arthur will never notice lack of dessert. "She spends an inordinate amount of time in the city."

"It's the doctor for Jon."

"Mr. Ross is surely capable of dealing . . ." What am I going on about? These were almost the exact words Tyrone Kendall had used last week when he gave her a lift to town.

David got a dipper of water, pawed about like a restless horse. "Can I go now?"

"May. Do put on a fresh shirt."

He went to his room. There was no fresh shirt, as she must know. The ironing was stuffed into two old pillow-cases behind the parlor door. She never seemed to get to it. He combed his hair.

"That's better. Tell Lilja to come to see me. I haven't seen her for such a long time."

He went to the door.

"Do you still play rounders?"

"Sometimes."

"David?"

Reluctantly, "Yes?"

"Be careful of that other one."

Her big light eyes were so intense he looked away.

"Darcy's all right, Mother, really."

Dark-haired, vivid, eyes narrowed by heavy lids, Darcy was his friend. Companion? Summer friend? What was Darcy? He had never had a friend before. Except Lilja. And now Lilja sulked. Resented the time he spent with Darcy. I'm sure you two will hit it off, the doctor had said. And they had. David still couldn't get over the wonder of Darcy, so foreign to Mouse Bluffs, yet choosing David as friend, companion, summer friend, whatever it was. For three summers now they had shared slow hot days, the asking Darcy's always. One didn't refuse Darcy. Couldn't even if one had wished to. David's mother knew that, that Darcy was part of the rest of it.

She was shaking her head from side to side as he opened the door. Then the coughing began. He stopped outside the door. Should he go back? He began to run pell-mell up the garden. By the time he had crossed the tracks and passed the depot, the quick lacing of fear was gone.

He saw Jacob standing outside his store, looking up the street as if expecting someone, and he started to run again, this time up the alley behind the store. Jacob always got the conversation around to his mother and the doctor and there was no explaining why his mother couldn't go to see Dr. Ross. It just wouldn't do. It was part of the code or something. The same code that wrapped him in silence, in interminable waiting. But he was sure she'd be all right. It was just mornings mostly. By afternoon she generally looked fine, healthier than most of the women around, and she was always cheerful, never downhearted or snappy like Lilja's mother often was these days.

CHAPTER 9

Prince followed Christine upstairs, his toe nails clicking against the hardwood. Saturday was the hardest day. The monotony of days was bearable, just, but not on Saturday, summer's night. She blew at a wisp of hair. Perhaps I should dress. It might ease the Saturday feeling.

Winter was bad enough. But midsummer, Saturday, when the air poured hotly through the windows of the cool old house, when the river was warm on her body, sometimes Saturday drew the nerves like a prison grill. The week-end feeling had its roots in childhood when time was patterned out to Friday after-four. Friday after-four was the beginning. By young adulthood the whole thing had become a sexual cycle, reaching a peak Saturday night, when hot blackness pressed down on the valley and on the big house blazing expectant and unfulfilled on the hill. In the city one might still have sought out the promised pleasures, or at least oblivion, but in Mouse Bluffs after marriage the pavilion and the Orange Hall were closed and young. One could hear and see the young seeking Saturday night and not join them. After marriage was only a film at the Wonderland, the band concert at the apex of Crescent, and the western road down the valley, where the townspeople sat on wooden benches or walked through the torpid mosquito-infested air, nodding greetings, stopping to pass banalities and smack insects: a sop to Saturday night.

But the pattern remained. On Saturday, around dinner-time, a dull steady throb began in her belly.

Standing before the closet, she decided against the gray silk; it needed a slip. Dress? For Darcy, Ian, Lilja, David? Or for Gavin? She unbelted her beach robe and stood undecided, then took out the blue tennis dress. It would do.

How hot it was. She examined her body in the glass. Smooth and hard from the swimming but getting a bit heavy. Too much of Cassie's meat-and-potato cooking. But one couldn't change Cassie. Not even Mary, with her hints about lobster and salads. Christine grinned belligerently at her own reflection; she liked meat and potatoes. And the resistance made Mary happy in some peculiar way.

"Getting lobster down from the city is more than I'm prepared to do for my stomach," Christine had told her flatly. "Sometimes I eat catfish if Billy is lucky," and Mary had shuddered.

But it gave her an excuse to describe the enormous difficulties involved in getting lobster to the new lodge at West Hawk. The lake full of fish and Mary serving Thermidor. Her pleasure, as far as Christine could tell, lay in the actual difficulties and in her ability to overcome them, secrets she cuddled against the ignorance of guests, who ate and praised and had not the money or organizational ability to imagine the intricacy of it all. Allow Mary her pleasures, she also had Charles. Christine pulled on the tennis dress. Without underthings it would be cooler. What would Mary look like without underwear? Without the stays, the massive boned brassieres? Ha! She looked into the glass again. Her hair had suffered a lot from the sun, bleached to straw. The permanent wave had done it no good. Permanent waves did no one any good, she decided, but everyone had been getting one and she had too, as she often did things, simply because she could think of no good reason for not getting one. She combed her hair back and jabbed a bobby pin at her temple. Just like Jean Harlow, she mocked herself. Her brows were white against the dark fringe of lashes. Maybe I should paint them or dye them or whatever they do. She picked up a thick lead pencil and made a pass at them. And go to Hell on Saturday night? She painted her mouth, a straight line across the bow on the upper lip, in defiance of Mary, whose mouth looked like two cherry halves, timid cherry halves.

"You're smart," she told the dog. He raised his head and looked at her, tongue lolling. "No flim-flam for you. But you stick too close. With this doglike devotion. I'd like at least to have a pee by myself."

Prince looked to the door. Gavin came in.

"When are we dining?"

"Soon." From the garden she could hear the shouts of the children playing some game. "Darcy's too old for that."

"He hasn't had enough of it in the city." Gavin placed his watch and chain on the dressing table.

"On the contrary, he's had too much of everything in the city. He's gutter. How can a boy from an expensive home like that be what he is?"

"Christine, I'm very fond of Darcy."

"The latest candidate for crown prince."

"Do you ever get an idea and not blurt it out?"

Her green eyes were glacial. "Most of my ideas I do not blurt."

"All the wrong ones." He threw off his coat. "This damned heat makes us all cranky. This terrible summer. Ominous." He left it at that. He seldom spoke of the news, made a point, she knew, of wrapping himself more firmly in practicalities.

She got him a shirt from a hanger in their closet. She slept in the dressing room on a small bed pulled close to the window so she could watch the river but, although there was a closet of sorts there, she still used the big wardrobe. "I wish you wouldn't," he had told her stiffly when she had Billy move the bed up. It was as much as he could permit himself to say. "Why?" "Because." "Because of Billy and Cassie? When I care more about what Billy and Cassie think than I do about how I feel then I'll drown myself. Besides," she added, pointing to the old oak-posted bed that had been Sir Richard's, "sharing that is rather pointless." He had no argument for that.

He took the shirt. It was one of the silk ones Mary had brought him.

"Don't wear a coat," Christine said. "It's too hot, even to please her. Do you know Darcy's shirts are handmade and cost ten dollars each?"

"No, I didn't."

"Doesn't it shock your good Scotch heart?"

"Scottish."

"That's the five hundred and eighty-fourth time."

She left him, the dog at her heels. He heard the bell in the yard and went to the window to call to Darcy but, as he did, he saw Mary step from the veranda and call, "Children! leave that bell alone. Lilja, I expect more of you. Now come along and wash up for dinner." She had more of the Gaelic in her voice than either he or Ian. Ian swore she worked at it. "How can a woman who went to Langley speak with Gaelic in her voice? Langley is guaranteed to uproot such provincial traits."

There was a perfection in Mary that defied analysis. Gavin never saw her without a lift of the heart. He watched her stroll into the garden, collect the children and then, arm in arm with her son, move towards the house; there was an easy grace in all she did.

He knew without her telling him that coming here meant as much to her as it did to him. Charles, of course, was a complete ass, regardless of how she built him up. Charles never came to the Bluffs. All Charles did was make money in large quantities. It was an outstanding characteristic in these times. Nevertheless it would be nice if he had other points. There was always a suspicion in Gavin's mind that Charles was perhaps not honest, a little too facile in his business affairs. Charles's only real accomplishment had been marrying Mary when he was overseas and he mightn't have achieved even that if she hadn't been so anxious to be near Gavin.

It's the old world, he mused. Only Old Country women have that quality of pure femininity. Brings out the best in men, even Charles. Makes one feel a gentleman. More, makes one feel that, if only there were enough Mary to go around, all mankind might be gentlemen. Even Mouse Bluffs flourished under her good gifts. The women admired her, put out that extra effort for her. What Christine received as Sir Richard's granddaughter Mary got merely by being Mary.

Downstairs he found the three having drinks on the veranda. Lemon cup. Ian had a smug look. No doubt he had laced his.

Mary said, "Cocktails are becoming more and more popular in the city."

Christine studied her drink lazily. "When I was a little girl it was my job to go down into the cellar with a pitcher and draw off a quart of beer for Daddy and Granddaddy before dinner. That damned cellar scared me half to death but I would have killed anyone who tried to take my job."

"How interesting."

"It never was cocktail or wine country, just whiskey and beer. People don't linger over their pleasures. They want them fast and furious so they can return as quickly as possible to work. No guilt about work. They take relaxation as they would a dose of salts, because they need it, not because they particularly like it."

"Gavin," Mary said, "do take your coat off. You look so hot, my dear."

He removed his jacket and hung it over the back of a chair and sat beside her. "I hope there are no calls tonight."

"I hope so too. How beautiful the river is."

Ian said sadly, "And how it smells."

"It's not the river smelling, it's the creek. Algae or something," Christine told him. "Where are the children? We should eat."

Mary smiled. "You're all so used to this. When I walk out that door I smell the sweetgrass."

"There's an orchid on every dung heap, Mary. All one needs is the eye for it. You're our orchid," Christine told her and went to look for the children.

Mary flickered her handkerchief in a fanning motion against her face.

Ian said sourly, "She's not being sarcastic."

"My dear! I know she's not."

"Christine has a way of scraping bottom always. She has the truth but she can't make even nice things palatable," Gavin said.

"We all dig our own graves," Ian observed.

The other two ignored it; he was given to enigmatic remarks which they knew from bitter experience they must ignore. Gavin pushed his brother's chair to the dining room. The three children were waiting behind their chairs. Darcy drew out his mother's chair with a sly look at Gavin.

The doctor said, "David, as you are our special guest perhaps you will say grace."

David bent a white face over his plate.

"God bless the master of this house,
The mistress bless also,
And all the little children
That round the table go.
And all your kin and kinsmen,
That dwell both far and near.
Bounty on the table,
God's blessing all the year. Amen."

"Old English, isn't it?" Mary smiled at David.

He was watching Gavin. All your kin and kinsmen. Ross nodded and picked up a roll.

"And how is you mother, my dear?" Mary asked Lilja.

"Fine."

"It's too bad of her not to call me when she's in town so often."

"She's called and can't get you in," Ian said. "That's her story."

"Shame on you. You know I'm home a great deal, because of Roselee. She is a difficult child."

"She sure is," said Darcy.

He had long, very dark hair and wore it pompadoured; it glistened now with water, the quick even clefts of a hasty comb. His eyes were dark, had a hooded look, and he was extremely thin, with a sinuous unboyish quality to his leanness.

"Now, son," Mary said.

"We've lost track of you on the society pages," Christine said. "It must be Roselee."

Ian said slowly, "As I so aptly put it, we all dig our own graves."

"Of course we do," Christine assured him. "What a genius you have for the obvious."

"There's my epitaph."

Mary sighed. "How serious we all are."

"No, if we were serious we wouldn't sit here in this backwater while the world digs, as we all dig . . ."

"You needn't sit here, my dear," Mary said. "You always have a home with Charles and me."

Ian laughed. "And leave Gavin?" His eyes found Darcy's, met malevolence with malevolence. "How would you like that, Darcy boy?"

"I should like it," Darcy said stiffly.

Gavin ate with deliberation, not really listening, except when Mary spoke. He watched her, his head to one side, hearing her voice but not the sense of it, as if its lyricism, its evocations, were quite enough.

Cassie came and stood stolidly in the doorway till he looked up. He had not heard the telephone. She nodded towards the office.

"Damn. Excuse me." He folded his serviette and rose.

David watched him go. He looks tired, he thought, and it's always somebody not really worth it.

"How tired Gavin looks," Mary said and David glanced at her, startled.

Ian began, "We all dig . . ."

"Oh shut up," Christine told him quietly.

Mary's eyelids fluttered. "You're tired too, Christine."

"Saturday night."

She observed the children. They too were frustrated by Saturday night, she knew; already the pattern was there, the night drawing powerfully; it was in the delicate flush on Lilja's cheeks, the glitter in the boys' eyes. The Newman boy. Appalling. No child should be so polite. Darcy was. But of course one knew Darcy didn't mean it. Saturday night was calling them and, although its promise would not come this night, it was waiting for them. She felt her breast heave in a spasm of regret, clenched her wet hands together in her lap. Her mouth moved silently.

After a moment she said, "Finish up your ice cream and you can go into the parlor and play the gramophone."

They looked at each other gladly and left.

She heard Gavin coming from the office, Sir Richard's office, and excused herself.

"I haven't the faintest idea of what it's about," he muttered. "I'll be at Herson's store. Get Billy will you? I don't want to leave the car parked there." Their eyes met; he did know and he was carrying the special bag, the one he took to the country for emergency deliveries; she never questioned him. "You know—if anyone calls have them call the hospital, have Rita talk to them. I may be gone some time."

"At the store?"

"Yes."

She stood in the doorway and watched them go. Soon the music from the valley would begin to trail up the hill. Music. It wouldn't matter what it was; it would rack her. The liveliest song could drive her into an agony of depression. Losses. Lost. Reduced to a mere organism. A thousand black blossoms fed the night with tawny perfume, brushed her arms to struggle against the moon. The path across the garden called. Tonight she must swim. The river and forgetfulness. Black and warm and waiting. To lie floating and watch the indifferent moon, sink gently, let the watery stars lie like cold wet coins against the eyes, then, never knowing why, resist! Throw the body in an ecstasy of effort up the low black road. Perhaps tonight. At least the point sought, the point of choice. A terrible lust grew in her to drive straight to that moment where unmeeting heart and brain might join once and for all in a frenzied squeal of panic, to see if she were ready yet. Ready . . . The thought for a moment erased the losses, the pointless urgency of the nights, the staggering pain of the dance-band tuning to banal heartbreak. Once, twice, how often? Each time so brutal that the last time remained the only time, she had clawed on all fours up the bank to lie panting and weeping and vomiting river, while the clever night dispassionately looked down on the worthless thing it had won back. She placed both hands against her neck, rubbing the warm night against her flesh in a gentle shaking motion. Tonight. The music came. Her nails bit her flesh. She turned and walked quickly to the dining room. The curtains stirred softly against the screened windows in the faint evening breeze, as hot as the day.

"Where's Ian?" she asked.

"He's gone to the summerhouse," Mary said, sipping her coffee.

Christine sat down heavily, toyed with the silver serviette ring, running it over her index finger. A strong night. She shrugged, threw the ring down. Alone with Mary. Her carping about Mary annoyed her for she knew Mary was a very good and wonderful woman. But she could not stem the childish impatience.

Mary began, "Basil Waterman and I had a talk before I came."

"And?"

"He wants to come down to see Ian."

"Oh God."

"He's sure he can help him."

"He's been sure for five years. Last year he came and helped and Ian didn't draw a sober breath till after Christmas."

In the parlor the old records began: *As I walked out in the streets of Laredo.*

"But he didn't do as Basil asked. Basil wanted him to write it all out, his whole life, do you see? Rather like long-distance treatment."

"Oh Mary, there's a time of not going back because it no longer matters. You can't save some men because there's nothing on the far side of saved."

"Everyone has value," Mary said firmly, in the tone of one who will never be angered, whatever the provocation.

I saw a poor cowboy wrapped up in white linen,
Wrapped up in white linen, as cold as the clay.

"Have they indeed? I'm not so sure. It's in our mouths, that sort of statement, not in the way we live. Have you seen the men at my door begging for grass to cut, wood to chop? Hundreds. And they're not trash, Mary, I know what you're thinking. They're men, that's all, and must live or die as men, not as cases or something of value."

Beat the drum slowly, play the fife lowly,
Bitterly weep as you bear me along.

Mary gestured impatiently. "Of course they are, that's what I've been saying."

"Can they be saved? I've seen their eyes. Like Ian's eyes. There's nothing on the other side of it. They've been robbed. But life robs us all sooner or later; whatever the blow, the method, it's over. Maybe the smart ones resign early." Jesus, two girls in the dorm, she thought bitterly.

Shot in the breast and I know I must die.

"Nonsense," Mary said. "Things haven't always been easy for me. It's simply that I do not let down. If one lets down the next step is giving up."

Christine refused the message. "So you and Basil will save him? You're welcome. You know the Chinese story about the man who was busily committing suicide and his friend came along and saved him?"

"Basil is a very clever psychiatrist. He has a splendid reputation."

"The friend was forever responsible for the man's life. He got nothing but vilification, certainly no gratitude, and was morally accountable to the man's family forever afterwards."

"Gratitude? One does not do these things in the hope of gratitude."

"Really? Why does one do them?"

"For their own sake. Because every human life has value."

Christine looked past her into the night. A myriad moths fluttered meaningless patterns of death against the screens.

Mary said at length, "That, of course, is what has governed Gavin's whole life, that belief."

Christine merely looked at her. "Excuse me, Mary," she said finally. "I think I'll go to the river. Prince!"

Mary shook her head sadly. "Will Gavin be late?"

"I won't wait up for him. He said he might be late. Saving valuable life is time-consuming."

Mary sat a long while over her cold coffee cup. How unhappy Christine is, she thought, and the thought made her feel unhappy too. For Gavin's sake she must find a way to help. She felt rather let down: the first time she had talked, really talked to Christine in several years. However it was a beginning, perhaps a hopeful sign. The children were very quiet. She wished they would play the Galli Curci records.

She called, "Darcy?" and a moment later the raucous notes of "Barnacle Bill the Sailor" ripped through the house.

She sighed. They hadn't bought new records for years; the old gramophone was hand-wound and frequently began to groan to a discouraging halt during a record. Of course they hadn't bought anything new for the house for years. She thought of poor Richard Rashleigh with his bright dreams of an estate, of all the thousands of pounds he had spent bringing his people out, building the opera house, the bridge, not knowing really what he built. Assuredly the result was not what he had planned, a great socialist community, every man a landowner, buying land through service to the whole. It hadn't worked. Or had it? For Richard it hadn't. How cruel to lose his son. And Christine. Well—the town did not forget. Whatever she did she was still a Rashleigh. There wasn't a man in town who wouldn't knock a stranger down for criticizing her and not a woman who wouldn't be pleased to have her for tea, however mad she became. Mary had spoken to Basil about Christine. He had promised to think about it. But of course that did not free Mary of her duty as Gavin's sister. Not that Gavin was unhappy; it was as if it never occurred to him to consider happiness. She thought of how different he was when he came occasionally to the city and was free of duties. One thing was clear. Gavin belonged in the big house, as successor to Richard; he was more than enough of a gentleman. There was immense strength in Gavin; things would straighten around.

She went to the parlor. The lights were out, the gramophone silent. She heard a giggle.

"Darcy! Lilja! Come along now."

She found the light switch; they came from the alcove sheepishly. Mary looked from one to the other.

"Lilja, you had better run along to bed. I heard Mrs. Ross say she promised your mother you'd be in bed early. Darcy, you and I can walk David to the tracks."

David shifted uneasily. "That's all right."

"No. We'll go along with you." She was thinking of Christine's comment about the hoboes. "Besides, I do rather enjoy a walk at night."

Lilja said good night reluctantly.

"Where's Aunt Christine?" Darcy asked.

Mary said with mild impatience, "Now Darcy, I don't know."

"Bet I do." Darcy poked David's ribs suggestively.

The cinders creaked beneath their feet as they walked through the darkened streets. Crickets chirked them along the way.

"I want you boys to promise me not to play games in the dark with Lilja. You're getting a little older now."

"Why?" Darcy asked.

"Now Darcy."

The two boys walked wordlessly by her side. David felt his face flame for Darcy's impertinence as if it were his own.

Darcy said, "Wonder why the lights are on in the Jew's store."

CHAPTER 10

From where he sat on the sofa, chin cupped on his palm, Jacob could see through the bedroom doorway. Silence at last. The baby slept. Elsie slept, her small body barely showing under the Hudson's Bay blanket. He heard the doctor on the telephone and thought wearily, past caring, the operator will listen.

Gavin spoke to the matron, told her to prepare for a post partum and a prem; he called his home and told someone to get Billy Treleven to come for him.

"Mary, I have a premature baby here. I'm going to move it to the hospital. Get the laundry basket, Billy will know which one, put some water bottles in it—you'll find them upstairs—warm not hot, just so that they're warm when they get here. Lots of fresh towels. Yes, thank God it's a warm night. One big blanket. No, don't come. Billy knows. No. Good night, don't wait up."

He returned to sit beside Jacob. The sofa creaked under his weight. Neither spoke. Jacob almost said again, the number of sayings lost, "Believe me, Doctor, I had nothing to do with this." The assertion had been lost in the strange sounds Elsie made against the Black Mask magazine she clenched between her teeth; the doctor had finally snapped, "For the love of God, man, shut up and make yourself useful!" So there he was like some lousy sharecropper in the latest Hollywood film, boiling water, hacking off lengths of new flannel and warming them in the oven, filling old vinegar bottles with warm water and wrapping them in towels.

Presently Ross said, "It's all right, Jacob, she only came here because she had no other place to go. Thank Heaven everything was normal. I was afraid I might have to use forceps."

Jacob's mind flooded with the picture of them trying to move the girl from the bed, or, worse, having to use the forceps on the bed; his shoulders heaved with silent relief.

"Yeates really threw her out?"

"And beat her."

Jacob rubbed his palms over his face. "I can't figure it out. Damned funny nobody noticed. How far?"

"Eight months maybe," Ross smiled wearily. "They'll be all right. She's tough stuff. Had it like a pup."

Jacob winced. "I don't understand—she was here last Saturday."

"Sometimes a woman—I remember a nurse in Glasgow who went full term and stayed right on the wards. When her time came matron and the chief surgeon paid for a lying-in hospital—she was back on the job in two weeks, looking a bit wan but no one any the wiser. Sometimes it goes that way."

Jacob leaned back abruptly, tried without success to infuse the scene with reality. Gavin Ross sitting and chatting with him in his sitting room just like two old friends, the unapproachable Gavin Ross. Suddenly the flaw was clear. It came to him with surprising bitterness; if you were all you're cracked up to be, Ross, she'd have gone to you. His eyes slewed sideways to catch the cold detached look on Ross's face as he checked his watch. He had yearned for a friend and often, passing the big house on his lonely walks, had dreamed of this man's friendship; he had always had an almost religious reverence for professional men, now in the breaking of days saw for the first time that the profession in no way identifies the man, no more perhaps than religion.

He said slowly, "I wasn't specially good to her," and for that moment all uncertainties were gone from his voice.

"But you couldn't know, could you? Each of us has different terms of reference. You were probably kinder to her than anyone else has ever been."

Jacob felt his breath stumble in his throat and for a moment he thought he might cry.

"Jesus," he sighed. He had a picture of her pushing through town with an endless number of prams. Anything for a dime, a quarter. "What'll I do? It's not mine."

"Nothing then."

"Just nothing?"

"Not much else you can do, is there?" Ross's eyes narrowed over the cruel sense of it. "He's a fine boy."

Their eyes met. A fine boy. The new life moved between them in the small hot room. Jacob looked away.

"You understand me, I can't afford to get mixed up."

"I understand. It's a story so old only clichés will do—they're wild flowers, these girls—bloom and, poof, gone. They have two generations to our one. Old Phoebe, Elsie's mother, is the same age as my wife. Yes. And here she is a grandmother and my wife looks —a girl. Such a small meager time they get and no one can afford to get mixed up in it." He rubbed his eyes wearily. "In any case, it's a good thing she did keep it secret if she wanted the child. Phoebe is the town expert on hot baths and slippery elm and sterility."

Jacob swallowed. Mouse Bluffs. "The boy. It'll be the same life for him."

"Seeds itself from generation to generation. And it's no concern of mine. I do my job and withhold judgment. There's only one trouble with withholding judgment, I also relieve myself of the possible charity or mercy. Still, it's the only way a man can function in this job."

There was a discreet knock on the door.

"Like you," Ross concluded and went to the door. "Mary." He sounded annoyed. "You ought not to have come."

"It's all right, my dear, let me help."

She carried the basket in one hand, the blanket over her arm. Billy followed her. Jacob rose to his feet and came forward. The night would never end, he knew. The humiliation would go on forever. The doctor's sister. He waited to be introduced.

Ross said, "The child is in that room. Make sure the bottles aren't too warm. You know what to do. Now, Billy, fetch the rugs from the car and we'll move the girl."

Billy looked neither right nor left.

"Should you move her?" Mary whispered.

"Of course I shouldn't but she can't stay here."

Jacob stood in the doorway, bereft of speech. Oh get out, just get out.

"Elsie," the doctor murmured.

The girl stirred, said, "Yes, Jacob," and Jacob paled. As they took her away, all of them ignoring him, just so much background, she called once, "Ma," and was quiet.

Ross said, "Good night, Herson."

Jacob locked the door. His legs, as he returned to the bedroom, moved stumpily as if he had no joints. Not here. God he was tired. He couldn't sleep here. Numbly he stripped the bed and put clean sheets on it, threw the bloodied linen and length of oilcloth in the corner. He would burn them. Burn out the memory with the blood. His brain cricked again sharply with the picture of the brown thighs spread, the queer white sack bulging and bursting, then the small head, the slime of blood everywhere, and over it all the terrible groaning sighs. For a moment he thought he would vomit, fell heavily against the clean bedding, buried his mouth against the white pillow. A screw is a screw anywhere except Mouse Bluffs. No! She'd been town property. Very quickly he went into the store. The bolt of flannel still lay across the counter, marked by the zig zag of his frenzied chopping. He found the scissors on their chain against the counter, sliced the edge and tore off the jagged piece, put it in the stove. He turned out the lights, went to the bedroom, set the alarm for five-thirty so he could get up and burn the soiled linen before the town was awake. As he struggled for sleep he thought, everyone in town knows I have no time for it, I'm engaged to a girl in town. But they'll all know. They'll all know she came here. He began to sweat. Build it up about Yeates kicking her out, no place to go, no one to turn to. But don't say too much. Play it low and close. A good deed. He thought, I'll pay the doc. Inexplicably he found himself thinking of Brace Harvey's hands, strong and big but the flesh firm and pink and uncalloused, the hands of a man who did hard work but always with gloves on. Beautiful hands. I'll talk it over with Brace, man to man quietly, sorry for her and tell him I'm wondering if I should pay the doc, maybe he'll offer to help and I'll say sure, somebody ought to help the poor kid out but let's keep it quiet. Play it low. He had barely closed his eyes when the alarm rang.

Phoebe Yeates, on her way to Reese Todd's Sunday morning, did not yet know she was a grandmother. She had been busy in the park the night before when Jack came home and found Elsie in the throes of unmistakable labor. By the time Phoebe got there, weary and with only a dollar twenty-five for the night's work, there was no sign of Jack or Elsie and the boys were asleep. She had been mildly puzzled as she quietly got out the laundry tub to fill it and scrub her body. It wasn't like Elsie to leave the little ones alone so late. She wondered then vaguely what Matt Henderson had wanted Elsie for. Left his truck in back of the pavilion and caught her as she made her way through the park.

"Where's Elsie?"

"How should I know?"

He spat. "Some mother you."

"Keep a civil tongue in your head, Matt Henderson or I'll set Jack on you."

"Just do that, Phoebe, I'll fix his hash better'n he got last winter. Where could she be?"

"Home."

"Home. She's not home. What'd she be doing there on Saturday night?"

"Well look for her then. I got better things to do."

"Listen, Phoebe—"

"Take your hands off me."

"If she's home when you get back, you tell her I want her."

"Not likely." She hurried off into the dark. "You leave Elsie alone, she's a good girl. Too good for the likes of you."

"Just tell her, you!"

Old enough to be her father, Phoebe clucked. Maybe they wanted her to clean. Elsie was a good cleaner. The Jew had given her an extra five dollars last Christmas. A good girl. Never a girl like her for turning a dollar. She'd do near anything, minding babies, working in the gardens, helping Mrs. Spence with spring cleaning and canning. It'd be better if Elsie could get a place to live in, away from Jack. He was hard on her.

It was a pretty morning, hot already though. She thought of the breakfast waiting to be made at Todd's and grinned. Maybe she'd be able to bring some oranges home for the kids. She robbed him blind, old Todd, and he didn't care. Lately she'd taken food openly, daring him, and although he didn't like it much there wasn't a whole lot he could do when you really got down to it. He didn't want to rile her and in turn she didn't want to rile him. She didn't go too far. She wished Jack wouldn't keep on about her going to the park. It hadn't been too bad and it wasn't every week and just summer but she knew Todd wouldn't like it if he found out. She didn't want him to think bad of her. He might have his quirks but didn't all men? His were better than gambling or drinking and he was a decent old man, clean as a boiled soupbone. Between the stuff Herson gave Elsie, fruit and bologna and things that wouldn't keep over Sunday, and what she took from old Todd, the kids did pretty good. She was vaguely troubled that Elsie had not put in an appearance even this morning. Jack would give her a strapping, sure. But Jack hadn't come home either so he wouldn't know, if the two kids kept their mouths shut. Uneasily she wondered if he'd been with Ian Ross again. He shouldn't. Jack was a gambling man, not a drinker, and Mr. Ross was what you might call an expert at drink. Sometimes they were pretty foolish together. Like Jack betting somebody would assassinate the King on the royal visit, "Him on a gold throne and the working men starving," and the two of them sitting in the summerhouse every night listening to the radio and getting drunk, then Jack coming home stumbling and cursing, "The bugger's still alive," and she never knew whether he meant the King or Mr. Ross because he was always saying Ross had almost died in some kind of choking fit.

She passed St. George's and saw Mr. Backhouse fastening open the doors. He nodded to her but did not smile. Every Sunday he held early communion service. Only the Pike sisters came. What they needed so much church for Phoebe could not imagine. Maybe they pray for other people, she thought suddenly, and felt warm inside with the idea. Maybe they'll speak to me over the fence if that's why they pray. I'll go out next time the little one runs out with some garbage. I just never figured it out. It would be nice. But it was pretty hard to keep Denny from going through their hedge and they sure didn't understand that, not ever having had a baby. The Pike sisters with a baby. She was laughing aloud as she turned in at Todd's gate.

Daniel Backhouse looked up the street after Phoebe. A fine morning. He wondered if Solveg would be going to early service in the city. Perhaps not. He couldn't blame her really. She had to spend such a lot of time in the church in Mouse Bluffs and so much of that time expended upon issues and causes which seemed to yield few tangible results. Not that one looked to the church for actual rewards but sometimes a woman found it difficult to get the broad picture. The willow beside the parish hall did not stir. Another scorching day, he feared. He hoped Lily was behaving herself at the Rosses' but of course she usually did. It was always his particular prayer that Christine would drive her to service and come in with her but she had never done so. Perhaps today Mrs. Rushforth would bring her. It was better in any case than Christine's dropping her off at the door and driving away.

Perhaps Solveg would change her mind and return tonight. Not likely. The negative sank like a small cold stone through his mind. Probably Tuesday's train.

He had telephoned her at her brother's last night. At nine-thirty. He always called between nine and ten. She was out, as she usually was at that hour, and suddenly he couldn't bear it. He had left the call in, had the operator ring the number every twenty minutes until Carl's housekeeper called to tell him in furious tones that she would leave a note for Mrs. Backhouse to call the Reverend Backhouse as soon as she returned.

"Dan, what's wrong!"

He rubbed his eyes sleepily. "Wrong?" He blinked at the clock on his desk, rubbed the shin he had bumped on the edge of the bed. "Solveg, it's after one o'clock!"

"Is something wrong with Lilja?"

"Where have you been?"

"At a movie. For heaven's sake. I thought something awful had happened."

"Well, I left the call in, you see," he told her lamely and wondered how it had come about that it was he who was in the wrong. "It's one," he repeated cryptically, mindful of the operator.

"Carl and Helga took me to Child's after the show, we had toasted cheese sandwiches and coffee in which I took cream and two lumps of . . ."

"There's no need to . . ."

"But apparently there is. Lilja is all right?"

"Of course. I just wondered."

"I'm sure you did."

"How the boy was!"

"The doctor says it's a matter of time. It's not just his stomach. The doctor thinks it has something to do with his asthma and—"

"Asthma!"

"Yes, all that snuffling and snorting and . . . It may be something he eats. Look, Dan, I'll explain it all when I get home. It's late."

"Of course. Give him my love."

"I will."

"And hurry home, my dear."

"On Tuesday if I can. Call Christine, will you? Only don't mention anything about what I've told you, you know how Gavin is."

He hung up slowly. It was all right. Certainly it was all right. And he couldn't have asked her straight out if she'd seen Leo Frank. He'd never ask her, afraid not to after that first, "I saw Leo Frank the other day in the city. Remember the architect who was next us at the lake?" and at the same time afraid to ask for fear of drawing attention to the man. Of all the men's names he had confronted her with, his tongue lurched over this one, the stranger's.

He thought vehemently, I won't, but knew he would. He always told himself he wouldn't, then something, some unknown, would trigger the whole thing and he would find himself accusing her; waiting, waiting for the reassurances, watching the most minute changes of expression as she answered. I won't, he said so fiercely to himself that his tongue moved silently in his mouth, I won't. With that he had gone to their room, knelt beside the bed, prayed briefly for peace and for Solveg with whom there was no peace.

How trifling the fears of night seemed in the morning light. He looked across the churchyard, lying still, green and lemon in the bright morning, and wished again that they had placed the cemetery here instead of on the other side of town past the tracks. It seemed too typical of Mouse Bluffs. The dead should rest beside the church, so the churchgoers would see their peace and be reminded of the transience of life. Besides, the cemetery might be kept in better order if they saw it each Sunday. "But the Presbyterians and Methodists might not like to be buried in an Anglican churchyard," Solveg had said once and he was reminded of another disadvantage of the Mouse Bluffs cemetery, a common ground. "If they did they would be showing better sense dead than alive."

At times he thought of Solveg as two women. Even her voice sounded different when he phoned her in the city. He knew she kept a wardrobe at her brother's and he didn't mind that so much; there were things she could afford and could not wear in Mouse Bluffs; just so long as it didn't become a passion, things. She never complained. Perhaps she might if it were actual necessity that forced her to wear the same summer frock, the same cheap hat, every Sunday. Though she looked splendid, even then. It was the absence of worry, real worry. He always felt a pang when he saw Scott's wife from St. Andrew's. They were so poor it had gone beyond shabbiness. The United Church wasn't meeting Scott's salary, Dan knew. He made it a point to avoid the Scotts. He had quite enough shabby, thin women to look at on Sunday without going out of his way to feel miserable about Presbyterians.

It was only after morning service, as he stood shaking hands and saw them collecting in sober groups in the churchyard, that he realized something was in the air. The news from Europe, the weather, the crops—these wouldn't detach the women from the men in solemn clumps. A scandal. He could smell it. In a moment of cruel panic he wondered whether Solveg had done something rash. Of course not. Here was Mrs. Spence wiping her moustache and telling him she always liked that sermon. She would not if Solveg . . . He sighed as the groups began to break up. He would be the last to know. The town protected the one to whom it should come in time of need. An undefined sense of failure fell over him as he went into the vestry. Lilja sat there with Mrs. Rushforth.

"Dear lady." He took her hand, genuinely pleased to see her. "I had quite forgotten I was to go to the Rosses' for dinner. Forgive me. All the handshaking. So good of you to wait."

They picked up Darcy, whom they discovered throwing stones at the chimney of the Parish Hall, and drove first to the rectory to collect some items of Lilja's clothing that Christine had asked for.

"Why do all the men talk together and all the women talk together after church?" Darcy asked and they all laughed, but the little needle of worry lanced Dan again. They didn't always.

"You have a lovely garden," Mary told him.

"Yes, although I . . ." He caught Lilja's flush and did not add that Arthur Newman helped him with it. "I do love flowers. But of course flowers are the least of it. Come along and allow me to show you our winter's vegetables."

Mary allowed. She was very good and gracious and he found himself telling her of Solveg's prowess with the preserving kettle.

"The rector's wife, you know, must practice economy," he said and immediately wished he hadn't. Why am I always apologizing? he wondered frantically. She knows and it must sound like an outright lie. "Solveg's charities are exceptional. You wouldn't . . . What she saves is by way of a gift to others," he muttered.

"I'm sure," Mary answered calmly. "The gardens are better this year, aren't they? At home we've only had to water half as much as we seemed to a year or two ago. Is it possible the drought it over?"

"I do believe our prayers are being answered."

He remembered with piercing clarity a special service for rain he'd been asked to conduct. An overalled farmer standing on the church steps afterwards and looking dispassionately at the cloudless sky. "Taken too long, He has." The way the white hairs grew thickly from the man's ear. Daniel began to talk hastily about his tomatoes.

Darcy watched them, drove one sharp black shoe into the peony bed. "Why do they always do that?"

Lilja said, "I know."

"Dad does it too. Everybody who comes to our house. 'Oh, so that's a petunia, wonderful. Will you look at those begonias!' Big thing. Only Dad's worse. He doesn't do a damned thing except pay the gardener."

Lilja's enamel blue eyes looked through him; she wouldn't tell. "You're not supposed to say that."

"God damn." Darcy's eyes glittered. "Watch out, you. Remember what I was telling you. After they all get to sleep I'll come and do it to you."

She went white. "No, you won't."

"I will."

"I'll yell."

"Naw, you'd like it too much."

"No, I wouldn't. I'm not ready yet," she said steadily, "and you said a girl had to be ready."

"Not if I make up my mind."

"I'll tell Dr. Ross on you."

"Ha! He'd call you a little liar and send you home. He thinks I'm I-T. Get it?"

"Then I'll tell your mother."

"She thinks I'm not ready." He laughed softly. From the corner of his eye he saw the clergyman and his mother returning and he whispered, "You haven't a chance."

"I'll tell David!"

"That squirt! Listen, don't you know when you're being kidded?"

"Yes."

Driving to the Rosses' Daniel made it a point to pass the ruined opera house and tell Mary all about it; she knew all about it but she had an easy interested way of appearing to listen.

"What a waste," she said.

"Well, you might consider it that," he said thoughtfully. "However I feel it was a triumph in a way. Like dressing for dinner in the jungle, only more so."

"Perhaps." She liked to appear to agree.

"And, dear lady, that is what we all do in Mouse Bluffs, dress for dinner in the jungle."

"But think of what all that money would do now, a soup kitchen or a free clinic."

He shuddered slightly. "Of course."

Billy Treleven knocked on the garden door of the summerhouse.

"Come in!"

He opened the door but did not go in. "You coming up for dinner?"

"Can't you see I'm entertaining a friend?"

"Yeh, I can see."

"Convey my apologies to my dear brother and Sir Christine."

Billy slammed the door and put the hook in place. If those two wanted out, they could go through the street side. It meant a hard haul with a wheel-chair on a hot day.

"Blast you, Billy, unhook that door!"

Billy went slowly up the garden, pausing here and there to check his plants. Let 'em yell. No one at the big house could hear. He saw the preacher's car come through the gates. That must be one mighty rich man, the preacher's brother-in-law. He ran to fine cars. Good idea for a preacher to marry a woman with rich relatives, kept the wardens in their place; it was something fierce the way them Presbyterians starved old Scott and hated him for starving. Then nobody looking at Backhouse's wife thought for one minute he married her for her money; still she was some sort of bohunk and it had to be taken into account; gave up the Romish church according to Cassie but Cassie went on intuitions not facts, "Something about those slanty eyes, I swear she's a dogan," and everybody knew they never really gave it up. "Them as lives in glass houses," Billy often told Cassie but there was no arguing with Cassie. Having a drunk in *her* family wasn't the same thing at all as being a bohunk or a papist. You could change over from being a drunk. Not that there was any sign of change in Ian's case, even with that expensive head-doctor coming all the time from the city and explaining about him being sick. "Sick in his will power," Cassie had told him plain. Cassie wasn't afraid of anybody. Not even Jack Yeates. But that showed her ignorance. Billy wouldn't go into that summerhouse with Jack Yeates sitting there drunk as a pig, not by a long shot. Maybe he ought to speak to Doc about Yeates always hanging around. He threw the thought away. Doc didn't follow up on little things like old Richard used to. Besides Doc was too busy. He had enough on his mind without Billy Treleven reminding him his brother was going to Hell on wheels.

"Jack, alter ego, incubus, we are alone. Locked alone." Ian banged the empty bottle on the table.

"My old lady's part Indian, that's what makes me drink," Jack explained laboriously. It was a theory he had been developing for some time.

Ian raised an insolent eyebrow. "Phoebe? Phoebe that was Goldie? Please, Jack."

Jack's eyes glinted with menace. "Her all right."

"Indian Jack." Ian folded his hands across his lap. Jack slowly drew out the knife, stroked his thumb along the blade, looked up at the vine-shrouded window. Ian's lip trembled moistly. "Go ahead."

The other got clumsily to his feet, went to the couch, pulled the apple-box from beneath it and brought another bottle of whiskey to the table. His hand shook as he poured.

"Got to win. Just once. Then slice."

He drew a filthy finger across Ian's throat, sucked in his gaunt cheeks till his big nose gleamed like a hook of bone.

"You'll swing," Ian whispered, "swing, swing, swing." His gray hair hung damply over his ears. His trousers were soaked with urine. "Win? Takes some thought."

"Ever tell you about my horse?"

"Countless times."

"Won every race I ever ran her in."

"Something to engage the whole man. And drawn out. Let's not be hasty with my life."

Yeates reeled to his feet, went to the corner and micturated against the desk.

"What the hell you always scribbling at here? And why don't you get that damned battery charged?" He stabbed the lifeless radio with his knife.

"No more dog races."

"Well, how was I to know Henderson would go to the Mountie? Matt hates that Mountie."

"Button up, Jack, your privates are public."

"Ar—" Jack feinted with the knife.

"And who would buy your booze? Or let you sleep in his summerhouse? Your dear old pal gone. Better prolong the affair."

"No more of your kind of bet. Will some bastard shoot the King? Will it rain in Saskatchewan? You got no feeling for it."

"Will there be a war!" Ian shrieked triumphantly. "How's that, Jacko? By the end of the month. Ten dollars says no. You can't miss that one."

"Balls. Make it the end of the year."

"You're on."

Yeates looked crafty. "Bet you four bits your brother comes down here and gets you up for dinner."

"Unfair," Ian whispered. "You heard him with your Indian ears."

Jack grabbed his knife, the bottle, lunged for the small door set in the far wall.

"Bring back that whiskey, you bloody thief!"

Ian wheeled for the door; it banged behind Yeates.

Gavin said, "Come along and get washed up for dinner." He sniffed. His voice was gentle. "Come along now."

"Sometimes when you speak I almost believe you love me."

"What sort of a way is that to talk?" Gavin said gruffly.

He took a blanket from the couch and threw it over his brother's legs, wheeled him from the close, rank place.

118

"It's what I used to care about. Snot-nosed and alone in that awful bloody school and later over there. All I ever wanted. Be brave. Gavin writes such brave letters. Do or die, Gavin will love you."

"Yes, yes, pull yourself together, lad."

"Lad? The minstrel boy to the war is gone. Didn't come back. All he had to do was be brave, buckle on his father's sword and Gavin would love him."

"Stop that. Mary's here and the minister. Billy and I will give you a good bath and you'll feel better."

At dinner Ian was pale and drawn, his fingers trembling over his cutlery and Daniel Backhouse expressed the hope that he was not unwell.

"You see, Father, I'm writing my memoirs. It takes a lot out of me," Ian explained and was gratified to see Backhouse flinch.

"Oh quite, you men who were there must have a great deal to say now, perspective and so on. With the world on the verge, I very much fear—"

"Father, it was bloody. Absolutely bloody."

Backhouse cleared his throat. "Yet the heroisms, the personal victories of battle in some way diminish the horror, do they not? One thinks of men, pressed beyond human endurance and rising to finer things in terms of sacrifice."

Ian crumbled a bit of bread. "You might have been there, you put it so well."

Gavin glowered.

Mary smiled vaguely. "But that's all of life, isn't it? Really it makes the whole thing worth the candle, doing something for others."

"Always," Christine murmured.

"Now, Christine. Remember what we talked of last night? It's a privilege as well as a duty. I haven't told you but I went out and helped Gavin last night," she said proudly while Gavin watched her with the air of a doomed man, his fork hanging in fascinated mid air. "I went over to that store—Herson's—where Gavin had delivered his wife under the most primitive conditions. I helped him take her and the child to the hospital. Such a lamb of a baby. So tiny you couldn't believe it. And Gavin as calm as you please. I felt as if I were a character in a play. Honestly. A darling baby, I almost feel as if he were a part of me."

Ian watched Gavin; Christine watched Gavin; Daniel Backhouse watched his plate while Darcy and Lilja stared goggle-eyed at Mary. Cassie, in the doorway with a hot dish, moved smartly and placed it on the buffet; with infinite pride in herself for rising to superhuman effort under pressure she said, "Coffee or tea, Mrs. Ross?"

Much later Gavin said to a tearful Mary, "You couldn't know."

"But it's so basic, Gavin, not to talk. So basic with a doctor's family. Oh, I am an idiot."

"My dear, the minister was the only outsider and he's fairly conversant with such things."

"That poor child. Oh! There must be something I can do for her."

"Leave her alone."

"But everyone will. She'll not have a friendly face. You haven't even a branch of the Salvation Army in Mouse Bluffs!"

Gavin smiled briefly. "No, we're very disorganized."

"I'll go to see her."

"Mary, I mean it: keep your kind feelings for the city where you can direct them into properly organized channels."

"Gavin!" She began to weep afresh. "I was trying to show Christine how she could help you. She must think me a prize fool."

"Christine isn't even thinking about it."

"You are cruel!"

"Nonsense, come along now, wash your face and come downstairs. I want you to help me with Ian. He's having a bad time of it lately."

"I am good for him, aren't I?"

"Wonderful: you know how we both love you."

"I know. Gavin, dear, I am so lucky in my brothers."

He kissed her gently.

CHAPTER **1 1**

The screen door was still banging. The kitchen table teetered, and Matt removed his seat from it impatiently. A new set, waterfall walnut veneer with cardinal red trim; he constantly forgot it wasn't the big old trestle table his daddy had made and which was now relegated to the tool shed. Herb didn't look up from his ledger. Matt put his foot on a chair, leaned against his knee.

"I just came from town," he announced.

"I know."

"Elsie Yeates got a baby."

Herb studied his fountain pen. "Bound to."

Outside the dogs in the run yelped. They had heard Matt come and would yipe and fuss till he came to them.

"Better see the dogs."

Matt gave Herb an exasperated glance and went out. He couldn't talk with that noisy demand going up. Herb gazed at the slapping door. He didn't close the ledger till Matt came in a few minutes later.

"First," Matt took a deep breath, "he steals my chickens, then he tries to race one of my dogs with a couple of curs for money."

Herb put his pen aside carefully.

"Then he kills that boy of his. Now he throws Elsie out in the street and her having a baby."

Herb waited. Matt breathed heavily. The old cuckoo clock ticked indifferently in the warm kitchen. Their eyes held.

Herb's slid away and he said mildly, "Somebody'll throttle that bastard some day."

Matt sat down suddenly. "I figure that's my kid, Herb."

"Your kid?" slowly.

"Yeh, Elsie and me..."

Herb got to his feet cautiously, stretched. "And every other buck in town."

Matt said steadily, "That ain't the way of it, Herb. She's a nice girl, clean as a whistle."

"Why didn't she come to you?"

"It's beyond me, Herb," Matt said. "I just don't know. She kept talking about going away to Winnipeg to get a job. She was saving up for it. Herb, a kid like that, raised the way them Yeates are, maybe she didn't know properly about it."

"You paid her."

"It was like a present. She was saving money, see?"

Herb wiped the sweat from his face. "You're more'n twice her age."

Matt smiled slowly. "I ought to do the right thing."

"She's a Yeates, Matt. What're they saying in town?"

"That's it. See, it was Jack throwing her out. There's a lot of talk about him being unfit to have kids."

"How about grandchildren?"

Matt ignored it. "Nobody's blaming her."

"Nobody blamed Phoebe either when he used to send her up the line to the bunkhouse but I figure she didn't mind."

"Even the preacher said bad girls don't get into trouble, it's ignorant ones with bad folks. Billy Treleven told me he heard him say it over at Doc's place. Now Herb, you know Daddy used to say that, bad girls don't get into trouble."

Herb staggered under it. "That's why Daddy told you to stick to bad girls."

"She's a pretty little thing, Herb." He got up and began to move around the kitchen nervously, lifting the stove lid, kicking the wood box. "She sure needs someone."

"She know about the money?"

"Money!" Matt flared. "Money ain't everything."

"Maybe. You figure to marry her?"

Matt stopped. "If you let me."

"Can't see how I could stop you." And after a long moment, "Billy doesn't usually tell what he hears at Doc's place."

"There's a lot of talk. Everybody's talking."

"Talking how?"

"Jack might get himself another licking or worse."

"Worse?"

"Tar and feathers?"

Herb slapped the ledger. "Nobody's been tarred and feathered around here for twenty years."

"They ain't all like you, Herb, some of these fellas boil easy. They're saying a man wouldn't throw a dog out when it was having pups."

"Guess not." Herb was thoughtful. "Might be best to get the

Mountie. Maybe Doc will. Remember when the Mountie got those social people up from Brandon when Olly Manson went loony and burned the kid?"

"The Mountie!"

"There's a proper way to do things."

"Sure. Sure. And how do you know this, Mr. Henderson? Did you witness it? Who else will swear? Sign this paper. Come to court . . . You and me been doing things the proper way all our lives, Herb, and what's it got us?"

"Look around."

"Yeh. But what for? I never know what you got in mind at the end of all this work and buying and building."

Herb's eyes glazed over his plans. "Well, I can't stop you. The place is half yours."

"I don't want it that way. I want you to be glad. Look, think about that kid. I bring that kid here, it's like having a slice of the future, see?"

"You sure did a lot of thinking between town and here."

"I been thinking about it for a long time. About kids, I mean, and us not getting any younger."

"Our daddy came out here with Sir Richard."

"And her granddaddy was here before that. That's real old family, Herb."

"Some joke." Herb went to the screen door and looked out. "What about Yeates? You want him around here?"

"I'm going to deal with Mr. Yeates."

Suddenly the kitchen was very quiet again. Herb watched the bright sun on the bean rows and felt a chill.

Matt said, "You told me once you'd help me when the time came."

Herb slumped. "This isn't what I meant."

"You won't?"

"Not what you're talking."

"You don't want her here?"

"Sure, let Phoebe Yeates come and sit in Mummy's needlepoint chairs. Let Jack Yeates try out Daddy's pipes. Matt!"

Matt thrust him aside, raged out into the yard. Through the screen Herb looked smoky, unreal.

"You're letting me down, Herb."

"I never let you down. You let us down."

"Tell you something, you just get along to town and get yourself seen for the next couple of days cause I tell you I'm bringing that kid home and Jack Yeates ain't never going to come to my house. Daddy's pipes!" Matt bellowed scornfully as he threw himself into Henry, yanked at the gear shift.

Herb returned to the table, picked up his pen. All gone. One amateur. Just waiting for Ross to die wasn't enough. He should've told Matt. Matt didn't know what he was waiting for. He should have told him. Couldn't. Can't change your way of doing things. Can't drag a respectable woman down. He'd never quite got it straight what Matt would do when he married Christine but he'd always known she'd want to live in the big house and he'd been making a nice house for Matt all these years, a grand house. Nobody'd be able to say Herb Henderson married to go to a fine house. Maybe he should have explained it all. Matt had never been so bull-headed before—bull-headed but never unmanageable.

A proper way. He remembered as he did too often the night he and Doc buried Tina. He'd walked the banks and rowed the river day and night, long after the others stopped, and then gone to Doc privately. Doc sitting like a dead man on the bank of the river. "You're right, Herb, she'd want to see her. We can't let Christine see her." They sure couldn't, Herb agreed, after three weeks in the river. Even the doc. He'd puked himself; no way around that. Her poor little kid. He'd done all the digging himself up on the edge of the bluff, while Doc lay face down on the grass, crying without a sound, only now and then a frightening kind of moan. Before the night was out Christine's swimming had begun; they should have told her. But he'd given Doc his word. They should have told her. There's a proper way to do things, Matt; a brutal lesson.

"We're all dying out," he said to the waiting kitchen.

Up in the cemetery were ten Hendersons. Six of them had gone there—Mummy and Daddy and his four sisters—in the 'flu epidemic. That fast. Suddenly there was him and Matt and the big old empty frame house. Them not twenty-one even and with just each other where there had been so many.

If he could just be sure. If it was really Matt's kid. It might work out. They could all stay here and when the time came he could go to the big house. It might even seem more natural. This way Matt might feel obliged to pay him his share of the house. Doc was getting on. If he could just be sure. Moving quickly, he took the key from the hook beside the kitchen door and went out, latching it behind him, struck off for the center of town where he would be seen. It wouldn't hurt for a few days to play along with it, be seen enough to account for two men.

Jacob sat on the wooden stool behind his dry goods counter. It was Wednesday and he'd had only three customers since Monday, three railroad men and yes, Mrs. Newman, besides the general run of strangers dashing over from stopped trains. For the first time since he'd come to Mouse Bluffs there seemed nothing for him to do in the store. He'd cleaned the shelves, scrubbed the meat cooler, taken stock of the dry goods, wiped each and every can with a damp cloth. There was nothing left to do but look over the accounts and wish the slow ones would pay their bills and wonder when they'd start coming in again. All he'd done was play the good Samaritan and it looked like he'd go broke over it.

He was afraid and had endless conversations in his mind with the various people in town. All day Sunday he'd rehearsed his story to himself, getting ready for the men who would come. They hadn't.

Life had taken on all the terrible aspects of a brutal story half-heard long ago, so grisly you tried not to hear and later not to remember. Now he wished he'd listened, devoured the clues. If he had, he might have been better able to understand the awful thing that seemed to him like a savage dog, biting him towards a prepared corner.

He knew now that he was afraid of Mouse Bluffs. Always had been. Fear rooted deeply in the dark irrational places of his mind, placed there bit by bit all through his early life: when trouble came to the goyim they savaged the Jew. While he had told himself he hated these people, while he had told himself he was contemptuous of them, fear had been like a deadly drying wind eating his loins and brain. There was a barrier between these people and himself; he had made part of it himself, made it out of his fear of the differences, out of his determination that his own differences, separateness, should be maintained. Now he was unmanned, concerned with nothing but survival. There was killing in the air. He remembered how the men had talked of Jack Yeates when Brucie died. In one shattering image he saw the merchants from whom he'd taken business inciting the men, going about the town slanting blood-letting words into every ear. Even Brace hadn't been in. Only yesterday he'd seen a group at the roundhouse, talking together, sternly ignoring the store, and he'd imagined one of them was Brace. It had been Brace. Surely only one man stood so big, so much the center of a group. Elsie Yeates! Elsie Yeates only had value because of him, because it was he, the different one, who they believed had betrayed her. That damned chip. The Virgin Mary now.

The bell over the door tinkled. He rubbed his palms against his apron, looked up expectantly. His smile froze.

Jack Yeates strode to the counter. "I figure you and me better have a talk, Herson."

Jacob swallowed. "What about?"

"About my girl, that's what about."

Jacob fingered the cutting shears. It wouldn't end. He was in a long dark tunnel with no light to lead him. There must be a corner to turn but his brain stumbled against the fear that there might not be.

"I've got nothing to do with your girl!"

"Seems to me she brought it home to roost. It's worth five hundred dollars, Herson, with doctor's bills and all."

Jacob leaned against the counter. Jack wasn't talking marriage, anyway. He saw a possible corner.

"You're crazy."

Jack grabbed his wrist. The shears fell against the counter with a clatter.

"You'll pay."

"Be reasonable, all she ever did here was clean."

Jack released his grip. "They're talking around town, Jake. This is something you got to square up. Everybody used to wonder about you. How about that girl of yours up in Winnipeg? Figure she'd like to get wind of this?"

"Get out," Jacob whispered.

"I'm telling you. They're talking. Now you get your fat ass off up to the bank or you're going to be dead. D-E-A-D. All I got to do is spread the word." Yeates swaggered to the door. "I'll be back tonight."

"I want to see Elsie Yeates," Matt told the matron.

He'd been standing at the desk in the narrow dark foyer of the hospital for what seemed half an hour.

Rita Crisp looked at him impersonally. "Visiting hours are over."

She took good care not to associate herself with the town or the town's gossip. She was a nurse. There were no bastards, only babies, in her nursery.

He said implacably, "It's important."

"Wait a moment." She left him for what seemed another age, returned. "You're not the father, are you?" She flushed. "I mean Elsie's father: she's very upset that . . ."

Matt shook his head. She gave him a long intent stare and led him to the ward.

"You look fine, Else."

He sat down heavily, his back to the linen screen. How white she was. The woman in the next bed got her dressing gown and went from the room with painful slowness.

"That's Mrs. Ellis," Elsie said. "It's her seventh."

"Oh?" Silence stretched around them, fluttered mutely against the wet pillow under Elsie's dark hair. He cleared his throat. "I been thinking, Else, you and me better get married."

She turned her head away.

"You should've told me, Else."

"I'm not much good." She sighed, and the tears ran from her eyes without any seeming effort of weeping.

"You're all right, Else. I think you're all right."

"I thought I'd be away in the city before the kid came. There's a hospital there where they take you and adopt out the kid."

"That's no way to talk."

"He's a nice little baby. I wouldn't give him up, not after seeing him."

"Course not. What say, Else, you and me?"

"I don't know, Matt. Honest. I'm not crazy about you, like. I know you're a good man and that but it would mean leaving Ma and the kids with him."

He said quickly, "Don't you worry none." His breath chugged out as if he'd been working very hard. Was there no way to stop that crying? His hands worked mercilessly over his tweed cap. "I'm sorry, Else, we'll wait'll you get out. Herb's agreed. We got a nice house, Herb and me; even a washing machine."

"He licked me," she told him dully.

"I know. Just don't think about that part. Think about the little fella. Herb and me'd give him a good home."

She raised herself on one elbow, whispered feverishly, "I'm going to kill him. Soon as I get out. He licked me. I didn't mind lickings so much only now it's different. Look at my belly, Mat."

She pulled the sheet down and he saw she wore only the heavy cotton breast-binder. She was bare below the waist.

"Oh, Else," he pulled the sheet against her body, his big hard hands clumsy in new tenderness. "You rest. You ain't yourself. Oh Else!"

As he walked slowly from the ward the matron came to him.

"I want to see my kid," he told her.

"Of course," she said, and took him to the nursery window.

"He's okay?"

"Certainly. Robust. You wouldn't believe it. We took him from the incubator the second day."

She led him to the front door, glad of her watchfulness, that it had been she and not one of the rattle-brains who caught this.

"Else isn't in such good shape is she?"

"She'll be all right," matron assured him soothingly.

He shook his head.

"You mustn't pay too much attention to her wild talk. You know some women get a bit upset—nervously upset—after childbirth and there were difficult circumstances in . . . Another few days, as soon as her milk is established, she'll feel much better."

"It ain't that easy."

Another day and night passed. Herb was sick of the hotel, the Legion, the powerhouse, Joe James's garage. He hadn't seen much of Matt and he didn't seek him out. They were waiting for something to happen. The whole town seemed to be waiting for a sign.

He met Brace Harvey on the street.

"Evening Henderson. Seeing a lot of you and Matt around."

"Yep. Something up?"

"Seems like it. I don't know. I'm going out on the road tonight and I'm glad to be going." He moved away.

"How do you see it, Brace?"

Brace turned back, smiled faintly. "I don't know, maybe it'll pass over. He's sure made himself scarce. Now the women are collecting up baby stuff. If he just lies low he'll be all right."

"He isn't that smart."

"Maybe not." Brace sighed. "He went over to Herson's the other night and raised hell but Jake kept the door locked and called the Mountie. Jack saw the police car and bolted. I'm sure glad I'm going. Know something? There isn't one bo in the park. They know." He scratched his cheek. "I feel kind of bad about old Jake. You know. He's a city man."

Herb chewed it over as he walked along. The boes. The hair along the back of his neck stirred in a draft. Lippy Jones had been on his way to work when a black cat crossed his path and he turned straight around, went home and booked off. Times like this chewed everybody's innards. He found himself outside Herson's and after a moment's hesitation went in. He remembered Brace's words and flushed a bit as Jacob came forward. City man. Yeh, old Jacob must figure them a gang of savages. City men looked at things differently, couldn't help but.

"Where is everybody?" he asked.

"You tell me." Jacob wiped his hands. "Have a chair?"

One place was as good as another.

Jacob asked, "Like a bottle of pop?"

"Sure."

After a time Jacob said in a high voice, "Say, Henderson, why have they quit coming here?"

Herb shrugged. "They'll be back. Everybody gets riled up. It don't last."

"Is it because of me?"

Herb looked at him in utter astonishment, saw the deep circles under Jacob's eyes, the trembling lip. "God, no. What've you got to do with it?"

Jacob looked as if he might faint. "I thought they might feel I . . . Well, her coming here."

With Brace's words in his ears Herb knew a sense of humiliation so powerful he lost all real sight of the other man.

"This is a good town; it's just that they're burned up. You know, a town gets a bum like that, what the hell can they do about him? Sweet bugger all it looks like. Makes them mad. Most people try to be about as good as they can. Figure why should they put up with somebody like that stray. My daddy had a word for the likes of him—blackguard."

It was a long speech; Jacob felt he must be talking to Matt; his knees shook, although he was sitting on the chair beside Herb; a muscle jumped in his cheek. He lit his pipe carefully and placed his fingers against the tic, though he knew it didn't show. He had watched in the mirror many times to catch it but it must be deep, rotten deep, to jump and jump like that and not move the skin.

"I'm sure glad no one's mad at me."

Herb gave him a sidelong glance. "No reason why they should be."

"No." Jacob clamped his lips together desperately.

"What I think, you did the right thing. You see there was no place she could go. Not one woman in town would take her in. Not then. Now they're all het up. Collecting up diapers and that."

"A man like that ought to be stoned out of town."

"Don't let anybody hear you say so."

"Give him what's coming to him." Jacob rammed his palm fiercely against his cheek.

"Don't carry on," Herb advised slowly. "It'll all die down, you wait."

The following afternoon Jacob closed his shop, went to the bank, then to the hospital.

Elsie nodded to the flowers. "They're nice."

He began awkwardly, "Elsie, everybody feels bad about this."

"Sure, me more than anyone."

"Look, I—" He took an envelope from his pocket. "Here's fifty dollars. I want you to have it."

"Why?"

"Because I feel bad." He tried to put the envelope under her pillow.

"I don't want it."

"You don't?"

"No. I got my money I saved to go to the city. It's enough. I earned it too, hard and easy."

"Well . . ."

"You still want me to clean for you?"

"You're staying here?"

"I can't go now. I can't give up the baby and I couldn't leave him with Ma, not with him around."

"Sure then, if you want."

"You don't care what people say about me?"

"No," he said reluctantly.

"Saturdays still?"

"Take the money. I don't mind."

"No. I got a kid now. I'll earn it hard from now on. It's okay. You feel bad now and I know you couldn't marry me because of that girl and your religion and that but after a while you might not feel bad and say to yourself you gave Elsie fifty dollars and figure you got something coming."

Jacob's face went slack.

"I wouldn't," he said.

"I'll earn for him and me, that's all. You see, Mr. Herson, that's the way my old lady and him take it, the easy way, only in the end it looks to me like the hard way. You get free water but the old lady trots along to Reese Todd every Sunday morning. If that's the easy way I'm going to try for something really tough."

"It will be tough." His face was swollen with color.

Her eyes fell. "You're telling me."

"Good luck . . ." The chair scraped.

"See you first Saturday I'm up. I hope you remembered about that tile in the kitchen. The water keeps getting under that broken one and all your tile'll go."

"I'll get it fixed."

When he was gone she cried a bit. Then her mother came in. Elsie wiped her eyes. They sat looking at one another.

Phoebe's face twitched sadly. "Jack ain't been around. You know he never meant it."

"That's him, all good intentions."

"Elsie, he's your daddy." Phoebe's glance was mild. "He's away somewhere just licking his wounds. I know him. He does something like this, then he's sorry."

"Good intentions make good deeds. I know. I learned that much. Funny thing, I used to always have the feeling that other people knew something I didn't, that they had it all over me."

"You coming home?"

"You want me?"

"It's like the tomb without you." Phoebe smiled wistfully, the tomb in her voice, her eyes, the loneliness of being on the other side. "Young Alb's making a whistle for the baby."

"Yeh," Elsie breathed. "It won't be any harder for him than for us. We're changing things, Ma."

"Sure, as soon as we get straightened around."

"No. I've heard that before. Right away. The minute I get out of here."

"Sure."

Elsie smiled. "You're a grandmother."

"That's right."

"We better give him a name." Elsie laughed for the first time, a shrill splinter. "Maybe a couple."

"I'm getting me a stake. Sure am," Yeates assured Ian.

"You are?" He'd been all night and morning in the house and was almost surprised to discover Jack still in the summerhouse as another day died. "Give me a drink. Perhaps you'll buy me a bottle when you get your stake."

"Why? Doc buys this." Although Jack had slept off and on during the night and day there was a feverish taut look about his eyes. "No booze. Five hundred smackers. I'm going straight over to Cutters' stud farm and buy me a horse I can race. I ain't had a good horse in seventeen years. The tide's turning."

"Is it then? Take it at the full, man." Ian drank steadily and with a will straight from the bottle.

"Here, leave some for me."

"Why?"

"I reckon I'm the last man in town'll drink with you."

"My friend Yeates! What a world of illusion you live in. A

bath, a shave, a fresh shirt and they all know and love me. I'm not like you, Jack, I'm people."

Jack burped.

"What, no knife? Your sensibilities are stunted today. I understand there are some gentlemen around town looking for you, friend."

"To hell with them. It's that Jew they want."

Ian smiled. "So that's it. Five hundred dollars. Did he say he'd give it to you?"

"If he don't I'll cut him till he looks like a mess of bait."

"Illusion. The quick coup. The easy toss. We're not friends, Jacko, we're brothers. Each his own method, each his own reason, the result—invariably unsatisfactory."

"Talk sense."

"You won't get the money."

"That's what you think." The knife came out. "I'll bet you ten per cent."

"That's easy enough, I might as well give it to you now. He's reported you to the Mountie for attempted extortion."

"The hell he has!" Jack half rose. "He hasn't the guts."

"I imagine with Indian Jack hammering on his door he found reserves of another kind."

"Don't call me that, you; nobody calls me that."

"I must have heard it somewhere."

"He hasn't the guts to take it to court."

"Ah, but you know what dogged fellows these Mounties are once they get hold of a thing."

The knife flashed. "You want it now?"

"Stop being theatrical. I've given you up, Jack. Even if war came tomorrow you wouldn't fulfill that obligation. Even you are cunning enough to know you'd hang. After all, a cripple. How could you?"

"Easy as a dog's tail. Beats me how nobody's done it before." Jack threw the knife down with a clatter. "Give me some dough."

"What! You owe me eighty-two dollars in accumulated gambling debts. I fear you do not intend to honor your debts, brother."

"Cut out this horse. I figure I know why you're a drunk. Christ, you're even worse sober than you are drunk. Ten dollars?"

"Great Scott, you're ready for the bin. Ten dollars! Real money? Aren't you even going to try a nice little wager?"

"I know another reason why you're a drunk. You don't remember, eh?" Jack mimicked, " 'You can't know what it was like, Jack, we were just boys, all of us.' "

Ian closed his eyes. His pallid face took on a waxy sheen. "Go away."

"Just boys together."

Ian took a billfold from the pocket of his shirt, very carefully extracted ten dollars, placed it on the table without looking up into the leering dark face.

"Don't ever come back."

"Now look, Mr. Ross, I didn't mean—I just want to go down to the park and shoot craps with the boes. Most guys fool around when they's kids."

"Out," barely audible.

"Five dollars is enough."

Ian began to laugh. "Oh Lord, Lord! I'll bet that's the only near generous thing you've done; five is enough."

"Well, we're friends ain't we?"

"You're an Indian giver, Jacko. Go."

Jack snatched the money, looked surly. "Okay, call me names." He leaned towards Ian, his fetid breath harsh, his small eyes gleaming with rage. "Sod! Figure the town would like to . . ." He looked up suddenly, turned and bolted for the street door. "Sod!" he howled on the slamming door.

Ian did not look towards the door that led to the garden. "What a close eye you keep on me these days," he said, his hands clenching.

"I don't like your friend," Gavin said.

"He forgot his knife."

"You know the constable is looking for him?"

"That's why I deemed it wise to oust him. After all it wouldn't look well, would it?"

"I shall have Billy nail up that street door."

"It's too late."

Gavin looked through the vine-framed window. He could see the flat stretch of river where it rounded the bluff. It was a nice view with the water green-blue in the dying light.

Ian lifted the bottle to his mouth. "You heard!"

"No."

"You're lying."

"That's fine. Let lies serve us. They have for a long while."

"Lies serve all of us."

"Of course. What would life be without them? I certainly couldn't practise medicine without them."

"Leave me alone, Gavin, I'll be along soon."

"It hurts Mary. She won't be here much longer."

"Very well."

Dusk had fallen, a swollen vault of shadow, as Jack hurried from the summerhouse. He looked furtively up the rise of the hill towards Crescent, turned and padded into the valley. He was hungry. The sleeping did it. He couldn't go without food the way Ian often did. Food. They practically had to cram it into Ross's craw sometimes. The boes might have a bit of grub. Not likely. But he had money. He wished he dared go into town for change. Some of these bums would kill a man for less than a ten. The park was dark. Ross'd come around, need someone to drink with. Anyway, it was worth more than ten.

He went to the bank of the creek but could scarcely see the planks of the footbridge. It hadn't a handrail. No fire showed against the mound where they usually camped. He struck a match. It gleamed a brief light at the bridge, went out. The creek smelt rank. Trailing from the branches of the elms on the other side were some long ropes the kids used to play Tarzan. Mountie was always getting complaints from the mothers, some kid falling into the creek. He struck another match and, as it puffed out, hurried across the bridge. Black as a witch's box in the valley. No stars shone through the thick ceiling of leaves overhead. From over the riverway he heard the bullfrogs singing. He cursed the odor. No self-respecting frog'd live in the creek any more. He stopped and listened.

Maybe they were down on the point. The mosquitoes weren't so bad there. But a fire could be seen from the bridge. Generally the boes kept off the point. He paused, cursed again into the sodden dark. If I'm Indian, how come I can't see better at night? Everybody knew Indians saw at night. He was starting gingerly towards the point when a light burst into his eyes.

"Jack!"

"Who . . . Put that off, you got nothing on me, Mackenzie."

Matt laughed. "It ain't Mackenzie, chicken liver, and it ain't some little girl you can knock around. Come here." He placed the flashlight on the grass, rubbed his big hands together. The night seemed suddenly filled with the harsh whispering noise they made.

"Nothing doing." Jack reached surreptitiously for his knife, found nothing. His fingers rushed in frenzy over his belt, pockets. "Stay away from me!"

"Come here, I got something for you."

Jack hesitated, moved forward tentatively. "What?"

"Well, you might say it's from the Lord."

Matt stood, legs apart, waiting, his great body enormous in the trickle of light from the flash.

134

Jack giggled. "You drunk, Henderson? Or them four-square gospelers got you?"

"And again you might say it's from Elsie and Brucie and maybe lots of others."

Yeates froze. "What're you talking about?"

"The Lord seems too busy with all this outside work around Hitler and them to take care of Mouse Bluffs properly. So I appointed myself." Matt laughed, a thin slick of a laugh that slid like foam from his lips. "Come here, Jack, let's see how you can take it."

"No!" Jack started to run back to the footbridge.

Matt jerked after him. "Come here, you son—" he bellowed. "I'm just going to . . . Just . . ."

He laughed again as he caught Jack. It felt good, very good, to be working for Elsie and he forgot himself, forgot the years of working and saving and seeing the couples behind the pavilion, while he counted the nickels and trained the dogs and put it to old Nellie because she was professional and cheap, while he hoed the corn and sprayed the potatoes and shoveled the snow and filled the ice house, everything leading to nowhere, until Elsie. He finished off the pointlessness of it all, gave it value, working in the dark park for Elsie.

CHAPTER 12

"How do you think we can get him down?" Al Blake asked.

Constable Mackenzie struggled to discipline his face, keep his voice terse, as if he cut down bodies daily. "You fit now to help?"

"Sure." Al gritted his teeth. "Look, I'm not ashamed of being sick. You're used to this."

"You hold his legs while I climb up there and cut the rope. And don't let him fall. Hear? You let him fall and I'll have your skin."

"Why?"

"Bruises. Contusions. Oh hell, just hold his legs."

"Maybe we ought to wait for some other guys."

"And more kids? You're a prize. When Dr. Ross gets here he doesn't want to have to stand around waiting for us."

"He don't need no doc."

"But I do. When there's a body—" He turned away again and looked at the tree. "Let's get it done. Just don't look."

"Ha." Al watched him climb the tree. His stomach felt full of hot rocks. "I wish I lived next door to somebody else."

"Nobody wants to live next door to me. Are you holding?"

"Cut away."

Al gritted his teeth till his jaw ached, seized the legs. Jesus, the smell of that creek. The rope gave. Al gave. The body fell with a sickening thunk against the rocks by the footbridge.

"Nice going," Mackenzie said bitterly.

He climbed down.

"God, I'm sorry, Mac. Listen, I broke my arm a couple of years back and it's not strong like it should be. God, I'm sorry. Mac, you're not sore at me?"

Mackenzie looked down at the body with bleak eyes, saw only the stump of rope, thought again of the number of complaints he'd had about those ropes. A man used his judgment; kids needed a place to play; a man couldn't use more than common sense. The prospect of the coroner's inquest mashed his stomach; it would be brought up; if it was suicide there would be negligence in his book. Blake slamming the corpse around like a sack of cement. More for the book. He set his mouth firmly against the invective he would have liked to heap on Blake.

"No, I'm not sore. I wish the doc'd get here, that's all."

By mutual consent they turned away and walked a few yards from the body.

"Undertaker, more like it. Why do you figure he did it?"

Mackenzie didn't answer.

" 'Course there was a lot of wild talk around town but . . ."

"You think he was all broken up over the feeling around town? How bad was it?" Mackenzie's voice was clearly unconvinced, even indifferent.

"A lot of guys getting together. You know. He was a tough bugger on his kids."

"I remember. Brucie."

Mackenzie walked slowly around the area for what seemed the hundredth time, looking through the grass, pausing to touch the trunks of trees.

"Yeh, and he had that coming to him, Jack did. Smartened him up for a while. I sure never thought he took it this bad. But you never know about a man. Maybe he wasn't so bad underneath; he just couldn't help himself."

"Maybe not." There was a faint persistent question in Mackenzie's voice. "Who were the guys?" he asked idly.

Blake gave him a sharp look. "Maybe he was better'n any of us thought. Being out of work can just plain kill a man by inches." He was extremely conscious of the body in the torn overalls at his back.

"Now Al."

Al jumped to his feet. "Here's Doc."

Gavin met Christine coming from the river. "Have you seen Ian?"

"He's at the house."

"That's a novelty. I went straight to the summerhouse."

She pulled off her cap. Her hair was wet with the river. Her body shone with the river.

"What's wrong?"

"Jack Yeates hung himself last night or early this morning."

He climbed the veranda steps. Ian was reading an old copy of the *Illustrated London News*, looking pale but relaxed after his night's sleep. A pot of coffee sat on the rattan table at his side.

"Good morning, Gavin. Coffee? Mary's wanting to see you. You must have been out very early."

"I was." Gavin placed his fingers against the coffee pot.

"I'll get you a cup," Christine said quickly and left them.

Ian chuckled. "Mary wants to buy a pram for the Yeates bastard. There's no dissuading her. March 29th, 1936: out of 44,954,937 votes cast in Germany's election, 44,411,911 for Herr Hitler. A working majority, was it not? It seems a long time ago doesn't it? Well? I suppose the half million odd dissenters have already repented—they were, I should think, warmly remorseful."

"Jack Yeates is dead."

Darcy came to a running halt in the doorway. "Uncle Ian, Indian Jack——"

Ian kept his eyes on Gavin, raised his brows.

Gavin said, "Just dead."

Eyes blazing, dark forelock hanging over his brow, Darcy burst out, "He hung himself."

"Darcy, please," Gavin said gravely.

The muscles worked along Ian's jaw. "No respect," he said.

"Go and find your mother, Darcy, and give me your word that you won't discuss this with anyone."

"Why?"

Gavin articulated precisely, "Because I am telling you not to."

"Everyone is talking about it."

"You are not everyone. Now, fetch your mother. I've got to get to the hospital in a few minutes."

Darcy left them grudgingly.

"Thick," Ian murmured.

"Young." Gavin took the cup Christine brought him. She looked from one to the other and left. "What did you do with the knife?"

"Alas, poor Yeates. I left it in the summerhouse, you know that."

"On the table?"

"I think so."

"It's not there now."

"He probably came back for it."

"No. I locked the street door. He couldn't have gone through the garden alone without Prince getting in an uproar."

"What's wrong?"

"I don't quite know. I'm going to do an autopsy, Mackenzie has already wired Dr. Seldon. There's something about it . . ."

Ian expelled his breath. "Mouse Bluffs."

"The ten dollars was still in his pocket."

"I see. Knowing Jack it would appear incredible would it not? Hanging himself when he was ten dollars towards the shining goal."

"The Mountie is wondering about that ten. I think perhaps we should forget about it."

"Yes."

"He's full of himself. Thinks he's Maigret and Holmes all in one. I don't suppose he's ever seen a body before, let alone a—victim."

"Was he?"

"I couldn't say."

"Wouldn't?"

"Shouldn't."

"Something in the nature of an execution."

Gavin rose, drained his cup. "I don't expect there'll be many to mourn."

Mary came and stood hesitantly looking from one to the other. "Is it true?"

"Yes."

"That poor child."

Gavin put his cup down with a thump. "My dear, I know you want to do what your heart tells you to but—no more talk about prams. Is that clear?"

"Gavin, it's only a gesture. In the city there are . . ."

"This is not the city. Now, do you understand me? Stay clear of all this."

She swallowed. "There's no need to get upset."

Christine returned, a kimono over her bathing suit.

Gavin asked, "Where is . . . ? There you are, Darcy. You didn't go into the summerhouse last night?"

Stoutly, "No sir."

"What will happen to them? The family?" Mary asked.

"They'll manage. Better than any of us would."

Christine said, "She went to school with me."

Mary looked startled.

"Phoebe. Grade school. Her blouse was always hanging out and her sockings skewgee and her nose running, then suddenly she was thirteen and a beauty. Goldie, the boys called her. She was Goldie for such a short time."

Gavin touched her arm as he went out.

"*Carpe diem,*" Ian breathed.

He was rather relieved Jack was gone, yet could have wished it had happened twelve hours earlier. My secrets to the grave, he thought sourly. He saw Darcy watching him with narrowed eyes. I wish it were next week and that one gone. And Mary, love the old dear but she does smother. Good old Jack, doing his dirty work on his deathbed as it were. And damn Darcy's eyes.

"Mary, let's go to Henry's and pick up some yard goods," he suggested.

She glowed. She had been plaguing him to let her fix up the summerhouse. Make her happy. The way to Gavin. Gavin's peace.

Darcy started out.

"Where are you going, son?" Mary asked.

"To David's."

Ian snapped, "Remember what your Uncle Gavin told you."

"Sure," insolently.

The boy palmed something in his pocket and Ian knew without question he had the knife. It wasn't important. It didn't matter. Junior Machiavelli. Their eyes locked. Darcy's glance skimmed away.

Elsie said, "Doctor, you got to let me go home."

"I know. You'll rest?"

"Ma's good with babies."

"You'll lose your milk if you're up too much."

"The kids need me."

"Very well. This afternoon. I'll come and get you when I close the office. It may be a bit late." Gavin looked towards the screen, lowered his voice. "Don't worry about your bill."

She smiled wanly, "I got the money," drew a red Bank of Montreal bankbook from beneath her pillow. "I kept back nearly every cent I could from him for over a year. It won't be more than sixty-seven dollars will it?"

He squeezed her shoulder. "That's the way of it." Each day brought what was supposed to be abnormal, atypical, before his eyes. He no longer believed in norms, was no longer confounded by the uncommon, but he was never inured to this, a sudden show of pluck. He felt his throat move with quick warmth. "You're sure you're feeling all right? No more pains in the legs?"

Matron had told him she was depressed and when he came in to tell her about Jack she had merely gazed at him soberly and said, "Good." The thought of shock trickled through his mind.

"I feel okay."

He hesitated.

"He never meant to be like he was. Part of it was . . ." She slowed to a full stop, couldn't say, the drink and your brother. "We all got troubles."

"His are over."

"I'd like to think that. Is that what you think?"

He got up. "Yes."

"If that was it you'd think everybody would do it, wouldn't you?"

"No," sharply. "We all have responsibilities and while they're sometimes hard to bear—Elsie, you have your boy."

They were silent together.

She said with infinite pity, "It's more—Yeh, I see what you mean."

In the hall Rita Crisp swept past Gavin. He caught up with her.

"How is Mrs. Newman this morning?"

"Still hanging on."

Their glances clashed. She wanted no tuberculosis in her hospital.

He said, "It won't be long."

Rita said angrily, "She should be in Brandon."

140

"It would be easier just to shoot her than attempt that ride."
She thrust her jaw out. "I have my babies to think of."

"I know." And you're right, he thought, as he began his
rounds. They're more important. She followed him as he went
from room to room. He told her, "I'll speak again at the next
council meeting."

"Fat lot of good that does."

"Tell you what, you write a memo on the inadequate isolation
facilities and I'll see that they all get a copy. It might help."

"It would help more if I wrote the Provincial Health Department."

He gave her a quick glance. It would help her right out of
Mouse Bluffs but he didn't have to tell her that.

"Plenty of towns without hospitals at all."

"I know, I know; there is no money. There is no money!
That's all I ever hear. I sit in my room and it goes over and over
in my head, there is no money. Oh, why don't I clear out?"

"For the same reason I don't. You knew it would be difficult.
There's no easy way to it."

"But does it have to be so difficult? How do they carry on?
They brought that woman in last night rotten. Rotten through.
How she even walked I don't know. And there it was in her eyes,
there is no money."

"Hush. Where's my mask?" She brought him the sterile tray
with the morphine and a mask. Muriel Newman was in the small
room behind the staircase, which was kept as an isolation ward.
"Don't come in with me." Crisp looked at her hands, scrubbed
raw, and said very well. "I'm discharging Elsie Yeates this afternoon. She's needed at home and the baby's strong enough."

Rita gave him one loaded look of indignation and stumped
away.

He touched Muriel Newman's wrist. "You know what you
have?"

She nodded. A slow smile glinted through her eyes, touched
her lips dreamily, and he saw she was glad to go and wondered
what it was like, that urge to get it done. He hadn't seen it often.
He hoped it would happen quickly. She had suffered much. How
unnecessary he was. You should have come to me. I could have
helped you. Now it was reduced to, "Would you like another
needle?"

She nodded. There was nothing between them now, physician
and patient, except for the one to watch the other accomplish it.

She said, "The boy."

"He'll be here again in an hour or so. You understand he mustn't stay too long in here?"

"He's very strong."

'Yes, a fine lad."

"Tall and handsome, you'll see, just like his father." Her eyes turned from the bright shaft of the needle slanting its way into her slack flesh. "I think of home."

"They're managing."

"It seems more real now than Mouse Bluffs. Do you?"

He took her meaning now. "Often."

"It's queer, I miss the rain most of all. I wish it would rain."

"It would cool things off."

"How I long for rain."

As he left she said, "Thank Mr. Herson for me. You know, Arthur isn't good at it."

She was no longer embarrassed about the hemorrhage in the store. It was all slipping away. Soon only the courage to be gone would remain.

He said, "I will."

Darcy found Lilja sitting on a wheelbarrow beside David. Her father's car was parked near the Newman's fence, the grass fender-high. Behind the cottage ran a lane but in front there was no real road. The prairie thrust straight to the fence and drew to a lanky halt; the twin ruts used by farmers coming from north of the Iron Bluffs were invisible to anyone standing a few feet away.

"Hi."

They looked but did not greet him.

"You hear the news?" He felt it grow tasteless in his mouth.

"David's mother is sick in the hospital," Lilja said, her little pink and white face full of sorrowful satisfaction.

Within the house Daniel Backhouse could be heard talking in shouts at Arthur and Arthur's shouted replies, big clouts of sound born on the parade square.

"Gee, I'm sorry," Darcy said, sat down before them tailor-fashion, plucked handfuls of grass and threw them to the sun-threaded wind. "Sky's getting dark."

"It's only a dust storm," Lilja said contemptuously.

"Is she very sick?"

David's eyes met his mutely. Daniel came from the house. Arthur shouted, "Not now. It wouldn't do."

142

"Whatever you wish, Arthur. Just remember us."

Lilja went to her father. "Is he coming?"

"No, my dear, his father needs him just now." He placed a hand on David's shoulder. The boy flinched. "If you want us for anything, son, just give a shout."

David looked away over the fields.

"I know how . . ." Daniel stopped. "Come along now, Lily, your mother will be waiting."

"Can't I stay?" She looked at David. "She's got another head-ache."

"Come along."

When the car had turned Appleby's corner Darcy drew the knife from his pocket and began stabbing the turf.

"Where'd you get that?"

"It's Jack Yeates'." Darcy paused. "He hanged himself in the park last night."

David's jaw dropped. "You're kidding."

"Uh uh. Uncle Gavin went down there with the Mountie to cut him down."

"How'd you get it?"

"Off the body."

"Didn't they stop you?"

"Naw, they didn't see me. I was there first and Calvin Harvey came along and nearly crapped himself and had to go and get the Mountie."

David got down on the grass. "What was it like?"

"Blue. And his tongue was out like this."

"Was his neck broken?"

"Strangled. Just hung there maybe an hour kicking. They say he must have got up on one of those trees with the ropes and jumped."

David wondered as he often did how Darcy, who spent six weeks in Mouse Bluffs during the summer, saw more disaster, knew more dirt, got into more absolute wickedness than he saw or heard of during the whole year.

"Tell you something else." Darcy's eyes were like slits. "He had a hard on."

David thought it over. "Now I know . . ."

"David! Come and get washed up. Polish your boots. It's time to go to the hospital."

"I did them!"

"Do them again." The door banged.

David called back to Darcy, "See you later."

"Todd, I don't give a damn, I want this seen to now. That place is a disgrace."

Reese Todd scratched his head. "It might be better to let the ruckus die down a bit, Gavin."

"Let the ruckus die down, Elsie moves back and they all forget. This town has no relief housing but it does have at least three places empty, for back taxes. What about the old Rainwell house? Good God, no one could claim we were pampering them but at least it's got a toilet."

"Have you seen the mayor?"

"Blast the mayor. I know who runs this town. Now Jack's dead and old Phoebe a widow and there's a bit of feeling. That girl has the backbone for a fresh start. Do it now."

"I wish I could tell you what would happen. Taxpayers aren't human, Gavin."

"Neither are you, apparently."

"Why are you so riled up? Don't give me sweet charity, Gavin; you've got a heart like a stone."

"The girl's got guts, they aren't so common that I don't rub my eyes when I see them," the doctor said tersely and knew he had said the wrong thing.

Their eyes held. Todd hated him. Old hate: Todd had closed his door on a son no worse than Ian. Was the gutlessness in the weak boy or in the father who refused responsibility? I take it back; it was not a judgment. It is always a judgment, Todd's eyes replied. Why, Ross thought, should I feel more guilty about Tina, an accident? Why shoulder the world when I'm not easy with it and the weight of it turns me unlovable and unloving. Todd has the world on his side. He cares about nebulous opinion while I flounder in search of minute comforts for those who depend on me. He looked away.

"I'll see the mayor. You look over the deeds and get a bill of relief ready. I'm rather tired of you, Todd."

Todd smiled benignly. "My heart aches. All right. See the mayor."

When Gavin had gone, Todd fingered his lip for a moment, got up and put on his boater and went out. He found Legs Cruise working in his garden. Todd leaned against the fence. Legs looked up and down the street with a conspiratorial air, ambled towards him.

Todd said, "I want you to turn off the water in that Yeates place, from the street the way it was turned on."

"You do?" Legs's beady eyes carried a hard comment.

"Yes." Todd fanned himself with his hat.

144

"Not my job."

"I know it's not your job, that's why I want you to do it. You see the town might just find a relief house for them. Don't want it to seem too comfortable if anyone goes around there."

Legs smiled slowly. Todd reached for his billfold.

Legs said quickly, "That's all right."

Mrs. Spence walked past.

Legs said, "You think Chamberlain'll figure a way to get us out of it again this time?"

"Sure hope so," Todd answered.

They winked at each other.

Todd walked back to his office. There was a real dirty one coming up. The sky was a muddy gray and seemed to darken perceptibly as he watched. It might work out. He regretted his rudeness to Ross. Still, he hated the ones that always had some scheme to spend town money foolishly. Let the poor take care of themselves. Who made them poor anyway? Not the town. The word Todd hated most in the whole vocabulary of the time was relief. Gavin with a guilty conscience about his brother's tanking Yeates up day in day out, everybody knew Indians couldn't take it; the brother sure could: could talk pretty sensibly right up to the moment he fell flat on his face; Gavin couldn't control his own household so he had to run the world. Todd smirked. Nevertheless Legs's attitude had been a revelation. There was a feeling in town all right. If he handled it right it would work. The Rainwell house wasn't far from his place. Maybe he could get Phoebe up twice a week.

By six o'clock the sky was thick. The wind squealed through it like a sick animal and the dull red sun pressed a hole in the eyes. Gavin looked up as he went into the house. It wouldn't rain, he was certain. He'd seen too many dirty howlers to hope for rain. He told David to go upstairs and wash.

"You'll find Darcy about somewhere," he said.

Christine came from the kitchen, saw David going up the stairs.

"The father must stay at the hospital."

"It's all right."

"Is supper ready?"

"Almost." She sniffed, pushed her hands into the pockets of her slacks. "Cassie and I canned corn today. Smell?"

"Oh."

"Lie down for half an hour. I'll hold supper off."

At the table they were all rather quiet in deference to David, to the wind spitting against the closed windows, the oppressive heat.

Mary said, "I hate to have to leave."

"We hate to have you go," Gavin assured her.

"I've had a grand summer. And just look at Darcy's tan. Next year he must go to Major Hollowell's in New York. He'll miss this."

"When will Charles be home from England?"

"On the tenth. He says they're full of promises on the orders but he doubts whether they'll fill them. They talk of nothing but war and of course, as Charles says, if they talk enough about it it's bound to happen."

David and Darcy exchanged weighted looks. Ian caught it.

"No," he said bitterly, "it's the young who make it possible."

Darcy asked, "May we have the little parlor?"

"Go along," Christine said, "but if you use the gramophone put the records back in the rack, it's not Cassie's job."

David asked, "May I be excused?"

"No ice cream?"

"No thank you."

"Very well. Perhaps later?" As they left, she said, "He's hardly eaten a thing. God, it's hot."

Mary said, "You look exhausted, Gavin."

"I'm tired. Someone paid Elsie Yeates' hospital bill and Matron wouldn't say who it was. I suppose someone offered and Rita thought we wouldn't get it from anyone else. Elsie made a fearful scene."

"I should think she'd be grateful."

"No. She wants to be her own woman."

"Woman! She's a child."

"I went to the mayor about that damned shack they live in." Christine looked up sharply. A small acid smile spiked Ian's mouth.

"When I took her home I found they haven't even water now. Something went wrong with it today and they can't very well complain to the town because they had no right to it in the first place. The mayor says it's a shelter after all. If the blasted place burned down they'd all be better off. Then the town would have to help them."

"What is it, Darcy?" Christine snapped.

"Could we have our ice cream in here?"

"Of course. Go to the kitchen and get it."

"Thank you."

Ian ran a finger under his collar. "I wish I had a drink."

"You have coffee."

"Coffee is heating."

The telephone rang. Gavin looked towards the kitchen, then went quickly into Sir Richard's old office.

When he came back he said to the question in their eyes, "Yes. But don't call David. I might . . . It's not usually something for a boy to see. Keep an eye on him."

Elsie shook off Phoebe's hands. "I got to do it or I won't sleep."

"Doctor said you was to rest! You can't go out. I won't let you."

"You can't stop me." Elsie put on her coat, pushed the bankbook into her pocket. "I can't rest till I know. Everything's got to start off right."

"Listen! Listen to that wind."

"Look after the baby. I won't be long."

She had gone half a block before she realized how tired she was, how terribly tired, how strong the wind. Her eyes were full of dirt, the streets long gray cocoons of winding wind and soil, all the houses shut tight against the unnatural dark. At the corner of First she stopped and leaned against the fence. She didn't know. She hadn't thought of that. Maybe it wasn't Mr. Herson at all. Maybe it was Matt. Ahead lay Jacob's, to the right, Hendersons'. Still she had to know. She started along the way to Herson's and decided she would have to rest. The pains in her thighs were so acute she felt as if the skin had been stripped away and the wind were chewing spasmodically at the muscles. She sat on the grass beside the Harveys' fence and closed her eyes. It was there Brace found her when he came in off the road, his club bag in his hand, his engineer's cap pulled low against the dirty wind.

The two boys were wild with the torrent of wind, filled with the immense surge of it as they ran along the rim of the valley. Below them, as if they were looking through smoked glass, they could see the long grass bending under the weight of the wind and far off the oaks plunging together in its fury.

They halted at the top of the long wooden staircase.

"You want to go see where he did it?" Darcy yelled.

David shook his head.

The shops along the other side of the Crescent were closed. The street lamps, lit as always in a dirt storm, were grimy yellow pods in bloated gray husks. The wind tore frantically at David's hair. I'm the only person in the world, he thought with fearful exultation. We are.

Darcy flopped on the bench. The thin lilac bushes surged against his head.

"Think it'll rain?"

David sat beside him. No need to answer. It would not rain.

Darcy said, "Uncle Gavin says if that old store of Yeates' burned down the town would give them a house."

"I heard him," David said.

"My mother paid that hospital bill."

"I guess you're rich." He was worried about his mother's bill. Ever since she had had to go to the hospital, he had been able to think of little else. He had six dollars saved. "How much was it?"

"A couple of hundred."

David clenched his fists.

"Let's do it," Darcy said.

"What?"

"Burn down that old store."

"We couldn't," David said.

Darcy took a handful of kitchen matches from his pocket.

"Everyone's helping them," he said. "Come on. Let's do it, David."

The wind flung tumbleweeds across the Crescent with pointless urgency. We are the only people in the world, David thought. We are alone in the storm's darkness and we are the only people in the world.

"Christine, get the boy."

Christine clutched the receiver. "He's gone. They both are. I don't know. No! They wouldn't go near the river. I'll send Billy out. Yes, yes, I'll go too. We'll find them."

Mary was already at the front door.

"Darcy!" she cried and ran towards the suspension bridge.

The river was a torrent of twisted black and white. Below the savage whining of the wind the bridge timbers creaked an agony of protest.

"Stay off that bridge, it's not safe!" Christine screamed from the door. "Billy!" Then she heard Mary striking the bell in the yard and ran out on the steps. "Get away from that! Do you want the whole town here? Mary! They'll think it's a fire!"

The fire was blazing full before Phoebe, roused by the heat, staggered outside. Wind caught the flames house high.

"Albert! Denny!" she screamed, ran back through the flaming doorway. Albert groaned drunkenly. She slapped his backside. "Out! Out!"

She couldn't waken Denny, ten. She slapped and clawed at the bunk and finally caught him under the arms and dragged him to the door, collapsed over the step.

The Pike sisters stood speechless at their bay window. Reflections of the fire danced gaily over their neat rows of geranium pots.

One whispered to the other, "The telephone."

It was a full five minutes before the bell on the town hall began to ring and the wind was so strong only half the volunteers heard it. The others had to be telephoned.

Brace Harvey, bringing Elsie home in his three-year-old Ford, slammed on the brakes. Elsie opened her mouth, clawed past him.

"My baby!" It was a shriek he was to remember all his life.

Brace ran to where Albert was trying to pull his mother from the step, dragged her into the yard. He stared, stunned, at the sheet of fire before his eyes. And heard a baby scream.

Elsie went past him. He lunged and caught her by the ankles. It brought her head against the steps with a terrible sound. He was trying artificial respiration on Phoebe, tears pouring down his face, while Denny and Albert crouched over the unconscious Elsie when the fire wagon arrived.

Phoebe stirred. "That baby carriage," she said plainly. "I can't get round it," and without changing expression began to scream.

"Just spray the Pike place," the chief said dismally. "Try to keep the grass from catching."

"The main! There's something wrong with the main!"

"Jesus, sweet Jesus!"

Legs had overreached himself.

All the while the Pike sisters watched fearfully from their bay window.

"Darcy! David, come out from under those steps. David! What on earth? Darcy, get him out of there. Dr. Ross wants you at the hospital right away, David. Take my hand."

Mary panted through the schoolyard with the boys.

"Is she dead?"

"No. Come along, we must hurry."

"It's starting to rain!"

"Thank God."

Muriel caught Gavin's eye. "It's late."

Arthur said loudly, "He's coming," and stared stolidly at her again, his brown fists tightened against the sheets.

Gavin placed his hand against her cheek and turned her head gently towards the window. The first long streaks of rain ran in muddy tracks down the glass. She smiled.

"Tell him I was presented."

"He's coming," Arthur insisted.

She watched the rain and slipped away into it. As easy as that. Gavin touched Arthur's arm.

"She's gone?"

Gavin nodded.

Arthur said sternly, "Leave me wait for the boy. He'll want to say good-bye."

Gavin drew the door shut quietly. They made them of iron. She even closed her own eyes. A day where nothing conformed to text. Suddenly he realized what she had said. My God, the pitiful treasures we store against the world. *Tell him I was presented.*

He rubbed his hands over his face.

Nothing more. Enough. Straight home.

He heard a commotion at the foyer door. It couldn't be the boy! The door burst open before him and Brace Harvey, face sooty, hair and hands blackened and singed, staggered in with Elsie Yeates in his arms.

BOOK II

CHAPTER 13

David looked out over Prater's Yard. Across the small alley to the west was the women's residence; beyond the enclosure was the playing field. It looked very serene in the late afternoon. The air had a golden texture he couldn't remember at this season in Mouse Bluffs, where September filled the air with dusts and pollens, the scent of varied harvest. The light, too, seemed clearer. Perhaps because there was so little free weedy open soil. The prairie seemed distant, not just a streetcar ride away, as if the thousands of people between its vastness and himself constituted distance in some way. But even so Mouse Bluffs pervaded his mind like a fugue, lines and images dulled since he had stepped from the train at noon.

"Have a good time," Christine Ross had said, passed him an envelope containing twenty-five dollars and three addresses.

"Study hard, there's plenty of time for good times after you get a degree," the doctor said, frowned as he always did when face to face with the result of his reluctant decisions about David.

"Steer clear of Darcy," Ian murmured and gave him a copy of *Paradise Lost*.

"I want you to keep in touch with Mary. She'll be good to you, and Darcy knows the ropes," Gavin advised.

"Let him get going. He'll be all right," Christine said sharply, bored with this last-minute summary of recent wranglings.

"I'm not a rich man; you'll find lots of boys with plenty of pocket money and you'll just have to get used to not having it."

Above their voices he heard Prince, sitting at the corner of the depot, his eloquent eyes dismal. "The worst thing about you is that you're glad to go and leave me. I followed you and asked nothing but the following, the long hours in the bluffs without a word. You freed me of my watch by the river, I loved you and you leave me gladly." From the rear platform looking back, David saw, not the Rosses, not the old cottage to the north of the tracks, but Prince walking desolately past the sterile little circular C.P.R. garden, tail low.

"So you're going to Winnipeg. Going to be a doctor are you?" Lippy Jones, resplendently official in his trainman's uniform, puffed into the seat beside him.

"No."

"What's that?"

"Arts."

"Well, there ain't much call for art in Mouse Bluffs."

"Liberal Arts."

"That Mackenzie King's everywhere." Lippy laughed heartily. "You're a lucky boy."

"Yes." If he ever forgot, the townsfolk reminded him with annoying frequency.

"But in another way you ain't. At all."

"I know."

"Wish I was younger." Lippy heaved himself up, leaned against the plush seat-back facing David. He had a very long upper lip, slash mouth that gave him a jovial simian appearance. "What I figure, it's crazy sending our best men over there. You take the Chinks now. The Chinks go ahead and send all them morons and cripples to war, keep the best, cream of the crop, back home. It makes sense. What about that boy of Brace's off there in a Jap prison camp and them Japs starving and beating hell out of them all the time? Might as well be some old crock like me. I hear the government might get up a suicide battalion, convicts and that. I wouldn't mind, no sir."

"Someone's got to keep the trains running."

"That's it in a nutshell, boy. But it feels like pretty small potatoes sometimes, when I think of my boy Tommy flying them big planes. Although," he lowered his voice, "it's pretty important when you think of all the secret stuff we move."

David considered Lippy's regular run, the thrice-weekly Mouse Bluffs passenger train to Winnipeg, one coach, one mail and baggage car, one caboose.

"A slip of the lip." Jones returned his secret service work to discreet silence. "What do you figure on studying in art?"

"Literature, philosophy, languages."

"Beats me. You're welcome. I haven't the noodle for it. 'Course when you're young it comes easy. How old are you now?"

David told him. Seventeen.

"That's right, I remember when your folks came here in '29, thirteen years ago, just before the start of the bad times. A fine woman your mother was, Ty Kendall was just saying the other day they don't make them like her any more. Always a fine lady, always a kind word. Ever hear of your dad?"

David shook his head.

"Ever go to see him?"

"No."

"Guess there ain't much point." A moment of sorrowful frowning exaggerated the simian lines of Lippy's face. Let us remember now and then Arthur Newman, former Sergeant Major, who needs no remembering from us. "Well, I best get on the job," he said. "Watch those city girls. I remember when Sholto Todd went up to be a lawyer."

Twenty years ago Sholto Todd's excesses had brought expulsion from university, caused his father to disown him; no boy left Mouse Bluffs for college without being reminded from all sides of the awful fate of Sholto Todd. David was to learn that every prairie town had a Sholto Todd, whose perverse failure and ruin in the teeth of astounding natural capacities was a legend of retribution, a solemn warning against pride and learning. Learning and the city; the one rotted religion; the other destroyed character. Out of Sholto Todd, Mouse Bluffs learned constantly what it had always known. "And him the smartest boy ever came out of Mouse Bluffs High School."

David thought, some day I'll find out just what Sholto Todd did.

Though he'd been in the residence for several hours, he hadn't yet unpacked. He moved from the window, took up again the four mimeographed sheets of rules that had been handed to him by the harassed Dean.

Resident students will attend chapel unless parents or guardians expressly forbid it.

Resident students will be on time for meals in the dining hall—
7.00 a.m., 12.30 p.m., 6.00 p.m.—unless notice is given before 6.00
p.m. on the day prior to missing breakfast and before 10.00 a.m.
on the day of intended absence from lunch or dinner.

No smoking in residence. Smoking is permitted in canteen and
common rooms. THIS IS A CITY ORDINANCE.

Rules about laundry, toilets, class arrival, use of showers, use of
lockers, wastebaskets, girls' residence, checking in, permits for late
hours, fire drill, where to report for C.O.T.C., where and when to
attend blood donor clinics, rules against students having outside
employment.

The door behind him banged open.

"Newman, I presume."

A lank blond boy looked, as he spoke, at the typed sheet on the
door, stamped in. Gap-toothed, acned, eyes as pale as green grapes.

"So what?"

"So as one identical twin said to the other we are womb-
mates."

"You slay me," David said. "What's your name?"

"Bleeker, Stanislaus. Slaw. I tried for Stan but Slaw they would
have it. Cole Slaw Bleeker, third year arts."

"Maybe we can change it."

"Too late, much, much. Mother meeting Joyce's brother, see?"

"I mean the womb-mates. Resident students making special
petition to the Dean . . ."

"I say, you're a barrel of fun aren't you?"

"I'm working at it."

Bleeker threw his bag on the bed and stalked out. David
looked at his watch. Five forty-five. Time to go to the dining hall.
He walked down the four flights of stairs and out on to the common. Across the way a café sign blinked: Vicki and Joe's. It
looked worse than the Chink's in Mouse Bluffs. It was. The food
tasted of old tired grease; the two waitresses called one another
and the tall soiled man "hon"; the recruiting poster on the wall,
Be A World Traveler at Twenty-one, was covered with a yellow
film of grease.

No one glanced at David as he ordered, ate, smoked. It was
what he wanted. No one came in and said, "Fine day." "Baby's
over the colic." "Cookie Miles was bumped." The Wurlitzer
thumped wearily over an old waxing of "My Devotion" and two
airmen sneered at him as he paid his bill and went out.

He strolled along Portage Avenue. He had never seen so many
people in his life and under the neon and street lamps, they all
looked as if they suffered cramps. At the corner of Kennedy he

heard a dance-band pounding, more horns than the Mouse Bluffs band; it had a slick city sound. He bought a bag of popcorn from an old man with a vendor's truck, who merely grunted as he took the dime. Finally he went to a movie; Claudette Colbert patriotically welding airplanes beside an underprivileged Pole, who somewhat convulsively practiced the Gettysburg address, wet-eyed, while violins oiled the sound track with "America the Beautiful." At twelve-thirty he drifted back to Knox Hall, was disappointed to find the main door unlocked and upstairs Bleeker asleep in one bed, the light over his own thoughtfully on. Red flannels did little to improve Bleeker's complexion. The wadded sheet of rules still lay on his bed. David banged the door, switched on the overhead light.

Bleeker blinked, rolled over.

"With all the bastards in this bastard-ridden world I draw the A-1 model yet," he said sadly.

"It's just that I want you to be part of things. I'm not trying to force you into . . ."

Lilja pressed her palms against her temples. She refused to look at Solveg.

"I don't want to and I have to have a letter of excuse."

Solveg sighed. Curly had said, "It's beyond me," and could not discuss it with her; the many and seemingly morbid differences of opinion among Christians only confused her. Solveg wished, as she wished every day, all day, that Leo were home.

"Is it because you feel your father wouldn't like it?"

"I'm Anglican."

"I know you are," desperately. The thought flashed through her that Lilja had her father's genius for exploding trifles to disproportionate size. She shook it away guiltily. "Surely fifteen minutes' chapel service isn't going to make you any less an Anglican?"

"You wouldn't understand."

Solveg winced. There she sat, sixteen years old, scarcely a hundred pounds, skin as fine as cream, fine blond curls cut short, a halo, angel-like, and she had all the malleability of a Mack truck. Perhaps it was the name. The child was still ashamed of having taken Leo Frank's name and felt she must give Daniel this much.

She said, "Lilja, will you attend until I write your father? I'm sure of his answer. He'll want you to go. But if he agrees with you

I'll write the letter. It's just that . . . If you want to get accepted into a sorority you don't want to seem—peculiar?"

"I don't want to get into a sorority."

"Of course you do."

Lilja bit her lip. Of course she did.

She said, "They're childish. Leo doesn't believe in them. Cults of superiority."

How did she manage to choose whatever suited her purpose from either of the two men?

Solveg snapped, "Will you wait?"

"Yes. Can I write to him myself about it?"

Solveg's eyes narrowed. "You do all the time don't you? Write him about this if you wish. I've never restricted your . . ."

She left the room. I've won one battle, one in all my life, she thought, and it looks very much as if I shall pay for the winning for the rest of my life.

It was curious that she had never felt Lilja was like her until recently, until all the resistance and tension had come between them. As a child the girl had favored Dan, rather sweet and soft but tenaciously loyal, rapaciously possessive with all her sweetness. Solveg recalled the summers when Darcy Rushforth visited Mouse Bluffs, the intense jealousy Lilja had brewed over his relationship with David. "David's *my* friend!" The soft voice of reason, "But boys need to be together without girls to hunt and fish—it's the way they are," had had little effect. Lilja had transferred that same passionate identification to the absent Daniel, pursuing the lost past like a fanatic, demanding a return of what could never come again, a return indeed of what had never existed, a vision of her wise and good father dispensing pure love. Yet in the strength of her passions she was like Solveg. Where Daniel bickered and parried and slowly, even unwillingly, cut love out of the heart, Lilja wanted to uproot it in one fell swoop, heart and all, like an Inca priest before the gods, a quick excising. But in spite of the punishment Lilja inflicted for real and imagined losses, Solveg felt a diminishing sense of responsibility for her. The more bitterly Lilja treated her, however, the kinder Solveg became, for she sensed that Lilja did not believe that a parent could stop loving a child. With childish arrogance she believed that blood love could be flayed and starved and still live and Solveg, with a kind of habitual protectiveness, did not want her to discover that such love did not exist or, if it did, was scarcely worth having. She approached her daughter with a vague sense of duty, as she had Daniel latterly, but, though she knew that duty must be an adjunct of love, should not be its basis, she felt no real guilt in this. Some women, she knew, are born to love men; others take men as fathers of their children, suppliers of homes, and love them as such. Lilja would be of the latter sort, for loving requires great heart and loving merely as a means of extending the self requires only great will power. Even now the girl plotted her future in terms of sterling and linen and war bonds. Nothing would surprise her. The home she would own, the man and children she would own, were to her the promised land, freedom. Solveg hoped her daughter would be a long time learning that people-owners merely move from one prison to another, that the present prison of lost childhood, betrayal, was only one of the many cages her nature would build for her.

Curly Frank, who always retired to the kitchen during these wranglings, raised her thick gray brows.

Solveg shook her head. "It's beyond me."

Curly went to the oven, looked at her cake, slapped the oven mitts against the table. "It's her way of being loyal," she decided.

"I suppose."

"No letter today?"

Solveg shook her head.

"Look, go downtown. Buy yourself a hat or something. Forget it, she'll come around soon. After all it's only a year since you got married and she hardly got to know Leo even. First time she falls in love, bingo! it'll all be clear as rainwater."

Solveg smiled. "Curly, you make the world go round." She mocked affectionately, "Everybody should have such a mother-in-law."

"Isn't that the baby?"

"I'll go."

When Solveg was dressed for town, Curly, the baby snuggled against her shoulder, advised, "Don't bring her anything. She knows you're trying to buy her. Last week a cashmere sweater, a record album. Make her ask. Pretend she's about twenty-one."

"I know."

"Buy Ivan something," Curly patted the baby. "You're bending backwards not to make too much of him. She knows. You give in too much, you'll be sorry."

When Solveg had gone, the baby yawned sleepily at Curly and blinked his big heavily-lashed dark eyes. Solveg had said, "I never look at him but it surprises me, those beautiful eyes. Imagine me with a truly brown-eyed baby. His father's son." Curly kissed his brow. He smelled good. It would get harder, she knew. Solveg loved him more already. She blew the thought away against Ivan's black curls. It was just Leo's being away. When he came back it would be all right.

God watches, she thought slowly.

God had not been much of a part of her thinking until recently, until the uniform, and now she was almost afraid to think of Him. No woman ever had it so lucky. She was afraid to think of that. For twenty years a widow with just Leo and, when he joined the Army, she had seen, late in the cold nights, herself alone in the suddenly bleak house. Then without a sign, not really, along came a whole family and a baby, a real boy. She smiled. And me always nagging him to get married. Well, she wasn't lonely. Not with Ivan. Whatever happened, she had Ivan. And Solveg was pretty easy to get along with too. Jon was a nice little fellow, delicate but no trouble. Once they got the girl whipped into shape it would be a fine home for Leo to come back to.

She snapped her fingers. I should have reminded Solveg about the films. Maybe Eaton's. Shortages. Shortages. A person would expect the government to realize you had to have snaps of the babies to send to the men, many like Leo who'd never seen their babies. Tonight, she vowed, I'll write to that lousy Mackenzie King again; he's so busy playing the big shot he probably doesn't know I can't get films.

She went to the kitchen to wash up the lunch dishes. "Maybe I ought to polish this floor," she said to Ivan as she put him in his basket. Solveg would say, "You're not the cleaning lady." That was all very well. Curly shook her head. Without exploring the idea, she was convinced that, unless she worked as she had never worked before, God might get the idea she didn't recognize good luck when she got it.

So was she any different from other mothers?

The worst good-bye there is. You look at that boy and you wish he had been maybe a little bit crippled or older or younger, anything. But you don't say it. He stands there in a uniform, whose head once rested small and warm between your breasts, the world born with him. Today a man and desiccated Bible-reading old men sit in dark rooms over maps and talk of advances and beachheads, how much meat yesterday, how much today and what a feast tomorrow; the drawing-pins move over the maps, hooks for the flesh of our sons. "I'll write," he tells you, so strong, so perfect. "Get the man in about the furnace and have the thermostat checked. I won't be long." And you say good-bye, wishing maybe he had been crippled a little, that he wasn't so perfect, but you do not say it, because he mustn't get it into his head, nor do you think too much about it after he's gone, because it gives bad luck and

the dark horseman recognizes those who think of him and takes
them, slides a sharp knife into their heads for the God to leak out.
You work. And work gets to be a prayer and you're a better
woman than you've ever been, so God will know you're on the
good side, life's side. God gives you a baby to love. Who could ask
for more?

"Listen, I want to know." David scowled at the Army doctor.

"Don't talk to me like that. By God, six months under a good
sergeant would do you kids some good. You come raring along
here before you're supposed to . . ."

"Yes, sir. Why am I not allowed to take C.O.T.C. training,
sir?"

The doctor looked him up and down with aggravating care.
He looked dandy. Five feet nine and probably stopped growing,
shoulders full and a man's depth through his chest. Well built,
dark, gray eyes, tanned, clear skin, face nicely boned, lots of chin,
good nose, close ears. A good-looking boy, not handsome, you'd
miss him in a crowd, meat and vegetables, Sunday School and
tennis. Just a nice-looking kid.

"You've got shadows on your lungs," he said. "Both lungs.
Scar tissues, the radiologist says. You don't think I make everyone come back like this do you? Your sputum is negative so you
don't have to worry but you should live moderately."

"Scars? What are you giving me?"

"At some time in your life you've had t.b."

"But if I'm better, why can't you sign the papers? Listen
Doctor, I want this, I really do."

"No." He watched the boy take it, swallow his anger. "Look,
it's not so terrible. I see men every day who want to go and can't.
This is one thing I just won't do. You've got one pair of lungs,
that's all, boy. We take color blind, shortsighted . . . Oh hell, you
just couldn't make it. I know. Put those lungs up against some
rough living, even the English climate maybe, and you'd be flat on
your back."

"I wouldn't care."

"Maybe not, but I've got the rest of the army to think of. Now
you sit down and think about it and just settle in your mind that
you're never going to be able to live it up. If you get a cold go
straight to bed. Hell, it's not my job to give out medical advice.
The Dean has my report and he'll probably insist you see the
college doctor."

David got to his feet reluctantly. "You don't suppose he'll write to my guardian?"

What was the kid afraid of?

"I'm sure he will. Your guardian's a doctor, isn't he? It's funny he . . . He'll understand."

"Oh sure."

As David was going out, the doctor said, "And don't try any of the recruiting stations later. It's something we're pretty sharp about."

The charge went home.

The doctor sat down heavily. If they were all as eager. There it was. Those who had most were most anxious to throw it away. The hell. He wondered if his application for overseas service would ever go through. Well, that was different. He wanted to have one large fling before middle age set in, even if he had to be shot at while having it. It was rough over there right now. If the news got any worse—and it gave no indications of getting any better—they might get to the David Newmans.

CHAPTER 14

Alfredo's canteen was in the basement of Knox Hall. Against all the high dingy windows shrubs grew; even on bright days depressingly little light seeped through to war unpleasantly with the wire-covered drop-lights. Students pressed against the hot-table, bickering genially, jostled past with books and coffee held high, wriggled noisily through the jam of chairs to join friends. The radio behind the counter blatted weather reports.

Bleeker forked another chunk of apple-pie into his mouth.

"Better than the dining hall," he said. "By the way, someone's looking for you again. Still."

David picked up a copy of *Tumbleweed*. "Who writes this stuff?"

"Darcy Rushforth was up to the room at noon again." Bleeker's small eyes reflected keen curiosity.

David studied the paper. "What did he want?"

"To see you, presumably. He gave me to understand you were almost a brother."

"I know him."

Bleeker touched the paper with his fork. David folded it angrily, threw it down. Bleeker flushed.

"He writes that stuff, some of it. Damn near got a one-way ticket to the front last year with a juicy editorial: 'Extinction's Our Destination.'"

David got to his feet, pushed his way between the tables, started the long climb to his room.

On the third floor he met Darcy. He stopped. Darcy smiled slowly. God, David thought, he looks expensive, right from the handmade loafers to the clipped black hair. His dark eyes had a lazy assured glint; even the smile had an expensive indolence. David was suddenly aware of himself, sturdy botany V-neck sweater, heavy brogues, serge trousers, conventional haircut, and knew without question he looked what he was, a country boy. And even if he wore Darcy's clothes, he would never be six feet tall with the proud nose, the slow black glance, of a blasé eagle.

"David!" Darcy shook his hand. No one at Knox shook hands. "I'm glad you came here." He put his hand on David's shoulder and they went upstairs. "How's Uncle Gavin? Aunt Christine? You know he wrote mother and she's been wishing you'd call: you know what it's like trying to call in here. Now tell me."

He sat on Bleeker's bed.

There was something inevitable about it, the pursuit and the meeting. Even the conventional words that glazed the event had the quality of a dream remembered.

"Everyone's fine," David said. "I was going to call . . . You know what the first week or so is like."

Darcy studied him, smiling faintly. "Got a date for the frolic?"

"You're kidding."

"Maybe I can line something up. I'm on the committee. What about Lilja Backhouse? Lilja Frank, as she very sensibly calls herself. Seen her?"

"At a distance."

"A distance! I thought you two were headed for child marriage."

David blushed. "She didn't write much and after her father left she didn't even come for visits."

"She's come along very nicely these last years. Ve-ry nicely. They're talking about making her freshie queen, did you know?"

"No," David said. The thought rather alarmed him. "Maybe I'll ask her anyway," he said.

"Go ahead. We can go together. I've got a car."

He didn't want to go with Darcy, but he knew this was pointless, that he had no way around Darcy. He was possessed of a sudden vision of the future, knew Darcy would not let him go. The smile said so. Darcy had sought him out. Darcy would not be refused, could not conceive of rejection. He felt his throat tighten. Where are your friends? Three years you've been here. Why me? But he knew why. He sat on the bed and looked at Darcy, felt time peel from his hot brain. His hands knotted together in a passion to scream Darcy out of the room but he knew he could not, that this was part of the price. There was to be no escape from Darcy who stood in blood beside Gavin Ross, in blood and how much else beside himself. This is how the old man lives, he thought, and was glad he had learned so much. Then knew he was only making words, implying a choice where there was no choice. It's what everyone does, he thought. Take it and try to call it courage. It's what everyone does.

Darcy picked a book from Bleeker's desk. "Man, I'll bet it set the Bluffs on its ear when her old lady took off."

"It wasn't like that. We knew at—at home. But no one in Mouse Bluffs knew for a long time and by then they were divorced and she married Frank."

"They defrocked or excommunicated the poor old bugger, didn't they?"

"He resigned. He's working in a munitions plant in the East."

"Praise the Lord and pass the ammo. I wish my mother would do something rash and romantic. I could stand the change."

In the days that followed Darcy called; he lounged about the room; they went to dinner.

"No use getting serious yet," he said. "No one does a damned thing until after the freshman dance."

He gave advice. "Stay away from the physics demonstrator, he's a herbert . . . Don't drink in your room. Not worth it. Sodomy, fornication, anything but not drink, it's the one evil the Dean knows . . . Nobody here gives a damn if you fail—only you—so work every minute you've got . . . Don't ever be humble. Humility disgusts everyone. You're better than anyone here—except me. Let them know it."

David took it, even enjoyed it, for with it there developed a new kind of conversation, endless talk about books and personalities, the indignities inflicted on them by everyone over the age of thirty. He began to feel tall and lean and wise, discovering his own tongue. Only when he was alone or when, called to the telephone, he knew who was calling, did he feel again the desperate thrust of wishing Darcy gone. And sometimes something Darcy said or the way Darcy turned his head brought it all back and his stomach would heave with hate, though he told himself in the brooding nights that his hatred was an irrational projection. He dared not hate Darcy. They stood together.

"How do you like it?" Lilja asked.

David was slow with his answer. The newness of everything sloshed unstably in his head, the lectures, residence life, canteen, Darcy's trapdoor. She waited. How small she is, he thought. Even tiny. She had a woman's face, her head slightly large for the smallness of her body; it gave her a singularly striking appearance. Or perhaps it was her hair, nearly white, that made her face and eyes seem larger. Although she wore the almost regulation pleated skirt and sweater and loafers, she did not look like the other girls.

"It's wonderful," he told her, glad to be rid for a moment of the uneasiness he always felt about acknowledging pleasure.

She sipped her coke, smiled. Her eyes were as clear and deep a blue as a hot July sky over the valley of the Mouse. He felt suddenly very happy.

"Will you go to the dance with me?"

"Yes."

"I was talking to Darcy: he says you might be chosen freshie queen. If . . ."

"That's all right."

"Sure? I only have a suit."

"I'm wearing a skirt and sweater. Nobody dresses. War."

"He wants us to go with him. He has a car."

"Oh God!"

"I know but I don't know how to get out of it."

"All right."

But she did not smile and her eyes drifted, as if aimlessly, around the café.

Our Girl For Queen! the posters read. They talked of it indefatigably in the common rooms, the canteen, the dining hall;
throughout the college there was an air of not yet.

David resented the wasted time. He had no sense yet of a beginning made. At night, lying on the lumpy bed, he thought of
Ian, all the wonders that were Oxford, and wished desperately for
a beginning. Perhaps, he thought, it's me. A better head might
make a beginning alone, a head unpeopled by Darcys.

He wished he could talk to Ian about this blister on the starting point, this enormous expenditure of energy on trifles—dances,
queens, sororities, fraternities. He had not expected it; nothing in
his old home or in the past-raddled Rashleigh house had prepared
him to accept frivolity, let alone enjoy it.

"If you need money, write me. I have a bit," Ian had told him.
Perhaps he had anticipated this sort of thing without being able
to put it into words. "It isn't that Gavin's close. You understand,"
he added apologetically.

"I know." It's just that I'm not a real Ross, unclaimed, bargain
edition. He said earnestly, "I don't expect anything."

Ian's glance held his for a long speculative moment.

"You're like an old man," he said bitterly. "You're old inside.
I suppose there's no changing it. I'll tell you a story about a boy—
a boy very much like you only he laughed occasionally. He went
up to Oxford on a fine scholarship the year his older brother sailed
for Canada."

"You've told me."

"All he had after his parents died was this brother and a sister
who was careering in London; he never cared too much about her
but oh! the brother. That older brother was God and the Holy
Ghost and our Lord. Cut off your arm! The younger one
would have cut away obligingly. All he ever wanted was that
brother's . . ."

"Please! You've told me."

"Och, leave me, I'm not fit to talk." As David left, trying not
to hurry, Ian said gently, "It's the morbidity, d'you see, the morbidity of the unloved."

He would not fail as Ian had; he had a route Ian had not.
But acceptance was a long time coming and he had long ago passed
the point of asking or mentally framing queries that were in effect
a demand for recognition. Recognition, he knew, must be won;
Gavin Ross valued only the ability to earn all things. Often, in
spite of Ian's kindnesses, in spite of all the wonderful talking
hours, so strange and so precious to a boy from that silent little

house, David found himself appalled by the sickness of the man, the grotesque way the white fingers worked over the blanket, the blue glaze on the face. He would imagine himself in that chair, clutching the same morbidity like a demon lover.

When rain came and damp air crept through the valley of the Mouse the sick man would sit in the little parlor with a fire blazing, working painfully over his breathing.

"I've lived longer than any mustard gas victim in the world. Write a letter to the Department of Veterans' Affairs; I tell you the doctors will be down here in droves."

Cassie never smiled, never took up his grim humor. She merely put more wood on the fire.

"It's because you're Scotch and that's the end of it. They make them Scotchmen out of horsehide, cast iron and tobacco juice," she assured him. "You're good for another twenty years."

"Say it isn't so."

Now he wrote lengthy provocative letters. David had had three already, as if Ian had been waiting, wanting him to go, make this journey east, so that Ian could write to him. David remembered the psychiatrist Basil Waterman who came once a year and chided Ian about the letters he did not write. Yet Ian wrote a great deal down in the summerhouse or in the little parlor. What he wrote no one knew. No one was curious except the psychiatrist and he was refused access. The writing always left the sick man tense, his eyes hot with unexplained angers, his tongue ready to lick to cruelty at the slightest provocation, as if the inert heaps of paper were an emphasis, a physical evidence of whatever he was trying to clean from his mind, perpetuated his miseries instead of expunging them. Now he could write, and mail what he wrote out of sight. The letters came in clean lucid Old Country script, sometimes clever and clear, sometimes confused with quotations, obscure references to his own past.

"That boy has done more for Ian than you or I or Basil Waterman," David had once heard Gavin say to Christine.

After a long interval she replied, "That's nice—for Ian."

Although he knew she did not particularly like him, David always felt in her a sense of mild compassion for his injuries. He knew and felt no obligation in the knowing—she did not require it—that it was she who had made his coming to Knox Hall possible; Ian could never have accomplished this.

"We started something whether we knew what we were doing or not." Her eyes were quick with impatience. "We might as well finish up decently."

"It's expensive," Doctor Ross said but he meant more than

just money; David trusted the old man's enormous sense of the practical. It was his sanity that held the old house upright; his attention to small realities was the mortar in the fieldstone blocks that kept it from sliding right down the valley into the river. "It would cost more than a thousand dollars a year."

"Unless he lived at Mary's."

Ian caught this. "You've lost your mind."

"I wouldn't dream of it," Gavin snapped.

David, his face as still as he could make it, felt his throat fill with gratitude.

Christine demanded, "Well, damn, what's money anyway? I just don't want to do this on the cheap. It's his life. You brought him here of your own accord, now let's do more than just what the Court requires. Don't turn him loose to be a delivery boy at Watson's." She paused grimly. "Not out of this house."

Gavin looked at her strangely. "Very well, write them and get an accounting and we'll discuss it again."

The talks dragged on and on until David was almost weary of the whole prospect; he did not realize it was the first time in years the three had met a common problem. After the first private interview with the doctor, in which David, digging his heels in for the only time, said, "I don't want to be a doctor," all the discussion was distilled to, "You're young, we feel you should go up to Knox Hall and take your second year of Liberal Arts: you can do that with your grade twelve, then we'll be in a better position to determine what career you're fitted for." David intended to write. It was the one thing he had always wanted, not to build bridges or learn accountancy or take out tonsils, but he did not say this to Gavin Ross. Ross had too many doubts already, doubts that were all for David, never for his own judgment or wisdom. At least David was on the way to the things he wanted and by next year, he promised himself, he would have a point upon which to bargain.

Yet here he was, nervous and fearful of this new place, new way of living, hiding his nervousness as best he could under quick words, a determined refusal to seem impressed; waiting, waiting for the great thing to begin. And the talk around him was all of queens, dates, dances.

"How do you do, Mrs. Frank."

David shook Curly's hand firmly and realized, as he did so, that he was copying Darcy.

"I remember. Yes." Curly cocked her head in question. Her bright dark eyes approved of him. "It was 1936, the year Solveg and Leo met. But you're like a big man now. And fatter. My, you were a thin little boy."

David blushed and sat beside her on the low chesterfield, saw his knees in the air and wondered who made such furniture for whom, saw a glass box of cigarettes and wondered whether to take one, whether to ask if he might smoke as the elegant men did in the movies, knew it would sound ridiculous, began a search through his pockets for his own cigarettes, wondered if it would be rude and finally put his hands on his knees as if preparing to lunge for the door.

Solveg came in, smiling.

"I could scarcely believe it when Lilja . . . She won't be a minute. Do you know, I still have that little knife you gave me. David, it was wonderful. Will you have a cigarette?"

He did, relaxed under her warm glance.

"How are all the Rosses?"

"Great."

The radio fanned a wisp of music over them, yet he was convinced he could hear his own wristwatch.

Curly asked, "Would you like to see the baby?"

"Oh Curly, boys aren't interested in babies."

His collar tightened. "Sure, where's Jon?"

"He had to go to scouts. He was sorry but I promised him you'd come—can you?—for Sunday dinner?"

Curly was not to be forestalled. She took his arm and led him to the stairs. It was a big house, almost as big as the doctor's, but newer, not dark, and the stairs were carpeted. He was unprepared for the richness of it. As they passed along the hall, he looked into the bedrooms—rugs, curtains, shining mirrors, everything bright and fine with money and care. He was amazed to realize he had never been in such a house; it had a false familiarity trickled into his brain via movies and magazines; a dream seized his feet and conveyed him over the silent rugs.

"There!"

Curly opened the nursery door cautiously, David looked down at what appeared to be mostly a little rump of blue flannelette, a dust of dark curls, a pink ear. The air was full of a curiously fresh scent.

He murmured something, felt a small cramp in him loosen as they went out.

Down the long hall a door opened and Lilja stepped out. She blushed. He blushed.

Curly exclaimed, "He just loves Ivan!"

Lilja wore a white sweater, a white skirt, little red pumps. She looked as unreal as he felt. He remembered her that morning riding in an open convertible with flying streamers, a sash *Knox Hall* across her breast. How remote she had seemed, her hair brighter than the tawny autumn light. Standing on the curb, smoking a slow cigarette, he had been sorry he was connected with her, a stranger involved in a process he had no wish to understand. Now in the shadowed hallway she smiled shyly to find him so near her bedroom and he smiled back in memory of the big old house with its worn furniture, woods satin-soft with age, its Chinese rugs, all so old and used and so much a part of the dead Sir Richard that one never thought of their value, absorbed them merely as part of the dead man's vision and the house. Their memories fused across the warm dusky air. He took her hand as they walked downstairs.

"I'm so proud of her I could burst," Solveg said. "The telephone has been just . . . And my brother is certain Hollywood is next. Really!"

Lilja was embarrassed again. She fussed with her pearls and looked aloof, her cheeks brightly stained. Solveg paused, smiled vaguely at the radio. They listened to the news. Stalingrad. El Alamein. Like stones the far-off cities dropped into the room. At length the doorbell rang and Darcy was there.

"No really, Mrs. Frank, I still have to pick up my girl."

"Quite. Have a good time," Solveg said. When they were gone, she turned to Curly. "He didn't know, I suppose. If I'd thought I'd have bought her a corsage."

"She won't care. She likes that one."

"Unfortunately."

Curly was quick to pick that up. "Why?"

"Well . . . Oh, it's a mess from all angles. He's got a bad background and . . ."

"How bad?"

"Not degenerates or anything but . . . Well, his mother died of t.b. and the father—an old Imperial Army man—went haywire over trying to enlist. He came to Winnipeg and hunted the recruiting stations leaving the boy at home to look after himself as best he could. The man was sixty if he was a day and deaf to boot. When he finally got the idea he went home and shot himself."

"So?"

"Even that was a fizzle. The bullet went through the front of his temple and he lived. The boy found him, loony as a . . . They've got him in Brandon Mental Hospital. Now, I ask you?"

"So this is why his eyes are this way. Poor boy!"

"It isn't only that. It's . . . There is no money. Not a cent. They lived in a—a shack across the tracks."

"She'll never need to go without. And her—she won't."

"I remember," Solveg sighed, "what it was like to have money, to be able to have nice things and to have a poor husband. She loves nice things too. It's hell. I know it's stupid of me and I should be ashamed, but I'm not, not really. I can't help it, I hate poor people."

"I see. Why did you ask him for dinner?"

"Because if I'm not overly nice to him she'll fall in love to spite me. They were terribly close. The other one, the Rushforth boy, is more acceptable."

"Ah, you'll win. Because she's her." Curly listened a moment; they both listened, two women tuned to one baby. "Maybe we should pack the parcel now, eh?"

They went to the kitchen to gather up the tokens of love, the sweater, the chewing gum, the coffee, tins of salmon, meat, weapons against the secret of their mutual and solitary loneliness. The pathetic pilgrimages from store to store in search of chocolate or gum or nuts, the sense of triumph when they secured some small item; nothing was too much. They learned to knit and tend the sick and go about on trucks to collect salvage and old lard. Nothing was too much. Nothing enough. The hole remained. The great gap where the men had gone. Gum and bully beef and socks on the customs declaration to carry the weight of I-love-you. They worked and were never tired enough to sleep deeply; they read the news diligently and never saw what they wished to see; they saw other women who kept their men, resented it, made those others feel inferior, their men unequal to the work their own did. Politicians prated, bombs fell, men and women under many titles and guises trickled the message into films and books and news that murder was lovely, but all the while a kind of plain life went on, remote from, yet hinged upon, the battles and the words. They told themselves, these women, that it was worth it. After all it had to be. But whatever they told themselves they were not convinced, for they were women and the simplicity of the facts too clear: it takes twenty odd years to make a man and men should not, before God, destroy one another, smear away in blood and ruin twenty years of love and growth. It was practice of perversion on such a grand scale it stunted their brains, so they moved about kitchens and counted up the little symbols, hoped and suffered, bound up the parcels of I-love-you and were exceedingly empty.

CHAPTER 15

David's hands shook on Lilja's waist. He could scarcely cope with the clashing of recognitions. We're too young, he thought, and knew they weren't; there was no too young for this. Yet flight was in him, wild, to run out into the night, howl at the moon because the time was wrong, demanded delay, delay, though her hand stirred in his and her lashes whispered to his cheek, now.

"Do you remember . . . ?" Her breath tumbled into his ears and lost small memories of childhood shared moved from her brain to his. The past, so recent, sounded remote, as if they must pursue it frantically or lose it. Her eyes clouded and her body trembled as she caught the images moving between them. "The Bluffs, the Bluffs," she whispered and seemed to revolve in a solitary ecstasy, while the music and dancers bumped and swayed about them.

Then she was gone into other arms without a word. David's eyes tried to follow her white and red, lost them almost at once. A dull sense of coldness fell over him.

"Come and have a short one," Darcy said.

On his arm Deirdre Campbell said, "Darcy, you bore me. If you think I want to spend the night getting potted behind the buffalo cases you're crazy."

She flung away.

"What's eating her?"

"She's jealous of Lilja. You blind? Come and have a snort."

He looked again for her. There were two or three uniforms in the auditorium. The servicemen looked uncomfortable, hot, as if they wished they had not come. He saw the crowd through the eyes of these men—young faces with no trace of life's workings on them, shallow, no touch with anything but the moment's appetites. But the uniformed men looked odd, too, their faces slightly wrong, as if a handful of age had been flung at them and caught there out of focus.

Lilja was dancing with the Dean, her face tuned to the big old man with polite respect. He followed Darcy.

Darcy drank first from the silver flask and passed it over.

"Moderation," he urged. David took a brief biting drink. "First?"

David wiped his mouth with his hand. "We have all the sins and depravities in Mouse Bluffs, only I think we're more honest about them."

Darcy laughed. "You know there's a great deal to be said for Mouse Bluffs."

"You're right."

"Cigarette?" He took the cigarette from Darcy. "Light?" The match flared up between them with bright purpose.

Over it Darcy smiled slowly, radiantly, as if he had waited to give this one particular smile, to rouse the compact between them to second life. Through the blackened window beyond Darcy's head, David had a glimpse of street lamps swaying in the wind as other lamps had swayed in another wind that night in Mouse Bluffs.

A weight sloughed from his chest. He drew his first free breath since he'd known he must meet Darcy again. It was true there was no escape from Darcy. He must take it and show he could take it, however it went. His duties were as harsh as his deed. He had been waiting in dread throughout these weeks for Darcy's sign, possibly words, words so brutal in their renewal of complicity that he hadn't been able to imagine what they might be. Now he knew. There would be no words. Exposure, the smile told him, would only rest in Darcy's eyes; it could go no further. Darcy might use again, as now, the quick hot needle for his pleasure; he would never risk damaging himself. But the smile, too, held an element of desire that David recognized, had seen in others. Darcy had no friend, had waited, would overpower one. He met the dark eyes briefly, glanced away. Remind me if you wish, I deserve this, but don't ever ask the other. I am not your friend. When I see that desire in your eyes something inside me screams run! The streets were grim with blowing dust and tatters of litter. When he looked back at Darcy, he saw only a calm, rather bored indifference. And though the flaming match remained, a signal, a blaze on his retina for all time, he was glad of Darcy's pride of manner and sophistication that made it so easy to deny him his moment's pleasure.

David shivered against the flame of whiskey in his gut. The load is mine. Darcy is incidental. But he had been warned. Darcy wished to go with him, would work for this by many means, and he tried not to be afraid.

In the next week a beginning was made. There was a general air of getting down to business. Classes during the day, study in rooms or in the library in the evening and at ten-thirty, after most of the day-people were gone, coffee or cokes in Alfredo's.

Gradually David made friends, although it did not come easily. It seemed churlish not to, since people seemed to expect little of him. He began to see that the retirement and angers of his first weeks were clumsy posturings to cover anxiety; he hesitated to call it fear, though perhaps it was. Something inherent in his person or acquired in his past had made him abnormally wary of casual relationships; perhaps he had feared that demands would be made of him that he would be unable to meet. Or it might have been simply that his loves and hatreds had attained full stature too soon and he dared not expend himself in new directions lest he deplete the force of those attachments he already possessed. With no real friends, Darcy, he discovered, knew everyone. He had a sort of manic excitement that caught people up into his orbit; they seemed to talk faster, think more quickly under the sharp laugh, the cunning dark glance. Even the people who hated him could not keep the envy from their eyes. David watched him, learned with effort to talk effortlessly to others, found himself strengthened, rather than weakened.

For the first of many times he went to dinner at the Rushforths, met Charles, who puzzled him, and Roselee, who had Darcy's eyes set in a thin thoughtful little face and moved with a sinuous challenging air.

"Ballet did that to her," Darcy told him. "She walks as if she were eighteen and a knockout. I don't think she even knows she's a thirteen-year-old donkey without the equipment to walk like that."

"She's kind of cute."

"She's all right," Darcy allowed with the air of one discussing an inanimate object. "If she ever menstruates we might establish some rapport. Right now she's hardly human. Neither fish nor fowl, as Mother dearly loves to say. Mater loves euphemisms; she's the queen of euphemisms."

"You should try a few."

"Come up and see my room." Darcy led him upstairs. "Tell me, where did you get all this delicacy? You weren't so damned refined in the Bluffs when we used to climb the roof of the Parish Hall and watch that old bag strutting around in front of Todd or Aunt Christine swimming nude."

"It's not delicacy. I just don't kill myself trying to shock people."

David looked around the room. It was perfect. Of course. From the tennis rackets on the wall to the low revolving bookcase.

"But you do, just the same." Darcy smiled to himself. "That's funny. I never thought of it. I go around being rude as hell and people say 'dear old Darc, such perfect manners,' while you . . ."

"It's phony."

"I know. I'll probably end up in the Manitoba Club smoking cigars and voting Conservative." His eyes belied it. "Here's Pierre Louys, take him home and read deeply. Just what you need."

He picked up the old toothless cat he called Madame Bovary and rubbed her ears, placed her tenderly on the velvet cushion on his desk.

"Let's talk about women," he suggested. "How is it with you?"

"Not yet."

Darcy groaned. "You're not supposed to admit it! That's what I mean. Now let's start over again. Had your ashes hauled lately?"

David laughed. Darcy leaped to his feet and lunged for the closet.

"You bloody brat!"

He pulled Roselee by the scruff from a crouching position beneath the many suits and jackets. She cast one quick black glance of appeal at David before the palm of Darcy's hand arrived resoundingly on her bottom. She wrenched away, ran to the door.

"You'll be sorry!"

"*You* will, sneak."

"What're ashes hauled?"

"Out!" Darcy howled. She slammed the door. "See what I mean? Sub-human."

To David's astonishment they appeared quite genial at dinner; he had no experience of family fight-and-forget. The Japanese maid served with paralyzing formality. David strained to keep his eyes from her.

"Every Sunday morning while the family is at church," Darcy had assured him, "unless, of course, she's got the curse. Then I go to church."

Charles held the table during the meal. The interchange of stimulus and response between him and Mary was so tightly constructed it seemed effortless. He admired her, it was apparent, was perhaps a trifle in awe of her. He did not converse with her or, for that matter, with any of them. It was her role to smile, to draw David graciously within the circle, to chide one of her children from time to time, all as undercurrent to Charles's monologue.

His talk was trivial, almost entirely about money, yet he did not quite seem to qualify as what David's mother had called "common." Perhaps it was his bigness saved him, not the mere bigness of two hundred and twenty unflabby pounds but a certain steeliness about him, a raw strength, vigor. But he obviously had no talent for young people. Would perhaps have denied that such a talent could exist. He talked down.

"I can't imagine why Gavin buries himself out there," he said. "No money. None at all." And, "I bought that piano at auction only last year. Paid fifteen hundred for it. You can't get good pianos right now. Just got to keep your eye out for a good old one."

David looked at the piano through the doors of the music room with what he hoped was an intelligent interest.

"If it costs enough it's good enough," Charles expanded. "Always buy the best, there are no bargains; that's life."

David did not permit his glance to find Darcy. Through his mind skittered all the boy phrases of the four summers in Mouse Bluffs. "Dad went salmon fishing last year. Boy, he says that's real fishing." "Dad got a new set of golf clubs, he's a southpaw." "Dad says—" "Dad does—" . . . In the face of his own unfathered existence, of the father that was no father, there had always been this Dad. Now, too clearly, he saw the reason for Gavin Ross's assumption of Darcy's love. Further, he saw that in the patience of Gavin's time it might still work out and he felt a cold hand wander over his neck.

CHAPTER 16

Lilja read and reread her father's letters. He was happy, he told her, in the personnel office of the war-plant as he had never been in Mouse Bluffs. People came to him, let him help them, as they never had when he was rector of a church. She must trust her mother and her mother's love, he wrote. She must forgive all, as he had forgiven all.

Although his letters, addressed *Miss Lily Frank*—for him a double defeat—marked her days, gave purpose to her waking and doing, and she prepared her own to him with painstaking care, sometimes copying two or three times over, the letters in themselves were beginning to symbolize defeat.

Often she saw the bitter parallel with Solveg, in that they both wrote interminable letters, both watched the mails and both wished the men back. However, there was a difference; Leo would return to Solveg but Lilja could never cry up the past. This was the fruit of Solveg's love.

"Do you ever feel lonely for the Bluffs?" she asked David, and the longing for return, study of time past, was in her voice.

With him she could share the quick flood of memories that came and jigged senselessly across her brain, pick each up with frantic fingers, study the loved lines and place it to rest for a little while. October ringed the moon white as they walked through the dry cold streets; the wind, high and huge, carried the indefinable scent of snow.

"In a way. I get lonely for the people sometimes, the way they do things there. You know. They don't have to blueprint and verbalize everything they do or feel."

"Do you remember how we played kick-the-can in the field behind Hendersons' and the dogs barking like mad and old Matt standing on the steps glaring?"

David laughed. "Finally running over and taking the can. 'You're born to jail, every last stray of yuh!'"

"Everyone had it over me, they could always threaten to speak to my father." Her eyes shone with happiness.

"'I shall speak to my daughter.' But he never did." David remembered with solemn incredulity Arthur's beatings. He asked, "How is your Wordsworth going?"

"You don't like to talk about it, do you?"

"Sure."

"We were happy then."

"You can't go around playing kick-the-can all your life."

"Do you remember the doves in the early mornings?" She sighed. "And the time we . . . Oh David. David, I always envied you your name. Your royal name."

Yes, names were important. To her. Lilja and Lily, the war in her family. Backhouse, the war with the world. He smiled at her gently. But what good is a king's name to me when the King will not acknowledge me?

They sat on the steps of a church and watched the street lamps in the park sway against the wind. A sailor and a girl walked past, arms linked around each other's waists.

"Are you really a conscientious objector?"

He let the phrase quicken in his head. "Sure."

"Someone told me and I told them they were liars. I wouldn't believe it."

"Lots are."

"Is it because of your father—what he did?"

He remembered again getting up to light the fire, his job since his mother died, the house cold and dark, the bare bones of the lilacs scraping the windows, finding the small tanned man sitting at the kitchen table with his box and a dead lamp, crooning "—men of Har—men of Harl—men of—" the dried blood on the side of his cheek like a black finger pointing to the exit in the temple; and the letter, always that pitiful letter, leaving the box to David. But he hadn't been able to will even this much; he had taken his box with him on the quick hot trip into madness. The only other thing, an envelope, marked in Muriel Newman's handwriting: *for David when he is a man,* Gavin Ross had put away for him in Sir Richard's desk.

"I gather there are no relatives?" Ross had said.

"My mother used to get letters. From cousins, I think. They're dead now probably. She stopped writing letters a long time ago."

"Come to my place for a few days and we'll see what's to be done."

It was the manner of things in Mouse Bluffs; there was no other agency. Nothing else was done until the Welfare Department intervened and Christine suggested drily that too much time had elapsed, it wouldn't look well.

So, without apparent show of reluctance or enthusiasm, Ross had made application to "foster you. You are a ward of the Court. You understand?"

David had asked a day or so later, "When did you first meet my mother?" and seen Ross's startled glance.

"I don't remember."

David started to say, "I know it wasn't that day in front of your house," but with that empty man, former Sergeant Major, so recently removed, he felt unable to go on.

"No," he told Lilja now, "it's not because of that." His legacy, scars. "Let's not talk about it."

"You're not just being smart?"

"No." He got up. "It's cold."

She took his arm. "Don't be mad."

"I'm not. Only let's not talk about it."

178

"Are you in trouble over it?"

"For Christ's sake drop it."

You're not afraid? She wanted to ask it and did not. It was too easy for women to ponder this fear.

"I've thought about it," she told him. "Every morning on my way to the bus I pass one of those signs, you know, with the W.D. grinning and telling you they teach you office work and all that."

"Great. I can just see you, amenities for the troops."

"I'd be away from home."

"There must be an easier way," he said stiffly and she felt his fear for her.

She knew that he was idealizing her, making her fragile, and, though this pleased her, she struggled against it. She put her head against his shoulder and he bent over, tipped her face towards his. They kissed; her breath tumbled over his mouth.

"Oh Davie, you're the only one."

"Yes?"

His eyes narrowed; if he had the guts he'd drag her in behind the church, he thought. She wouldn't mind. He felt this in her and was troubled by it; he wanted her to mind. At the same time a man's needs were pushing him beyond endurance; the boys in residence seemed to talk of nothing but sex; it made harsher the strictures under which they had to live. He knew he must smash through, have done with talk, the agony of listening to the scufflings in the corridors at night. He hoped it would not be with her. He did not want to damage her or what they shared but she was too often with him, her invitation too clear.

"Let's get some coffee," he said and, saying it, hoped she would say no, let's go in here where the shadows are.

He clenched his fists. Lilja no. The night rested like a cold black cloth against his eyes.

Her resigned okay drenched him in a debilitating draft of relief.

"Are you going home for Christmas?" she asked.

"Darcy wants to go with me." He took her coat. "He hasn't been there, you know, since—for several years. I'm afraid the whole damned bunch will decide to come. A jolly old-fashioned Christmas Mrs. Rushforth calls it."

"Why is he always with you?"

Is he? Is that how it seems even to you, that Darcy is with me always?

"He's my friend," he said, and was surprised how well this simplicity could seem to cover it. There was no one else. "You still jealous?"

"Of him! Listen, if you knew what I know about him and that Deirdre Campbell."

Someone put "String of Pearls" on the machine in the corner and slick melancholy sponged over the tired café.

"I know they sleep together," he said.

"Well, don't talk as if it were *nothing*," she said.

He recognized the split in her—a schism obviously greater for her than for him between the teachings of the small firm past and the things of the real world. Confused, she reproached her mother because the world seemed to have changed or, finding in others sins she desired for herself, rushed to fix blame.

Gently he asked, "Who told you?"

"Everyone."

"Darcy doesn't tell."

"Oh?"

"She does."

Lilja tried with obvious lack of success to digest this.

She asked, "How does she keep from having babies?"

"God! What do you women talk about in the common room?"

"Well?"

He told her, his elbows propped on the table, the music of "In the Mood" churning through the yellow air, and wondered how he came to know so much.

"I wonder," she said at length, "how my mother got into trouble when she knew."

This was different; he felt a deficiency in her that she could mention it. "People get carried away sometimes."

When he took her home, they stood on the step kissing mildly, reluctant to part, and she said, "Let's try it."

"What?"

"You know."

"Well . . . That's not the way it should happen. I . . . It's not like taking a bus ride or something."

"You mean you want to be carried away?"

"Something like that."

"How can a person do all those things if they're carried away?"

"I don't know! Look, talk to your mother or something, I'm no expert."

"She is."

"Don't say that."

"She is."

"Stop that," he told her sharply. "Forget it and don't go around . . ." He kissed her and left.

His frustrations piled up hotly against the cold night as he walked home.

"Avoid respectable young ladies; not only are they a lot of trouble but they're no good at it," Darcy had said and offered to provide him with clean untroublesome girls, guaranteed proficient. "Dad set me up when I was sixteen."

Even in this, it seemed, there was no way around Darcy. He thought of the last weeks. Darcy, Darcy, Darcy in them everywhere. Darcy and his wonderful jazz collection; Darcy and his exquisitely literate pornography; Darcy taking him to concerts and art shows; Darcy saying blandly, "It's hard to eradicate hick when it's got a good start"; Darcy pouncing as they stood before a small El Greco—the soul of the man seen dimly through the long shadows, flaxen stretched limbs, hollow eyes—"You saw something. Good. What was it?" All good lessons.

And now this or he'd damage Lilja, a greater evil. But he wished desperately that he had the cunning to live alone.

The following day he telephoned Darcy.

Darcy laughed. "All right. Look, don't bother about money."

David said nothing. Well, give it all. All at once. Did it matter?

Darcy said quickly, "Of course if you'd rather."

"No. I can always remember that you bought me my first whore."

After a moment Darcy laughed and hung up.

"It sure looks crummy."

A seedy middle-class clapboard house in a declining district, very tall and narrow, set well back on a big lawn, a screened veranda and a small bare light-bulb hanging above the door. David looked around, almost expecting to see an abandoned wagon or tricycle and discover they had come to the wrong place.

"You were expecting maybe the Royal Alex?"

It was crummier inside. Visions captured and woven from the erotica Darcy had lent him slipped away into the sad stuffy air. Worn velour furniture, maroon and bottle green, the carpet a faded tangle of clumsy flowers, photographs of movie stars baring impossible rows of teeth, a faded landscape of bushy trees and isosceles mountains, the one garish note a magnificently vulgar record player purring "I Dream of You."

The madam, tiny with thin legs, looked like Mrs. Spence from Mouse Bluffs, had a fine moustache and a hefty bosom that preceded her like a bird's breast, quite at odds with the rest of her body.

"Falsies," Darcy suggested in aside. "I know they're supposed to be fat but that's life."

She took one quick look at the two boys and led them to a pleasantly furnished sitting room beside the kitchen because, she assured Darcy, it was more comfortable and moreover because of her great esteem for that wise and good man, his father . . . Actually they looked so young that she was afraid sight of them would make older clients uneasy if they happened to remember the stringency of the laws against contributing to the delinquency of minors.

She left them a bottle of beer and two glasses, promised they would not wait long and smirked with sweaty graciousness, "How's . . ." stumbled against school, ". . . tricks?"

Darcy winked. "Tell you later, Victoria."

She was laughing gaily as she went out. David had just one long minute to feel queasy, wish to hell he was back in residence, when she popped her head back in the door and nodded to him. As he went out, he saw her wink at Darcy.

The woman was behind a curtain racked across one corner of the room.

She called, "Take a seat."

He sat and fanned his amazed eyes over a tremendous heap of comic books. It wasn't much of a bedroom. But better than his and Bleeker's. He grinned.

She parted the curtains and came out. As she did so, he saw the bucket, the bottle of Lysol, the douche syringe on a towel on the floor. It rather cooled him.

She was tall, taller than he, and had short black hair, an extremely wide mouth, parted in a perpetual half smile to reveal enormous healthy teeth.

"I knew you were young when Victoria told me to wait up."

"I'm probably not up to it."

"How old are you, honest John?"

"Nineteen."

"That's okay then. That's my rule except with servicemen. How come you're not in uniform? Nothing wrong with you is there?"

"I'm in college."

"Is that right? You want to talk or . . . ?"

"Okay."

They were silent.

182

She laughed. "You're supposed to ask me why I'm at this work. They all do. The young ones."

"Why are you at this work?"

"Margie. Because there's good money in it."

"Good enough."

"I change it. Sometimes I got a bastard off in boarding school, a kid brother in college, a crippled husband. Any old thing."

He looked at her and they laughed together. Her eyes wrinkled mischievously at the corners and her whole face relaxed in unforced good humor. David knew abruptly that it would be all right and she smiled again as she saw him meet it head on. She let the cotton dressing gown slip from her shoulders. Her breasts were large and firm; she was younger than he had thought. Without embarrassment he took off his clothes and arranged them neatly over the chair. He recalled Lilja's, "How can a person do all those things if they're carried away?" and felt quite superhumanly the master of the situation, twelve feet tall and without a scruple.

CHAPTER 17

"Victoria Engles tells me you brought some boy to her place." Charles slapped it straight out.

"David."

"I don't want you to make it a practice. Some of the boys' parents get wind you're taking them there . . . You understand?"

"I wouldn't. Just David." Darcy felt himself blushing. I'll crack that old doll in the kisser, he vowed, and was in agony for fear she had told Charles the rest of it.

"It's all right," Charles said. "I just wanted to make it very clear. I don't mind about David. After all he hasn't a father to set him straight. I don't suppose old Gavin got beyond the birds and the bees."

They laughed together in memory of Darcy's account of Gavin's instructions in the facts of life. Darcy felt great relief.

"That's certain!"

"And another thing," Charles said sternly, "I want you to stop this nonsense about Mouse Bluffs. Your mother is upset that you don't want us along. A family should be together at Christmas."

"Okay, I won't go."

"No, I think we'll follow her suggestion and all go." Darcy groaned. Charles continued. "It would be nice for her, and I didn't want to have to tell you this but your Uncle Ian is in bad shape. No, it's true this time. Gavin wrote me privately and asked that your mother get down before next summer because it might be too late."

"That's too bad."

"Yes, he was a great soldier. Now, you give in on this, understand? It may be the last time your mother will have all her family together. And by this time next year you may be away overseas somewhere."

"Yes, sir."

"Yes, what?"

"Yes, I'll give in on this. I'm sorry, I didn't know."

He said no word about enlisting.

Charles was longing with a wistful irrational passion for the day when Darcy would be in uniform. Then Charles could put his son's photograph in the broad office window of his warehouse, as Brenner, in dress goods across the street, had done with his two boys' pictures. Each morning on his way from the parking lot, Charles slowed at Brenner's and the two solemn faces in their crisp naval caps, tastefully set against black velvet with two small Union Jacks on each side, looked out at him. Darcy, of course, was better looking than either of them. He fancied a solid purple velvet for Darcy; it had a rich royal look. Black was redolent of death, although you couldn't get away from it; it had class.

Charles watched Darcy leave the club dining room. He got it from Mary and his schools, that ability to say the right thing at the right time, that sure knowledge of when to laugh and when to be sober, when to play the rogue. He carried himself as if he had a certain select place in the world and knew there was no better; it was the way Mary did things. Sometimes it was hard for Charles to know what constituted the right thing but Mary knew intuitively. He simply followed. Darcy had that inherent quality but he was tough stuff too, some of the steel and pepper of his old man. Of course, men learned early that the right thing was not always the practical or possible thing. Anything was possible for Mary but the anything of her endeavors was fairly defined and limited. Charles often thought of her as a kind of flower, rather beautiful, still precious although fading. But not a wild flower. She had never known the wind. And never would. This was Charles's common ground with Gavin. Without liking the man, Charles met him here. Charles's function, both believed, was to keep Mary happy and rich. This Charles was realistic about. The man must supply the hothouse; without it there could be no Mary. As long as she was comfortably rich, she could be uncomfortable about the poor.

What a strange mixture of sinew and silk this product of North American society was; she could scrub a floor if she had to, and never had to; she could marshal a committee, attend to an incredible amount of administration, wangle endless hours of voluntary labor from friends and acquaintances and strangers, though the results of all the effort, even genius, she expended were often so minimal that in any sphere of business they would have been considered dismal failure. Through her good works and careful reading quite aware of what she called the seamier side, she believed that such things happened only to maladjusted strangers, never to those one associated with; if they did, one no longer associated with them. She took a hefty cocktail in her stride, smoked an occasional cigarette, cried when she turned forty and had to relinquish full activity in the Junior League, enjoyed a smart off-color story but would never repeat it; she wouldn't, Charles had told her, half angrily, half in admiration, during one of their rare arguments, say crap if she had a mouthful. She was a remarkable woman. It never entered Charles's head to try to live up to her.

Darcy had the best of both of them.

The young one—well, there was no accounting for it. He had always been close to Darcy but Roselee resisted him as she resisted Mary. She was a Ross, on the line of Gavin or even Ian. Anyway, it didn't really matter. Girls simply got married.

He wondered if Darcy would follow up his C.O.T.C. training and go Army. Charles rather hoped not. The Air Force was the place for quick promotion. It occurred to him that, with his obvious literary gifts, Darcy might do well in public relations. That would mean a commission and a degree of safety. Darcy, of course, would probably prefer the more romantic line, chasing about in Spitfires and winning D.F.C.s. Still, no harm in looking into the other. It would please Mary; she hated talk of Darcy's going. Charles could probably swing it. Just a bit of the old oil here and there. He smiled ruefully. Probably as soon as he got it set up Darcy would go rushing off into battle. He knew his boy. Still, for Mary's sake he should at least look the situation over.

"What's with you about C.O.T.C.?" Darcy asked.

David took another look at the redhead beside the counter in Alfredo's. "I'm delicate."

"Ha!"

"That's right. I'm sensitive, I don't want to kill people."

"Jesus, did you tell the Army that?"

"Sure."

"Come now."

"They said they understood perfectly, they don't even want zombies of that particular . . ."

"Listen, I sweated out two summers in Shilo in a stinking itching crappy winter uniform; don't give me this."

"Try it, just tell them you're yellow. They'll understand."

Darcy followed his glance to the redhead. "You're pretty damned sure of yourself. I've never seen tail affect a soph so much."

"And I've never seen a guy who liked to watch before."

Darcy, face livid, got to his feet. Who told? Margie? Victoria Engles? The hell. David, after that brief spurt, was silent, refused to look at him. Darcy flung away, stopped briefly to talk to the redhead on the way. He had that much, anyway; there wasn't a dame in the college he couldn't have.

"Blanche, lie down, I have something to say to you."

"Oh Darcy! You're the worst."

He leered comically as he swaggered away. In the hall outside he met Lilja and asked her for a date, letting his eyes slide slowly over her little pink sweater. She blushed.

"Giving the freshmen a break, Darcy?"

"Well, I've noticed you've had a little spare time lately."

He was right. Her eyes fell.

"Dinner dance?"

She agreed quickly. Unless he was wrong and he never was, she had a very low boiling point.

"You can do better work and you must. That last paper was a term paper and you did badly: you'll have to make it up on the examination."

Assistant Professor Phillips of the English Department chewed a paint-chipped pencil, ran a hand through spikes of sandy hair, looked worried. It was not David Newman he was looking worried about. He was not particularly concerned: the kid could make it up. Phillips was no longer happy at Knox. Something was gone from the whole world; it had been a long time going from the Hall but now it was finished—a quality of laughter.

The young women too often had a look of voracious cunning; the man-shortage had sucked their instincts to the surface. They were afraid for their own poor chances of fulfillment; they behaved badly with the boys, without subtlety. The young men were either guilty and sullen, made so by the pressure of their country's needs, or alarmingly cocksure, made so by the young ladies' persistence and by a conviction that a fast one had been pulled, that their immunity to draft indicated a superiority of some sort. They talked with morbid intensity, had what seemed to him a precocious, even if shallow, preoccupation with death wishes and guilt complexes. He had recently heard a group of second-year students wondering if they might get some laudanum and take a flyer in the manner of Coleridge. He had been shocked, not so much by the idea itself as by the apathy with which they spoke of it. A few years ago the students had had convictions, fears and hates, had expressed them; he thought of all the wonderful raving Marxists; whatever they had been against, they had at least been for something. These appeared to be against a great deal in a contemptuous way; for nothing. It was as if they'd taken their youth underground. They read the newspapers and never the war news; they studied history and never discussed the history being made; they studied sociology and never talked of the enormous social changes they were experiencing; they studied psychology and never the psychology of war; they lived with the mob at their backs, a jealous bereaved population that had no patience with their youth and immunity or with the quiet business of learning, and did not censure the mob; instead they practiced to be old, kept their indignations as quiet as their pleasures, to avoid offending the mob.

Paul Phillips studied the boy. What was he, seventeen? A quality of ageless waiting in his eyes. Too many looked like that, as if they had experienced tragedies and survived, barely intact. It was disquieting and annoying. What right had seventeen to look like that? He tried to prevent the annoyance, the conviction that they created and magnified their sighs and tears in order to conceal the guilt that corroded them.

"If you have some problem, something that prevents your preparing papers properly I wish you'd tell me. I'm your faculty adviser."

David took the proferred cigarette, wanting wildly to laugh at this thin kind academic talk of "problems." Suppose he told him, watching the kind academic face as the blazing words engulfed the academic air.

"I guess it's just sloppiness," he said, "I'll make it up."

"You've been up at the *Tumbleweed* offices quite a lot."

Tightly, "Yes."

"There's plenty of time for that next year. You should get off to a good start in your first year here."

David waited. Phillips saw the hope.

"I've read some of your stuff. It's not bad. But you need more background. Some of it reads like Darcy Rushforth."

David colored.

"I suppose that's inevitable. He's the white-haired boy up there. But he's scarcely a maestro. Look." He leaned forward. "You know how artists study and copy masters in order to understand techniques? Why couldn't a clever chap write satirically, say in the manner of Addison, just as an exercise in style?" It was far from inspired but it was better than the Rushforth school of slick vulgarity.

David's glance kindled briefly, then faded. "The trouble with that is that you might get to write too much like Addison and not be able to scrape it out when the—the time came. A lot of 'clever chaps' write like Hemingway and will always write like second-hand Hemingway."

"They write like Hemingway because they can't write like themselves. You can."

"Can I? One line in a thousand. I know I want to but it seems so far away I don't even want to think about it or talk about it."

"I see. Well, take it easy on extracurricular stuff and let's see some good work on the exams. How are you with exams?"

"Pretty good."

There it was. He should have affected some humility.

"Good luck."

Phillips watched the door close. As a wet nurse I'm a good assistant professor. He thought, with his usual wry amusement, of Alice Dufresne in the Economics Department, who kept the victim's I.Q. report right before her during an interview, advised against smoking and even, if she felt called to do so, discussed the evils of pre-marital relations. What Alice did not enjoy others could do without. Alice had never been quite the same since her first year at Knox when, young, she had identified herself too closely with the students and had developed a great joyous affection for a fey girl who wrote fey poetry and kept a full-scale cardboard skeleton in her clothes closet. One day Alice had opened the fey girl's door and found her stretched naked on her bed with a potato chip on each round pink nipple, a potato chip on her umbilicus and a neat little heap of potato chips on her pubis, while, kneeling beside her, an Amazon from the track and discus team nibbled delicately on the potato chip at the left. Alice had been a long time recovering. In fact, a portion of her had never roused to life again but concealed its death beneath a spate of negatives. It was her constant suspicion that homosexuality was rampant in the boys' dormitories.

Phillips looked at his watch. He had to invigilate an exam; there was just time for coffee. As he went out, his gown caught in the door; another tear; it was beginning to have some character. In Alfredo's he saw David Newman having coffee with Lilja Frank. Damn, at least the boy might study right after I talk to him. They were looking into one another's eyes with a kind of grave acknowledgment of lust. Well, at least Alice doesn't have to worry about Newman. But he should be studying for tomorrow. He can't be nearly as smart as he thinks he is.

CHAPTER 18

"Gavin has decided it's time for me to die," Ian told Mary.

He looked as if he might; something terribly old and used up about him. Yet his skin, stretched shiny white over the long fine bones of his face, was strangely unwrinkled. He couldn't weigh a hundred and twenty. It was hard to believe he was only forty-seven.

"My dear, you'll outlive us all." She kissed him, the frosty air trapped in her furs moving against his face fragrantly.

"What an appalling idea."

He put out a hand to Charles. Without excusing himself, Billy Treleven passed between them and handed Christine the mail.

Ian asked drily, "What, Darcy, no cat?"

Mary said, "Poor Madame Bovary. It nearly broke Darcy's

heart. He was like a lost thing for days. The old dear simply went away in her sleep."

"How sad."

"David, Darcy, Roselee." Christine took command. "Take charge of the coats, please. In the hall closet."

Darcy was already helping his mother with her coat.

David said to Roselee, "May I" and she shed her coat into his arms with a glance of confused adoration.

"Gavin is at the hospital. Shall we go upstairs and I'll show you the arrangements I've made about sleeping? Then we'll have lunch."

"Christine, you don't change," Charles assured her with heavy gallantry.

David caught her eye. She nodded and he went upstairs to his old room on the third floor. The house was decorated with greenery and red ribbons. Little pine wreaths marched along the oak bars of the balustrade. The room was chilly. On his window overlooking the garden was a small red tissue wreath; he had brought it from home that first terrible Christmas. He was glad she had remembered. On the floor in the corner was the tea chest full of scribblers, purple thoughts, ten years of infinite wisdom. He smiled. He hadn't meant her to save those. How white everything was. One could scarcely believe a river lay under that sprawling white brow. On the bed lay a parcel. He unfastened the string slowly. A new suit and three new shirts. The note said: *Not a word, Merry Christmas, C.* He hung the suit in the closet, noticed, as he did so, how shabby his cuffs were, put the shirts in his old drawer and was wondering what to do about the box when he heard Roselee calling "David!" so he pushed it under the bed.

"Knock when you enter a gentleman's room."

"If I ever find a gentleman I will." She jumped on his bed. "This is better than mine. I've got a davenport in the sewing room. Trade you."

"Get your boots off my bed."

"When you growl like that it makes me all shivery."

"Watch it, I'm hell with the thirteen-year-olds."

"I can't help being thirteen. I wish I was really old, about twenty, and I'd look like the Duchess of Kent: cool and beautiful and wear black and you'd be right at my feet: tell me what life's all about."

"What?"

"You know—you and Darcy are always saying that jerk doesn't know what life's all about tell me."

"When you're tired, old, twenty."

"You have to show me Mouse Bluffs, Mother said so, you and Darcy: it's your job to keep me out from underfoot. I've never been here before, never, it's so tiny: Mother always left me with the housekeeper; I'm such a trial, she doesn't like me much."

"That's reasonable. Do you like her?"

"Sure, only I like the housekeeper better than I love Mother."

"What about your dad?"

"He's okay. I told him I wanted to be a lawyer or a ferry pilot and he laughed and said there was no need, I should learn to get a rich husband: that was much harder than being a lawyer or a ferry pilot."

"Do you want to be a lawyer or a ferry pilot?"

"No, I've decided I want to be old and tired and beautiful and marry a B.A."

"God!"

"I did that Ruth one and sixteen thing with the Bible: you take a string and a key, you know, and the man I'm going to marry has initials D.N."

"Droopy Nickers: I know him well, I hope you'll be happy."

Her cries of "Mean!" followed him downstairs.

That night after dinner he talked to Ian in the little parlor while the others trimmed the tree in the drawing room.

"I'm sorry you feel so rotten."

"I don't. It's just Charles. Small doses of Charles go a long way." He mused, "It isn't that he's coarse or even vulgar. Never have contempt for men like Charles, lad, they're rare as rubies even if a lot of smart-assed novelists would have you believe they're dirt-common. He's got the hang of things, you see. No one in the world makes me as conscious of this chair as Charles does. Charles the merchant of smallwares. How we cling to old Bayard and his *sans peur et sans reproche*. He's dead dead dead and chivalry with him. Charles is the one. Charles flourishes. Charles is king. It's a different order of intelligence but that doesn't make it wrong, or us wrong. And it *is* intelligence, don't ever fool yourself about that."

He took a small plated flask from beneath his blanket and delivered himself a hearty swig. David watched the fire and wondered where to begin. He felt he had been away a long time and would not be able to pick up the threads of the fabric they used to chew.

"What's wrong with Dr. Ross?" he asked, his voice checked hollowly.

Ian gave him an ironic look.

"Welcome to the club."

"He's hardly let on I'm here."

"You're flawed."

David met his eyes, his own full of dread. Ian glanced away.

"How's that?"

"He's cold. He can't stand anything less than perfect." Presently Ian sighed. "Don't listen to me. I'm jealous. It's Mary. He'll get around to you when he gets through recherching of *temps perdu*. The old first. They have less time."

"What do you mean, I'm flawed?"

"Everyone is, forget it."

"Why can't you be honest with me? You used to be."

"Never. I've forgotten how to be honest. In any case you just want me to tell you what you're already afraid of so you can blame me for it." He was quiet a moment. "I thought I told you to avoid Darcy and here you are like Siamese twins."

"You told me a lot of things."

"I guess. Maybe we're all disappointed because we can't do it all over again properly through you."

"All?" David asked bitterly. "In other words I'm flawed in all directions."

"Imperfect instrument."

"I didn't know it meant so much."

"To him it didn't. That's the core of him. The one-way god, no hours for petitions. You've always looked for too much."

David's knuckles were white. "So did you then."

"That's my particular disease. You must learn to be straight while there's still time."

"Why is everything so different?"

"You are different."

David got to his feet. "And God fulfills himself in many ways."

Ian laughed. "That's better. Wheel me out there now and we'll proceed with the charade of happy family."

Christine served punch. It was the first time David had seen drinks served in the house. Mary became quite gay and Charles took the boys to his room, gave them a drink of whiskey, then brought Ian a glass. Gavin refused Charles's drink. David watched him and thought, it's odd how he and Christine rarely meet one another's eyes, and yet one always feels they are in contact somehow. Often he sensed hostility in their silent communications but he could not define it. Billy Treleven kept bumping into things and was teased for his low resistance while Cassie flushed about in a constant state of pleasure as Mary praised her shortbread, her fruitcake, her sandwiches.

The telephone rang for Gavin, and he said, "You can drive me, David."

"May I come?" Darcy asked.

"I'd rather you stayed, son," Gavin told him mildly.

"Another boy dead," Ross said in the car. "Tommy Jones. Lippy wants a sedative for his wife. I spend twenty-five years keeping them healthy; it doesn't take long to kill them."

David waited in the car. A few lights sprinkled First Avenue, a few dull red patches on the snowbanks where trees glinted from front parlors. Gavin returned, sat wordless beside him several minutes.

"I need a younger man to help me."

"Bad?"

"They could have held the news over Christmas and not hurt anything but the system."

David started the car.

Gavin suggested, "Drive over to George Lee's, there'll be no one there Christmas Eve."

He was right. The iron stove in the back of the restaurant was red hot. The air smelled stale with old cooking but George smiled a great welcome and brought them coffee and fruitcake.

"Very good cake, doctor, baked in old honey pails; very clean pails, pop on the lid and good, ready for parcel."

"You're an opportunist, George, also the best fruitcake-maker in town. Not a lady doesn't know it. Don't tell them I said so."

George did not argue the point. He smiled, asked David how the scholar did. The scholar did well. George retired to his kitchen, his tea, his Bible.

Gavin began, "You've done well, your term work is splendid."

"Yes."

"About these demerits, late hours, they're not really important as long as your work holds up. I gather you're not the worst offender."

"No, sir."

"You're doing as the doctor told you?"

"Yes." He waited.

"It's a bad one." Gavin sipped his coffee. "I should have caught it but I expect you were finished with it before you came to us. Perhaps we should move along now."

"How bad?"

"A permanent weakening of the lungs. Don't get tired, don't catch colds. That's about all I can tell you. Get X-rayed every six months."

David looked away, his throat tight. This was all then, this grave, rather indifferent advice. He remembered the doctor's saying to him once, "Some days it seems as if fifty per cent of my patients have nothing I can treat except with pink pills. Constitutionally inadequate. I'm sick of them. You can't damned well tell them they just didn't get enough in the beginning, they were shorted on quality. They feel tired, their backs ache or they're depressed. I can't put in what they never had." And remembered more, the tone, the utter contempt.

"It won't go? I've heard you talk about scar tissue being absorbed . . ."

"No."

"You know they won't take me in the services?"

Gavin was thoughtful. "They might in time, if you have some specialized training. They'll take myopic anemic doctors or engineers. It's a matter of having something to offer."

I offer myself. It's never enough.

As they were leaving, Dr. Ross said, "Don't excite Ian, that is don't argue with him or talk too long."

"All right."

The older man pushed his shoulders back. It was a cold night. Behind them George called, "Merry Christmas!" It sounded thin, even pathetic, against the silent town, the grieving Jones family huddled under the black time.

Gavin said, "It feels more like Christmas with Mary here. Still it never feels as it used to years ago."

Up treeless Main Street the wind blew darkly. The pine tree on the hotel steps clung sternly to the coal bucket at its base but the colored tissue cover fluttered weakly.

Ross asked, "You didn't want to go to midnight service, did you?"

"Not specially."

"At home we didn't make much of Christmas. Hogmanay was the time."

"Home?"

Gavin laughed shortly. "That's funny isn't it? But you know sometimes I feel as if I'm still back on that journey, setting out from Glasgow and always traveling, as if all I ever wanted was to make a great circle and end up back in Glasgow. But here I am and it's home. I doubt if I'll ever see Glasgow again. I only went back the once and it wasn't the same. It was to show Christine the old places: Sir Richard had always promised it to her. So we went. The summer before my daughter was born. After that it became—impossible. And now . . ."

How cold the wind was. David held the car door for the doctor. He thought, he's never said anything like that to me before. Never mentioned Tina or that summer. Above all, not that summer. It was the first crack. David felt very happy as they drove homewards, glad with Christmas, the small new hope ricocheting round his brain.

Christmas Day he and Darcy took Roselee walking through the town and found it hauntingly deserted under the bright winter sun. Even the rink, center of all winter life, was closed. They tried a few windows, standing on the seven-foot-high ridges of snow pushed from the roof. They found a shutter broken and decided to bring flashlights and skate that night but could not, for Mary drummed them into service at the bridge tables and sent Roselee, looking like a very small weary witch, her black hair in disarray, to bed. When David went upstairs later he found her curled up in his bed, grinned and carried her, snoring gently, to her davenport. On the sewing machine beside it he saw her diary and picked it up, folded it open and placed it beside her. At breakfast she spoke indignantly about people who stooped to reading other people's personal and private papers: he leered knowingly and she threw her toast at him and was sent from the table.

Boxing Day he went alone to see the old cottage. He had not been there since the day he'd collected his things. It was boarded up and the prairie had been unkind. The apple tree beside the henhouse looked dead. He tried the door; he couldn't remember its ever being locked but it was now. He didn't want to go in, anyway. He turned away but stopped on the slow rise beyond the road allowance and looked back, remembering that in March the crocuses grew on this exact spot and, unless you knew where to look, you could scoop snow for hours and not find them. To the west was the cemetery, the snow so deep only the tops of the stones and the stubby roof of the Rashleigh sepulcher showed against the sky. His mother was there in her corner of a foreign field. He recalled how, near the end, long after the royal visit was over, she had talked about it as if it were still to come. She couldn't really believe the King had come to her. It was as remote as her own going home, a dream, desire.

She wanted to go home; she wanted to see the King, part of her home come to her, but when the thing desired was within reach she rejected it, had not the strength to lose desire. Fulfillment is an ending but desire, like the long journey out of Glasgow, can go on forever.

He felt sad and sore for her and for all the snow and did not go to her, but rather wandered back past the depot and down by Herson's store. He wondered where Jacob had gone and why his mother's death had affected the man so strangely. That terrible day; everyone said, this is the worst, murder and burning and his mother dying, the worst day. But another week brought war and beside the enormity of war, death and burning dwindled to nothing; there was to be such a glut of death and burning.

Herson had packed his bag and gone. Just like that. At length a cousin came, a lean dark man who took inventory, collected the collectable accounts, sold the property to another Jew from the city. David could not remember his name now. He had already moved on. His mother had stumbled into the store and begun to hemorrhage, and for Jacob it was too much. He had to have more walls between him and other people, a city man. Too much. It was too much for everyone. Especially her. David was glad she hadn't known about the war.

He found himself on Center Street and passed the Pike sisters' house. On the corner was the old concrete base sticking up through the snow. Across town the sun turned the western horizon an angry red, burned the underside of high cold clouds a brilliant blue. His legs felt weak and sweat trickled down his back. "It serves no purpose to care so much," Ian had told him in the heart of the black promise never to speak of it. Or worse, "I did many murders once myself. Deliberately. You don't stop thinking of them but neither do you talk of them and perpetuate the murder. I absolve you, you need no other absolution. Some day you'll absolve yourself, alone in the clear noon of reason." It hadn't happened yet. Maybe it would never happen. Maybe he would always be walking in the cold silent dream of Mouse Bluffs and find himself standing before these cement blocks. He had no sins, only this sin; he had no past, only this event. Man's inhumanity to man dwindled to mere gossip and snubbings beside this. He could never deal with it, never find noon, only shroud and secrete it and be Siamese to Darcy. They talked of Germans, Krauts, bombing schools, raping children, burning hospitals, crimes against humanity's most betrayed trust, children: all the noseless corpses creaked a new-blooded squeal against the deed. I did not know, I did not know, he thought. I did not believe he meant to do it. It was all—all blackness, wildness and wind. But even as he went over the old, old thoughts, he knew it was no good; he could not escape from it. Whatever had been done, he had been there;

he had shared in it. There could be no plea of ignorance. In every corner of the flat world the children are beaten and starved and gassed and burned by my brother murderers; me first, me first. The western line of early dying day was full red, the sky sweeping to quick night now emerald-blue. Against the sky he saw a figure move darkly, raise its hand, and he knew it was Darcy, calling as he had then, "David! Wait for me!" and he turned as he had then and ran till he could no longer hear the voice and his chest ached with terror remembered.

CHAPTER 19

In the spring of 1944 Darcy graduated in two directions. He took a B.A. with honors, the extra year a playing for time, and he left his father's house. The latter was by invitation, issue of despair.

Over the past four years Charles had moved from confident assurance to mild anxiety to sullen frustration. His son was failing him.

"See here, I've got it all set up for you," he said. "Public relations, you won't even have to leave the office. Jesus Christ, when I was your age I'd been under fire for four years."

"Four years?" Darcy mocked. "The simple truth is, Father, that I don't want to die and I haven't your faith in that office."

"You won't, damn it! Why do you say things like that?"

"Further, it isn't simply a case of how you can swing it in order that I need not die, it's a principle, don't you see? I do not wish to die in—or even be involved in—a manifestation of pathologic homosexuality tinged with paranoia. It disgusts me."

"You talk mighty big while a lot of other men are out saving your skin."

"Don't I, though?"

Charles sputtered helplessly.

"What's wrong, Dad, are your friends avoiding you?"

"People think it's damned funny. They—look at me."

"Just tell them I'm an epileptic. I do. It saves a lot of unnecessary explaining."

Charles stared at his son, his mind flooded with all the images he could not express; the camaraderie, the toughening-up of barracks life, the wenching in anonymity, the sense in later years of having made history, the indescribable warmth one always felt for those who had helped one make it.

He said lamely, "I always hire veterans."

"Balls. In any case, it'll all be over shortly. I heard one of the history profs say so. Big invasion coming up et cetera."

"Listen, son, I won't have you make a fool of me. And don't give me this—history prof said so indeed."

Darcy gave his father a steady look. "I'm not going to do it. Not to please you or your friends. That's what makes wars, a lot of young men who allow themselves to be pressured or compelled or conned into thinking their good lives are cheap."

"Is this the stuff you write in that newspaper?"

"Not directly but I think I get my message across. It's not fashionable, to put it mildly, to disagree with the heroes."

Charles was speechless. How could this be Darcy, the perfect talented Darcy, calmly delineating treason?

He marveled, "It's a wonder you're not in jail."

"I may be yet. Don't worry, it'll all be over one day and people like me will be in style again and you'll understand."

"I won't live that long."

"Yes. As soon as the Armistice is signed the propagandists will lay down their pens and you'll try to revive the brains you put into deep freeze in 1939. Twenty years from now a lot of mental cripples will be writing slow methodical books about it to get us ready for another. The carnage. How awful, how brutal. But the message will be there—glory! Go back, do it again; it wasn't perversion, just tall clean young men dying in a tall clean way. I intend to be around to give it the lie. I'll be the one who sat at home and saw the daily roster in the *Free Press*, who made notes about the black marketeers and profiteers, the ones who said over an unguarded drink, 'It sure hasn't hurt me none.'" Charles blenched; Darcy lingered over it. "It hasn't hurt anyone in the pocket; the country is blood-fat and getting fatter. It only hurts the foolish young men. And I don't intend to be one of them."

Charles's well-manicured fingernails cut his palms. "Then I think you had better leave here."

Darcy was stupefied. "Leave home?"

"That's it. I'm sick of it. I'm sick of looking at you and wondering what's wrong with you."

198

Darcy got to his feet slowly, looked around the pleasant room. "Well," he said. "Well."

"At your convenience," Charles said stiffly.

"No, it had better be now or I won't go. You're right. I should. If I stay here you'll just start needling again."

Charles said harshly, "It's that Newman kid, you were all right until you started bringing him around. What's wrong with him, may I ask?"

"I've seen the look. He's not like me and he didn't lead me astray. He can't pass a physical. You don't like that, eh? He's so respectable he's abnormal. Why do you suppose the poor bugger went over to engineering? Not because he wants to be an engineer but because the Army wants engineers and he hopes to be able to make it that way. I tried to talk him out of it."

Charles's mind scrambled to readjust. He breathed sarcastically, "I'll just bet you did."

"He has a hero, you see," Darcy said, "one must have a hero. I have none. That's my trouble. I never wanted for anything, I've had no hungers and a man, I'm convinced, has to hunger for small things before he can learn to desire the big things. It's like learning anything. Baby steps. I don't even know how to be guilty because I've never in my life had a responsibility I could shirk."

Charles shrank into his chair. With every bald word the vision of himself and Darcy, man and son, was drifting further and further away.

"I thought," he said at last and, even saying it, was ashamed, "you admired me."

"No, never," Darcy told him gently, "but I always liked you."

He was gone before the humiliating thank you came from Charles's lips.

Darcy moved to the Y, tried to get a job, but no one would hire him now that he was subject to call-up, so he found an understanding doctor in the north end, who gave him drugs which he took before presenting himself for medical examination. The Army doctor told him seriously that he had a bad heart and Darcy said yes, he had a history of being bad-hearted which, due to his absolute keenness, had escaped the doctor who passed him for summer training. He got a job as announcer at a radio station. A beginning had to be made somewhere and, although the work bored him at times, he rather enjoyed the lack of restraints, the lively people he met. Finally, with Mary's connivance, he set up in a sophisticated bachelor flat, collected a weird hungry lot of friends and raised hell with the man-hungry women. On a regular basis he had the obliging wife of an absent serviceman, who wore her rings around her neck on a chain and was happy to convenience Darcy and depart almost without a word.

He went home every Friday night for dinner and, although quite often Charles contrived to be absent, there was no open enmity between them. Charles, whose misery had intensified after D-Day, preferred not to look at Darcy. He bought war bonds at a prodigious rate, sent packages to the sons of all his acquaintances and friends, became an arch-enemy of all black-market practices. Charles was unhappy.

Failure to make Charles understand his position was a sore in Darcy's days. He picked at it constantly, hoping to discover the reason for his failure. It made him uneasy and sometimes erratic. He was accustomed to dominating people; that he could fail so hugely was to him incredible. Socially he became almost overpowering, capable of lassoing an entire roomful of people, driving them under the bright whip of his tongue into whatever corral he chose. If the group was too large, he made his way through it, insinuating his personality into all minds. He was considered brilliant—perhaps, it was often hinted, a little too. Nevertheless, he was asked everywhere. And he went everywhere. He did not like to be alone. Alone he picked.

"Did you ever think that maybe you did win?" David suggested.

"I've been able to twist him—everyone but especially him—ever since I could shout. Look, he's a good guy. Oh, Christ, I know he's got loopholes you could throw a horse through but he's smart. I always thought he was wise to all this my-country-right-or-wrong crap." Darcy laughed. "It might not have been so bad if he'd kept up my tuition; I was preparing for my master's. I thought I could stay on at college till it was over, but I had no idea what an expensive fellow I am. It was quite a shock."

"I'll bet." David surveyed the apartment.

"One thing about it, I would never have been such a mighty scholar under ordinary circumstances. God, think of it. Ten years ago I could have drifted through without learning a damned thing, but with old Mars' chariot hurrying at my rear end . . ."

"Just shut up, eh?"

"Why *do* you stick around?"

Yes, why? David looked at the dark face, eyes. He no longer quite knew. The balance between them had shifted and he was uneasy about what might come. Darcy had been for the first time thwarted and Darcy, thwarted, might—What might Darcy? Who could say? Some new violent uncaring act, this time open? I must watch, David thought. Watch for Gavin Ross, who counts on him. Pay off my guilt this way. Is that what it is?

At any rate he stayed, endured needling, rudeness; grew stronger, he hoped, through the needling.

"Maybe I don't like to hurt your feelings," he said.

Darcy laughed, said indolently, "I was up at Victoria's last week. So you're still seeing old Margie. Really, boy, you're a sticker."

David knew these tactics. "Saves a lot of trouble," he said. "Besides it's largely psychological, love. Even just taming the beast it's nice to know and like the woman."

"Aren't you the one, though. Psychological, ha!"

"What isn't a psychic or a moral involvement—war, love, dying? Maybe not going to war is worse than going. Maybe when all men are insane the sane man is a cripple. Say it's about 1800 and a lot of silly types are going to America to fight Indians or die of scurvy or get land. Say it's the thirteenth century and a lot of silly types are going to free the Holy Land and die or bring back chunks of civilization. Say it's 2500 and a bunch of crazy jerks are going to Mars. Say its 1944 and a lot of bare-fisted mad-men would rather smash themselves to bloody pulp on Normandy beaches than let a lot of perverts run Europe. How do you stop being involved and who's smarter?"

Darcy laughed again. He laughed a great deal these days, a wild separate laughter. "You're not kidding it's psychological, boy; you've had it, the whole course."

"Maybe the instinct to fight is as basic as the instinct to mate or eat. Jesus was against it but His men are out blessing the battle-ships and taking sides and still fancy they have something to do with Jesus. They split their minds down the middle; maybe yours is more split because you think they're wrong. When you give me that manure about not fighting I want to believe you, I'd like to see what you've done as some kind of crusade."

"It is."

"No. You're alone. Picture of Darcy saving Darcy. If you got married and had a bunch of kids I could maybe believe part of it."

Darcy was livid. "You know, if anybody else said that I think I'd kill them."

"You can't join the race that way. That isn't the sort of killing that's in the air."

"Christ, you go at everything with all the staid bloody calm of a Sunday School teacher and you get the Sunday School teacher's answer. Just take my word for it, it is a crusade and I'll win and in about ten years you'll see what I was getting at. You, my God, you—Other guys go to a house and drop it, not you, you damned well get to like the chip and *it saves a lot of trouble*. How does Lilja feel about it?"

David looked at him.

Darcy said, "Go on, tell me—how does she feel about it?"

"I don't know. You tell me, how does Lilja feel about it?"

"I haven't discussed it with her—yet," Darcy said.

"Tell her if you like: you like to see people bleed."

"And cook myself? You know wild horses couldn't turn that girl from you." Darcy poured smoke through his nostrils reflectively. "Do you know what a really ordinary little girl she is? No. I guess not. With you she's got something. Maybe you excite her gonads but she's quite something when you're around and quite nothing without you."

"All this means is that you haven't made it," David said.

He looked away. And she's supremely beautiful. You don't understand that, how I can stare and stare and not get enough of just looking at her; drink it in, as they used to say; the modern trick of depreciating physically beautiful people must have originated with the ugly. Of all he must bear from Darcy, this was the hardest—continuous attempts to make him feel apologetic for Lilja's loveliness, for loving it. And Darcy knew it.

"True enough, I haven't," he said, "but you know what a persistent guy I can be. I expect it's her early training, heavy on Mosaic law. Still, I'm plying her with erotica—it shouldn't be long now. There's a key to all of them. Maybe hers is Mouse Bluffs." His eyes glided across David's face. "She really gets her mammaries in an uproar when I let her prattle about it."

David laughed, intentionally low, derogatory. It was a sort of duel they fought these days. Lunge, lunge. And who will win? I do not, nor do I lose.

"Comic books work with Margie," he said.

Darcy looked at him narrowly. "You know you're getting hard; I imagine it's those slobs in engineering. It was much better, although I must admit unnerving, when you were discovering Eliot and Gertie. That was tolerable even though you do immerse yourself—all heart, boy. Do they talk about anything but their squalid affairs and senseless drinking bouts?"

"They're all right. You're beginning to talk like a fruit, you know that? It's that arty-farty crowd you hang around with."

"That's show biz."

"The hell it is. Those characters haven't got their feet in the door. Actors who can't act; writers who don't write; dancers who practice only the goose. Don't give me show biz. You read the news and yak at a lot of old women to buy soap, conduct drama courses for sex-hungry housewives on Tuesday nights. Drama yet! What're you wasting yourself for?"

Darcy's eyes hardened. "Am I? This is the burning question. Am I wasted? I begin to hear a hollow sound. Tell me about the bridges you're going to build in the jungles of South America."

"Cut it out."

"You don't like that do you? All right, let's go over to Alfredo's and sneer at the freshmen. It's sport I never weary of."

In Alfredo's they discovered Paul Phillips talking to Lilja. She wore blue and looked flower-fresh and David wondered why all his images of her were so commonplace—flower-fresh, milk-white skin, sky-eyed—for surely there was nothing ordinary about such beauty. Even Phillips had hooked his heels around the chair-rung and kept shifting his body as he watched her.

"After all, people must marry," she was saying. "There has to be a touch of glamor to it and if there's no money or brass anklets or cows to offer as a show of worth then why not the love theme? It's evidence. It works. People still marry for children and homes and sex made comfortable."

"You shock and surprise me," Darcy mocked. "I agree with you, but of course with more right; I've done such a lot of actual field work. It's very bourgeois, romantic love. I'm glad you have such a growing understanding of it. One day you'll be a great lady, like Mater, part of the middle class but running the show because you have such understanding."

Phillips turned to David. "How are things?"

Bloody awful and you know it. "Okay."

Darcy went to the counter. David followed him, not wanting to remain under Phillips's question. Darcy leaned against the counter, facing Phillips and Lilja.

"Do you know that when Eskimos go on a hunt they take lactating women with them? Think of it, so much nimbler than a cow or a goat, can be packed in a kayak; have teats will travel."

"Some day I'm going to knock you down."

"I wonder."

The bottles were beaded and dark, and cool against the hand. Phillips teetered his chair; his cold pipe clicked against his rather long yellow teeth. Darcy studied him through half-lowered lids.

"Miss my touch in class?"

"Rushforth, I didn't teach you. Your brain was one big sponge sucking everything in. That isn't teaching. You didn't need a teacher."

Darcy paused between offence and pleasure.

"Think that one over," Lilja drawled.

"I think everything over."

"That's part of it," Phillips said enigmatically. He got to his feet. "Come and see me, David. I'm always in my office Tuesday nights."

"Counseling?"

Phillips nodded pleasantly, too perceptive to be provoked. David watched him leave. The spiky sand-colored hair always looked as if Phillips were overdue at the barber's. Shoot the bull. Talk of destinations. Life. Art. He did not want to talk to Phillips, resuscitate the still twitching corpse of his future. He could wait.

"I bide," he said to the other two. "I'm the best bider of time east of Mouse Bluffs."

"Next to me." Lilja's eyes met his.

Darcy asked sarcastically, "Do you two want to be alone?"

Lilja said, "That's a good idea."

"After all the money and time I've spent on you."

"Mother asks about you," she said to David. "She says we don't see much of you. She's right."

"It's a long way in from Fort Garry."

"Sunday?"

"All right."

"Ask me," Darcy said.

"Saturday's enough for you. Besides you're never bearable on Sundays."

"True."

"By the way, thanks for writing to Dad."

David grinned. "The answers are an experience."

"Aren't they?"

Long grave letters about duty and persistence and sin and obligation to the church, proud poems against pride, none of it offensively paternal but rather heavy weather after a time, David found.

Darcy lighted a cigarette with deliberation, held the match till the flame touched his fingers. "Your father writes such volumes

I wonder he has time to make guns or whatever it is he does. He writes pounds to my Aunt Christine. I do believe he thinks he'll save her but he's wrong, you see she's not really wicked or willful, she's crazy."

"No, she's not," David said slowly.

"And parsons can only save the wicked, not the insane or the insanely wicked."

"She's not crazy."

"You say. Any woman who swims night and day to commune with the dead is not my idea of Mrs. Mental Health."

"It's not communing, it's mourning."

"Is there a difference? And for Christ's sake mourning must stop somewhere."

"How would you know?"

Darcy's eyes were expressionless. "How do you manage it? You're getting worse and you afflict all of us. It's chronic. You're always making me wish I were something else which is preposterous. Or that you'd drop dead. Which has a point."

"Let him go then!" Lilja said.

The two looked at her, astonished.

Walking her home, David said, "Get off it."

"All right. It's just that you're together in some queer way I don't understand."

"Queer?"

"Don't be clever." She took his arm. "Why do you stay away from me?"

"Because. You know why, we've been over it a million times. And another thing, I haven't the dough."

"I don't care."

"Much. I don't blame you, you're pretty and you've got everything and you should be going around doing everything, dancing and sororities. I'm just not in that league. I can wait."

"What about me?"

"Can't you?"

"I don't know. You don't mind all the other fellows? Darcy?" They stood on the steps of her house.

He said, "I mind but . . . You'd pretty soon get tired of all I've got to offer and then there'd be nothing."

"You're lying, you're afraid of being bored."

It shook him. He said hotly, "You couldn't bore me."

"Not right away. I love you too much?" She waited but he could find no answer, so she said, "Come on in."

He shook his head but went inside. The need to apologize

toiled in his throat; he could not find words that would not confirm, in his own mind at least, the truth of what she had said.

She threw her coat over a chair. "I even went out with Cole Slaw Bleeker last year and you didn't mind."

"Cole Slaw!"

Suddenly they were laughing together, clinging to one another's hands and boiling quietly in a delicious union of joy. She placed her fingers over his lips.

"Where is everybody?"

She whispered, "In bed. Let's have a drink."

He watched her as she moved through the shadows of the gray and rose room. How small she was. Her little hands, fluttering over the glasses, seemed oddly inept.

She murmured, "I daren't get ice, the tray rattles like bones. Curly would be up like a shot."

They touched glasses. The laughter nudged them again, then changed subtly. They smiled slowly and desire grew in the warm gloom.

"To waiting," he said hoarsely, and it was a mistake for they could wait no longer.

She slipped off her shoes and went to close the glass-paned door. His arms and palms ached over the supple white warmth and speed of her.

"It's okay?" he asked but didn't hear her answer.

Later she said, "So that's being carried away."

"You'll never come any closer."

She brushed her mouth against his cheek. "Now what?"

"I used to wonder why they made these damned great low chesterfields."

"Shouldn't we hunch over the deed and make plans of some kind? I'm new at this. I expect to be married over it." Her small laugh snuffled against his neck and every inch of his body flamed with heightened sensibility.

"You will be; let's not talk about it right now. Kiss me."

"But I want to talk about it, it's all I've ever wanted to talk about. I want to be married in Mouse Bluffs at St. George's." She sighed. Her whole body quivered. "I don't want to just go on dating other men and knowing some day years from now we'll be married."

"Kiss me." She did. He rubbed his palms against her silvery curls. "The first time I was ever aware of a girl, of wanting a girl was when we were at the lake. Remember the quack doctor and after? First time."

"You were precocious. You still are. Let's talk about us."

He turned his face from her, all the tender whiteness of the hour just gone sluiced away; they had come a long way together and in five minutes rushed apart at such speed he could no longer comprehend her words.

"If you keep this up I'm going to slap you."

Very slowly she got up from the chesterfield and reached for her sweater.

As she fastened her skirt she said, "Lock the door on your way out, will you?"

He pushed his face into the pillow.

As she went upstairs, he heard a door close. Her footsteps paused, then flicked briskly on. When he heard another door close, he left.

When he telephoned on Sunday morning she said she was sorry but Leo Frank had been killed overseas and would he mind taking a raincheck. He said that was tough and he was sorry and was there anything he could do. No, she said, she would call him but she didn't and the next time he saw her she was with one of the early returned veteran students, who limped slightly and looked very old and dashing and glanced at David as if he were scarcely human when she introduced them. He waited.

CHAPTER 20

Ian hung on.

"Sheer stubbornness," Gavin declared in admiration.

"I've seen out V-E Day. I'll live till V-J Day," Ian promised and went on with his maps and drawing pins keeping track of the war.

He had removed all the black thumb tacks from the map of Britain, each marking a bad raid. The thin red line of pins had gone from North Africa and Italy, halted in Berlin. Japan remained. Then Hiroshima and Nagasaki were bombed and black thumb tacks, previously reserved for Allied suffering, seemed only appropriate.

Each night for years he had gone to bed saying, "It'll be over tomorrow."

He did not mean the war but his life. It was a form of prayer. He was making it clear to God that he was as nimble as He, and anticipated such underhand tactics as taking a man in his sleep. God, he was convinced, would wait until he was thinking of something else or until he forgot to issue the contemptuous pronouncement. He had a deep dread of going out as one came in, dumb, without time to compose the mind and consider the fact, so he pretended to God and the world that his life was hinged upon the war. Nevertheless, he knew what no one else seemed to know, that war went on forever. 1919 slid without effort into 1939; 1945 into what? 1965? Probably. When he died this malignancy would still be chewing his vitals.

He had a secret. The secret of prolonging his life in war. He was needed. The others, with their prating about the will to live, analysis, decent life, had never come near it. David needs me, he thought early each morning when he discovered he had won another erasure from God. Without me there'd be no one who had a share of the horror; he might feel that need again. Without me he might confide in a Jack Yeates during some bottomless moment, live to regret the telling more than the crime; the Jacks understand no trust, gag those around them with the poisons they draw from such moments.

"The drive to confession is sheer egotism," he'd told the boy. "A nasty plot on the part of the Almighty. We betray our prides. My sins are not the world's worst but He put something in my head that makes me hunger for them to be the worst. After all, they're mine."

David wrote to him the first week in September:

This summer job may be gainful but it plays hell with my thinking processes. Sometimes by the end of the shift—"Two hamburgers and! Four to go!"—I'm stunned and find myself wondering whether it was worth it. The people I've met are pretty staggering but I don't want to make the mistake of assuming that the seamy side is *life*. I keep telling myself that women like Mrs. Ross and your sister are as real as the tarts who roll into this joint every night at the start of their peregrinations—of course they are, no more no less, I hear you say.

The big fact is that I can't simply accept people. How does she live? what is her background? what sort of furniture has she? does she read? go to church? listen to Bing Crosby records? make dolls? how does she love? and more important, how does she talk? How does one describe the long upper lip, the pocket of flesh on the jaw which squares the face, the way the green-gray eyes conceal secrets with that cunning that began in the first cave and still calls stranger enemy?

Perhaps one of the reasons I cannot rest or accept things and people is my lack of identity. This is personal but it is also part of a larger concept that I began to develop soon after I left Mouse Bluffs. Lack of identity seems to be endemic to this country. I have seen so many people—Ukrainians, Icelanders, French, Jews, Irish, ad infinitum—trying to place themselves by identifying with their ethnic group. I want no part of any of this. I cannot accept labels, either for others or for myself. The cult of nationalism, of the elect, should have died its proper death when the last fire went out in Germany's ovens. When the Icelanders start their trek to Islendingadagurinn each August it is Lourdes, the Buddha and the start of the march to Belsen all over again. We need a new beginning.

Darcy wants a different sort of cult—page Rimbaud—but it is too foreign or too late. Systematic derangement belongs to another time and place and is as puerile as the others. I have no heart for the beret and the absinthe—it seems too bloody conventional.

I am coming out next week and you can shoot me full of holes because I ramble and have not your rapier-like thrust against the world. I am tired. I'll be glad to leave this job although it's had its points.

The other you asked about is okay. X-rayed last week and the dr. flatteringly drew attention to my horselike lines. Augmented no doubt by all the steaks—the cook weighs 300 and considers himself a fine figger of a man, he looks at me daily and shakes his head. He's crammed steak into me till I expect all cows to moo hopefully if I happen to get in a down wind.

I'm getting out of engineering. Now the war is over I can see no purpose to it—there never was, you say, but let's not cudgel that to death. The point is, how will Dr. Ross take it? I'll have my cap in my hand when I get there.

David.

"David wants to go back to Arts," Ian told Christine.

She turned it over in her mind. "Gavin won't take it."

"I know."

"Why change now?"

"Because he should never have left in the first place. He's a thinker and a watcher, not a hydro-project builder. It's more important."

"Gavin won't think so."

Ian was silent a long while. "No one can be won that way, I've told him so—especially not Gavin—but everyone has to try it once in life. Gavin's never understood, he only thought the boy was crazy to get himself shot, would go to any lengths to get shot."

"He did it to please Gavin? To—win him?"

"Because Gavin is the only one here who doesn't love him."

She set her lips firmly. "It's not that simple."

"I know, I'm a mean old man." He smiled. "I thought you might—work on Gavin?"

She laughed outright. "I've forgotten how. And besides it wouldn't do any good."

"I suppose you're right." He wheeled past her. "I'll be at the hotel thinking."

"Maybe Solveg could help: she's coming down this weekend."

Ian said emphatically, "You know and I know that Solveg has no time or compassion for anyone's problems if they hinge on money in any way. Poverty isn't a crime or a pity to her, it's just so distasteful she will not think about it. She used to hide it pretty well but not any more. Well, at least she's honest."

Christine picked up her bathing cap and went through the veranda to the garden.

She knew perfectly well what Gavin would say. David was old enough to decide a course of action and carry it through; this vacillation indicated a weakness of character; and it was expensive; also there was no real obligation. It was not as if the boy belonged to them.

She waded into the river. The friendly mud sucked at her feet. Sometimes, when she went to the mouth of the creek and stood in the shallows, the fish came and brushed her legs and remembered, she knew, the flesh. At first she had imagined Tina out there. She had imagined Tina small and moving softly on the river bed, her thin brown hair floating to the river's touch, still wearing the little salmon-colored sweater, her eyes large and almost but not quite afraid as she wandered and wondered how to break the shining tight mirror above and return. No way to break it. But Mother could go to her. And Mother had. She had dreamed of one day having the courage to go deep into the murk and stay with Tina; but fly after it, bleed for it, that kind of courage would not come. Still she went each day and it was a comfort to Tina and to her that she came, was there, would always come, would never leave the river's side. Three-year-old girls get lonely with only a river. However, as time went by she knew that the river had absorbed Tina, that Tina in her loneliness had given her flesh to the fish, joined her world. Now Christine did not visit the child. She bathed in the great fullness of Tina. Each molecule of water, each animal and fish, had been made Tina in the sharing-out. Once, in one of the bad years when the river was foul, the water low, a number of long leathery leeches had caught on her legs and thighs. She had dragged herself beneath the old elm, watching them feed as their progenitors had done, wondered if they too remembered, if they carried the memory through their generations, that Tina had helped God in his work of building the river's people. Billy

Treleven had seen her and run frantically for salt, carried on. He meant well.

No, David was not theirs.

Neither she nor Gavin had ever assumed, as the townsfolk, speculative, assumed, that he took Tina's place. It had even been mentioned a few times, as if this made it fitting, that he was within months of Tina's age. What nonsense. Tina was three years old. Tina was the river. David, of course, had never assumed any such thing. There was that. Perhaps that was why she stood him so well; he had created a place in the house, not taken one. This was the root of her obligation to him, and it would not be for much longer; he was a man now. Of course, he'd had a man's ways from the first. That father was a harsh devil.

In the beginning, he had been silent to the point of invisibility, with none of them caring enough to help him from the grim prison of child misery. Often in those early days she had been surprised to find him at the table or walking quietly through a room. He was so withdrawn he was scarcely in her consciousness and she had felt he would one day disappear, leaving no mark of having been with them; then, through Ian, in some curious way he had come out of the shadows and made his place.

She would not like it if things went badly for David. If, from her house, he joined the grim skeleton of Sholto Todd among those who left Mouse Bluffs and did not succeed. She would not like it at all.

Herb Henderson hailed her from the cliff.

He raised his cap, a barely discernible salute. She waved back but did not swim to the sand-strip as she sometimes did. He always stood in exactly the same spot.

She remembered the first time she had seen him there, raising his hand. As she waved back, she had had the impression that he had stood just there and waved before, perhaps many times, that there was something permanent in the image of him standing just so in the long strong rays of the late yellow sun. If she turned in now, he would come down the narrow footpath, moving like a powerful nimble-footed animal, and sit on the sand beside her, quiet for long intervals. Sometimes they did not speak at all but sat, while she rested, breathing out the long swim, watching the river and sky familiar to both since birth. Then she would say so long Herb and leave him. When he saw she was not swinging in, but going on downstream to the springs, he put his cap back on and in a few minutes was gone. For some reason she felt a comfort in his watching. He was not like the others and, when they sat on the beach, she had a sense of communication with him, as if she gave something of the river to him and he did not question it.

Once she said, "You walk a lot, Herb."

"Like swimming, it clears the head."

He said two things; she took up the one, "I suppose the family keeps Matt pretty busy," and she wondered if this were the basis of his loneliness.

"He's a good daddy. And she's all right. We get on fine. Never would have believed it. Runs Matt and me and the little ones just like Mummy used to. Matt's a good man. Steady."

"I'm glad."

No one would have believed it, that the day Elsie Yeates was discharged from hospital after her concussion she would marry Matt Henderson and go to the house no one in town had been inside for years, settle down, beside big and silent and perhaps disapproving Herb, to raise a baby a year. Church on Sunday, W.A. on Tuesday, I.O.D.E. on Thursday and Mothers' Union on Friday; this was Elsie Henderson, and what the ladies of the Bluffs remembered they didn't talk about; in Mouse Bluffs gossip and scandal do not preserve luster when they reach the proportions of tragedy. Phoebe lived with the younger Yeates children in the Rainwell house, for which presumably she paid rent to the town, as she now kept house daily for old Reese Todd; even Phoebe had attained a degree of respectability. Others had taken her place. She no longer plied the park, perhaps, it was suggested, not so much because of Jack's gruesome demise there as because the hoboes no longer roved the country in such droves and paused to take heart in the oak grove. Phoebe went only occasionally to the Hendersons': although she received her mother civilly, Elsie did not like her coming and Phoebe did not want to strain the relationship. Too, the powerful air of virtue somewhat exhausted her. With the rest of Mouse Bluffs Phoebe had ceased to wonder who had murdered Jack; no one for a moment believed he had had sense enough to commit suicide. After the coroner's open verdict the Mountie had seemed to keep up his inquiries forever; every now and then the new man asked a question or two. Even Gavin Ross had been unable to explain what was only whispered through town as "them bruises." Mouse Bluffs chose to consider Jack well gone, as if he personified the bad times. Where formerly scarcely anyone had had a good word for him, now no one had a word for him at all.

Now and then, to titillate the girls, the town boys would pretend the park was haunted but the legend never really took hold. Mouse Bluffs was ever practical. The small park in the valley was the prettiest spot for miles in the flat prairie; it would be sheer stupidity to let a ghost have it. Jack Yeates was up beyond the tracks in the town portion of the cemetery. Between him and the town the living freights thundered. It would take considerably more spirit than Jack had possessed to launch itself against the C.P.R.

Sometimes the Mountie, now Nat Farland, came and talked to Ian, for everyone knew Ian and Yeates had been drinking mates; it was, no doubt, on file. Ian could offer no information about Jack's enemies. They were legion, he supposed, all of Mouse Bluffs whom he had offended by his constant misdeeds. Nevertheless, he talked volubly to the constable. A Mountie, like a cripple, is a lonely man in Mouse Bluffs. Farland was of the new order of policemen, a university graduate; his negative virtues were noted; no one was beaten in the cell behind the fire-hall these days. He often brought books and magazines to Ian, perhaps as an excuse to visit. Ian read them keenly, especially the copies of *Scarlet and Gold*, and in return plagued him incessantly with criticisms, ironical references to Plato's watchdogs.

"What a crazy history you policemen have!" Christine once heard him say. "Part of the development of the country but not part of the people. Like everything else in the West, no continuity. The law came from the East, another immigrant. The fur traders didn't stop to become ranchers; the policemen didn't bring out their families to fill up a nation, they were an occupation army. The pattern's still there; the ranchers' sons didn't stop to be farmers; now the farmers' sons don't continue to be farmers; always the younger generation picks up and goes and someone else comes along. Now machinery is depopulating the prairie; it needs fewer men to crop it each year. They're going in droves. We move backwards. The automobile is depopulating the towns; the farmers can run to the city at the drop of a hat and what of the little merchants? Dying. Dying towns. What will it be in a hundred years? There was nothing here seventy years ago. Seventy! There's no reason to assume that Mouse Bluffs is permanent."

"You're wrong."

"Yes," Ian sighed. "It's just that I'm out of it. The old families who came out with Sir Richard still go strong. And you feel it, they'll be here forever, the Joneses, the Blakes, the Hendersons."

"You know those Henderson twins well?"

"Can you never forget you're a policeman?"

Farland laughed genially and waited and, of course, got very small change.

At length he said softly, "I've played this game with men

before, the game of wait and watch, and never seen one who wouldn't break. But I can't play it when that man is two men. It doesn't work."

"What put Henderson into your head?"

"Which? There it is. One of them knows something."

"Everyone knows something."

"Too right." Finally Farland relaxed and smiled his way around it. "Tell me about Sir Richard Rashleigh." It was his favorite topic.

"I don't know a Sir Richard! Sir Richard is a myth, a folk tale, a song from a mouth organ whispering through the park on a summer's night, a figment of Mouse Bluffs' collective imagination."

Farland's eyes danced. "Come now!"

"I never saw him."

"Never?"

"Only in my cups. Once I looked into the office and saw him at his desk, late, an oil lamp by his elbow and his eyes black hollows of dreams that never came true."

"But they did."

"Not his dreams, there's the point. Not his. He set the goal, saw the prize and when he got to it some fault in his soul, some crookedness in his road had altered it and there was no other chance and he did not want the prize. He knew then what I, the wisest man in the Bluffs, have aways known—that there is no prize, not only because none of us wants to take it at that moment but because if we do tomorrow changes it and us. The real prize is death."

"*Breeding lilacs out of a dead land*," Farland said, then mockingly, "You are old, Father."

"Too old now to see Sir Richard," Ian said shortly. "I save that for the likes of you who pretend they're great historians and at bottom are scarlet-coated romantics wildly pursuing fancies."

"Fancies?"

"Ay, you don't mislead me, Nat. One day you'll find that man you're looking for and he'll be no more real than Sir Richard, no more real than Nat Farland, arm of the law who came under orders and stopped a while in Mouse Bluffs and went away again, under orders, leaving no mark and taking nothing with him."

Listening to the two men wrangle, Christine had wondered how much any of them might leave or take, even Richard Rashleigh's granddaughter, clenched in the myth as tightly as a head in a hemp loop. She would leave only the river; Sir Richard's issue, the fruit of all his giving, Mouse River.

When she pulled herself up on the lawn below the house, Prince came forward to stand respectfully in attendance.

"David's coming to see you," she told him and he cocked his head politely.

The dog and the boy, it hadn't offended her. Nothing offends me about David, she thought.

What a warm soul I am, my most generous hour, he does not offend me. Scarcely anything offends me. Except Darcy. And it's not even Darcy personally, he's harmless, but Gavin's tacit assumption that Darcy is somehow his heir to the future, son through some mystic union with Mary, and the further assumption that I must feel this too. She did not grudge him the former; she knew that the big house, she, the last one, could not, through magic or willpower or marriage, give old Richard what he could not have of the prairie, survival.

Perhaps Gavin was just more cunning than others; he would have his survival, however much mental adjustment was required.

As she walked slowly through the house, she thought, I wish there were some way I could manage this, give this unoffending boy a chance. It isn't just the money. It's Gavin himself must approve or say he approves. This would be enough for David. Small things could so alter a young life, approval withheld or a wrong meeting, and suddenly one was weary and used up, all the hopes gone. Like, she thought for the first time in years, meeting an older man, a doctor, a man from the old places, and imagining he was just right for Sir Richard's house, when all the while Sir Richard's house needed a Hoyt or a Jones. She shrugged it away. What nonsense. Sir Richard's house, like Sir Richard, belonged to the river in which all Mouse Bluffs bathed. It was an experiment founded on a false premise, and continued to absurd lengths after the faults were clear.

In the hall she discovered a note from Solveg saying she could not come Friday but to expect her Saturday morning. She was pleased; it would be nice to have her friend visit. Someone too to take the edge off things if Gavin got unpleasant with the boy.

"But my heavens, wouldn't Calvin rather have peace and quiet?' Solveg asked.

"Not a bit of it." Gavin roused suddenly out of his preoccupation. "Brace is quite right. I assure you if I'd been in a prison camp for some four years I would not want to get into bed and think, whatever my physical condition. People around me, people talking, people smiling, people telling me they were happy I was home. And all my own people. No, we must all go and share this."

David asked, "Is it true he's hired the Orange Hall?"

"Not only that, he chartered a plane yesterday to bring Calvin from Winnipeg—landed on the highway. Nat Farland was close to nervous prostration with his road blocks. I've never seen Brace so happy."

"No man deserved it more," Christine said.

Ian poured cream in his coffee. "I for one feel we should make an early start. I plan to go early and stay late. Brace has ordered ten kegs of beer from Jaques."

"In the Orange Hall!" Solveg cried.

"Further, he telephoned me this morning that he has two cases of champagne and one of whiskey."

Solveg swept her forehead dramatically. "Mouse Bluffs!"

"That's all right," Gavin nodded. "Mouse Bluffs hadn't any organized celebration at the end of the war. People ran out into the streets willy-nilly, and after they got done shaking hands and shouting and speaking to people they hadn't had a civil word for in years there was nothing left to do. Some went to church and some got drunk but it was anti-climactic. The Bluffs needs a celebration; there's not been one since the King and Queen passed through and that didn't amount to much. Personally I'm rather looking forward to it."

"Gavin?" Solveg regarded him intently. "Yes, I can see you are. Bless you."

The doctor flushed.

She said, "But surely Brace hasn't this sort of money."

"You'd be surprised. He's doing the lion's share—his son and his idea—nevertheless a few interested citizens are, shall we say, showing their interest?"

"Not you!"

"Well, the bingo prizes. They'll be playing bingo in the Legion."

Christine watched carefully. David and Ian felt her concern. Would Brace Harvey's glad, once-in-a-lifetime joy in survival remind Solveg too much of all she had lost, scrape the newly whitened scars to bleeding disbelief once more? Ian shook his head slightly, smiled at Christine.

"Come along, Solveg, people will be glad to see you."

"Do you really think so?" There was mild mockery in her voice.

Christine said quickly, "Of course. And David. Brace particularly asked for you when I saw him at the post office today."

"There's nothing small about Brace Harvey, it's an open invitation to the town." Ian looked at his watch, "I've got to go, it's seven-thirty and I have a special function to perform; I must be there before anyone else."

"What?"

"Bartender." His bony face split in a great grin. "That's Brace—homespun psychology. Who must be put on his honor? The man should run for office."

The others laughed as he wheeled out with great pretense of fury.

David asked, "When are we to go?"

"Eight-thirty should be near enough," Gavin decided.

Christine asked, "You really are looking forward to it, aren't you?"

"I intend, waistline permitting, to dress. You ladies should do the same."

Christine and Solveg exchanged a delighted glance.

David felt an immense happiness with this unexpected celebration, the unusual lightheartedness at the table. It seemed a good omen that he should have chosen this particular day to come to Mouse Bluffs to present his new plan to Gavin Ross.

Christine said, "Is Mrs. Harvey dressing?"

"Is she dressing!" Gavin rolled his eyes. "She has her first evening gown and handmade slippers to match. I saw and admired the lot when I dropped in there this morning."

"And Brace?"

"Brace will wear his kilt, I expect."

"His what? Harvey?"

"Stewart clan—distaff side."

"But Brace went to St. George's."

"He's a great man for peace."

Solveg teased, "I had no idea you felt keenly about such things."

He answered her with exaggerated loftiness, "I'm not saying the Presbyterians are right, I'm a verra broad-minded chappie, I merely say they're mair right than others."

The two women groaned suitably, rose. Gavin told them they must hurry because he and David intended to dress with great speed in order to stand at the door and nag. He accused them of prodigious clack-a-wagging, suggested they might hold up the entire celebration if the gentlemen were obliged to wait. The old man was in a humor quite unlike anything David had seen. He decided he would have to wait till the following day to approach the doctor and, even as he thought this, he wondered why he was always waiting for something, why he was so good at it, or whether perhaps he waited because he was so good at it.

"Poor Daniel would have enjoyed all this," Solveg told Christine.

"I suppose he would."

Christine gave her a sidelong glance. It was most peculiar that, with Leo dead, Solveg talked not of him but of Daniel, as if it were he who had died. In the days of their old intimacy she had seen Solveg pass through the special tortures of her love for Leo, seen her break all points of identity with Daniel and go, after an indecent interval, to become Leo's wife. Christine had been more perplexed than shocked by the affair. She had never felt so about any man. She remembered Solveg's telling her once, "He—he touched my ankle . . . Oh dear God! What am I to do?" Ankle. Often in the night on her narrow bed in the dressing room, Christine thought of it: *he touched my ankle*, the agony of breathlessness in Solveg's voice, but, however hard she tried, she could not discover the secret of it, that touch, that explosive male touch that had blown Solveg clear of Mouse Bluffs, changed Dan, brought a new life into the world, created a new family and now was gone. It affected her in much the same way as the novels she read all winter—sword fights, daring men and voluptuous women, love, battles, all part of a fictional world that must be accepted with powers of disbelief and criticism suspended. However, she knew a kind of terrible doubting pity for Solveg over Leo's death, terrible because she knew something wonderful and rare was gone from Solveg's life and doubting because she hadn't really any idea what it had been.

She told Solveg, "He writes to me, you know."

"Dan? Yes, he told me."

"He told you?"

"Yes, he came to—comfort me. All that way. He was a nice man."

"Is. He wasn't. I used to think him a sort of—stuffed shirt, you know? But his letters—really, I look forward to them more than anything. Everything seemed so—empty, just empty and always was, it seemed, and suddenly there were Dan's letters. It makes things a little less . . . Every Tuesday's mail." After a long moment she said, "The forties are the worst time of life, too late to do anything about all the mistakes and too early to be resigned."

As they were going upstairs, Solveg said suddenly, "He wanted me to marry him. Again. Dan, I mean. But you know I couldn't."

She sounded as if she were about to cry.

Christine said, "Of course not."

"Brace—I remembered it when Gavin was talking. Dan, one day after church, 'I saw you looking at him.' Me, small voice, 'Me? Looking? *What* him?' Dan, sad voice, 'You know who.' Silence. 'Brace Harvey.'" She laughed. "Oh how foolish it all was. Brace Harvey! The only man in Mouse Bluffs who still believes God puts them there, babies, after one goes through the proper Christian ceremony."

Christine put her arm around Solveg's waist and laughed with her. It wasn't really funny, she thought, and they both knew it but Gavin's mood had caught up with them. There was happiness in the house; it had been a long time since she had sensed it. Abruptly the thought came, nothing can prevent our holding it for just a little while if we try, and she was astonished to find this following so quickly upon her admission of emptiness. She had not, she realized, had such a thought for years. Perhaps, just perhaps. If we try.

David stood outside Ross's bedroom door. The women stared.

Gavin boomed, "Kilt made me think of it. Ian's dress kilt. Perfect. Kneel, lad." David knelt as for the accolade. "Barely touches the floor. You'll do."

"You're magnificent," Christine exclaimed. "David, I shall wear my white silk, you demand it."

David bowed. "It's drafty." But his cheeks were flushed, his gray eyes shone with pleasure as Gavin thumped his shoulder in approval.

Christine studied his face: what a strange boy he is, he'd wear the armor if Gavin suggested it. Perhaps the powerful austerities of his early years warped out his boyishness. He sends out his love like Whittington's cat, a small everything, expecting no return.

Christine discovered her white silk slightly yellowed.

"Damn, it's grown old while time stood still!"

Nevertheless she wore it and Solveg assured her she looked beautiful.

"It was cut from a sari Daddy brought from India," she explained, and Solveg looked judicious and said that with all the gold threads no one would notice the yellowing; a good piece of silk was ageless.

Occasions calling for formal dress in Mouse Bluffs were almost non-existent. Solveg had nothing with her so she settled for a full skirt and a daringly-cut blouse belonging to Christine, which showed a great deal of the upper regions of a figure that had already shaken Mouse Bluffs once. Christine winked and said hot damn and brought out her jewelry.

"You should have some of these stones re-set."

Christine said with mild surprise, "Well, no—I couldn't."

"Why not?"

"It isn't done. They're not really mine—it's a kind of trust."

She looked beyond Solveg, her eyes blank. Trust? For whom? She wondered how many other dark pockets of unreason were housed in the sheltered gloom.

"I don't understand."

"It's not important."

"I'm sorry." Solveg sighed. "Dan would have understood perfectly. But Curly's always telling me I mustn't live in the past. I just parrot her, forgive me. Hard not to, isn't it? But at least it's my own past I live in. There now, let's forget it. Is David really going to wear that rig?"

"You're awful: of course he is."

"Why is he always being different?"

"I suppose because he is different."

"I'm glad Lilja stopped seeing him. I had to—it was more or less forced on me—take steps, and you know I think on the whole she was relieved. Couldn't see him going to the office or kissing the babies, I expect, and that's what she wants."

"They're through?"

"Oh, quite. She's made her mind up and I think she's chosen well; he's a good man. Don't mistake me, I like David. I just couldn't see it."

"You're right, he won't be ready for it for a long time. I don't think he really knows what he wants yet."

Solveg fretted a moment. "He makes me uneasy. I often wonder if he's one of those—oh, you know, they think it's clever to go around calling people Babbitts or Yahoos or Philistines and missing the whole point."

"He's not like that."

"They used to sit and talk about Dostoevsky and other unpronounceables with fantastic intensity—that kind of thing, Love and Life and Art, and I always felt—closed off? Lilja always closes me off but more when she was with him. And of course they talked a good deal about sex—oh, quite openly. They all do it, talk that is."

Christine turned away. "I suppose that's the modern city way of it."

Solveg smiled. "Maybe it isn't even preoccupation with sex so much as a frenzy for honesty; they're so honest they're dishonest. And it makes things a bit rough on old Mother, I mean you can't say 'Be careful, my child, of men; take long walks, et cetera,' when you've just heard that child engaged in a clinical discussion of the whole thing."

Gavin called from downstairs. They were still laughing as they went down.

Billy and Cassie were dressed and ready; Cassie in her blue Sunday silk and a summer straw took one look at the other women and removed her hat. They crammed into the car, waved good-bye to a desolated Prince and were halfway to the corner of Main when Christine remembered her gift for Calvin and they had to go back.

"A pair of slippers; his mother was telling me that for years he's had to wear those bloody Jap things without backs and he has a thing about proper shoes."

The others felt their empty-handedness, so Billy drove to Deacon's and they bought up the last of the chocolates. Cassie announced triumphantly that she had made a pair of red flannel pyjamas because he was such a tall boy and could never buy them long enough and had worn them little Nip pants up to his knees all this while, the heathens. She had just begun to describe how she had lined the jacket with canton for extra strength when they drew up outside the Orange Hall.

Through the open windows they could hear the fiddlers tuning up. Tyrone Kendall with his wife, son and two girls drove up. The boy was in uniform.

He said ironically as he shook hands, "Ma says she knew I'd come home but you see she gave all my clothes away."

"Nonsense, you don't fit them. And me thinking the Army wouldn't feed you." Mrs. Kendall told them brightly, "Ty's been in a stew all day. Dancing and drinking in the Orange Hall, my goodness."

Ty frowned, laughed uneasily. "It's just a thing I can't get away from, see. And Doc, you see I live to get to confession."

In the hall they saw Father Graham drinking a coke and talking to Calvin. Ty turned white with disbelief.

"All the way from East Coulee. If I'd stayed home and heard about this I'd of . . . ."

The band played with dignity, a slow beginning. The ladies, a row of various shades of muddy-colored crepes, smiled from their chairs around the walls, chattered, watched the newcomers, the youngsters who sped up to the little shadowed balcony; after they had seen how Christine was dressed, many of them would go to play bingo. A buzz went up as the Ross party came in. Brace hurled himself through the crowd of men around the improvised bar.

"By God, Doc, you look like a movie star. Come and meet the boy, folks."

They shook hands with Calvin and placed their gifts on the card table.

"He's fat," David said and Gavin looked glum.

"Ay, that kind of fat. Like suet. Filling up on sweets and milk so fast he's a balloon."

Calvin removed his jacket, stood grinning at them all with a happy stupefied look.

"Doc, that vitamin shot this morning set me up for fair."

"Easy on the refreshments."

"Don't worry about me, I'm not taking any chances, not now I'm this far. I'm drunk just being here."

"Let's dance," Brace thundered.

A silence. Then a clamor went up for him to start. After some hesitation the band sprang with all feet into "Highland Laddie."

David turned to Christine. "May I?"

Brace and Mrs. Harvey circled the floor once, Brace's kilt flying, his feet more enthusiastic than talented. The girls looked hopefully at the servicemen, and the town boys turned a bit sullen. The weight had shifted; the men were coming back. Solveg, dancing with Gavin, thought, it does look right, the kilt is right and romantic and redolent of foreign ballrooms and parties for other soldiers returning from battles long ago. Even Brace Harvey, his bald head gleaming with effort, looked tonight like some wild foreign chief.

David stood beside Calvin's chair. "How does it feel?"

Calvin teetered back. "Like I died and went to Heaven." He sipped a coke, tipping the cold bottle against his mouth with a look of exquisite satisfaction. "My old man's all right."

"He sure is."

"A tiger. But damn it I wish he'd quit saying, 'That's all right, boy, don't talk about it.' He thinks he's sparing me. Now everybody's saying it. Cripes it's all I've got to talk about. You do something for four years, what else are you going to talk about?"

David laughed. "Go ahead, talk about it."

Calvin grinned. "Well, not right here."

"They're afraid."

"I guess they figure my mind might snap or something. I got an unsnappable mind, I'm here."

The band chugged through "You Are My Sunshine" and Calvin hummed dreamily.

"They've heard some pretty grim things, they're just afraid now that they're true," David said.

Calvin gave him a sidelong glance. "They are. But that isn't what I want to talk about. There were guys, friends—well, you just don't get them out of your head and come back all in a minute. Things we did. One day I stole a box of oranges. It was climbing Mount Everest. Sounds nothing here. Specially when everybody keeps saying, 'Boy, you don't have to talk about it.'"

Brace came up. "Let's not get serious, you fellows, this's a party."

"See what I mean? Okay, Dad. Listen I want to get at those parcels, I'd like to share out the candy."

"You don't . . ."

"Well, you see sharing out is . . . Once we got a Red Cross parcel and Jesus things were tough . . ."

"That's all right, Calvin. We'll do it. Don't worry none."

Mrs. Spence pointed herself at Calvin, breathed heavily over him. "Don't you worry is right, Calvin: the Americans are getting even with those Japs."

"I guess."

"Just let those monsters think about it now."

Calvin smiled mildly. "I guess we were all monsters."

"Now don't you talk about it. The things they did to you boys." She shuddered.

"That's it, see? War is a sort of craziness anyway, Mrs. Spence, no reason why the prison camps would be any different than all the other crazy things. Men go nuts. They're nuts when they're out killing each other; they're nuts when they get each other in the stockade."

"Please! You don't realize . . . We know what you brave boys did, now don't talk about it any more. It's a lovely party."

"Sure. They're not crazy in Mouse Bluffs, not as crazy."

David went to speak to Ian. He nodded towards the spigot. "You've found your calling?"

Ian swung his chair, leaned forward, creating, as he could do so quickly and so readily, the sense that they were alone. "I was asking myself who the handsome lad in the tartan was. He looked like a boy I knew long ago."

"You don't mind?"

"Welcome. But aren't you the boy who wasn't going to have any part of the cult of ethnic groups?" He gave a low laugh.

"Maybe a man without defined antecedents can go into any court."

"Without conviction, there's the hole. And you did it for someone else, there's the second. It doesn't count. Nothing done that way counts. Learn, lad, before it's too late."

On his face was that obsessed white look that so often was preliminary to a tirade of self-pity and regret, to another and still another drink, evenings at the hotel, black days in the little parlor.

David said quickly, "Have you had a chance to speak to Dr. Ross?"

Wearily, "No, let it rest a bit, David."

"Registration starts next week."

"Well, have a beer and we'll think about it tomorrow. Here, you'd better take the ladies a glass, they can't come for one but I don't suppose Mouse Bluffs is feeling critical tonight."

David took two glasses but by the time he got across the room Christine was gone, so he gave one to Solveg, kept the other.

She said, "I shouldn't."

"No one . . . It's all right."

He sat beside her.

"What enchanting legs you have," she teased.

Across the room he saw Elsie Henderson with Matt. His gut clutched up in a knot, the old always-new spasm. You've got to face it and go out and never avoid her and always remember that she doesn't know, that it would be worse for her if she knew, Ian had told him. And he had done it. Yet he could never leave the house, even for a walk, without feeling weak with the dread that he might meet this woman, be reminded afresh of her terrible sorrows and that he had caused them. She was stout and looked much older than her years, her hair half gray, but her plump little face had an air of brisk determination. She was pregnant again; his eyes feasted on the swollen waist. Fill up, Elsie, you can never fill up too often.

"David, you're a million miles away," Solveg scolded. "Don't you know I'm supposed to be a *femme fatale?*"

"What?"

"I was asking if you knew Lilja has her ring?"

He got to his feet.

"Alvin Marshall, you know him, don't you?"

"No. But I'm sure he's just right."

His eyes glittered. She thought for one appalling moment he was going to cry. Then she saw that his glance was on the girls around the door, not on her at all, and that he was smiling. She turned away in confusion.

"He's a good . . ." she said slowly, but he was gone.

Groups of boys, the odd girl, stood around the corner and down Center where the shadows melded thickly. Against Rose's bakery across the way David saw the dark smudge of Ally James's big body as she hunched slyly towards the lights and people. Did she ever speak, poor brutalized Ally, locked in the tower of her epilepsy? Her eyes, dull pits, told him: alone, alone is ugly; ugly is alone. She seemed to sense his thought and flopped hurriedly into the dark. He saw Calvin come out of the hall with Jessie Talmadge, knew Calvin was at last happy; Jessie was listening; she would listen and walk off into the night with him. Jessie was only fifteen and Calvin probably wouldn't remember that. Nevertheless, David decided, she was just what Calvin needed, not talk of vitamin shots or parties so much as someone just like Jessie. The fiddlers bucked vigorously through "Avalon." The music drifting through the windows was transmuted, a honeyed thread of melody spilled into the big sky.

On the hotel steps Charlie Jaques sat, looking glumly at the Orange Hall.

David said, "Go on over, Charlie, I'll keep an eye on things."

Charlie didn't hesitate. "I'll only be half an hour. Thanks, boy."

David sat on one of the rockers on the porch, elbows on his knees, thumbs against his mouth. He felt quite detached from Mouse Bluffs and its people, a god's eye view. Their joys were as changeless as their tempers; they went on forever, never questioned one another or resisted the paths set out before them. He knew for the first time that he didn't belong in Mouse Bluffs. He could almost leave. But not quite yet. He must take something with him, treasure he had been promised from the beginning. He must be claimed or he would be nothing, would carry rags of the unloved past with him wherever he went.

Earlier Lippy Jones had said to him, "Shame your daddy couldn't be here, David. He surely would have enjoyed it being over."

David had agreed with him, knowing Lippy was thinking of his son, knew no other way of speaking of him except through references to other dead. David had watched Gavin, the townsfolk making pleasantries for Gavin, thrilled that he had worn a dress suit to distinguish the night, yet as always intimidated by him, by the dress suit, by his inability to be one of them, however much he smiled or chatted. Maybe they sensed that the strong man was on that long journey out of Glasgow whereas they were rooted.

Lippy said, "Biggest party this town's seen since Sir Richard married Christine away."

Then David knew what he had never quite known before. Why the old man was trying so hard tonight, laughing and talking; quite out of his usual fashion. Why the years had brought up such weary shadows in his eyes. Proud strong man, he had always seemed remote from Mouse Bluffs, ministering to its sorrows and its joys but never sharing in them. Always journeying out of Glasgow. Glasgow. It was characteristic of the man that no one knew more of his past than this word. Parents. Past. He never spoke of them unless to Mary in their long low-voiced conversations. Even Ian said nothing, or almost nothing. And one did not ask such things of a Ross. Something in Gavin, borrowed or absorbed by Ian, forbade it. Even I, David thought, have never asked.

He understood now something of the pain of the old man's journey. He had not desired that it should be a circling back, out of Glasgow and back to Glasgow. He had sought to root himself in Sir Richard's vision and Sir Richard's line, but Sir Richard's house and Sir Richard's river had defeated him. His throat ached for the old man, trying to plunge back across time into that marriage that the river had destroyed. He needs me, David thought. More than I need him. Much more. Why can't he see it, say it?

On the steps of the hotel, with the music twining about him, David waited. Surely tonight, with the news about Lilja lying like lead in him, he could make the old man pause, abandon the fruitless past and claim the future, keep the trust that had howled to hot life on that cold January night of long ago.

Above the town stood a great harvest moon, all copper and fine. So large one knew even in the darkness that the sky was gauzed with golden harvest dust rising from the thousands of bushels of wheat being gathered in; the noise of the celebration was only a faint spangle against the prairie night of good harvest.

Jaques returned and David refused the offer of a drink, went to walk through the quiet side streets.

Nothing so silent, not moon or cold space or mountain top so silent as the streets of Mouse Bluffs at night, nothing so small as the sound of feet on the cinder paths. Whatever man had built was lost against a horizon so vast no house or pathetic valley could hold the eyes. Eyes and heart, like the two live lines of steel that braced all together, must follow the sweep west, forever traveling over immensity, proportionately nothing.

Roots? Who could be rooted in such vastness? Mouse Bluffs is a journey.

"My God, boy, you nearly knocked me down!" Nat Farland caught his arm. "I've been looking for you. Ian Ross is dying and wants you."

David stared at the big dark man, the brown jacket black in the dark, the buttons winking.

"I'm wearing his kilt," he said.

"I see you are. Come, here's my car. We must hurry."

CHAPTER 22

Outside the hospital Herb Henderson burst from the night and caught Farland's arm. "They told me Doc Ross is dying."

"No!" David cried.

"Ian," Farland said.

Herb seemed to sag against the white pillar. Farland shrugged and urged David towards the door.

In one of the three private rooms Ian whispered to his brother, "Burn my papers."

"Aye, now keep this nozzle on your nose or you're done for," Gavin said gruffly.

"I am. Take the bloody thing away. Tell—tell David that——"

He turned his head in surprise and could speak no more as his exhausted heart failed again, his lungs filled with the disasters of another war, another ruined boy's returning, and he thought, even as he died, how foolish it had been to have had one chance and go like this, a victim not a man. He wanted to tell Gavin about the one chance but he was very tired. Suddenly he was aware that there was a lot of blood and no air and he was making a great fuss.

Gavin cried, "Don't come in here!"

Bewildered, Ian clutched Gavin's arm and thought he said, "I loved you once," and died under the doctor's futile hands.

They buried him on Tuesday morning in a downpour, with all the town out in their old clothes against the rain, a stumpy flock of black umbrellas. The cortège left St. Andrew's and walked north with Ned Luke's old gray drawing the coffin on a small old-fashioned carriage, for no cars dared cross the prairie along the rut road after so much rain; the minister went bareheaded and the town followed, the umbrellas finally bobbing up the street with awkward haste, for the gray seemed rejuvenated by the rain and set an unseemly pace. David held an umbrella for Mary and Rose-lee while the rain ran down his neck, soaked into his shoes; Dr. Ross walked firmly behind the minister, Christine at his side; neither had wept nor would weep. Behind them the psychiatrist, Basil Waterman, walked through the rain negligently in an expensive lounge suit; he had driven down in the night and had either forgotten a coat or didn't care. A small balding man, his eyes gutted with grief behind horn-rimmed spectacles, he wept as he walked. They buried Ian to the left of the Rashleighs, as near as a Ross could come, nearer than any of Mouse Bluffs.

No bird dared sing into the full air for fear of drowning and, as the minister spoke over the coffin, his arm over his Bible held off the rain. His words were lost in the steady sloshing of water into the raw grave, the hammering of rain on the coffin. As they turned to leave on his last Amen, a colorless huddle under blobs of black, thunder rolled again in the west and they hurried away in twos and threes after quick handclasps with Gavin, Christine, and Mary.

"Bad day."

"Sorry."

"Sorry, Doc."

Back at the house Waterman started up the steps, stopped blankly, looking at the wheel-chair ramp. His face was bloodless and withered, like flesh soaked too long in water. He glanced once at Gavin, turned slowly and went down the drive to his car. He did not say good-bye. Gavin shook his head, looked as if he might call out, but did not.

Cassie brought tea to the drawing room and the doctor clasped Mary's hand a moment as they sat side by side on the sofa.

He said wearily, "I wish Darcy had come."

Mary blew her nose and her eyes filled again. "He simply couldn't, he was terribly upset."

Roselee looked at David without a vestige of expression and he knew that Darcy had not wanted to come. He didn't blame Darcy; it was grim and Darcy hadn't known his uncle too well or cared too much. David watched the doctor's face and his tongue felt swollen with its own inertia. Darcy, with a quick disrespectful quip, a crazy inappropriate story, would have been able to win up the smiles slowly on that face; the Christmas the Jones boy was killed Darcy had sat late in the kitchen and tossed Gavin wild and wonderful and almost true stories out of Knox, roused him at length to bellowing delight. Darcy should have come.

The night before, two telegrams had arrived. Gavin read: *Deepest sympathy to you and Aunt Christine, Darcy Ross Rushforth;* David's: *Holy Ghost gone, come I shall set you on a pinnacle of the temple.*

It was supposed, David knew, to be funny; he had torn it to very small pieces under the doctor's dull glance.

"I'm giving Darcy Ian's medals," Gavin had said.

"He'd like that," Mary answered tearfully.

"You should bury them with him," Christine said unexpectedly and the others looked at her curiously and ignored it.

"Darcy wanted to go himself," Mary almost whispered to Gavin in the small private world they seemed to inhabit right in the midst of others. "He made a great show of not caring when they wouldn't take him, the government considered his work essential, but I know how he felt."

Gavin nodded. "It's the only way to take it. I was always too young or too old or not in the right place when great things happened.'

David resisted the "Damn Darcy to lying hell," that rose so strongly in his mouth he was afraid he had said it, caught the cold amusement in Christine's eyes, got up and went outside.

After a while Billy came to the summerhouse, looked in and said, "He was a heller but all right for that."

"Yes."

"Figure I might have been worse with all he had." He sat in silence with David, smoking a slow cigarette, while they thought of the heller and how vacant the house seemed. "Looks like rain for the funeral. Doc, he don't say much but it hits him in the heart, like. Scotchmen, they don't like to show it much when they hurt. I sure hope it don't rain."

David smiled slightly. None of them liked to show it when they hurt; he watched the muscles working along Billy's jaw.

Looks like rain. No rain for years, now she's raining every time there's a funeral. Looks like rain. Rain. Through the town like a litany. It still rained. The lights flickered and went out and the whistle on the powerhouse let out a long whine of lament to inform the town of what the town knew, that the storm had cut a line or flooded a generator in the decrepit building. Cassie brought candles and Mary began to cry again so Gavin helped her to her room and stayed with her, talking the old hours up, easing the journey he was making out of the warp of their child times together.

"They're talking about the Old Country," Roselee told David.

"Are they?"

He wondered desperately how he might approach the doctor and get the gnawing problem off his mind. From the moment Gavin had cried out at the hospital for him to stay out he had been out. There seemed no way to speak past the massive fact of Ian dead. He sat in the little parlor and saw the untidy heaps of books hanging half in, half out of the bookcases. There was the carpet, the flowers and scrolls in deep reds and blues and flashes of yellow, the worn leather chairs and no Ian. The carpet, the brasses, the windows, the lace curtains, all the objects that had surrounded Ian and never been noticed. Now the objects. And no Ian. No man to hear the heart speak a volume behind the sparse spatter of words. No Ian. Two Rashleighs in foolish hand-on-sword poses looked blandly out of the eighteenth century but no Ian.

Far away he heard the telephone, hoped it was a call for Gavin, that someone needed him.

"Are you very sad?" Roselee pestered.

"Very."

"Did you love him?"

"Yes."

"How do you know?"

"Look, you're fifteen now and you shouldn't been so damned rude."

"Almost seventeen. I didn't love him."

"How could you?"

She flung herself into the chair opposite him. "That's right, how could I? Are you a good lover?"

"What?"

"Well, you love people. Uncle Gavin, Ian, even the dog. And that blonde—I know. You're good at loving, I'm not."

"You fascinate me."

"But I meant the other too, lover. Are you good? It saves embarrassment. I don't mind about the blonde. Lover, I'm in love."

He looked her over. The strange heavy-lidded eyes, so like Darcy's fastened on his with sultry excitement and color pulsed into her cheeks. She wasn't as brave as she sounded. But she had grown up. He hadn't been noticing. Tall, small in the waist, full-breasted, her hips narrow, still a girl's hips. Another couple of years and she would be a nice meaty piece of woman. She pushed her legs over the arm of the chair provocatively, scanned her own ankles approvingly.

He grinned. "Are you now? Are you enjoying it?"

"Not yet."

"Pull down your skirt."

"Why?"

"Because you're liable to get knocked on your back if you go around doing that."

"What?"

"That."

"By you?"

He bent forwards and gave her skirt a tug. "By me. Behave yourself."

Gavin came into the room.

Roselee murmured audibly, "Damn."

David asked, "May I drive you?"

"I wish you would."

Roselee put her feet on the floor. "Can I come?"

"No," David said firmly.

It was a confinement case and he had a long wait. He found himself wishing he had brought her. When Gavin finally returned to the car, he looked weary and sated. Activity had washed the bitter controlled look from his craggy face.

David said, "The rain's letting up."

"He had an an almighty dread of having to go to a city hospital and getting some bright young man who would prolong his misery; that's why he would never go to Mary's." The doctor's voice was measured, heavy, as if he were reading the words. "It's something we used to understand, the right to die."

"I never thought of it quite like that."

"The hospitals are chock-a-block with smart lads who think only in terms of cases. A thousand dollars of this and a thousand of that and a last ditch operation for two more weeks of 'life.' If they had to live cheek by jowl with the families they'd learn of the want and misery they create to build up their wonderful books of cases. I hate more than anything else having to send a man or a woman to the city. Common sense seems to be dying out there, even common decency, the right to die."

The old man sighed over the impossibility of conveying this to anyone. Against his advice Alice James had gone up to the city last spring with a suspicious sore on her tongue; some horrors you checked and watched, some horrors you were cautious about giving to the scalpel, but she had panicked and put herself in the hands of one of the new brand of surgeons who, biopsy in hand, had suggested removal of her tongue. What he had not told her beyond what her own sense told her, that she would never talk again, was that she might also never eat again except through a tube. Save the organisms. Radical surgery; a good report it would make; then what? Lymph gland involvement probably in six months' time. Perhaps the antibiotics were a factor in making them so free with their knives. Thirty years ago a man thought more than once before operating and, when he did operate, it was pretty soon clear whether he was competent. Back in Mouse Bluffs, face to face with all possibilities, Alice James had elected to keep her tongue. Perhaps to die early is better than to live as a case triumphant.

"Some of these brats with degrees think existing is everything," Gavin said. "I gave my brother liquor as I give people in pain morphine. Only a fathead talks of addiction in such cases."

After a moment David said carefully, "I see that. But it's pretty dependent upon a man's judgment, isn't it? As a principle . . ."

"I don't develop any of my points of view in that way— leave that to preachers. I do what I know is right and the devil take the soft ones who must form up a school before they can stand the weight of an idea."

As they drove up to the house, David said, "I must talk to you."

It had to be announced, specific.

"Later, David. I'm tired, as you can see."

"When?"

"After supper."

He waited again and after supper they sat by themselves on the veranda, as the sky cleared and late sun washed the tops of the elms.

"The days are getting shorter."

"I've got to get back to Winnipeg."

Gavin nodded.

"I want to quit engineering and go back to Knox."

Gavin drew a quick breath, abruptly angry. "For the love of God, why?"

David said, "Because it's what I want," and thought frantically, it will go badly. They were both scraped to nerve-ends.

"It's nothing. It gives you nothing to work with," the doctor snapped, alive now, as if all of him had been waiting for a signal to slough off his sorrow. "My brother had the humanities and it did nothing but enable him to spout Lucretius when he was drunk. No tools. If he'd had medicine or engineering he might have done a man's job even in a wheel-chair. He was wasted through his gentleman's education. Being a gentleman is no profession in this country and that's the end of it. You stick to engineering, David."

"I can't."

He knew he was without an argument that could reach this man. Long ago he had declared he wouldn't study medicine. He'd made it stick; the doggedness had been reasonable then. Too, he'd had an ally; he had none now. Worse, it was the very characteristics he loved and admired most in the old man—strength untainted by self-doubt, self-questioning—that made him unreachable.

"Now see here," the doctor said, "I've had enough of this. If I've learned one thing over Ian it is this. You're in no position to educate yourself for education's sake. You need tools. Much more than Ian ever did."

"I can only get what I want at Knox."

"I won't stand for it. I've lived a long time and I know what's best. David, you've got no family and you have a couple of precious years to help yourself get some background. Don't drift. Don't change horses in mid-stream."

"I'm not."

"I can't sanction it. Damn it, I won't. I pay the bills and you'll do the right thing or nothing."

David flinched, said at length, "That's it then."

"That's it. You'll be glad of it one day." His voice was already disinterested, convinced of the victory that was always his.

David felt his eyes cloud. He said bitterly without thinking, "Do you remember my mother?"

"I do. What's that got to do with this?"

"Only that I know."

"You know what? Good God, David, what is this?"

David searched the old man's face wildly, trying to say it: I know. I've always known it. You were there that summer, the right summer. Don't think I haven't counted and counted and counted. You told me yourself you were there. It happened. Don't ask me how or under what circumstances but it happened. My mother told me so herself, came as close as a woman of her loyalties could ever come.

But he couldn't say the words and, looking at the old angry resistant face, a terrible doubt lanced his brain. The conviction had been part of him for so long. How had it come? What had his mother said? His mind, searching for that fall day, could find only the sound of rustling leaves, a mild sad gentleness overhead. No words. Suppose I imagined it all? With the sting of Arthur Newman's dog-whip on my hands, I wanted a father. Suppose I just reached out, chose arbitrarily . . .

His mind reeled away. His throat closed. Give me the letter, he almost shouted. That letter my mother left for me. Then realized that to Gavin Ross twenty wasn't a man.

He said harshly, "I know Arthur Newman wasn't my father."

Gavin rubbed his whiskered jaw. David pounced after the gesture. He's relieved. Of course. He doesn't want to claim me yet. Acceptance must be won.

"How do you know that?"

"I remember the day she met him. I was just a kid, maybe three or four, and he asked her to marry him right in front of me."

"This has nothing to do with me. I should prefer not to hear of it. David, it's been a bad couple of days."

And there's a line you still won't cross. I know. Okay. You win. David set his teeth.

234

"All right. And I don't mind about the other."

"I knew you'd see it."

"I mean I don't mind giving up college."

"Now, just a minute!"

"No, you've got your ideas. And you're tired. Don't worry about it." I must never get angry, don't let me get angry when he's done so much, I owe him so much and from his position he's so right.

"We'll talk about it again. You're upset about Ian but you'll see that I'm right."

"No. You're almost always right, Dr. Ross, I've got to quit kidding myself. I've got to do it my way."

Gavin gave him a long steady look of surprise. "Go ahead, lad, do it your way and more power to you. I like guts. But remember I'm not footing the bill. Not when I know I'm right." Two spots of color rode high on his cheeks.

David smiled into his own rage: we've never been so alike as we are right now.

He said softly, "To hell with you then."

As he left, he heard Ross roar with laughter and felt his stomach, clenched up with fury, suddenly burn with joy. His mouth twitched; in some way he'd gotten closer than he'd ever been. Perhaps it had been telling Gavin he knew. He didn't know how, after all the desperate trying, he had accomplished the moment. Nevertheless, he realized that he had chosen a hard path. Harder than ever now. It scarcely seemed important. With the harsh delighted laughter at his back he knew he could manage. In resistance was the strength of challenge, the old man's love of challenge and respect for those who could meet it. Roselee was standing on the stairs, listening too, her mouth half-open with curiosity and surprise.

"And with you, too," David said.

She raised one brow suggestively and he slapped her bottom as he went past.

CHAPTER 23

Darcy was creating. He sat in his shirt sleeves at the typewriter, the desk a welter of yellow copy-paper. Early in the summer he had found the new apartment, the top floor of an old mansion that had been converted into three flats. The living room ran along the entire south side; it was pre-eminently a room with a view, elm trees bowing in sleepy jungle towards the gray-green waters of the Assiniboine. All summer he had worked a night shift at the studio so he could sit at this window of river and trees and create. He created with great fervor innumerable radio plays, which he submitted with persistent hope to the C.B.C. and which the C.B.C. as persistently rejected. Sometimes in a mood of what he called utter white heat, he tore off a poem or two but these he considered private affairs, unlikely to bring return or recognition; he read them to David when David would listen.

During the summer, while he worked at the hamburger joint, David had slept in the small corner room. Now that Gavin's financial support had been withdrawn, it looked as if the arrangement would become permanent. This was precisely what Darcy had hoped for when he moved into the new place. Alone, he had not created. The other apartment with its smaller rooms had always seemed stale after a shift. He would find himself going out in search of people or filling the place with them—people he didn't particularly like but who, at least, provided an audience and, at most, material for copy. But now there was David to listen to him and be shouted at, girl with, get drunk with. He was at last, he declared, free to create. And create he did. The number of yellow pages grew.

"A million words, that's the climax," he told David. "From then on its easy."

David said once to Phillips in anger, "There are two kinds of men who want to write. The kind who always have because it's in them, they couldn't conceive a future in other terms. Me. Okay, smirk. And Darcy. Who wants to write because he likes to read or because he has some compulsive desire in a thing-directed society to produce something above the level of things. If he'd see himself in this category it might work out, but he won't. He wants divine inspiration so he writes stories full of incomplete sentences ending with three stops and enumerating the heroine's pubic hairs —sensitivity and realism, by God. He suffers. He suffers like hell, just like the books say. But it's no good."

He suffered with Darcy because he was oddly humiliated for Darcy. He always felt, when he came into the room and found Darcy at the typewriter, as if he'd happened upon a midget trying to make love to a six-foot woman. So he endured the fits of temper as Darcy wrestled with his muse, endured the endless boredom of listening to Darcy flay an idea till all freshness was stripped from it and it lay in tatters on the floor like Darcy's most recent rejection slip. And saw Darcy's growing frustration, his rage against his own incapacities, turning like a searchlight to focus upon their relationship.

Their relationship had changed, was changing. The old wry condescension rarely rose now to cover contempt. Darcy resented silence, he resented comment, but most of all he resented David's daring to believe he could accomplish anything in what Darcy considered his field. Darcy who always succeeded, who was born succeeding. The weight of Darcy's resentment grew between them like substance, a great circular table they ate at, talked over and around, fought over, but could not leap or escape. Sometimes David looked over the edge of the table, saw Darcy, and felt the sweat break out on his brow, his tongue curdle with abuse for Darcy's ego, Darcy's sneer, and sometimes too he would see Darcy's brow wet with the same hate, Darcy swallowing the same bitter phlegm, the things that could not be said lest civilization between them end forever, old fires revive to new holocaust.

"Why don't you let me help you?" Constantly from Darcy. "That bloody Phillips doesn't believe anyone wrote a line after 1895. Show me your stuff and we'll go over it." The threat barely concealed, I'll put an end to this nonsense once for all. You don't belong. I do. Let me tell you so.

David's refusal would send Darcy prowling through the shadows on the other side of the table, shadows from which he would rush only to lunge, thrust, and retire with the hope of eventual triumph undimmed.

When Gavin Ross came to town on one of his rare visits, Darcy would give him the full steady pressure of learned winsomeness, would return from dinner at his father's house, dinners to which David was not invited, full of the old civilities, and David, tensed against their sudden evaporation, would wonder if the intense life they shared were not similar to the marital relationship. Together they were different from the men they were with others; had different manners, eyes.

"It fascinates me."

Warily, "What?"

"Uncle Gavin. The paternal image—country doctor. The whole town running up to the well with their sloppy buckets and always coming away empty, yet always going back, always hoping."

"All they go for is water."

"You kill me! What do you go for—the elixir of life? You go for the same damned thing they do—on a grand scale. Just a man. Sane and solid right down to his ankle bones. But the myth persists. People believe what they want to. When he drops dead they'll all go around saying he never sent a bill. *Dominus vobiscum.*" He mused, "I'll bet the old boy never even made a pass at any of the bottoms he's looked up."

"No, I don't suppose he has."

"I don't suppose he's even wanted to."

"No." David thought again. "Maybe you're right."

"Of course I'm right." Darcy laughed uproariously. "It isn't just that he thinks he's better than anyone else, he *is* better. If you define good in Presbyterian terms. Oh, the hell with it, he disgusts me."

"Sure."

Darcy's eyes slitted. "I suppose you know he's going to die and leave me that mausoleum. It's all he's got and I want it. I shall have the satisfaction of selling it to a madam."

The mild torture never really let up. But there were two kinds of torture, David knew—the sort he gave Darcy which, though less explicit, was unremitting and abrasive and made Darcy's eyes saturnine with unspoken hate and the sort Darcy gave him which seemed to be entirely guyed within the concrete world, the shared blazing past, the unloved present. And all the time Darcy carried his desire to create like a torch that ignited everything within reach, reduced all to burned stubs. At times when David saw him pawing through Bartlett or Roget or pacing the floor in a fury of concentration, he would feel humiliation so keen he was certain Darcy must see it. He tried to pretend that Darcy's torch Darcy's agonies, did not for him exist; it was all he could do and it inflamed Darcy.

"Hi," casually, as he came into the living room and saw Darcy at the typewriter. "Creating again? Still?"

"How did it go?"

"It didn't."

"What?"

"I mean I got the job and two hours later lost it." David threw himself on the chesterfield.

Darcy strode over, looked down angrily. "What did you do?"

"I went in and said, 'Mr. Salt?' which was pretty silly because there it was on his desk, James Salt, City Editor. 'Mr. Charles Rushforth suggested that if I came to see you, you could tell me if there are any openings on your staff.' So Mr. Salt—thin and fat at the same time, you know, thin frame and rosy bloated cheeks, all veins, beer probably—looked as if he wished he weren't a lodge brother of your father's or as if he wished I'd go away but I didn't so he said, 'Here,' and wrote a note on a piece of paper, 'go out to this place and get a story of the meeting.' 'All right,' I said, all capable and calm. 'Get a street-car pass at the front office, here's a chit,' he said, so I went out and got a story and some character in the sports department let me use his typewriter and I wrote it up and Salt said I'd better try something else. I agreed with him. All done. Career as a newspaperman."

"What did you write?"

"I got out to this hall in the north end and found it was an Orangewomen's meeting; there were two other reporters there, kids, and we wait and wait around and some old guy rushes out and says Mrs. Somebody has been elected keeper of the robes or some such crap. I asked the other guys what the hell and they tell me the Orange ladies don't allow reporters into their meetings. So I went around to the back and climbed on a garbage can, just a real keen kid. Here's the story." He pulled a sheet of copy from his shirt pocket.

Darcy read, " 'Destruction of the Roman Catholic Church was aimed at in a series of resolutions passed in secret by the L.O.B.A. today at 2 p.m. at Union Center. Attempts were made to bar the press——' You're nuts!"

"That's what Salt thought. I believe there was real anguish in his scream, 'The Ladies' Orange Benevolent Association! For the love of God!' "

"In other words you didn't want the job."

"No."

Darcy threw the paper to the floor. "Damn you, after I went to dear old Dad on my bleeding knees."

"I thought I might. You know, you read stories. But as soon

as I got there I knew I couldn't. All those characters screaming around and looking important, hammering away at typewriters with an air of Here is Where We Do It. For a nickel on any street corner you can get what they do and it's crap."

"I know it's crap. They know it's crap."

"No, they don't. They think it's a Calling. You can see they're thunderstruck by it, the power of the press."

"It's a living."

"It's that."

"And if you were any good, I mean—foreign correspondent?"

David laughed. "You should do it. For God's sake, you believe it. Running around Bucharest in a trench coat with your hat pulled down? No matter how you slice it it's still crap and it's still expensive at five cents."

"So all right. Look, I've thought it over, I've got some bonds. You could pay me back later. You can live here and go back to Knox as a day man. You don't eat much."

"No."

"Plenty of businessmen invest in medical students and stuff, it's done all the time. I don't need the dough. Take ten years."

David lit a cigarette, trying to hide his twinge of unease.

"I'll get work and I'll pay my way here. Only not that kind of work."

"Something nice and honest, I suppose. Like a pick and shovel detail?"

"Maybe."

"You could go into Dad's place."

"No thanks."

"He pays well."

"Would you?"

Darcy caught it; his tension eased away; he grinned. "No. Are you coming to Greenway's with me tonight?"

"What is it?"

"The usual, I suppose. Gin in many different disguises, Harvey getting obstreperous. Mother called, by the way. You must come to dinner with me Friday. Such a dear boy. Such a help in her sorrow. And there's a letter for you."

David sat up, "From where?"

"City."

"Oh."

Why do I keep hoping? he asked himself as he took the letter.

Darcy watched as he put it in his shirt pocket, then went to the desk. Good manners belonged to a former world. Any privacy, however trivial, provoked Darcy now. He questioned David intently about everything, how he felt about a party, a woman, what he was thinking, and before handing him his mail, always fingered it deliberately. David waited until Darcy had begun to type, then opened the letter. There was another sealed envelope, wrapped in a sheet of stationery inside. Across the sheet was written: *If you should ever wish to see me, call. I'd like to talk to you about a very good friend. Basil Waterman.* David fingered the closed envelope, knew who had written. It looked slightly yellow, not old. He opened it slowly, carefully cutting the edge with his penknife.

January, 1941, New Year's Day and a resolution, the only one to be carried out. I shall give this letter to Basil and when I die he will contact you. Out across the valley the snow is thick and whiter than your hopes. A veritable superfluity of snow, a vulgarity of nature; she always goes to vulgar extremes on the prairies. It is twenty-eight below zero outside. I see the summerhouse, just the eaves showing. Unbelievable that I sit there on evenings so hot the leaves on the trees hang limper than my hands and no bird sings for fear the desert will rush down his throat and dry his little insides to dust, like mine. I feel quite godlike. A dead man's words are so powerful. I should plague you with all manner of portent and injunction: be wise, be good. But I can't foresee what it will be like. I wish I could. I hope you are a man now and better able to do without the people a boy must lean on. I hope I've seen it that far. All I wanted to say was that if you ever feel compelled to share the darkness go to Basil. I've told him nothing. I never do. But he is a good man for all my wicked treatment of him and although he may not understand it on your level he has a warm touch when the spirit is cold. Never speak to Darcy. Or anyone but Basil. But especially not Darcy for that will serve to increase the deed. There's no relief in Darcy, speak to him and your heart will begin to erode with evil where there is no evil even now. Believe this. What else must I say? Be kind to Christine? Never let Gavin know; I never did? Don't kick dogs or children? Yes, and if you ever get to France have a look at the spot where they killed me and ask why I never got a decent burial. With love, Ian Duncan Ross.

David folded it carefully, his heart scalded with the pressure of this remarkable care, seared with the reminder of the man gone, the reminder of the strictures on him now, alone in it again. He tore the psychiatrist's note to shreds on the ashtray, carried it to the bathroom and flushed the shreds down the toilet. The other he would have to secrete or carry a while. While he had it, he was not entirely alone. Only when he had read it to memory would the force of it be gone; he might have to see Waterman then. He hoped not. He pressed his forehead a moment against the cool mirror of the medicine-chest. He hoped not. He touched the letter once more.

Darcy was still at his desk, his back rigid. David waited.

"What was that?" lightly.

And lightly back, "A love letter."

"And she all set to wed."

"No." And lies forever. "Dean Summers. No bursary. Only if I declare my intention of going into theology."

Darcy turned it over suspiciously, accepted it. "Don't you see he's giving it to you on a platter? He can't tell lies but you can, that's what he's trying to tell you. Why didn't you let me read it?"

Because it came two days ago while you were out.

"I cannot tell a lie," he mocked. "I will not mislead the church, the holy United bursary-poor church. Contemplate. Some worthy might lose his chance if I took it, some fellow all China is waiting for."

"I'm beginning to think you don't want to go back."

"The mission fields crying for. The pulpits empty for."

"You don't!"

"You're right. I'm through with it. I don't want my brain all chopped and screwed into Schools of Thought. What have I to do with seventeenth-century thought or seventeenth-century thought with me?"

"Pick and shovel."

"We get our deserts. Here you are *cum laude*, radio *and* creating. Always creating. Darcy, the world is yours. You flourish. You create while I am steadily diminishing, dwindling to—soon I shall be three inches high, soon an inch, then nothing. I never happened. A misbegotten bastard from a womb that had better remained empty. I'm living backwards in time. Watch me disappear."

"Where's the rye?"

"You're so right. Bring on the equalizer. Why are you always right, Darcy? Incredible that you should create and be right. Unfair distribution. Take it up with Heaven."

Darcy went to the kitchen. He called back, "Not only that but I'm rich and handsome."

"God did not skimp on His Darcy."

"And well loved by all who know me."

"Exactly. A triumph of body and mind."

Darcy brought back a drink. They glared at one another.

Darcy said, "Drink, scum."

"Why?" David demanded. "Why me?"

"Because in all this perfection I need a reminder of how poorly endowed others can be. It keeps my feet on the ground."

"There's that. Maybe that's my function. Hear that? I have no control over it."

He gulped the drink. Darcy poured another straight from the bottle.

"This must be quick," Darcy said. "Shall we get drunk very rapidly and go to Greenway's and show Harvey what really obstreperous types are?"

"How come you're wenchless tonight?"

"Deirdre'll be there. I'll back her into the linen closet for a couple of minutes."

"Why don't you leave her alone now she's married?"

"Because she's in love with me, she's constantly telling me so. Mind your own business." Darcy reached into his pocket. "Shall I wear my jewels?"

"What is it?"

"Uncle Ian's V.C." He pinned it on his shirt.

"You son of a bitch."

"Uncle Gavin wouldn't like that."

David leaned forward, glass poised. "Take it off."

Darcy smiled slowly, took the medal and handed it to David.

"Here. Mind, you mustn't wear it out. Special delivery this morning, a positively eye-shaking stack and a touching letter from Uncle Gavin about the Ross family and my responsibilities. Uncle Gavin has poor eyesight, he can't see my father, my father's name, my father's house."

David fingered the bronze cross on its crimson ribbon. He had never known of this. How typical of the man that he should not mention it.

"He just sees my father's wife," Darcy went on. "Now our Freudians would . . ."

"I don't want to listen to that bilge again."

"I like you best in your ugly moods. What's wrong man, jealous?"

"Sure. I told you. All this and you create. How could I not be jealous of the refined, well-loved scion of a fine old family?"

"You lack conviction," Darcy said.

"Do I?" David reached for the bottle. "Here, put your medal away."

Darcy shook his head. "You keep it."

"I don't want it."

"No—I meant to give it to you. I didn't even know the poor bloody crock."

"Dr. Ross meant you to have it!" he exploded. "What the hell are you always trying to buy me for? I'm here aren't I? Let it do!"

"Stop shouting!" Darcy shouted.

"I don't want the stupid thing. Take it. Wear it to parties. Who cares?"

Darcy snatched the medal from him, strode to the window.

"I'll throw the goddamned thing in the river."

David said softly, "You do and I'll throw you in the river. Throw it. Go ahead."

Darcy hesitated, opened the drawer of his desk, flung the medal in.

David's breath whistled through his teeth.

"Everything you damned well do is unforgettable," he said. "Some day I'll kill you."

Darcy laughed. "Try it." He shoved the desk-drawer to. "Come let's get over to that party. Let's get out of here."

CHAPTER 24

"Of course I'm going to marry him," Lilja said, "but not until next summer. I want my degree."

David studied the other man. Alvin Marshall was tall and fair, hair cut close to his head, military brush, military shoulders, the thickness through chest and shoulders of a man in his thirties, the promise of more heft in the square frame. He held a glass, listened attentively to a young intense matron in a flowered gown.

"He looks old," David said.

"Old enough."

"And rich."

"Rich enough."

"How?"

"Clipping coupons."

"Perfect."

"You're so right."

He raised his palm, brushed it against the side of her slender throat. Her pupils dilated. He moved his lips in a silent kiss.

"I love you."

"I know," she said. "I love you too. Take your hand away, people will talk."

"Too late?"

"Much."

She took a cigarette from her little silver evening bag, offered him one. The scarlet-tipped fingers trembled as he brushed them. Distantly, beyond the welter of bodies, someone was singing about a slow boat to China with doleful lack of tune; in a far corner Darcy was openly wooing Deirdre while her husband, only feet away, looked murderous.

David reached forth to touch Lilja's hair, rubbed one white curl between his fingers. A long sigh escaped her.

He murmured, "It doesn't take much with you does it?"

"Not with you."

"Him?"

"Stick to the book."

"Rules yet?" He bent towards her till he saw her mouth begin to tremble and felt his own vitals burn, then said in a low bitter voice, "Is he any good?"

"Next June."

"Invite me. I wouldn't miss it. You'll be so beautiful. How did you grow so beautiful? Maybe you should marry Darcy, you look like Hollywood together and just think of what it would do to me."

"Darcy?"

"He talks."

"You told me once he didn't."

"This was a special case, as you well know."

A slight flush rose in her cheeks. "Did it hurt?"

"Quite a bit. But that was why, wasn't it? For both of you."

"Yes." She placed her hands against her rib-cage and pressed gently as if in pain, bent towards him. "You won't give, will you? Anything. Well hurt, hurt like hell. That's all I ask."

"Is it?" He brushed her arms.

"You two are quite shameless," Darcy said at David's side.

"Go away."

"I've come to save you from yourself. Don't thwart me."

"Save yourself," David said.

"It's too late. Lilja, I admire your taste in fiancés. Solid. Absolutely solid—bone probably. He's just the kind of thing Mother would love."

Lilja lowered her lids. "It means so much, from you."

Harvey Greenway passed, came back with his tray of drinks. They each took one.

"You might at least say it's a good party," Harvey implored. They ignored him. "Rude buggers. Why is everyone rude to me? I invite people who can be perfectly charming at other people's parties and they come to my house, drink my liquor, act rude, make passes at my wife. To hell with all of you."

He left. A self-styled quartette moaned nostalgically about Old Black Joe beside a drink-laden gramophone.

"That's the kiss of death." Darcy looked at his watch. "Let's go. Let's get in the car and drive up to West Hawk. There's a jolly idea. We three discovering the laws of the isosceles. Seriously, the folks have closed up but there's plenty of tinned food and we can swim or fish tomorrow and drive back tomorrow night."

David looked at Lilja. She turned slowly to glance at Alvin Marshall. He was placating Harvey with a charming smile and taking another glass from the tray, while the beflowered woman at his side rubbed her thigh against his.

"God, what white teeth he's got," David said.

"All right." Lilja nodded to Darcy. She looked a question at David. He shrugged, nodded. "I'll get my coat," she said.

"We'll be outside in the car." Darcy searched his pockets for his keys, avoided David's eyes. He had a look of barely controlled exultation.

As they let themselves out of the unquiet house, David said, "How would you like a good sock on the jaw?"

"Come now, be a good boy. We'll laugh a lot and have some fun. Just forget you're the son of God and we'll get away from this boring bloody town."

"You're drunk."

"Not as drunk as you are."

"She'll be sorry tomorrow."

"Not her." Darcy smiled. "She makes it a point never to be sorry, that's why she's marrying old gotrocks."

David leaned against the car. It was true; she wouldn't be sorry. Stripped of the right to indignation—Darcy was so right, so cruelly right about so many things—he felt what? Along with distaste a growing alarm. I could have asked her myself and she'd have come. She as much as told me so. But I let him do it. Do I let him do too much? Serve my own purposes? He's up to something. This is not a whim; he planned it. The night was all ink and gold, tissue-brittle with fall. The star-stippled sky moved with grave majesty. Another drink and it would start to revolve.

Darcy yanked open the car-door. "If you don't like the idea, stay home."

"She wouldn't go."

246

"She would."

Lilja ran along the driveway.

Darcy whispered, "Ask her."

"No."

Darcy laughed, a great shout of joy. "That's just as good."

David held the door for her without a word. She sat between them as they crossed the city to Darcy's apartment, wheels moving irrevocably over all the asphalt points on the line of no return. They waited in the car while Darcy went upstairs for bread and whiskey.

"Shouldn't you call your mother?"

"I did."

"What did you tell her?"

"That I was spending the night with you and Darcy."

"You hate her."

"Why do you say that?"

"I can hear it in your voice. Why? Because she had the courage to take the man she wanted?"

"Because she hadn't the courage to resist him."

"It all depends on your point of view."

"Exactly."

He took her by the shoulders and kissed her on the mouth with gentle deliberation, let his mouth trail over her cheek.

"Love me?"

"I have to," he said hoarsely, "or it's no good is it? Anything. For you."

"He took the keys."

"I noticed. I thought of it too."

She laughed against the side of his throat.

"Was it her? Your mother? Who watched us that night?"

"No. I think it was Jon."

"God," he murmured. "I'm just a boy from Mouse Bluffs."

"You don't belong in that place."

"I do. *Here* I belong in Mouse Bluffs. There I'm a stranger who walks around with a lamp in his outstretched hand hoping he'll run into a mirror."

"Don't go back. I won't. Now."

Darcy got into the car. "Break it up. I brought some eggs, too. Can you make bacon and eggs, my love?"

"Perhaps, my love."

"Why do you seem so old?" David asked her. "I'm a whole year older than you are, I have no job, no education, no family and people keep calling me a boy. You're a woman. Some day I'll be over thirty too and have the start of a double chin."

"A boy from Mouse Bluffs."

"That too. Is it such a drawback?"

"I can feel it in you. Order. The town's teaching."

Darcy laughed, eased his foot on the accelerator. "You're right. Damn! That cop isn't after us, is he?"

"Your conscience, he's turning. I didn't know you had one, Darcy. Keep your arm there, David, just there and your hand—that's right. In Mouse Bluffs they don't need traffic cops, each man is his own constable."

"Hear, David? The policeman in your soul. Uncle Gavin and Anglican Calvinism."

"What I'll do," David said, "is find a very rich, very dull woman and marry her; it's as good as a knife."

"I have just the one for you," Darcy said. "I've had her in mind for you for a long time. Come I shall set you on a pinnacle of the temple. When the time comes. And watch it boy. Son of God or not you'll . . ."

David said sharply, "Cut that for God's sake."

"Why? Scared you will?"

"It's just I'm sick to everlasting death of that particularly unfunny . . ."

"Okay. You're not the son of God. I never said you were. But this particular little temptation I have in mind for you, you'll yield to it, boy; you'll yield to it."

"Well don't talk about it," David said. "Just let me think it's all unplanned—like tonight."

They fell silent, the long black road east feeding their silence. Lilja fell asleep against David's shoulder while Darcy drove through the long sobering hours. It was after five when they arrived at the cabin. The sun had not appeared; the morning was cold; the snap of winter cricked through the cool wind.

"Cabin?" David touched Lilja's eyelids with his lips. She stirred. "It looks like the house of Usher."

Darcy calmly broke a window. The place smelled stale and stuffy and did not welcome them. They looked around but not at one another and wished they had not come or that coming had taken less time, for time had rubbed away the glow of impetuous decision.

"Shall we have breakfast?" Darcy asked.

"Later," Lilja said shortly and went to one of the lower level bedrooms. "Fetch me some blankets, Darcy my love, I'm going to sleep some more and see, when I wake up, if last night's two lively lovers survived the trip."

Darcy brought her a blanket from the cedar closet and she went into the bedroom, closing the door firmly behind her.

"Hell," Darcy said.

David got a blanket, kicked off his shoes and threw himself on the lounge.

"That's it. Hell. Good night."

When he woke, he felt stiff and his mouth tasted limy. Late morning light filtered through the shutters, trickled through the close air. He got up slowly and looked for Darcy. No Darcy. All the doors along the upper level were shut. It felt as if he were alone in the place, the homespun curtains unmoving, the pale furniture steadied to death for winter. He went to the door of Lilja's room. His hand rested a long moment on the handle. And then? "Excuse me, gentlemen?" Something tactful to show that boys from Mouse Bluffs had the social graces. He opened the door cautiously and hated himself. She was curled up in the red blanket, her face as pale and smooth as white silk. He closed the door behind him and went to her, leaning forward till the warmth of her flesh reached him. She opened her eyes, the blue so dark she looked drugged.

"You smell good," he whispered.

"I felt you near me."

"I know." She raised the blanket and he lay beside her, took her in his arms. "Your dress is mussed."

"That's all right. Hold me tight."

"I wish it weren't like this."

"I know."

"I wish I could plan or had something to offer but I haven't."

"You have. But not for me. Don't rub it in. You told me a long time ago. That night I gave up resisting the inevitable. Maybe that's growing up—people say it is—but it sure felt like growing down."

He thought of his future, the extension of a present he had only barely begun, and he knew she was right, it had no properly marked lines; burdened as he was, he would play it as he must, as each day told him. Nevertheless, there was order in it and the courage at last to see past sidetracks.

"How wise we are." She giggled. "You scratch. I wonder if Darcy brought a razor with the whiskey and bread."

"You're the wise one. Women are. This thing about a home is built in with you. You go after it like tigers."

"Can you see me stumping around in brogues doing case work or sitting in an office with a bunch of seat-sprung kids yukking about dates and pimples? I don't want to be your trollop, hang

around and wait and wait and live with Mother, while all my
vital organs seize up and forget what they're there for."

"Babies?"

"Babies."

"That's plain enough."

"I just don't fool myself, David."

"Couldn't you fool me, a little? Come on, illusion me."

She laughed, pulled his face down to rub his cheek. "I'll have
no skin left."

"You never wanted to marry me, did you?" he said.

"Oh yes."

"No, I've been doing some learning about loving the last
couple of years. If you had you wouldn't have seduced me."

"Seduced you!"

He said, "If you had me in the ring position it would be someone else here now."

"You're mean!"

"Am I mean? Illusion me some more, come on. Oh, God, I
love you."

"I hear Darcy. He'll suspect the worst."

"He always does. I want to go to England. Not right away. Not
till after all this . . . I have to feel a certain way about my work
and myself, mostly myself I think, before I go. Identity maybe,
something—something has to—let's pretend we're asleep exhausted with our efforts and see if he'll make breakfast."

She stared dreamily at the ceiling. "He's found out."

"What?"

"That you've got it—what he's wanted. Maybe he's known all
along, ever since he first came to the Bluffs and latched onto you.
What he hasn't faced yet is that he hasn't got it, that's going to be
worse. Get away. Go to England now. He hates you."

He kissed her. "Are you at it again—managing?"

She sat up, tried to speak. He pulled her down beside him
again.

"Fight me off," he urged and she laughed with him.

Darcy shouted, "For God's sake come out of there and stop
that giggling. Coffee's ready. Lilja, come along and do your
chores."

"Tell him you are."

"Tell him we're busy," she suggested.

"I wish we were." David called, "Coming dear."

Darcy made a vulgar noise. "To you. Both of you. In
quantities."

The sun was well up and strong; the warmth of it strolled lazily through the veranda as they ate the crumbly tinned bacon and eggs.

Darcy said, "You're a pretty animal even without lipstick."

"A girl can't think of everything." She glanced slyly at David. "Sometimes she gets carried away."

Darcy poured milk from a can into his coffee. "Mater would shoot me down in flames if she knew we were using up this stuff. Emergency rations. The hospitality of the bush. Well, I suppose we constitute an emergency."

"Tell her. I'll tell my mother."

"Must you?" Darcy looked pained.

"I always do. Don't you? Tell, I mean."

"Almost always. After all where's the point?"

David intercepted their glares. "And your father?" he asked Lilja. "Is he on the revenge roster?"

"He just tolerates everything out of existence but he's a dear."

"Nice of you to say so."

The low windows were flooded with creamy white light. Across the lake a haze clung to the gray water, absorbing the sun; a film seemed to lie between the eye and the heavily wooded shore and hills. Only the evergreens had color and even that was bleached pale by the long hot summer gone.

"He thinks it's in the blood, you know. He's never said it but I think he feels I'm just a bit wild with the furrin strain."

"That's not fair."

"I know."

"To him. Lay off."

"Nevertheless it's true."

"Do you like anyone?"

"You."

Darcy asked, "Me?"

"Not you."

"All this proves that young ladies should not go to college. Girl, learn your place, honor thy father and mother, keep the kettle boiling, be on time—definitely be on time."

"I couldn't agree more."

"That's your trouble—insight. Down with women having insight, all they require is intuitions. That's good, I'll use it."

David stretched. "You better, no one else will. Who's going swimming?"

They swam naked from the dock and lay on the rough planking in the sunlight in their underthings while the sun rolled through the sky to the south. Lunch was tall drinks of rye, mixed with water dipped from the lake, and chunks of tinned Camembert.

"Do you remember the sky when the geese come home, gray as if with the breaking ice?" As he spoke, David shaded the sun from his eyes with his palm, watched the slow rise and fall of Lilja's breasts under the thin lace slip.

"It's not that way anywhere else," she said.

Darcy murmured, "I thought you at least had that place exorcised."

It came to David suddenly that he had never been so happy, that there was an irrational element in it; Darcy's presence in some way made his happiness. Was it just knowing where he was, what he was doing? A circuit fused, lodged deep in him to return again and again in the time to come.

"You stand and look at that sky," Lilja said, "'and you're only ten and you shouldn't be sad but you are and you'll never be ten again.'"

David gave her a long slow look. When had it ended, that trembling desire for what was gone? His palms ached. A boy on the stairs, he thought. A great service, if I had known it. I might never have realized how short-changed I was. I thought your body was singing the first silken song of love but it was only uttering the harsh bright spasm of escape.

Darcy got to his feet slowly; his lean body moved easily, the muscles hard and firm against healthy flesh.

"Man, I'm baked. I'm going to get the rifle and go up the hill, see if there's anything to pot at. Come?"

David said, "I don't. I nearly shot Arthur Newman once."

Darcy turned languidly. "Your father, you mean. Why do you have to make such a production of things? Why can't you just say you don't like it?"

He walked across the dry grass to the cabin, very slowly as if the sun-powdered air had texture.

"Have you ever seen a baby on the toilet?" Lilja asked. "Ivan sits there and looks all rapt, all by himself with a difficult pleasure on his little face as if he were listening to someone talking about wonderful things in a world all his own. That's how Darcy looks at you."

"You spoiled it."

"I meant to. You'll never have it—what you want—until you get away. I doubt whether you even think as far ahead as next week. I'm afraid—terribly afraid."

The sun shattered. From behind the cottage a blast, simultaneously the whine of the bullet over the water.

Lilja gasped. Something like a whimper crept through her lips. "That was close?"

Silence. Another shot. The top of one of the dock posts splintered away. David began to curse.

"Darcy!"

They waited. After a few minutes David felt his fear drip away; his blood slowed; his flesh seemed to melt against the dock like warm wax. Lilja tried to speak; her teeth chattered.

"He's crazy!"

"Just a bit."

"Let's go."

"No. Stay here." Don't move. Don't let him know you're afraid. "He's just horsing around."

"Some fun."

He waited again. Surely there would be no third shot.

"Stop hating Darcy, you've got no right to it," he said dully, working against the possibility of a third shot. "You've got no right to anything about me, even hating Darcy."

"None?"

"That's the way you wanted it."

"I'll consider myself told off." Her hand found his, curled inside his palm. "Love?"

"Always." He rolled over, his body tight against hers; it covered her head at least from the hill. He traced her eyebrows with a slow finger.

"They're white."

"I'm white all over."

"I know." He kissed her. "Why do you nag?"

"Just me. Plan. Get away from him. It comes naturally to me." She was breathing rapidly; he placed his hand against the thin silk on her waist. She said weakly, "Don't."

"Like that?"

"That. He's coming. By a pricking in my thumbs." She closed her eyes. "Do you remember the quack doctor? 'Girl, the hand of God is on you.' I always thought something wonderful would happen to me. Then when it did I wasn't the one. Maybe I planned too much."

"It may yet."

She laughed shakily. "As Cassie used to say . . ."

"Pigs might fly but they're not likely birds."

"Kiss me."

Darcy said, "Would you rather I watched?"

"Sneak," Lilja said.

"I see more that way."

David shaded his eyes. "And hear more."

"I'm quite a villain. Perfectly cast."

"We should go," Lilja said, stirred under David's hands, her skin roughened as if with cold. "Unless of course you want to do some more potting," she said and her shivering increased.

"You know I didn't really see you, just your hair shining. I thought it was something else, I wasn't even thinking about you. Funny." Darcy laughed. There was none of the recent high note of strain in his laughter and his face was cool, dark eyes quiet. "Let's finish the bottle."

As darkness began to fall they dressed. Then Darcy hammered a board over the broken window while David and Lilja looked out over the lake.

She said, "I know why it's so hazy over there. Fires."

"Yes. Fires."

"Now are you going to get away from him?"

"Not yet." He took her in his arms, looked into her eyes. "I may never be with you again," he said and sounded rather surprised.

She averted her glance. "I can't help it—the nagging."

"Don't cry. I can't do it. You see, he's a kind of—I couldn't tell you. He needs someone. He looks all right but . . . And it has to be me. You see, Dr. Ross counts on him."

Her eyes were incredulous. "God damn Gavin Ross."

His mouth went white. "You don't understand. You're strong, you've always had . . . You . . ."

"I understand all right. What do you think you are, a temple maiden? God damn him."

"Darcy's waiting for us. Kiss me good-bye."

"Not with him watching."

"All right."

They turned and walked towards the car. She wept and David could think of nothing to stop her weeping. Without a word Darcy gave her his handkerchief and they got away quickly, driving through the long low tunnel of trees towards the highway, as night grew and the smoke of distant fires filled the air.

CHAPTER 25

It was almost three years before he saw her again. He went one night to Knox Hall to talk to Phillips and she passed him as he came through the front entry. She did a perfect double-take, stopped, reached for his hand. She had done something to the white curls; they no longer fanned an aureole about her face, ready to stir in the faintest breath, but lay back against her head.

"Having a baby hasn't hurt your figure."

"What are you doing now?" she whispered and kept her hand in his, clutching the side of his thumb as if he might disappear.

"Writing, all the time. I work as night watchman at Green's."

"Is it any good? The writing."

"Not yet."

Scarcely aware of what he was doing, he moved towards her. She said abruptly "I went to England. I missed you over there."

"Was it fun—the honeymoon?"

"I said . . ."

"I know. Women have to be first, they have less time."

"That sounds like him." She said flatly, "You're still with him. Tell me, what did he do when Deirdre killed herself?"

He let his eyes linger on her mouth as she talked, heard, taken again by its unforgotten loveliness, "Nothing."

"My sorority is arranging a series of classic films, we're trying to get the auditorium." She withdrew her hand uneasily. "Did he get you the job?"

"He introduced me to Green. He's a strange man."

"I know all about Green the fur tycoon. And Green's daughter. He's some kind of foreigner isn't he?"

"What?"

"You know what I mean."

"I don't. Perhaps you mean it on two levels. He's an Englishman—I think."

"Maybe that's part of it." She fumbled, steadied. "Let Darcy run everything. Go on. Let him. Find your jobs, your friends. Take everything. Choose your rich stupid wife like he said he would..."

"I told you you had no right. To anything about me." He smiled, his mouth pinched with the strain of it, and moved towards the stairs. "What is it like? The baby."

"Wonderful." Her small gloved hand went to the handle of the door.

"You don't look big enough to have babies."

Her mouth moved as if she were about to speak or attempt a smile and she was gone. He looked after her, feeling bereft. The spring night pressed blackly against the small panes of glass in the door.

Upstairs in the office Paul Phillips looked up and smiled. David took the other chair, all age-chewed leather with the stuffing peeling through the arms.

"What's in a name?"

Phillips offered a cigarette. "Tell me."

"Or the obverse of the same coin, when is a woman not a woman?"

"You're ahead of me."

"When she has a compulsion to marry and change a name she only just got. Deed poll and marriage being vastly dissimilar. Even then there's a kind of deadly honesty about it. And babies too. Plans. Nothing like plans. Have you a match?"

"When can I read you?"

"When I'm printed."

Phillips smiled. "It might be a long wait."

"Wait. My thundering bloody destiny is waiting. I sit in the Almighty's anteroom waiting for an appointment that never comes. The incinerator over at Green's does a brisk business. Some day if I work and wait long enough something will go snap! and it'll all come out like a string of pearls."

"Modest fellow."

"Darcy used to talk all the time and hand his stuff around to anybody literate. It siphons it off and anyway my career is being the antithesis of Darcy."

Phillips lowered his eyes. "How were things in Mouse Bluffs?"

"As usual. The ice on the puddles cracked underfoot all the way to Easter service and the river is black and gray, aching and groaning in the night for break-up."

"Did you go to Easter service?"

"It's a candle I can't light and if I could it would burn away and leave me lightless before I saw more than the little glow in the small corner. I wandered through town and wondered where all the people were, then remembered there were hardly any and the quiet was why I went."

"I'll go some day."

"You'd only see a dump."

"How was the family?"

"He thinks I'm no good. Maybe I'm not but I wish he wasn't so certain." I wanted to say, Give me my mother's letter, you have no right to it now. But thought, no, not like that. And went on waiting.

"Why don't you tell him you're writing?"

David smiled at last. "Because it's the same as nothing to him. And in a way he's right. It needs men with pitchforks and scalpels and good strong hands. It has no time for the watcher. Probably no need. The unconcrete."

"The unconcrete," Phillips murmured. "By the way I thought you might be interested in this." He pushed a folded essay paper across the desk. David picked it up. Phillips said tentatively, "Odd."

"How odd?"

"Three pages. This has been going on all year. I get twenty or more out of the best in the class but only three from her, yet she's got it all there. When I remember how Darcy used to come up with young novels for his assignments—all this tells me is 'I was at class and didn't miss a single relevant word.' Is she really like that?"

"Roselee's okay. She's just one of those kids who knows everything. They sent her away to New York a couple of summers to a special school, just like they did Darcy, and she was told what pictures were good, how a poem should sound, how to drink a glass of sherry and she thinks she's got it made. What she wants she gets and God help the bystanders."

"Like him?"

"Not at all."

Phillips lit his pipe. "She sits and writes it all down, just the important words. She's like one of those Siamese cats, all sinews and eyes looking dispassionately around and finding people, especially professors, very trivial."

"It's just that she's—sane? I don't know, you get the impression of bags of common sense and a keen old brain behind it." David got to his feet. "She worships Darcy, that's probably partly

257

why she's here, his approval. He hardly knows she's alive. I'll have to go. I have to punch in at midnight and there's something I want to do."

Phillips urged him to stay, fiddled nervously with the essay paper as if he had expected more of it than it had yielded. "I didn't want to tell you but he's been around here. Not that I mind but . . ."

"What did he want?"

"He stayed an hour and told me about his work and asked me if I'd like to read it and I said yes, and finally he asked me what you and I talk about."

His eyes slewed from David's. The room felt suddenly cold.

"See you," David said.

"Any time," Phillips called after him and thought, I shouldn't have.

But the trickle of danger was there. Even though they might mean David's going he couldn't quite wish back the words.

The students were starting to laugh again. The tide of veterans had passed its full, those hard-eyed men who, like Roselee Rush-forth, knew what they wanted. More student cars in the parking lot each day, it seemed. He wondered if the golden youth would come again, if he'd see another wave of those wonderfully careless young people of long ago. It hardly seemed possible in this present of big bombs and standing armies. The universities, it often seemed to him, were beginning to churn out mere technicians, and intellectuals, always scorned in the marketplace, were beginning to be scorned within the institutions of learning as well. His high postwar hopes were reduced to a prayer that he wouldn't have to watch another generation being stunted, holding their youth out of range of a death-dedicated public, too young to know they were civilization at work saving itself. He wished the group to which David belonged could learn how to laugh, knew they could not; once it is taken away, it does not come back. There remained the bombs, slipped away to wait like meat-pies in the cold cupboard, the generals and politicians who had been careful not to die. And, he thought sourly, the Darcys. He knew that David should have gone. Some should fight; it was in them to join the race, whatever madness it engaged in. But he might have died. Yes, he would have died. It was a chance they couldn't take. Phillips laughed. Now all agnostics will kneel and say a prayer; ask no more for laughter, just be glad to be alive, accept the necessary evils and the Darcys without question.

He picked up Roselee's paper and wrote "Brilliant" on it, gave her five out of ten. That should stir her imagination.

Marvin Green looked up. A glint of light slanted from his eyes and he pushed the newspaper aside. John Crossen, his secretary, watched him: God, he's like an animal, he can hear and smell, even see, long before the humans catch the stimuli.

"There's David."

"Yes, I expect so."

Green strode nervously to the mantel. No one else could have seen the nervousness. Crossen caught it in the way the long clever fingers snapped the cigarette against the wrist.

"Do you want me? I could get on with some work."

"Stay."

Green smiled to himself. He was a tall man, lean but large-boned, his shoulders stooped; the pale scar of his hair-line remained in the smooth shining flesh on his forehead; his face had great strength, large nose, the cheeks sunken a bit, emphasizing the power of the big bones through jaw and cheeks; his eyes were a very light intense brown without a vestige of humor.

Crossen asked, "You think he'll do it?"

Green gave him a sharp glance. "Of course he will. But not yet."

Crossen nodded. He probably would. Out of twenty years as Green's secretary he had learned that Green, who never failed at anything, would not fail in this.

"He has no family," Green said as if to himself.

Crossen felt the quality of the threat. The gray dust of a thousand premature wrinkles made him look like a child in grotesque make-up. Even his eyes looked white and unhealthy and wrinkled.

The housekeeper opened the door of the drawing room and David came in.

"Good evening, sir. Mr. Crossen."

He took his seat.

Crossen relaxed, as he always did. It was astonishing the way the boy eased things between Green and himself. Although, he reminded himself, there'd been nothing to ease before David began to come to the house. Crossen had moved in fifteen years before, had accepted the tensions of the household without question. Then suddenly they became unbearable and only the cause of the strain could relieve it.

"Good of you to drop in like this," Green said warmly. "You don't know how Crossen and I get on each other's nerves."

"Do you?"

Green smiled that aside, said, "Pamela enjoyed the park today."

"I did too."

Green floundered. Crossen watched with immense satisfaction. It was nice to see him flounder.

"How are you liking the job?"

David laughed. "I just sit there and write, then go to look at the vaults and windows twice a night. In a word, cushy. You, sir, are a gentleman and a patron."

"Good." Green smoothed his hands together. "A glass of wine?"

Crossen was on his feet in an easy motion, went to the credenza where a bottle stood on a tray, prepared each night on the chance of David's coming. Three glasses. Two if Crossen was to be out. Whiskey had been their nightcap in the old days but the boy wouldn't drink it before "work."

"I was twelve years old when I came here," Green said, "and I was alone. I came out from the Old Country to an aunt and she died before I got here. I went on the street. I sold papers on the corner of Donald and Portage. In those days a boy had to fight for his corner. I mean fight—fists and bleeding noses and black eyes and the gangs screaming kike or bohunk or goolie. There was a lot of race feeling back then. The factories in Orange, Ontario, used to have signs: *No Englishmen.* Maybe it was the Scots started it all; I don't ever remember hearing any shouting about the Scots. God, they were a tough bunch! Bushy used to take a bath twice a year whether he needed it or not. It was on that street corner that Bushy Mackay found me and took me with him into the north. The street corner was no place for a boy but neither was the north; you pretty quickly got to be a man in the bush."

David studied him, intrigued. He was always puzzled by Green's train of thought, all the filling, as if to stand rich in his expensive house and drink good wine out of a life's work was not enough. Darcy had been right, as usual; there was something compelling about the man, about the whole situation. David had asked Darcy in effect the same question Lilja had asked, "What is he?" and Darcy had said, "A tycoon," which was no answer. "A tycoon with a tiger biting his ass then. But that's not important. It's what *you* are that's important. All think, no achievement, no money, no give in. Study up on Marvin Green. The old man tried to peddle me to him, but I was all wrong. He recognized me: I'm the second generation of him. But you're not."

David's eyes were alert as Green talked on about his early youth, hardships; it told David nothing. There was a renegade somewhere, he knew, under the artificially tanned face. He was still trying to find it.

Then Green said, "I met someone last week who knew you a long time ago. Jacob Herson."

"Yes?"

"Do you remember?"

Remember what?

He said, "It's a long time ago."

"Not too long."

"It seems long to me." He met Green's eyes, "You're not trying to find out about me, are you? There's nothing for you to find out and I don't like it."

Crossen suppressed a smile.

"I assure you, I wasn't," Green said coldly.

David smiled faintly, watched the knuckles whiten on Green's hand over the wine glass.

"Is Pamela in bed?"

"Yes."

Green passed his glass to Crossen, who caught the signal, took it carefully back to the tray.

"I wonder if you would excuse me?" he said.

"Of course."

David glanced at his watch. "I'd better go, it's eleven."

"Crossen will drive you."

"Yes, I'd rather like a breather. Half an hour? I'll have the car out front." He closed the door softly.

Into the silence David said, "How's Jacob?"

"A man with no stuffing. Something must have happened to him; he comes from a solid family but he drifts. He never seems quite 'there' if you know what I mean."

"He was in the war."

"That may be it; some of them will never settle properly." Green dismissed it with an air of boredom. "You understand about Pamela?"

"I think so."

"What is she like? Out? Say at the park?"

"Just as she is here. Perfect."

Green leaned towards him. "You know how much perfect costs?"

"I have a fair idea."

"I'll tell you anyway and remember I'm not talking about money."

"I understand."

"Every morning at eight-thirty Pamela has her breakfast. At nine a physiotherapist comes and she exercises. At ten her teacher comes. A Ph.D. He's the very best. A psychologist. He taught her to read and write a bit and do needlework." Green pointed to a little framed picture of silken flowers against the wall. "Much, much more. And trained therapists . . . It's taken all these years. There was something to work with, do you see?"

"He does on a grand scale what Mother with her good works does on a small scale," Darcy had once said. "It's what the whole of our society does; down with superiority, up the cretins. Anything to fight nature. Kill off the cream in war and set up the mentally retarded in silk-lined boudoirs. It makes the ordinary types feel so charitable. Of course it's a big fight, nature is a formidable enemy. It takes indomitables like Mother and Green but in the long run they'll probably win."

"You needn't tell me all this, sir," David said.

"No, I like to talk to you. Do you know I have no one to talk to? I pay Crossen too much to talk to him. I don't have that trouble with you." He laughed.

"It's just that I can see why, you don't have to spell it out."

"I suppose you can but I don't want you to misunderstand me. A person meeting Pamela might not guess. Now anyone seeing Pamela on the street wouldn't know, would they?"

Not unless they looked into her lovely big empty eyes. "Perhaps not."

"Everything is perfect. Nothing has been spared. There are four people whose whole living depends on Pamela. When she was little there were seven. Have you ever heard them crying? The ones like her? No? Well, I have. The little ones, they cry outside a door no one can open; even without intellect they have heart and their hearts break, break, break. It's a terrible thing to hear that continual weeping. You understand? There has been no weeping here. We don't stop loving a child because it is a child for good. Growing up's a potential. Pamela had not the potential but she's a very perfect thing for all that."

"Yes, when I walk with her I feel—I don't know—peaceful?"

"That's it. Does it matter that Pamela doesn't know about bombs or business or poetry? Does it really matter?"

David felt a surge of excitement; he was on top of it now.

"Well," Green expelled his breath as if he had run a great distance. He rose. "Just so we know and say it. I don't like people who pretend my girl is something she isn't for my sake. It's enough that she is what she is. Transformed and perfect after her fashion."

What a curious way he talks, David thought, as if he had phrased and written all this out, memorized it, a testament. There was something almost beautiful in this calm expression of sorrow turned into a moral triumph.

Then Green added, "You know it's not hereditary, don't you?" and destroyed it.

David said abruptly, "No, I didn't," and got to his feet.

"You know about the fire?"

David's eyes glazed. He sat down slowly.

"No."

The idea scorched through his mind that Green, with his enigmatic talk of Herson, was about to peel away the scar-tissue's ragged fringe. He missed the next words.

". . . in the fire. Pamela's mother—you see we were living in a frame house, a nice place but very old, like tinder. Her mother died but they saved my girl. There was a doctor living right across the way—he slashed—performed a Caesarian right there on the lawn with the house burning down and my wife screaming hurry. She was terribly burned but wanted the baby to . . . Then Pamela was as you see. The doctor said the blood supply was bad because of the smoke and shock, oxygen cut off so there was permanent brain damage."

David rose and moved leadenly to the door, his brain charred meat.

"You'll come again?" Green asked, the note of pleading in his voice belying his stiff exhausted smile.

"Yes, I'll come again."

CHAPTER 26

"I'm glad you came," Basil Waterman said.

"I didn't want to but you see how it is. If I could just say to Darcy 'You knew, you son of a bitch,' but I can't. Ian was right, I can't speak of it to him."

"Do you know why he did it?"

"For the same reason he's done everything, because something was left out. Because he had—has—everything and can't do a damned thing with all his gifts. Because he loves no one."

"Are you sure he doesn't?"

David met Waterman's eyes and smiled briefly. "Quite sure. Don't lapse into that sort of thing or I may as well get on the couch and let you rattle your gourds or whatever you do."

Waterman laughed. "I can hear Ian Ross when you talk, he must have had an immense impact on you."

"He taught me to read good things and to distinguish between the King and God, and that the highest calling was not killing wogs for the Empire and that no one would beat the ass off me if I dared to think otherwise. But I was never impressed by his— histrionics? He fancied himself a great blackguard and drunkard and half the kids in town were a bit scared of him because they'd see him rolling along the street singing, generally in Gaelic or French to add spice to it. He just did it for courage—a protest. A heller in a wheel-chair is a lot different from a cripple in a wheel-chair. I liked him and I think he liked my accepting him as a heller without being afraid of the wildness. It was real. He suffered a lot. He was smart too."

"He was more than smart. He was . . . I was in the trenches with him." Waterman looked at the picture on his desk, a big fair woman flanked by two handsome teen-agers. "But all that was long ago."

"I remember you coming out to see him. You probably don't remember me. He would say you were trying to save him and I used to think of the gospelers who came from Brandon and hooted their state of grace in front of the post office."

Waterman smiled. "I remember you all right. And I did try to save him but he had that attitude, you know—why? What for?"

"I know."

"How's the doctor?"

"Fine. I get the train of thought but that—obsession of Ian's was only part of his trouble, not its root. Something to blame. He couldn't stand alone and I don't mean this physically; he was always talking to me about walking straight. The weakness must have been in him from the start, a need for approval. And when he didn't get it, he put the blame in the wrong place."

Waterman's eyes pinpointed behind his horn-rimmed glasses. "Gavin's a hard man."

"Not really," David said slowly. "His duties are harder on him than other men's. I know he's considered hard, inhuman, austere. That's his strength. He's never been weak, can't understand weakness, and that's not the same as being hard."

"Perhaps not." Waterman's eyes still probed. "Do you get close to him?"

"Not with this sort of talk. That's what I'm telling you. To him it would seem like undressing in public."

"Is that why you stayed away from here? To be like him, bottle it up?"

"No," indignantly. "I've got to take it alone sometime."

"Then why do you stay with Darcy? That's worse than taking it alone."

"I'm big enough."

"For both of you, is that it?"

David got to his feet, "I feel better anyway."

"Good. And I didn't rattle a single gourd."

"You came damned close to it." He smiled. "And you're subtle. I'm used to cocktail-party Freudians, the left-overs of the thirties, and they're short on subtlety. You get to what you want without all the muck."

"Just remember that I'm a friend before doctor. I'm the wailing wall, if you like, or the seashell you put to your ear to hear the song of your own blood. Take your choice."

David thought, "You're also a nice guy."

Waterman went to the window and looked out over the dingy rooftops of the city. "What about Green and the girl?"

"That's all right, he put it all on the table. He's okay."

"Are you sure? Sure it's all on the table?"

"It's hard to describe how he affects me. I can't stay away from him. Maybe it's just that I've never met a millionaire before. A classification; new, I don't like classifications. I like to see around the big fact: millionaire or drunk or schizo. He's not coarse with it either, things haven't taken over if you know what I mean, he knows how to make everything work for him, on his terms."

Waterman let it lie a moment in silence. "Did you hear what you just said?"

David flushed in confusion.

"Did it ever occur to you that Darcy might have told him?"

Into the long cold wait David said haltingly, "He wouldn't."

"He might. I offer it for what it's worth."

"He wouldn't." He felt the weakness of it and crashed on, "Because Darcy doesn't think about it, that's what I've been trying to tell you, that's why Ian told me not to talk to him, it's a wall, he knows or remembers but not the way I do because he doesn't care."

"That isn't what Ian meant."

David went to the door. "I may be back again."

"I know. Because you haven't been entirely thorough have you? There's something else, another aspect."

"Yes."

"Perhaps I can help you with it."

"I'm not sure I need help."

"We all need help."

"He was right, you have a warm touch."

They shook hands.

"Keep it," Waterman told him carefully. "We all have some— hazard in our lives. We learn to bear it and discover our identity in spite of it. My own hazards haunted me many years and perhaps humanized me. Yours is worse than most and requires more bearing. You can't drop it or exorcise it, there's the secret. You learn to lug it on your back through the years and it never gets lighter but your back gets stronger."

"I hope." He felt foolishly like crying.

"But not strong enough to carry another man as well." Waterman's eyes did not spare him.

David sighed, "All right, I'll file it," and left.

I won't go back, he thought. It's done and I'll lug it. My way. For us both. For the good man too. Even if not for myself, I would have to do it for him. Darcy's clear cool face after he'd fired the shots sprang into his mind and fear cramped his brain. I must remain on watch. Only I can do it. I do it for the good man and do it gladly. It is my trust; I accept it. Wise man, Waterman, what has all your subtlety to do with this?

One June day a month or so later he was surprised out of bed at noon to find Daniel Backhouse at his door. He shook Dan's hand delightedly and put on a kettle for coffee.

"You stopped writing me a long time ago," Daniel said.

David apologized, "Letters—take it away."

"Yes, you wrote such long ones."

"So did you. I enjoyed your letters." And sought light from your candle before I learned what a little light it shed. For me.

"We do our duty as we are called," Dan said. "I hope I helped you a bit. You've had a difficult row to hoe, my boy. And it's still difficult."

Mind your own business, David almost shouted and saw the line of gray on Dan's chin, the faded blue eyes blinking with concern behind the thick spectacles. I must watch myself, he thought.

My wound is raw again. I suspect everyone. No one has knowledge but Wiseman Waterman and Ian-Ghost. And my brother and I.

"You're looking well." He passed Daniel a cup. "Instant stuff, hope you don't mind."

Daniel sipped, smiled. "I'm living here now, you know."

"No, I didn't."

"I'm at Solveg's."

David couldn't control it. "You're what?"

"Just as a friend. Her mother-in-law's there of course so it's perfectly—I have work here now, I wanted to be near my grandson. Solveg herself suggested I stay at the house. She's very good, we get along well."

"I'm sure."

"And Ivan needs a man about. Jon is going into the ministry but of course you know that. I'll tell you why I came, apart from just wanting to see you; Mouse Bluffs is celebrating its seventy-fifth anniversary and Reese Todd has written to ask if I'll serve on the committee. It's next year. We'll be mailing invitations and announcements then, of course, but it's a matter of getting everyone working on it now."

"That's nice." David ran his fingers through his sleep-tangled hair and wished Daniel would come to the point.

"I thought—well, if you might write something, perhaps a little essay on the pioneers, for our anniversary book."

"I'm not very good at that sort of thing."

"Nonsense, I have all your letters and Lily has told me you write. Now you think about it, David; it might be your chance. Writers have had smaller beginnings."

But not much. David stirred his coffee. Dan, relax, let hell roll over all of us. An essay, a chance, a light in my darkness, Oh Lord.

"Of course we couldn't pay you. Have you—I hear there's good money in fiction."

David asked, "How is he—Lilja's baby?"

"Beautiful. A beautiful bouncing boy."

"Did she nurse him?"

Daniel's eyes jerked, snapped against David's face. He said faintly, "Why I really don't know."

"I just asked."

Dan surveyed the untidy room. "You and Darcy must have quite a Bohemian life here."

Darcy's art: fishnet curtains, rather droopy; African masks; nudes; a series of glum green Egyptians all suffering from priapism; endless piles of books and tattered magazines, pocket books piled up in the corners; the open chess set with a cigarette butt lying in the middle of the board.

David said, "Not very."

"It looks Bohemian."

"I guess." But you're not Bohemian at all, living with Solveg yet.

"Well, think about what I've said. Christine Ross has all Sir Richard's papers. It would make a splendid article if she would let you work with them. As I'm sure she would. You're almost a member of the family, as it were."

"Yes." As it were.

Daniel prepared to leave.

"You must come to dinner, you and Darcy. Telephone me any time, under Frank."

"Sure. It was good of you to think of me." Under Frank. Poor bastard. "Give the family my love."

"I will."

David went back to bed and was still asleep when Darcy came in from work at seven.

"My God, you sleep a lot."

He opened his eyes and Darcy's face was less than a foot away.

"Were you dreaming?"

"I think I must have been."

"What about?"

David yawned, stretched, scratched his chest and pushed his feet over the side of the bed. "Let me have my dreams, eh?"

"You were smiling."

David gripped the mattress.

"There are two coffee cups dirty."

"I dreamed Dan Backhouse came here then," and he told Darcy. Darcy laughed inordinately and David couldn't laugh with him and was sorry he'd made it snide to distract Darcy briefly. "Make me some coffee, will you? I'll have to get on my horse."

"You've got till midnight, for Christ's sake."

"That's okay."

He got up quickly. There was a dangerous suggestion of breaking in the obsidian eyes. As he shaved, he heard Darcy going through the flat quickly, soft silent padding up and down. He probably had his shoes off, looking for clues to what had happened during the day.

David called, "The mail is on the kitchen table."

"Thanks."

When he had showered and dressed he found Darcy had his toast, eggs and coffee ready. It was a deal. When David came home in the morning he made Darcy's breakfast.

"Dan thinks we're Bohemians."

"Aren't we?"

"You might be."

Darcy said, "Did you go out today?"

"No."

"You must have been tired then."

"Well, I worked all night."

"Why don't you bring it home? I could help you maybe?" Darcy laughed deprecatingly. "I've learned something out of my own mistakes."

David refused to go into that one, which usually resulted in a screaming rage against publishers, editors and the Jews and pansies feeding at the public trough of the C.B.C.

"I got a letter from Uncle Gavin."

"I noticed."

"Why didn't you read it?"

"Why should I? It was yours. And sealed."

"I don't mind if you open my letters. I have no secrets from you." Darcy pushed the letter across the table, "Read it."

"What does he say?"

"Go ahead."

"You tell me."

"The same crap he always drips out. My boy you're all we've got, your mother writes that you have a great future in radio work, keep it up. He understands. He hears me constantly. I'm the master communicator of world events to the entire West. I fill a great need. I must come and see him."

"Why don't you?"

"God! Five minutes of it and I'm gorged to here. My old man is more bearable."

"You hardly see him either."

"Why are you drinking your coffee so fast? Are you going somewhere?"

"Yes."

"Where?" David did not answer. "Where, I asked? What's wrong with me? Why does everything turn out wrong? Look . . ." Darcy leaned over the table. "You've got to quit going to Green's. I knew, God damn it! You are going there."

"Isn't that how you planned it?"

"No, and you bloody well know it. It was a—a gag. You said you wanted a rich dull woman. I was—kidding."

"You weren't."

"I was. I didn't think you'd keep going."

After I found out. "The hell you didn't."

Darcy put his head in his hands. "Stop torturing me," he said, his voice muffled. "It was supposed to be funny. You're only offered the kingdoms of the world, you don't take them."

"Darcy, I'm telling you. I don't intend to. Go and lie down, stop making such . . ."

"Listen," Darcy said urgently, reached for David's hand. David withdrew. "You don't know him."

"I do."

The small light from the stove cast moving blotches across a suddenly unknown face. David thought, I should turn on the top light, it would change all this, but he did not move.

"He's a maniac and a genius," Darcy said. "He does just what he likes with everyone. Go ahead, laugh, you'll wake up married to that cretin and never know what hit you."

He flung Dr. Ross's letter at David's chest.

David picked it up carefully. "Darcy, for God's sake . . ."

Anxiety about the new element in Darcy's rage ran a poker over his brow. There was usually a point at which he could get the upper hand; it had to be soon. He fingered the letter desperately: my boy you're all we've got.

"Darcy, listen to me," he said. "He's talked to me. He told me all about her. I like her. She's like a polite little kid."

Darcy's eyes shone wildly. "So you take her to the park? To the beach? I'm watching you! Why do you think I broke you up with Lilja, eh? Why? Shut up. I did. It's not for you, that's why. Neither is Green and his Pamela. Davie, I'm on my knees; don't let him have you."

"Have me? What in hell is this? Darcy, get a grip on yourself. And while we're on the subject, I'm sick of you following me around, really sick. Take your sick head over there and wash it under the tap."

He got up from the table.

Darcy laughed. "That's it, that's what I get, eh? I've done everything for you. Everything. Given you a place, food, clothes; got you jobs, women, saved you from that white-haired bitch and you crap on me."

The room was silent.

"Go on," David said.

Darcy made a curious sound, a sort of moan. "I thought it all

270

out today. I walked and walked. I wasn't at work at all; I haven't been for a week. If you ever listened you'd know. I thought it all out how to explain to you and it's not supposed to go like this. I know I haven't done all those things, but sometimes I think it's true because part of it's true, see? I know you've got it. Alone. You don't even mind it, the being alone, because that's the way you are. You've got it. I faced that. See? It hit me one day. I just knew, all of a sudden and it was like dying and that's why, you've either got it or you haven't and if you're big enough you see it. Room at the top; some of us are on a sawed-off ladder. That's me. I'm jealous." He worked his hands together rhythmically. "Jealous. Can you imagine it? Darcy's jealous. And I'll always be jealous but I want to be part of it. See it. *See it.* Everything I've done was because of that, because I knew long before it sneaked out into the open. Introducing you to people. Getting you to see what Lilja was really like that time at the lake. Teaching you to listen to music, look at paintings. All of it. And now I'm telling you *watch Green.* Do it. For me. Just one thing. For me."

David said at length, "I can't let you—what you're suggesting —it's wrong."

"I know but I can't help it. I want to be there. Being able to recognize it takes almost as much guts as having it. It's remarkable. I'm the only one."

"I don't know what you've done or think you've done, how you've twisted it in your mind, but whatever I've got it's mine. Alone. You said it. It's all I've got and it's the one thing you can't wangle a piece of. My conscience, my insides, my li . . . Darcy please. Just leave me alone for a while, will you?"

The air in the small room seemed rank. His arms and stomach ached with taut muscles he could not quiet. Darcy thrust his hands in a powerful spearlike motion over the table. Dishes fell wildly to the floor; coffee soaked into Dr. Ross's letter. The muscles grew so rigid they burned David's flesh like cramps. Darcy's palms spread slowly, trembled as if they held a massive bowl. Tears ran down his cheeks. David thought wildly, if I could just relax enough to turn on the radio he'd be in there talking suavely about soap. Darcy's hands closed.

"There you go again. Why can't you see that I'm your best friend? That we're together, that we have to be."

"I have—seen it." David's throat closed over it; his chest heaved.

"Believe me about this then."

"I've got to get out of here." He lunged for the door.

Like a big silent animal, in his stocking feet Darcy went after him. David sucked in a huge clout of air as the fingers ripped into his arm.

"I'll kill her first," Darcy said.

"Darcy! I've told you. I go there for—for the peace of it. It's almost like being alone. She doesn't count."

"She gives you peace?" Darcy's hands fell away. He chuckled. "Of course there's peace in stupidity, that's the world we live in. Peace you don't need! It's a silk-lined padded cell and when the door closes it's shut for good. Peace!" he shouted. "I'll give you peace!"

Silence and they looked at each other. David felt violence burst through him, like an abscess breaking. He put his arm against his eyes briefly, then turned shaking, afraid to look at that face again, and went out of the flat quickly, slamming the door behind him.

CHAPTER 27

The night spread itself out plainly under the closing sky. Green sat in the back of the Cadillac with Pamela, waiting, and Pamela smelled like fresh-cut flowers, smiled, put forth her small hand with childish grace.

"Good evening, David."

Green said, "I though you weren't going to make it," but his voice was serene. Of course people kept engagements with him.

Instead of begging off as he had intended, David went to the concert, sat on the other side of Pamela, who was still and quiet in tender green silk, her amazing white hands a poem in flesh, and felt fear and horror flow out of him into the music. All the way to the auditorium he had been possessed of a need to be alone. Something was gibbering in his head. If he could just be silent he would hear it. He had a curious sense that the message wasn't new, that he'd heard it and run from it again and again. But Green and the girl steadied and soothed him. Or perhaps this clear high place of ordered music soothed him; the fluttering of programs, the nods, the lowering lights, the detached watching of half-faces and backs of heads, here a beautiful crown of silver, a lovely soft withered old arm raising opera glasses, all as rigid and cooling as a Mass. He did not think of Darcy. He was conscious in a peculiar way of not thinking of Darcy, of mild pleasure that he was able to sit beside the grown-up child and her secretive father and think only of the music. Even when he glanced up towards the balcony as the intermission lights lowered and caught the glow of a pale vicious face, eyes malignantly on his own, he was not thinking of Darcy. Darcy did not belong with Green and Pamela. He glanced upwards again into the semi-darkness and saw nothing but the shining balcony rail, let the music trickle coolly over his hot mind once more.

They drove to Green's house and Miss Berkeley met them at the door, smiled, asked Pamela how the concert was.

"Lovely, wasn't the music lovely, David?" Then, as she was preceding the housekeeper obediently upstairs, Pamela turned and looked back, her large eyes as happy and helpless as a pup's, said, "I love you, David, and you, Daddy."

David felt his throat swell. "Good night, Pamela."

"Good night, my dear." In the drawing room Green said, "You're good for her."

"She's good for me." David sat down wearily. "It makes you wonder about our values. It's odd—you don't mind my saying this? You never feel the pity of it when you're with her."

"There isn't any," Green told him casually. "That's what perfection means."

David looked at Green steadily. "Do you really feel that?"

"Yes."

"Mr. Green, what do you want with me?"

Green met his glance. "You're tired."

"Yes." He felt as if a bright clear wind were coursing over his brain. "You haven't talked to Darcy Rushforth about me, have you?"

"Never. Only about the job, in the beginning when he contacted me."

David felt himself drifting down, put his hands against his face, rubbed his eyes. He must be going mad, not an explosion of nerves but a contraction that would leave his head no bigger than a match-head. He could scarcely remember a word Darcy had said today but right before his eyes was the picture of Green and Darcy talking. If he listened a moment he would hear what they were saying. A throb began behind his eyes. He wanted to go home.

Home where it took no magician reaming out Liszt to ease the day, where the slow thick river holding no cloud shadows flowed by forever under the big sky.

"You should take a rest, David, all this writing at night—you're getting thin."

"What is there about me that everyone takes one look and knows exactly what I should do better than I know myself?"

"Sorry." Green smiled indulgently. "Drink?"

"No, thanks, I can't work after it." He said abruptly, "I need the job just now."

"You've got it."

"But that's all I want."

"Don't look for what isn't there." Green poured himself a drink, chucked the glass against his palm. "Has Darcy been filling you full of nonsense? He's a bad lot. His father's no better than he should be and I expect it's catching if not hereditary."

David gave him a sharp look. "What's changed you?"

Green hefted the glass, said drily, "You have."

"How?"

"Because I didn't know a man could be so good. Disinterested? Maybe that's the word but it doesn't quite get across . . ." He seated himself beside David and said after a brief silence, "I had a crazy idea. I've had it for years. The irrational in any man's make-up. How I've studied it in other men. The soft spot. The way in. Mine is Pamela. I worked at it. My soft spot had to be bigger than any other man's because that's the way I do things—even madness had to be an achievement. Others saw it. Darcy knew and I think his father sensed it. I knew one day I'd find a young man just like you and his soft spot would be a great need for quiet, even a need to love, then I would manipulate him till I could say, I've got eighteen million dollars and no son and I do not want to leave my perfection with hired help and trust companies and boards of directors who will manage to create a one-woman prison and let the crying start. Let me buy a different sort of trust for her, someone who sees the pity and the perfection; only marriage can do this, only a man I trust as I trust you can do this." Green's face was a study in control yet his eyes looked red.

David rolled it slowly in his mind. "Am I really like that?"

"Yes. And eighteen million isn't enough." Green smiled very minutely and David realized that the man was relaxed now as he had never been before. "Now it's off my mind for the first time. I had to find the man before I could see how foolish I was. If I hadn't found you I might have gone on for years thinking it pos-

274

sible. It's been hard to tell you but I had to because I knew you'd understand and because I've seen your eyes—only the truth would satisfy that question you're always asking. It sounds pretty raw but it's not really, no more than any other man's weakness exposed. Crossen damned near cried when I told him."

"Crossen?"

"He's known me twenty years and didn't know I couldn't do it."

"Mr. Green, is this the first time in your life you've ever wanted something and decided not to take it?"

Green laughed. "Almost. Let's leave it at that. Benevolence. If we go on I shall have to admit you couldn't be had and that would bother me and then I might forget what a splendid fellow you think I am."

David said slowly, "Maybe I will have that drink, very light."

"It is rather an occasion isn't it? For me anyway."

"I just realized . . ."

"Yes."

"You're my friend."

Green splashed out a mild drink. "Any time."

"And I didn't even work at it."

Green looked at him quizzically.

"Don't ever. That's a maxim." Presently he said, "I want you to come here as you wish. Let it be a home or not. However you like it. But you owe me nothing. Remember that. When anyone owes me anything I make it clear. You and I are simply friends. There's a gap here, you see; I've never had young people about, it just didn't work. You bring it all to me. A young man wants to climb mountains or write books or hitchhike around the world. It's good. I forget—or never knew—how the dreams come into a young man."

"You had them."

"I never was young, David. And money, thinking money, corrupts the qualities of youth."

"So many do—think it."

"The measure of our time, the little power, things. Almost like medieval demon possession, money. Maybe it's the death throe of the Protestant ethos—they prated about good works and giving and taking and healing, the treasure box full of solid gold coins and gems, the march away from ideas. I know because I'm the heart of it, I'm the success of it. I talked a while ago about that idea I had, it was no idea but—obsession, the last limit of my function, buying the only unbought soul I could find. I build and build and build and I'm the destroyer in my own building, the worm in my own wheat."

"We all are," David said.

"Please." Green smiled. "Don't butt in on my private flagellation. After all, I'm eighteen million times worse than most men in this town, don't count me down cheaply."

David laughed.

Green said, "I mean this—this youth thing. I want you to come here. Now let me drive you to work. It's late." In the hallway he said to Miss Berkeley, "I'll only be half an hour. Go along to bed, Agnes, and I'll lock up when I come in."

The night was now sodden black, weighted with the smell of rain. As the car rolled down the driveway, David caught, or thought he caught, a movement in the trees. His breath clotted.

"Mr. Green!"

"What is it?"

"Nothing." The trees were steady. He must have imagined the movement, whiteness fleeing the headlamps.

"Light me a cigarette, will you, David?"

"Have you a watchman here?"

"Why would I need a watchman? There's Blue, he sleeps over the garage; I guess he'd know if anyone was hanging around. Why?"

"I just wondered."

He let David out of the car in the alley behind the big squat Green Building.

"Remember, whenever you like. Move in if you want to."

"No, I wouldn't do that. Thanks."

"Good night."

David watched the car drive away. As if this were its signal, the faceless panic began its chewing again. I've got to stop this. I've started seeing and imagining things. As Green said, don't look for what isn't there. It occurred to him that eighteen million was a lot of money, many times more than he would ever see, that it took an order of genius to acquire that from a beginning on the fighting streets. But there was no Horatio Alger here; within that perverse proud mind there had never been rags, and riches knew their place. He wondered if he could as easily give up a dream as Green had done and, hard on the heels of that, knew it had not been easy, knew too that Lilja was right, Green was some kind of foreigner, his own kind. He knew as well what Green wanted of him now, what the debt would be, and the obligation was already beginning to spread through him like sour milk. The

276

night mists crowded up against his face. In a blaze of honesty he admitted for the first time that no human relationship could be perfect, that men should not run from imperfections. Yet he could not relieve himself of the desire for perfection. Just once. There was Darcy—imperfection of the highest order, the purest of imperfect relationships. Surely this paradox was almost proof that he could do it.

He rang the night-bell and the evening man let him in. They toured the building together and David signed the watch-sheet, checked the revolver. Alone, he took his papers and books from the desk. Facing him was the electronic panel with the windows and doors of the building designated by small spots of red light. If someone tried to break in, the affected window or door would begin to blink at him and an alarm would go off in police headquarters.

He looked down at the work he had done the previous night.

It won't do, he thought. I shall leave here soon. False pretenses. Each hour brings me closer to being in debt to Green; my debts are already manifold. The suggestion of movement in the glowering garden troubled his mind again. He shook his head, picked up his pen. When the telephone rang an hour later, he was in the midst of his work and answered it grudgingly.

"David, Crossen speaking. There's a constable coming there. Let him in and show him the fur vaults and the grills, then come here in the police car."

"There?"

"There's been an accident," Crossen said.

"No."

"A murder."

"Mr. Green?"

"No."

He replaced the receiver, leaned his head against the cool concrete wall, pounded his fists against it with a dull monotonous thudding. As he had longed for those moments in the doorway to smash them into Darcy's face, smash and go on smashing until there was nothing left of my-boy-you're-all-we've-got. This was the savagery that had blazed for that interval through his brain, run from tonight and always run from. He hated and feared Darcy, had always hated and feared him. He had wanted to kill Darcy. And he had done it. I saw him, he thought, and did not stop him.

When the policeman rang a few minutes later, he had stopped crying.

"Really Darcy, you're the limit," Mary scolded as she moved around the kitchen in her dressing gown, her thick hair tousled, pins glinting from the temples. Her face, clear of the usual careful powder and color, was very white, faintly creped like a piece of tissue; she wore an incongruous pair of diamond earrings, as if in her confusion she had swept them on, not wanting to be without some mark of her intense femininity. "You must have known I'd be asleep."

"Aren't you madly glad to see me?"

He leaned back in the breakfast nook and watched her, blowing smoke through his nostrils languidly; he wore no coat; his shirt sleeves were rolled.

"Always. Stay the night, dear, your father would be delighted. You know you're both so proud you'll just neither of you give in. Your father didn't understand and you were bad to be so proud and not tell him why you couldn't enlist."

"I came for one of your Denver sandwiches, not a eulogy on Dad. You're the best short-order cook I know."

She paused, gave him a puzzled glance, a short graying woman, rather stout, her face a study of kind years. "You haven't been up to some mischief have you?"

"Am I not always?" He rested his chin on his palm.

She ran her hand over his hair impulsively. "You're a good lad."

"Don't you believe it." He caught her hand in his for an instant.

"I wish I knew what you're laughing at. You're very full of yourself tonight." She broke the eggs, brought him the toaster and plugged it in beside the table. "There, you do the toast, I'll get the butter."

"I'm happy."

"Darcy! You've met a girl."

"You could say that."

"I'm glad. You should settle down and get away from that dreadful Chelsea crowd; that's all very well for a few years but a man needs a home of his own."

"I will. Mother, I—I haven't felt so—cleaned out, so good since—for years as I do right now. I want you to rem . . ."

"What's her name? Oh dear, there's the door. I expect your father's forgotten his keys again."

"Let me have the sandwich."

He took it to the table and began to eat. Mary looked at him again, a short doubtful moment, then pushed the swinging door.

The bell rang again. Darcy paused in his chewing. Someone was on the back step. He crammed the rest of the sandwich into his mouth.

When she returned, they were with her and she said uncertainly, "There are some policemen here," then saw they had followed her and gave the man at her side an indignant glare.

Darcy wiped his mouth with the back of his hand and got slowly to his feet. "I know."

"Darcy Rushforth?"

He went to Mary and kissed her brow. "Outside," he said to the man in blues.

"Darcy! What do these men want?"

"I think they want to hang me."

The policeman exchanged a quick glance with the man in plain-clothes. Roselee, a dressing gown flapping carelessly over her nightdress, pushed between the policemen and stared at Darcy.

"They won't say it but that's the gist of it, Mater dear," he called back over his shoulder. "Get Dad and tell him I've killed someone. He'll be pleased."

The two men who had remained just inside the front door opened it for him and went out at his side. The first two closed the door and turned to Roselee and Mary.

Mary was crying. Roselee looked at her helplessly.

Mary sobbed, "It must have been in his car. That terrible little sports car and I bought it for him and that awful crowd! That David. He's nobody and he's been bad for Darcy from the start, Charles was right. We mustn't let Darcy cover . . ."

"Hush." Roselee took her by the arm firmly. "Where can I reach Dad?"

"Call Gavin. I must have Gavin."

Roselee shook her. Mary looked at her angrily.

The girl said sharply, "Stop it. There'll be plenty of time to cry."

Mary shuddered convulsively, shrank into her dressing gown as if she were withering before Roselee's eyes.

At length she whispered, "Thank you."

The detective said, "Mrs. Rushforth?"

Roselee started. "I'd forgotten you." She fastened her gown.

"People do. I'm Inspector Day and I won't keep you, I know all this is rough. Just tell me what time your brother got here."

Mary said, "Just a few minutes ago. I was in bed and heard the doorbell and . . ."

"Did he seem upset in any way?"

"Not at all. He hadn't his coat but it is warm. He told me he wanted a snack and went straight to the washroom under the stairs to wash his . . . Dear God!"

"Leave her alone!"

"You better get a doctor for her," Day said. "She's in shock."

Roselee took her mother and led her into the sitting room.

"Lie down, dear. There. You stay—I'll call the doctor." She hurried towards the hall telephone, stopped beside Day, her back to her mother. "Can you tell me what he's done?"

Day averted his face, said calmly, "Killed a girl."

She asked weakly, "What girl?"

"Pamela Green."

"Oh!" She placed her hands against her breasts and pushed; a sob exploded in her throat. Day put out a hand to steady her. "How do you know it was him?"

"He's made no secret—a Mr. Crossen saw him as he left the house. He wasn't hurrying. And as soon as he stepped out that front door he started to talk."

Mary wailed, "He told me he was getting married. I don't believe he could have, Darcy never takes a drink when he drives."

"Get that doctor," Day advised.

David watched the door, hating it.

"Come in. Oh, it's you." He pulled himself to a sitting position on the chesterfield.

Roselee looked around the room, her eyes cloudy with fatigue. "I thought you might phone. They're taking it—hard."

"You should see how Marvin Green is taking it."

She sat down slowly. "That wasn't necessary."

"I'm sorry. It's six a.m. and the cops have been yakking at me for hours and Green—oh Jesus, he just sits there and looks at me."

"I called Uncle Gavin."

"Damn, damn, damn!"

"I had to. It'll be on the radio by now."

"The radio?"

"He's made a confession of some kind and will be charged right away. It'll be 'brought in for questioning and held' or something but everyone will know. Daddy's frantic. He's got the house full of lawyers—well, two lawyers."

"Why did you come here?"

"I needed you."

"You what?"

"I needed to be with someone. You. Dad's a horse's neck and Mother's under sedation and I wanted to cry."

He saw her face was wet and swollen, said wearily, "Come here," and took her in his arms.

She cried a long exhausting while and said, "It was all right to come?"

"Yes, there was no one else. You were right," he told her, and was astonished to find her so soft and pliable, shaped to his shoulder. She had always seemed so distant and solitary, saying the wrong things and trying too hard, and yes, as Phillips had said, feline. "Come on, let's make a pot of coffee and pretend we can do something to make it all go away."

"We can't."

"No, you look into Marvin Green's eyes once and you know."

"Don't you feel—bad—about Darcy?"

It shook him so badly he thought for a moment he might vomit up the mouthful of brandy Crossen had poured into him.

He got to his feet unsteadily, took her hand. "All my life I've felt bad about Darcy—now I feel worse."

"And the worst is to come. It's—one of the lawyers said the jury thinks of the victim." She began to cry again, put her arm around him. "You'd feel better if you could."

"There'll be lots of time for it."

"That's what I said to Mother. You're so—so dead."

"Is Dr. Ross coming?"

"Yes."

"How did he—take it?"

"You know."

"He'll blame me."

"He can't."

"You'd be surprised," he said and felt again the hot sorrow rise up in him that whatever he had done was not enough; his accomplishments in this partnership were nothing, his existence in it a guarantee of failure. Now he thought bitterly, now wise man, teach me how to walk upright with the load. I saw him again and did not stop him.

"Why! Why!" Roselee cried and he couldn't answer.

They drank coffee and were frightened together and she repeated the things she had heard the lawyers say. They tried to solve their fears with sensible talk, but what they spoke of was so irrational, so unnatural, that no amount of talk could leak sense into it.

At last she took her purse and said she must go, fumbled with her car keys, and, at the sight of her bewildered search, pity bled through his head once more. He kissed her gently and told her to come again. She said she would.

"Uncle Gavin is driving. He may be there now. I should be there for him."

"Yes."

After she was gone he lay again on the chesterfield and smoked, looked at the ceiling and wondered if he would ever sleep again. An hour passed.

The telephone rang and Roselee said, "He's here."

David thanked her and they paused a moment with nothing now to tell one another and hung up. By night he still had not slept. Inspector Day called and told him to come to Central Police Station. He shaved, put on a fresh shirt, put off leaving as long as he could, finally picked up his coat, looked at the telephone and knew Gavin Ross was not going to call.

CHAPTER 28

"Thanks, Inspector."

"You understand what I've said?"

David understood all right.

Day continued. He spoke in a quick husky voice as if he had something wrong with his throat. "It's a matter of using your head; believe me, you've never needed it more. You and I know that if you'd really thought he was going to kill her you'd have done something about it. Just don't exaggerate or dramatize yourself or you'll wind up before the fact. If I wasn't sure you're in the clear I wouldn't say this. Not so very long ago you'd have stood a good chance of hanging."

David turned away sickly.

"Is he crazy?"

He hadn't known he would say it, how foolish it would sound, putting him back in that world beyond the line where one stood very small against the furniture, insignificant beside the big ones, the ones who coldly administered a justice unintelligible to one's own bewildered why, what for.

Day shrugged. David looked about the office again and wished it were solid, that it held some point of familiarity.

"Thanks, again. Should—should I see him?"

"You don't want to, do you? It's not my department. If he wants to see you, I guess. You'll have to talk to one of his lawyers. Not right now anyway."

David almost said thanks again and bit it off. As Day said, a crown witness. Why then did he feel like a prisoner?

Day held the door. "It should go quickly."

"Isn't that the doctor I saw at Green's?"

"Kerr."

"Suppose he'd give me something to make me sleep?"

"He might," Day didn't move. "Ask him." He started to close the door. "I'll be in touch with you."

"I know."

He caught the doctor and was told to get his own physician to prescribe a sedative.

"I have no doctor." He reeled and Kerr said, "Oh damn it, come in here," led him into his office and gave him a phial of phenobarbital. "These will do you a few days."

His brown eyes sagged at the corners, but his face was sour, not sad, as if he knew about the eyes and resisted the doggy look.

"I'll be all right in a day or two—I'm just not used to . . ."

Kerr gave him a quick look. "A day or two! You're just starting, Newman, don't let anyone fool you. You're out on your feet now but just wait . . . Oh go home and go to bed."

He wandered the streets for nearly an hour before he collected his purpose, found himself standing at a bus stop and realized it was past one a.m.; no buses would be running. Cars flipped past in endless idiot procession. What did so many find worth rushing through the night to reach? The warm sick smell of exhausts fouled his throat. Overhead a network of wires clutched arthritically at the city, holding off the sky.

A man stood in the cavernous doorway of a bond house. All gray and wasted, phlegm spat out on the pavement, blank-eyed, head nodding in palsied ruin. I should go home, David thought, and he was thinking of Mouse Bluffs. He stood looking at the derelict, their eyes upon one another, no comment in either. The man moved farther into the shadows, his back against the wall as if he were climbing in a far place; then by inches he lowered himself into the dark corner, gave a little high-pitched giggle of achievement. If I ask him he'll tell me he's Sholto Todd or David Newman or . . .

He bent forward from the waist and whispered, "What's your name?"

No answer. Only the slithering urgency of rubber on asphalt, far away a clarion horn. David raised his hand. The cab stopped down the street and, without looking back, he ran to join it.

Gavin Ross was sitting by the window at Darcy's desk, one hand resting on Darcy's typewriter.

"It's you at last."

David's fingers curled around the phenobarb in the pocket of his tweed jacket. His tongue stumbled against his teeth. No sleep yet. He stood in the middle of the room and looked at the doctor's back, went to the closet where he knew Darcy had a bottle of whiskey.

"Drink, sir?" His tongue felt thick.

As he brought out the bottle, Darcy's coats churned. A tangle of wire hangers clattered to the floor.

Ross got to his feet. How old he looks, all uncolored and lined and cragged with a mountain of living. The doctor looked at the bottle and shook his head. David poured a drink into a soiled glass he found on the coffee table and gulped it down. He began to cough.

"That's the way of it, I suppose." Ross's eyes were on the bottle still. "Out guzzling this night."

"Well, it's A Way."

"Don't fool with me. Sit down. Now, I've got some questions to ask you."

"I know."

"By God, you're impertinent." Ross's big hands tightened convulsively. "What's this thing about you and Darcy?"

"What thing?" Good man, do I lay out my bones for picking all in an instant?

"You know what I mean. He says he did this terrible thing because you were going to marry that girl."

"He'd better plead insanity." David reached for the bottle between his feet again.

"Leave that muck alone! I'm asking you something."

"You're asking me if I'm homosexual. I'm not. I can bring several young women to testify for me and one very nice professional I've used for years. That is I did until a couple of years ago when Darcy decided to share . . ."

Ross looked ill, said scornfully, "I expect you could."

"I can't speak for Darcy. Do we know our brothers? He apparently speaks at length for himself."

"You know what the Crown is going to do with this?"

"Two gay boys. One gay boy and one foolish one."

"You're not boys, you're men and it's time you faced up to it." Ross struck his fist against the chair-arm. "You've had half a dozen different jobs since you made a fizzle of putting yourself through college. You can't stick to anything."

Except Darcy.

"Sir, I know how you—but it doesn't help getting worked . . ."

"I'll get worked up if I damned well please. By heaven, I do not understand you. Your mother was a fine woman."

David felt his face burn as if he stood too near a fire. "Maybe my father was a son of a bitch."

"Ach!" Ross made a deep guttural sound in his throat, got to his feet. "You were a stray and I took you in and you've acted the part. I knew better. All my instincts advised against it. You've poisoned the well."

"Is that what you came to say?"

"I came to say that Charles is trying to drum up an insanity plea and you're not to help him."

"You'd rather he hung."

Ross moved his shoulders wearily.

David took the bottle and drank from it. Ross's eyes flooded with utter disgust.

"No flaws, even on the gibbet," David said.

"There's nothing wrong with that lad. All that's wrong is you and your capers and juvenile delinquency at the age of manhood. He's as good as dead. There's the gay life and the guzzling for you. You might as well have shot him."

"I might as well, you're right. You're always right."

Ross went to the door. "Don't ever come to my house again."

When he was gone David studied the phenobarb and the whiskey in turn, heard again and again the closing of the door, then realized it was still open and banging gently against the wall, in the breeze that blew over Darcy's desk and Darcy's typewriter. Wondering if there were enough phenobarb, he got to his feet and closed the door. Maybe phenobarb and booze simply interacted and he'd bring the lot up, then have neither. Yes, like Arthur Newman he'd contrive a lash-up. Lash-ups like bad lungs and bad-heartedness were in the blood, his blood and Arthur's blood, laced together by the double-tongued dog-whip. He sat down and gave the whiskey another try. It worked. Bare bodkins do not become me. Darcy and the bare bodkin. Where had Darcy got the knife? Lots of knives. But this one performed so well. Cut Pamela's useless pretty head right off Pamela's useless pretty body. No insanity in the Ross family. If members of the Ross family go mad, we hang them for their foolishness. No, not their foolishness, for allowing their drunken fornicating friends to drive them to such delinquent acts as cutting off a woman's—child's—head. Darcy and the grand scale. Couldn't even fail on a mediocre level. Darcy would go out with the sun darkened and the veil of the temple rent, sane but temporarily foolish. My brother.

The whiskey wasn't going to do it.

His head jerked back with a howl that strangled in his throat; he smacked his head back and forth between his palms. When the spasm was past, he picked up Darcy's bottle and heaved it over Darcy's typewriter and Darcy's desk right through Darcy's window.

At noon the telephone rang. He roused, looked at it and let it ring. It rang on forever, stopped only to begin again. A sweat of rage sprang over his eyes. He grappled with the receiver.

"Waterman here. Do you need me, David?"

"Frig you."

He hung up and rubbed his face. Now why did I do that? I have to go to the toilet. Maybe I should do it right here. Who cares? He tried and found he couldn't. Habit. Habit takes us to the backhouse. Backhouse. He staggered to the bathroom.

"You look like hell because you are hell," he told the face in the medicine-chest glass. Shopped around for bargains, even in hell, hell in Darcy, hell in Arthur, and here was the free-with-every-purchase standard model.

He turned on the shower, pulled off his clothes with awkward fingers, stood for a long while under the stinging spray. When it was over, he felt better.

"What did you do to Uncle Gavin?"

Roselee stood in the doorway of the bathroom.

He pulled the towel around his waist and said, "That's a nasty habit and you've been doing it since you were so small it didn't matter."

"Does it now?"

He went to his bedroom, yanked on a pair of jeans. "Not much. What did I do to Uncle Gavin?"

"He had some kind of an attack when he got home but he's all right now. He was out like a light."

"Probably a sudden attack of heirlessness."

She looked confused.

"Don't mind me, I'm always like this two mornings after a murder."

"Don't be hard."

"Sackcloth? Daub my brow with ashes?"

"Do you know they can't bail him? Anyway mother couldn't have him—she's prostrated. He wants to see you."

He was silent, said at last, "I don't know whether I could."

"Would you try?"

"Not yet."

"Was Uncle Gavin mad at you?"

"He thinks I'm a gutless wonder who took evil delight in leading my-boy-you're-all-we've-got into the paths of—wherever I led him."

"I'll tell him."

"No you won't." He glared at her. "Because you don't know."

"I do."

"It's all he's got. Now. Don't take it away from him."

She fumbled for a cigarette. "Why are men always so rational?"

"They're not, as you must know by now. Roselee, I'm sorry; clear out, will you, and let me be."

The telephone rang again. As he answered it, he hoped it would be Waterman. It was Lilja.

"David? Do you want me?"

After a moment he said in a low voice, "No. Thanks. Stay out of it. Thanks. It—well, you know."

"I know. Davie?"

"Yes," he said, "I do."

"Good-bye."

Roselee looked at him curiously, her face flushed. "That was a woman, wasn't it?"

"Go along home."

"Was it her?"

"Yes."

"Why doesn't she leave you alone?"

"She does."

"Not really."

"I'll tell you then," he said savagely, "just to set your mind at ease. Because I'm in love with her and have been since I was eleven and always will be. Is that clear?"

"It's wrong," she said whitely and went to the door. "I'll win."

"What?"

"What I set out to win. I always do."

"Well, bully for you. Convey my respects to your mother. She'll forgive me. She's a very forgiving woman."

"Yes, after she's decided what to forgive. Often it has nothing to do with what offended her in the first place." She smiled briefly and looked very hurt and tense and he wished there was something he could say to set the world right for her. "I'll be back," she promised.

The newspapermen began their phoning and finally ringing of the doorbell, so he dressed and went out and walked without destination till he was exhausted, then discovered that he had walked himself to Green's.

"He's gone to the funeral parlor," Crossen told him and asked if he'd had lunch.

David said no, and Crossen rang and ordered coffee and sandwiches, which a strange woman brought on an enormous silver tray. David took the coffee. It tasted bitter and old and his stomach refused it; he tried to eat a sandwich and found he could not.

"You look ghastly."

"Do you think he would want me to go there?"

"No. I do not."

David nodded. "I've got this—this floating . . . The feeling you have when you've slept too long and wake up in a strange room. I didn't really want to see him. It's a nightmare. I don't know why I came here."

Crossen said steadily, "Go away then."

"You don't like me, do you?"

"Whatever gave you that idea?" Crossen smiled tightly. "I might have. But you're another one who lives alone. I've had twenty years of it. It's quite a bellyful."

"Why do you stick it then?"

"There's a good question." Crossen studied it. "Maybe because he fascinates me. No. Let's be honest. I just hope some of it will brush off on me and if it doesn't then at least I've been part of it."

David laughed and, when Crossen looked at him oddly, said, "Just—echoes."

"Oh? Well." Crossen gathered his thought, said, "He'll be all right. After a time. I know him. It's just that he's been at it for over twenty years, his perfection. Only there was never any perfection and I think he knew it when he decided not to buy you. That's when he really knew. In a way . . ."

"You're glad."

Crossen didn't fight it. "Yes."

"There'll always be you, eh? Well, well."

"There never could be you."

"No."

"And to tell you the truth I don't think he wants to see you. Oh, he'd be perfectly splendid about it, you know him, but he wants to get it done with and you could scarcely help him forget. I hope they don't drag out this beastly trial."

David rose. "Excuse me, I feel a sudden attack of nausea coming on."

"I shouldn't wonder. Good-bye, Newman."

Outside he stopped, his breathing heavy as if he'd come from physical combat. Pretty soon there'll be only Darcy and I'll have to go. The others don't want me or I don't want them. There's just Darcy. And that fits no category of wanting.

Now all I need is for Charles to come and tell me to remember Darcy's schizophrenia or manic-depressive psychosis. No doubt they've picked out a category by now. All they require is someone like Waterman to give him the once over. He's mad. He's sane. Waterman can play it either way. It figures too. He was. He wasn't. He's as sane as I. Ha. *And do you qualify as an expert?* No one more expert. He took a shot at me once. *Did you not take a shot at Arthur Newman and, even as your finger pressed home on the trigger, see that he was in the line of fire?* I missed. *Didn't Darcy?* Darcy has done murder. *And you? Murder is old hat for you and Darcy Rushforth.* He does not honor his father and mother; he drinks and fornicates; he loved his brother in crime which manifolds the sin. *Is it better not to love your brother? Say this much for Darcy. He loved. You did not.* I carried his burden for him. *No man carries another's burden; that's a dream two thousand years old. You did what you did to save yourself; how long must you live to learn this?* It is bitter. *Is it not more bitter for Darcy who had no burden? It's worse not to bear the burden; hasn't Waterman tried to tell you this? While you carry your guilt as a load upon your back, you may become a man; without guilt you are a brute and men must destroy you. Pity Darcy because he is not mad, not guilty, not loved. Darcy dies twice without your pity.*

I sat in a warm car with the idiot-dedicated Green and saw Darcy's face by the light of Green's headlamps, saw killing in Darcy's eyes where I have always seen it, heard again those words: *I'll kill her first*, knew the time had come again and did not stop him, saw my dark brother waiting to do his work and let my mouth close over the warning, saw him in the shadows as I have seen him now for years, watching, waiting, and did not catch his hand warmly in mine to stay it. I feared that handclasp, told myself that whoever survived it would be a killer.

Pity Darcy who would not suffer idiots? Pity Darcy who sprang from his emptiness at last to passion and guilt? No. Pity rather the one who had to destroy Darcy or live forever too near the sucking vortex of Darcy's empty heart.

Gavin, good man, I give you Darcy, my dark brother. I killed him for you.

No! I killed him for myself. Sing, howl at me of time, of Darcy dying, dying, never dead.

"What in the world are you walking along talking to yourself for?" Charles threw open the door of the Buick. "Get in, boy."

David got in. "I won't do it."

"That goddamned Gavin."

"No. It wouldn't work because I don't believe it."

"You've got to. It's the only sane answer. Come on, David, pull yourself together and we'll get Darcy out of this bloody mess."

"Us boys. Another parking ticket to fix."

"It can be done. My lawyers . . ."

"You've got a phantom limb, old man. He's going to die."

"For killing that moron! What kind of bullshit is this? Listen, you may think you're a poet or something but my boy is in jail and you helped put him there and you can help get him out. This is not the time to get poetic."

"You're right. I'll bake him a cake. A sunshine job. Something practical. You know I knew you would come along right here on this corner and tell me Darcy was temporarily insane. A warning, an aura. Tell me this, does Darcy want a cake?"

"By God, I'd like to punch your snotty nose."

"My pleasure. Everyone else has had a go at it. Honor thy father and mother. Old man, what old ears couldn't hear on Sinai I hear. Honor thy children. Unless we honor our children they die in dishonor and posterity will not know us. All. Especially

Darcy. Must I be his little father forever? Howl it. Especially Darcy."

Charles cried in alarm, "What's wrong with you?"

"It is late. Too late for you. Too late for the good man. The twentieth century rolls on, we kill the little bastards one way or another. I am temporarily insane."

Charles looked aghast at the inert form and panicked. Couldn't take him home. Couldn't leave him alone at the apartment. Or take him to a hospital. They might find him really crazy and he wouldn't be able to testify at all. Keep him from talking to anyone, the lawyers had said. He bent forward and smelled David's breath hopefully. After a long perspiring moment he remembered Solveg and took David to her without considering whether she would want it or not. What Charles decided upon Charles did.

CHAPTER 29

It was two months before David visited Darcy in the jail. The city was in the grip of an August heat wave. A blister of a day. He carried his jacket along the street but, once inside, he felt cold, felt that moisture must drip from the dark walls of the police station. Yet the policemen in their blues looked hot and Day mopped his face with a linen hand-towel. The window above Day's head, shelled molten by the sun's glare, showed the ragged top of a distant elm, limp and motionless, as if the intensity of the heat had glued its leaves.

"I just thought I could make it easier for you." Day mopped again, looked at the thermometer. "It must be good for the crops." Everyone said it, acknowledged that this city was particularly dependent upon the crops, sweated and mopped and beefed and took in each other's laundry on a million-bushel scale; guilty because they did not harvest or help with the harvest, they allowed weather reports to grow like parasites in their brains. "Figure at this stage rain would do them more good."

David put his jacket on. "What was it you wanted?"

Day found himself wishing violently that he could leave well enough alone. Not since the boy-killings right after the war had there been a case with so damned many people to feel sorry for.

"Don't get him wrought up."

Color stained David's pallid face. "I'm not liable to."

Day returned awkwardly, "What I mean is—try to go on about —ordinary things if you can. There's a pretty fine line."

"Mr. Sherman told me."

Talk about ordinary things, he told himself as the turnkey led him along the dank concrete way, keep him sane enough, just; all right; the crops, a fine crop we had this year, Darcy man.

Darcy looked so much himself, so ordinary, the white shirt immaculate, open at the throat, the thick mat of chest hair showing darkly as he turned and smiled, that David could think of nothing quite ordinary enough to say.

He sat at the other side of the table and Darcy said, "Hi, glad you came."

"Hi." He managed to light a cigarette.

"You look like hell, you must be taking this hard."

"You know me, mountains out of molehills."

Darcy laughed, an old low ironic chuckle, and placed his palms flat against the table. Disregarding the officer's gesture, he leaned forward, eyes still full of gentle laughter.

"Still think you're the son of God?"

While David was reeling in pursuit of this, "You're not, you know," Darcy said. "False premises, man. Remember what I told you once, there's no elixir of life, just water in that well. Are you still at the apartment?"

"No."

"Why not?"

"I've been sick. What the eminents used to call a nervous breakdown I guess. I'm staying at the Franks'."

"You should have stayed there! I think of you there."

"I couldn't."

"Why are you shaking? Sherman says it's a pity I'm not a veteran, juries are often favorably affected by it—sentimental, you know. It shows you how much our age loves the specialist. How is it at Franks'?"

"All right. I'll leave soon. Dan wants to come and see you. Would you?"

"Not yet. Maybe. If I start to chicken. Is he saving you?"

"He tries but he's too bloody good now to save anyone."

"Ha! That's my boy." Darcy's eyes glinted. "Maybe he's not

too good to save me. I need the best unsullied Daniel to save me. Only weaklings feel their sins have to be understood before they can be saved." He watched his fingertips and hurtled on in a low voice. "I've done a lot of thinking, that's why I asked to see you— about us. The first time round," his eyes met David's and flickered back to his hands, "there was no ignorance of the law—and you know I don't mean Day's law—but also no imagination for the consequences. It never bothered me but this time I knew and I knew what would happen and I went ahead and I could have stopped myself but it still—the victim—doesn't bother me. Sometimes I lie there and I think of all of you and how I've got you in my palms, you'll marry and have kids or die early or late and this will be part of it all, it'll go on Darcy forever, the alterations I've made will still be felt five hundred years from now and whatever you write I'll be there in it for good, you'll never be shut of me. Maybe I thought of this at the time: call it power if you like but I knew what I was doing and I knew what would happen so it must have been worth it to me, do you see? I don't suppose you could get the old man to shut up about mental hospitals, could you?"

David said presently, "I don't have much influence."

"He's trying to buy psychiatrists all over town. It's just that I might fall for it in a weak moment and you know . . . Well, you know."

"Yeh."

"I just don't figure I'd be good at it." There was a small grudging note of pleading in his voice. "Are you working?"

"No."

"Not writing?"

"No."

"But you've got to, otherwise there's no point."

"I will again, some day."

"Some day!"

The officer got to his feet.

Darcy flung himself back in the chair, one arm draped over the back, "Okay, see you around."

David said good-bye.

"They won't let me have my typewriter here, you have it, I won't be needing it. Maybe I'll make a statement. *On the Eve of his Execution*—that sort of crap's got to be writ by hand. It'll bring me to near my million words. Big deal. And listen . . ."

The officer touched his arm.

". . . even if you're not the son of God at least you thought you were and you had the guts to look, see—even if you looked in the wrong place, you looked; that's it, see, you were right even when you were wrong, a capacity to look. There is no God, man, only the animal who coupled with Mother. Tell Roselee to stop coming here! I'm sick of her loving face. Do that, will you? She'll do it for you. I don't need any of them."

"Take it easy; I will."

"Sure. You will. And don't come here again even if I ask for you, let them do it fast. I can't wait and wait like you. I chose this, get it? I chose it and I want it and I want it quick. Think on these words, you slob, they're more important than any I've said this day." He grinned as if in mockery of their old ironies. "And remember. Don't come. I'll remember your face, you son of a bitch." His voice was low now, his eyes full of a strange softness.

David tried to speak but a cold hand seemed to close over his mouth. The officer nodded brusquely and the turnkey was waiting.

Roselee came that night and stayed till dawn with David, sitting and talking and sometimes lying with her head in his lap, while they rambled through old disjointed memories, half-shared and having nothing to do with Darcy, until at last she fell asleep and he dozed with his palm on her brow.

He saw Darcy next in court. There were serious gaps in Darcy's audience; Mary, Gavin, Marvin Green did not come to witness Darcy's justice. After considerable argument between counsel, Darcy's statement on the night of his arrest was admitted as evidence . . . "She was an animal. She had no brains." And with the words, the person of the victim walked through the courtroom and went to sit with the jurors. David, numb, learned how Darcy had taken the sharp, sharp knife, a knife he had had since boyhood, kept with him always, and removed the head without brains, brains being the prize and the worth in the time of Darcy; Oh Lord, without I.Q. we are as sounding brass. Basil Waterman, distinguished in precise morning coat, delivered the *coup de grâce*, pronounced Darcy sane within the meaning of the law, and the jury did what it had intended to do all along, gave Darcy the achievement he thirsted for. In this place, contrary to Ethics and Moral Philosophy as taught at Knox Hall, the law neither punishes nor reforms but eradicates, and responsibility is the coat left outside in the hall with the briefcase and bus tickets. Darcy stood, "pale and drawn," the newspapermen wrote, as Mr. Justice Cornish delivered sentence, wished mercy on Darcy's soul. Darcy turned as he was led away to wink at David, and Roselee clutched

David's hand, as if it were his heart or hers and she could hold off its breaking. If the newspapermen saw this, they did not write it; they were having trouble conveying to their readers the Crown's infusion of the sexually abnormal into the crime and had no wish to include details that would spoil the effect.

The trial took two and a half days and the jury considered for thirty-four minutes, fast enough to suit all victims.

"Mr. Green wants to see you," Solveg said.

"Well, I don't want to see Mr. Green," David told her softly. "Look, Mrs. Frank, I'm not being rude. I just couldn't stand it. Tell him I just couldn't. Maybe I'll do it after but not now."

"He means well."

He continued to stare at the ceiling. "Nobody ever meant as well as Mr. Green. It's just—I don't think I could stand to be forgiven. You tell him. Dan Backhouse dishes out more forgiveness than a man can sanely bear."

"Oh, David," she murmured reproachfully. "Very well, I'll talk to him." She went to the door, turned and asked with an air of bewilderment, "Are you waiting for something?"

"No."

She went downstairs. Marvin Green stood beside the enormous floppy fern at the mullioned windows, looking out over the yellowing garden.

Solveg began, "He's . . ."

Green turned and smiled faintly. "It's all right. I just wanted to tie up . . ."

She was a magnificent woman, her golden brown hair still thick and glossy, her body heavy but graceful, full with living. He looked at her eyes again. It's the eyes, he thought, the way they go up at the corners; it makes one think of old and primitive courts and regal women of faraway places. She gave him a long steady glance in exchange.

"You've had a dreadful time," she said and it was just right. She told him, "He simply lies there as if he were waiting for something."

"He is."

"Not that. And whenever I ask him what it is he says there's nothing. He won't even see my daughter and they've been friends for years. He talks to Jon but only about football games or chess and sometimes to Roselee—the Rushforth girl."

"I understand how he must feel. In any case, I can't help

thinking he would like to see me. Sometime soon. I'll call. May I? You can keep me posted."

"Of course."

"He's as innocent in all this as my girl was and she suffered only a moment. It was her only suffering."

"I believe that."

He picked up his hat.

"You're a very generous man."

He smiled briefly. "Not really."

"Would you—like a cup of coffee? In the kitchen. I mean," she laughed, "I always make a pot at this hour, I put it on just as you came in."

Her smile was gentle and assured. She had sensed his loneliness and touched it instinctively with warm certain fingers.

"Yes. I'd like that very much."

He threw his hat down and followed her and, while they sat and talked, he felt something relaxing within him. I've been at it again, he thought. I never give up. A plan had been growing to put Crossen in the offices and take David as his secretary; now, for the first time, the plan lay cold and impossible. How we go about our devious ways to get our slaves. Those nights of talk with youth in the house were gone. David would never be young again; the impediment of his lost youngness would lie between them like a rotting corpse. He watched Solveg as she sipped the thick black coffee, her slow almond eyes touching his briefly, and was glad he had come to lose this last illusion.

That night the newspaper carried word that the defence was appealing the judgment in the Rushforth case on the grounds that Mr. Justice Cornish had erred in his direction of the jury.

The following afternoon Christine telegraphed David: *Gavin has had another stroke. Come if you wish.*

Daniel rushed around worriedly and offered David money, would not believe, in spite of firm reassurances, that he had enough. Jon drove him to the bus terminal.

He was just in time to catch the six-thirty bus going west. His mind felt cleansed and weightless suddenly, as if some old greedy fungus that had slowly been absorbing more and more of it had been abruptly excised. Mouse Bluffs was the source. There he would draw deep breaths of past and present, find a clue he was still seeking, clue to Darcy, to Darcy dying. As soon as the bus, picking up speed, had passed the outskirts of the city, he fell asleep; he did not rouse even when they sped past Headingly Jail where Darcy waited.

No one met him.

He walked through the evening-splashed streets of Mouse Bluffs and smelled the gold of a hundred piles of burning summer.

Christine opened the door and said, "Hello. Your room is ready."

He took his things upstairs and washed, then went to the door of the big bedroom on the second floor. Dr. Ross was in the bed and Cassie sat in a rocking chair, very still. She placed a finger to her lips, so he stood for a moment watching the old man's chest rising and falling, listened to the whistle of the old man's breath and felt purged, full of enormous energy.

He left the room quietly and joined Christine downstairs in the little parlor.

He asked, "How is he?"

"You know strokes, forever or tomorrow."

"What did you mean, another?"

"The doctor says he must have had one before."

"What doctor?"

"There's a new man here. Elliot. He came in June, straight out of college."

"Why does he say that?"

She looked very old and tired and he saw, in the slanting light from the lamp, that the blonde hair was filled with gray.

"Because he says he saw it at the hospital. I never noticed. He says Gavin had lost some of the use of his right hand and that his eyelid drooped. I never noticed."

David bent towards her. "He told me not to come here, to his house, ever again." It was a question.

"It was the newspaper. The appeal. He started off on a tirade against Charles. He wants Darcy to hang."

"I know."

"He's quite inhuman."

"No."

"Yes," she said. "Could I try one of your cigarettes? I've always wanted to try one."

He lit a cigarette and passed it to her.

"You are the only one." She sounded mildly surprised.

"What do you mean?"

"I couldn't think of a solitary soul but you. He'll need some-one."

"Even me. Why do you hate him?"

She started to cry and he went to her. "He took the river from me."

"Tell me. Here. Use mine."

"We had a row. You know—Darcy—and now he talks Roselee as if the dead ones or the ones without children don't count. So I told him flat the river was all he'd ever have and he said—he said he found her years ago and he and someone else buried her on the cliff. He says he did it to spare me!"

David held her in his arms a long while. "I expect he did," he said at last.

"He did it to have her to himself."

"She's dead."

"Now she is. Now she is. He and his Mary and his posterity! Oh God, now it's all nothing again."

"Mrs. Ross—Christine, a man makes a decision in a—a hot moment and it seems like the only decision and once it's done . . . Even if he starts regretting it five minutes later, it's done." Her shoulders shook. He promised, "I'll help you."

"You had better help him, there's no one else."

"I see." After a pause he asked, "Did you hear what I told you? That he doesn't want me in his house."

She got up brusquely and looked down at the ashtray. "Maybe I'll take it up. Don't worry, it's not his house. It's my house. Grandpa left it to me. It's never been his house and never will be."

After a long while he went upstairs, looked into the bedroom where Gavin Ross slept in Sir Richard's bed. Cassie rose, gave him her chair and went away with a whisper about tea.

When Ross opened his eyes, they focused for one malevolent moment on David's, as if he had expected or sensed David's presence. Then his hand moved to the bedside table. David saw a pad and pencil there, held the pad while the doctor wrote painfully across it with his left hand: *stray*.

David leaned over him. His gray eyes were wet but his voice was calm. "Old man, you're stuck with me. I'm here to help you." Ross turned his head away. "I'm all you've got."

Later that night Dr. Elliot came and left drugs and told David, "He may pull up a bit, he's got the constitution of an ox."

Elliot was a tall thin young man with a perpetual air of frantic haste. His thin blond hair stuck up in tufts and was receding above his temples.

"How far could he pull up?"

"Well, he'll never work again but he might get to use his hand again, maybe even walk with a cane. I've seen some fantastic things happen—for a little while."

"He'll get plenty of care." David went with Elliot to the door.

"Are you a member of the family, Newman?"

"In a way."

"God, the old boy's a tartar isn't he?"

"He can be."

"When I first came I went to him and asked if we could work out a deal, me taking calls for him and him helping me in the O.R. You know what he told me?"

"I can guess."

Elliot laughed. "He said I might need him but he had no need of me. Boy, it was rough. But he was right. I did it myself—with numerous referrals to him, I must admit—but I'm glad now. I'd be in a hell of a spot now if I'd chickened in the beginning in the O.R. You take care of that prescription and give him the other stuff every two hours. I'll be in tomorrow."

He rushed down the steps two at a time and hurled himself into his car. Prince, lying on the veranda, lifted his aged head with a look of utter disgust. David wondered how long it would be before Mouse Bluffs taught Elliot to go slowly, to wait and let life run through his hands so gradually he could feel its texture.

David was about to close the door when another car drove up. A Mountie got out.

David asked wearily, "Who are you?"

"I'm George Shale and you're David Newman and I want to talk to you."

"Come in."

"How's the doc?"

Everything in David was suddenly alert. Shale's eyes. His chest seized as if someone had struck him a sledgehammer blow: Darcy was talking again. He led Shale to the drawing room and closed the door. The room seemed stuffy; in the fireplace a mass of baby's breath was like clotted dust.

"What is it at this ungodly hour?"

"About the Yeates case."

A mighty hot wind of relief sucked through him. "Jesus, you guys never give up, do you?"

Shale grinned. "We have that reputation. Darcy Rushforth has told the Winnipeg Police that he killed Jack Yeates, that's how he got the knife."

"Are you re-opening the case?"

"It's never been closed," Shale said softly. "Do you remember anything you could tell me?"

"No."

"He could have done it, you know, he was sixteen and a big kid even then. And wild," he added suggestively. "They say he was into everything in town during the summers, girls, drink, gambling in the park."

"I don't remember anything about it. Go and see the Yeates'."

"I have. Elsie Henderson told me what she's told every Mountie for years, to get off her place."

"He's only saying it because he doesn't want the appeal made," David said.

"Are you sure he couldn't have done it?"

David's head was a giant turkey house, a million windows with Darcy in each. One fell open abruptly; he paled. Shale jumped after it.

"You've remembered something?"

"Just him showing me the . . ." Knife. The sharp, sharp knife, taken from the body in the oak grove of long ago, saved against the day of slaughter, to remove the head without brains.

"Go on."

"A knife. I remember him showing it to me. He said he'd taken it from the body. It was the sort of thing he did say."

"And . . . ?"

"That's all." His stomach began to heave. He saw a puff of satisfaction skitter through the constable's eyes and asked. "Is that why they move you around?"

"Move me?"

"The R.C.M.P. So that you never get to be part of a place. The town closed the case."

"That's why. Now look, if you think of anything else, give me a call."

"So that you can't change. You're always the same man with a different name. He had no reason to kill Yeates."

"He says Yeates stole ten dollars from him and they fought. Say hello to Mrs. Ross for me, will you and tell her I asked after the doc."

"I will."

He went upstairs again and took his place at the bedside and, when Ross woke, he helped him on to the bedpan, gave him a drink of water, sponged his face and told him with his eyes, there's only me, I'm all you've got, and felt his chest burn with the fury in the old man's eyes.

CHAPTER 30

Darcy was hanged early in the morning of the ninth of November. At daybreak the skies of Mouse Bluffs were a heavy whitish gray; wind flicked maliciously over the frozen ground to shake desiccated gardens. By noon the first flakes had begun to fall and in a matter of hours winter was a mile-high blinding over the prairie, howling menace at the town over the dead lip of the valley.

When the doctor woke, David whispered, "He's dead," and saw a grotesque mixture of sorrow and relief wash into the eyes.

Gavin Ross slept through that day. At suppertime he woke, sensed the winter outside, the new absorbency in the air.

David nodded. "It's storming."

Ross ate and slept again.

By Christmas he could work a little blue sponge in the fingers of his right hand and Christine would come into the room and stand beside him while he clutched at her hands. The holiday passed without a celebration in the big house. On Christmas Eve David walked to George Lee's restaurant and bought a small tin of fruitcake. He had a jar of Mrs. Wright's jellied chicken and with these Cassie made the doctor a Christmas lunch. Christine gave David a small red-wrapped package. He opened it and saw it was Sir Richard's watch which Gavin had carried: he thanked her without looking into her green eyes and, when he went upstairs, replaced it on the chest beside Sir Richard's bed.

Sometimes, while Cassie sat with the sick man, David led the old dog through the bluffs, walking the cold hours away; although he carried a rifle, as if he must have a reason for the walks, he never raised it. He tried, in the lonely woods, to discover the pattern of life through his own but could not recall with clarity any of the major disasters he had experienced. Once when he was a boy it had snowed in June; the saucer-big flakes clung to the surprised garden for an hour of incredible soundless beauty. Once he had got up before dawn on a Sunday and walked through the town, while the wonderful peace sang with tender urgency, go, go, go, and turned a corner to see Mrs. Spence on a stepladder, scrubbing the outside of her house in her best dress, her arms tied around with the legs of an old pair of longjohns to prevent the soapy water running down her arms, singing sonorously, perhaps as penance, "All Things Bright and Beautiful." Once, on a green and yellow summer's day, he and Lilja had hidden behind the caraganas back of the Hendersons' and watched the dogs coupling. These were the things that came, trickling like beads through his mind, while he searched for the terrors, the meaning of Darcy dead. They moved with minute majesty through his brain and all else had the quality of old newspaper clippings, dry and dissociated. Once he caught a flash of red through the trees and for a moment it was Arthur Newman in the old pyjama top; he sat at the foot of a tree to wait, while Prince's yellow eyes queried him, but of course Arthur too could not come. Arthur was with the dead unreal things and Prince was old and got cold easily and must be cared for.

Roselee wrote often; short notes, but he rarely answered. Now and then he got a letter from Jon, full of details about his studies, sometimes suggesting he write to Phillips, cheerful letters asking very little except the receiving of them.

On New Year's Eve he went to the hotel and drank too much, telegraphed Waterman: *Am okay. Noon came November nine. At absolute zero all molecules stand at attention. Stop writing. Please.*

In the morning a reply came: *Best news, Happy New Year.*

For a long puzzled moment he couldn't remember his own wire. It was evening before he recalled the words and was half-sick, half-relieved, wondering if they were true, if indeed Darcy dead were the light of noon for him.

Later he took one the pads of paper he bought for the doctor and wrote: *Hear this, Darcy. Sometimes too exhilaration tunnelled deep through the double man; the texture of young times together, the slow summered hours of boyhood, was drawn across time present like gauze over a lens.*

He reread the words slowly and put them by, to be taken out, he knew, again. This was the first he had written of Darcy; he would never be done with him. Had the double man, four-armed, four-legged beast, dissolved once for all in the hemp-woman's embrace? Perhaps this was noon, the only noon a man could know, the clear simple awareness that the beast lived still.

I hated you, Darcy, he thought, then shaped the words aloud, letting his lungs fill with the health of them. I tricked my hate in many guises but I hated you always for what you told me of myself.

He thought then, as he did often, of Darcy's words to him at the last: *I chose this, get it?* Still without meaning, yet he felt he ought to understand, that it was all quite simple, as if meaning stood, smirking and sidling, close to the words but refusing to be one with them.

He formed the habit of going to the hotel two or three evenings a week. He knew he was drinking too much and with cheerless determination. He was afraid to drink; he didn't like it and was subject to minor blackouts. But at the same time he was afraid not to drink.

Often he looked at the pitiful ruin of the old man and thought of Darcy's Eskimos, how, when one's father became old and sick and unhappy, one fulfilled the last terrible obligation, offered the right to die.

When the ice began to move, he found himself looking often at the old suspension bridge, still in use, still unsafe in a bad wind. The town used it but would not repair it, because it belonged to the Rashleigh estate. One day he went to the shed where Billy kept his tools and looked around. When he found what he wanted— saw, hammer, nails, two planks—he took them to the bridge, methodically measured and replaced two footboards. The bridge was a tyrant; the more he did, the more it revealed its sickness. Occasionally Billy came to watch him work, shake his head, say, "Davie, it needs a new bridge, can't patch up a thing as far gone as that. Not one man." Or loafers from town came and were amused and thought him nuts but none interfered or helped. He wanted no one. He spent the savings he wryly called his "England" money on ropes and timber and nails. The bridge carried one day into the next, kept him out of the hotel. He had vague plans that some day he might have it in fairly decent condition and could then approach the town about supplying new main posts but he didn't think too much about that, just about each day, each inch of victory over the rot.

By spring the old man could sit up and, when June brought Daniel Backhouse to Mouse Bluffs to help complete plans for the celebration in July, Gavin could get about with David pushing him in Ian's old chair. He could speak only with great difficulty and preferred to write on one of the little pads David kept handy.

Christine sat many hours at a time on the veranda or under the big elm at the riverside but she did not swim.

"My dear, you simply have to forgive him," Dan said.

"Why?"

"For your own peace of mind if for nothing else."

"I've never had peace of mind except for a short time through your letters. You're a fake, Dan, you always seem to be offering something wonderful but it never pans out."

"At least be kind to David. He's done a wonderful job."

"He does it because he wants to," she said with surprise. "Dan, I owe David nothing. No one does. He loves Gavin. It's more than either of them deserve. He's one for you. Hint away at him, he still thinks Heaven is just around the corner. He's out a couple of hours every day at that broken-down bridge patching away, as if he thought there might be something on the other side."

"Have you tried to do any of that work I asked you for?"

"*The Life and Times of Richard Rashleigh.* Please."

"I thought—you know when David couldn't."

"Wouldn't. I asked him to sort out that junk in the office as a start. There's a letter or papers or something Gavin's been keeping for him. I told him he might as well have it if he could find it. I don't think he even tried. When I looked in that evening to see how he was doing he was gone, out on that damned bridge."

"You know more about it than he does. I thought . . ."

"You thought what excellent therapy it would be. Will you please stop running the world? Dan, you're a quack doctor with a cure for which there is no disease."

Daniel went away undaunted; he made it a point never to be daunted.

The town began to catch the spirit of the coming celebration. Signs appeared in shop windows, in the Parish Hall, in the *Bluffs Era Press.* Townsfolk wrote to their relatives and invited them to come. The usual harbingers of gloom said it wouldn't be a success; Mrs. Spence tramped up and down in a rage, looking at the signs and snapping indignantly about waste and nonsense and johnny-come-latelies. City papers carried notices and press releases, prepared enthusiastically by Daniel and de-purpled drastically by sour editors. British American Oil, Purity Flour and other industries, under mild coercion from Reese Todd, promised floats for a parade. Families brought pioneer items, old spinning wheels, millstones, primitive farm implements, an old shawl someone's father had brought from an unspecified country in the Middle East, a tiny velvet box full of old English coins—all to be placed in a historical exhibit in the Orange Hall. Cassie nagged Christine and at length got more than a cold stare. Christine dumped a heap of shabby leather jewel boxes in her lap and Cassie proudly carried the last of the Rashleigh fortune across dusty Main Street. George Shale, summoned, took one look and began to swear; a town boy was hired to act as custodian. Old guns and old letters, even old marriage certificates. No one's treasure was refused. Reese Todd and Daniel and Brace Harvey, now mayor, drew up long and repetitive memos to one another and were tired and happy and wished volubly it were over but had never felt so useful or involved so many people in their schemes. After many days of deliberation the Henderson twins brought Daddy's carved buffalo-horn pipe-rack and chair to the Orange Hall and Daniel received both graciously, pressed them into service as helpers in the parade. "Scarcely anyone knows how to ride a horse properly but you boys do, we're getting some fine riding horses from Cutters' and we want some real cowboys." Matt and Herb grinned and admitted they could ride, went home and ordered cowboy suits from Eaton's catalogue. When the C.P.R. delivered them, the two men paraded before a delighted Elsie and a capering crew of little Hendersons and felt like boys again. Everybody loves a parade. Charlie Jaques bought paint and painted the hotel's hitching rail; if there were to be decent horses there again, they surely deserved some appreciation. Even the Indians from up Goose Plains way were to come and march in the parade. The government handicraft expert who had been sent to re-teach them the skill of beading found that all at once her pupils were in great anxiety to bead the lovely soft factory-made leather she had brought from Winnipeg. She felt quite flushed with success and wrote long letters to the department about how splendidly they worked, how work had given them pride, how under her gentle urging it was all coming back to them, till one morning she drove to the reserve and found the shacks deserted. Her pupils were gone and so were all the leather goods and head-dresses. Everybody loves a parade.

"Would you like to see the parade?" David asked Gavin and the old man wrote: *No. Dancing tonight. Save self.*

David nodded and helped him to the bed.

"If you want me, pull the cord."

The cord ran to the end of the garden and was attached to a small bell that David could hear from the bridge. Gavin nodded and closed his eyes. Downstairs David saw Cassie and Billy leaving for the parade and went to get his carpenter's box. He took off his shirt and had started towards the bridge when a small green English car with a Winnipeg license swung into the driveway.

"It seemed like a good excuse," Roselee smiled. She wore a

pink cotton suit and was fuller in the hips. Her face was tanned and her hair longer than she had worn it. "What a male man you are, lover, such a lovely hairy chest."

He grinned. "You sound like the old brat again," he said and kissed her cheeks, French fashion. "Do you need excuses?"

"For Mother I do."

"Why doesn't she come to see him?"

"Because he was against her, he wouldn't help save Darcy."

"He was right."

She turned towards the house. "But he was her—her everything and it's been hell for her. You know, all her friends being so damned good and not mentioning it; I think she'd rather they were cruel. She hardly goes anywhere. It's terrible to see her. I sometimes wonder if she's part of it, if no one can be as good as she is without life bringing about this gruesome—balancing."

"Your father—how is he . . . ?"

"He's never got over Darcy pulling that—gag?—and wrecking the appeal. I think he feels worse about being balked—no, that's cruel. He's all cracked up inside about Darcy. God, it's wonderful having someone I can say it to!"

She came very close to him, waited. Their lack of embarrassment during the bad time was gone, he discovered. Her nearness now had a sensual quality.

She turned away, as if sensing his unease. "Have you seen her?"

"Who?"

"She's in town. I saw her on the street with her father."

He started for the gate. She laughed and went up the steps.

"I'll announce myself."

He found Lilja and her father at the corner by Deacon's Drugstore. She looked very small and exquisite in white, very unBluffs-like.

Daniel beamed. "David, would you take Lily to the parade? I'm afraid I must be in one of the official cars and she insists she doesn't want to ride in it."

They sat in the summerhouse and listened to the bands thumping past the corner of Main and Crescent.

He said, "You're lovelier than you've ever been."

"I'm pregnant again."

"You said you'd never come back."

"Dad wanted me to come. Mother's getting married again. I thought I should come for him and—"

"I didn't know."

"Some women have it in abundance it seems."

"Are you still so jealous of her?"

"No." Her glance ticked away uneasily. "The Premier is coming. Daddy has to meet his train at noon." She took his hands. "I was wrong, you know that?"

"No you weren't. You did the right thing thinking it was the wrong thing, most of us reverse the process."

She flushed. "Can't I beat him even now when he's half dead and there's no—no Darcy?"

"You never had to."

She laughed and picked up her gloves, took his hand and placed it against her abdomen. "Another boy."

Without knowing why, he felt a sudden terrible pity for her, got up and took her in his arms, held her very tightly, that love might not flounder away into pity. She raised her head to meet his mouth.

After a long while she said, "That's what I meant. I was wrong. Can I turn back?"

His breath caught. "You know you wouldn't."

"I would."

He touched her waist with his hands. "Even with this?"

"Because of this."

She put her small smooth arms around his neck again. Far off the Legion band played "When Johnnie Comes Marching Home" and in the garden the birds cried answers with witless abandon.

He told her, "I can't leave him."

"Is he so perfect?"

He stared. Love has nothing to do with perfection; I have loved his good imperfections as I loved your imperfect beauty.

"All right, you win, I wouldn't." She laughed but there were tears in her eyes. "I'll go to church on Sundays and drink too much on Saturday nights. Sometimes I'll read Dylan Thomas to the children and teach them the difference between Rembrandt and Van Gogh. Sometimes I'll winter in Florida, and sometimes I'll have sordid little affairs. But mostly I'll be half-happy because I do like him and when I'm near him I tell him I love him and I mean it, but sometimes I'll think about you and for a minute I'll know I never come near happiness, then I'll have to tell myself it was only sex and I can go back to being half-happy again." She went to the door. "One thing, I'll never drive hell-bent for election the wrong way down a one-way street. You do that because you want to see their faces but it just makes me frantic. I'll be all right now; it's the excitement I miss. Would you kiss me, just once more?"

He kissed her and his arms ached with longing for the return of the keening joys she had always promised. He knew that her coming had been a test, a minute war she had won on the one-way street, saw how small his own part in it had been. Pity sprang tall; he could not now prevent it.

It's the way I have to go, against them, watching the faces so the journey will have sense. If there's the odd collision, that too makes sense and there's no frantic excitement to any of it; it's the quietest way forward I know.

The day wound slowly through the town. Visitors arrived and, when the hotel was full, were billeted in the homes of the towns-folk. The Premier came and looked stonily important as a premier should, stood under the scalding sun without flinching to unveil a cairn to the Rashleigh Group, delivered a ponderously eloquent speech as a premier should. In the Legion rooms back of the Wonderland and in the Prince Albert the men congregated and drank beer and promised one another that there would be a hot time in the old town tonight. By ten o'clock the crowds were thickening up along Crescent and Main and the town band played indefatigably beside the post office. The heat was oppressive; Deacon did a brisk business in mosquito repellent and the young people, tired of waiting for someone to start the promised street dancing, began to drift by twos down the long wooden stairway into the darkness of the valley.

Roselee stood on the darkened landing of the staircase, looking through the tree-tops towards the lights.

"Are you practising Juliet?"

"I'd forgotten how deep your voice was."

"You never knew." He stopped beside her to look out. Along the dusty heat-drenched street Japanese lanterns glowed orangely, surrounded by puffs of misty insects. "He wants to see the street dancing. They haven't danced in the streets since he was married."

"And won't for another twenty-five years."

The same people. She turned towards him and raised her arms. Wordlessly he took her embrace. The big blinding good yes burst through him. He had always know she would stand one day in this dark place and he would go to her and love her.

"I love you," he said without hesitation and her dark eyes bloomed. Her mouth opened to meet his.

"Is it over—the other?"

"Yes."

Her eyes turned smoky, believing. I would like you now to say it wasn't love, but it was, first love which clings to the mind long after first and love are without meaning. Lilja, I love you, always will. He kissed the silky underside of Roselee's arm. Not like this. Women as beautiful as Lilja must be loved; even when they shame themselves as she did today we don't stop loving them. But not like this.

"How is it that you didn't smell or hear or feel me loving you?" she whispered. "It's been all of me for so long."

"I think I did."

"I went to your room today." She turned and leaned against the round pane of glass. "Have you put up with that ever since you came?"

"Nosy."

"You don't hide things any more. Somehow I knew you wouldn't mind."

"I have nothing to hide."

He passed her and went up the second flight to his room. She followed. He sat with all the messages, the little sheets, torn from the many pads of paper, in his hands. *Drifter. Stray. Your mother was a fine woman. Fouled my house. Everything to Roselee. Leave my house.*

"Why do you keep them?"

"No reason. He has to have someone to blame and he hated to be nursed, me giving him his shots and enemas. He's always hated sick people, imperfection." He threw the papers to the floor. "And there are the things I said between notes. I'm no saint. I remember them."

How is it now to know the flaw was there all the time? Perhaps my father was a son of a bitch. Keep your own house in order. For you disorder is always somewhere else. Giving the right to live is the most terrible work we can do for others; your whole life long you've been at that work. Old man, honor thy children. It's late for honor.

"I haven't always been kind," he said.

And there's still one thing I must have from him. A dozen times I've begun to demand it and been afraid. If he rages, it will kill him.

"What does he mean, everything to Roselee?"

"He feels you're his heir. Though he has nothing to leave. To you. Do you want to go with us to watch the dancing?"

"Love to." She touched his cheek with her fingertips. "God I love that. Touch. Tell me we'll see a minister soon: this bodying part is hammering away at me like..."

"I'll see one tomorrow; can you wait?"

"Can you?"

"Just."

He kissed her, studied the lines of her face with a learning finger. Her dark eyes were a loving bright warmth in her dusky loving scented face; her subtle beauty fluttered through him like the pages of an illuminated book: you lovely, oh you lovely woman. He saw Mary's beauty in her for the first time, a shadow, the immense strength of this fragility.

Her voice, when she spoke, had changed pitch; love had moved lovingly into her throat. "Find me a priest all shaven and shorn."

"So right. Me, all tattered and torn."

"Me, all forlorn and such a maiden. That's what made her forlorn! I never guessed."

He turned her towards the door with a laugh. "Go get dressed before I take advantage of you. Tomorrow we'll ... Listen, I can't leave here. You know that, don't you? Even for a honeymoon."

"I know." She turned to go, stopped quickly. "I haven't been all honest. I came partly because Marvin Green talked to me. Partly. I was aching to come."

He flinched. Glanced away.

She continued pleadingly, "He asked me to tell you that whatever you might have taken, you gave more in return, he's going to marry Solveg Frank: it didn't sound so corny when he said it."

"Jesus!"

"He's nice. He feels badly about you, David, why don't you see him or write—make peace, he calls it?"

He began to laugh.

Her eyes blazed. "Oh, what's wrong with you?" she said but she knew and the pain of Marvin Green's forgiveness was in her too.

I should practise to be old, David thought, study age. The refinements of being old and nimble. The older you get, the better your footwork, a paradox. He got to his feet and walked through the papers on the floor, went down to the sickroom.

Cassie was putting out the doctor's clothes.

She whispered, "He wants to know where she is."

"Down by the river, I imagine."

Cassie made no comment. However life went, she was with Christine, part of Sir Richard's legacy. She left and David went to the bed. The old eyes followed his movements alertly, on guard.

David thought of Cassie, her loyalties, and how he had almost blurted his news to her; it boiled in him like sunshine. But his tongue had faltered; the old man must know first. The old man must approve, at least be worked into a position where he would consider it, would believe his opinion could aye or nay it.

A quick disgust flung itself against David's brain.

Why need I lean and hover and manipulate? Why can't I make him admit his responsibility in me? Darcy's gone. Mary, Christine; none of them count. There's only us. We two. He can speak when he chooses. He must speak. How can someone like Green, who moves as deviously as a European diplomat, be straight in these matters and we others, who have no guile, no eighteen millions accumulated out of a lifetime of astute manipulation, we who carry our straightness like our middling poverty, a flag, must pick and hesitate and shade our eyes from the hot glare of love?

Give me your full estate, old man. I've won the lion's share, Roselee. Give me your hand in love, all that's left.

"I'm going to ask you something important."

The doctor's eyes gleamed, waiting, but even with the bold clearing words in his mouth, David's tongue failed under the demanding helplessness of the man and he sought a distant point.

"Do you remember the night the old King died?"

The doctor's face began to work with desperate twitchings.

"Danshing," he bubbled through the slack mouth.

David felt his eyes begin to ache. He went to the window. Tomorrow then, after he had finished working on the bridge. He always felt tranquil then. *Danshing.* The old man had said it several times before but always casually, never like this.

David took a deep breath, returned to the old man. When he had finished dressing him, he rang for Billy and together they carried the old man down to the chair.

Roselee walked beside them, glancing at David often to share a heavy-lidded look of love discovered. The spokes of the chair's wheels glinted to the street lights. He thought, it's her genius, giving like this. He felt himself grow love-tall under her eyes, knew why she had always seemed so sparse, three pages in an essay, that all of her had been waiting to love. She gave as much to others and to objects as they required, waited her time with an honesty so straight it had seemed unintelligible.

At the corner of Crescent and Main the doctor raised his hand in signal and they stopped in the shadow of the big elm that marked the beginning of the Rashleigh estate. Because there was no sidewalk on this side of Crescent, only an occasional person drifted over to nod and speak to the heap of flesh in the wheelchair. The doctor reached for Roselee's hand and held it, as he watched the people far along the broad way forming up squares.

Matt Henderson's raucous voice began calling the do-si-dos into a microphone while Elsie, at the top of the grandstand, clapped happily. Beside her, the six children shouted with zestful abandon. David did not count them, as he used to, to see how many there were, whether now there were enough. There could never be enough. The scar ached. Still. Would always. Hear this, dark brother murderer. The twentieth century rolls on. We kill the children one way or another. Me first, always me first. He stood there, looking at Elsie, complacent among her children, felt the load on his shoulders, knew that, as Waterman had said, it would never grow lighter. But it was his load now, no longer the other man's. Darcy's words: *I chose this, get it?* slid into his mind again. Was this why Darcy had flung himself at death? So that David, alone, might carry his own load? No. Darcy had never joined the race, could not die for an idea or for another, could die only for himself.

Flanking the little Hendersons, Elsie's two brothers grinned approval of the festivities. The boys lived with the Hendersons now and worked for the C.P.R., Phoebe having gone to live at Reese Todd's as permanent housekeeper. Todd was old and frail but carried his work well; he had seen fourteen mayors come and go and had $93,500 in a bank in Winnipeg. Only rarely now did he ask Phoebe to get out the soft old shoes that had been his mother's and walk naked before him. They were old; the status quo flowed around them like milk and honey. Mayors come and go but town clerks go on forever; trulls come and go but housework goes on forever. Phoebe walked beside Todd today and nobody was disturbed. She nodded amiably to Elsie, saw the expensive silk dress covering Elsie's pregnancy and was glad. Elsie had a good man. Under the grandstand crouched Ally James, her little eyes spearing the dancers and strollers with hate. Her great suety body ached from twisting to peer through the slats and moving legs. Brace Harvey, the first railroad man ever to be mayor of Mouse Bluffs, stood at the corner and shook hands with all comers. Al Blake lingered for a while, recounting in loud voice all Brace Harvey's good works, including the cheque of long ago and hard times: it was safe now to admit having been poor. Calvin Harvey stood at his father's side and smiled a wonderful happiness; people had long since stopped asking Calvin what he was going to *do*;

whatever nature had intended for Calvin had been expended in grim yellow prison. Daniel Backhouse carried a glass of tepid lemonade to a drunken Indian woman lying on the steps of the Wonderland, under the impression that the poor soul had fainted. Herb Henderson in his grand Eaton's cowboy outfit saw Roselee and David and Gavin on their corner and ambled through the music and heat towards them. He pushed back his white stetson and nodded to David.

"Where's Mrs. Ross?"

David gave him a look of studied coolness; he was somewhat fed up with Henderson's asking this whenever they met. Herb leaned towards the doctor to shout as many did, under the impression that, sick, he couldn't hear.

"Remind you of your wedding?" He stepped back, pulled off his big hat. "For Christ's sake, he's dead."

Swing your partner, then you go, then you go. The glassy look in Henderson's eyes. Roselee's gasp as she withdrew her hand. *Allemande right and allemande left.* The way the whole town tilted as the long fire went out, shifted to slide dancers and strollers and pitiful celebration into the hushed immensity of the waiting prairie. *Swing your partner and promenade home.* Herb pushed the chair and Roselee hurried ahead through the night, the lacy white bloom of her crinoline brushing the air like cooling wings. At Sir Richard's house she waited for them, her dark eyes large, her breath coming in little sobs, and held the door as Herb pushed the chair up the weathered ramp.

They carried him between them up the stairs, the big old head rolling limply from side to side, as if in some wonderful child-deep sleep. Herb held the body against his chest while David pulled down the sheet. As he did so, one of the little tablets of paper rolled to the floor. Herb reached forward to close the mouth.

"You'll need a piece of lint to bind his jaw for a bit." David could smell Herb's pomade, hearty male scent redolent of barber shop and pool hall. He had dropped the white hat somewhere. "Where's Mrs. Ross?"

David picked up the tablet and turned it over. On it in the shaky familiar block letters: *What king?*

"She'll be down by the river, the big elm."

Herb glanced around the big room. "This is Sir Richard's room."

"It's his room."

Herb went to the door. "I'll tell her."

"No," David said, "I should."

Herb pursed his lips. "There's something I got to tell her. He made me promise not to but I figure I can now."

David watched him narrowly. "I guess I know. You tell her. Thanks Herb."

Herb hesitated, turned back, his shoulders twisted against the door. "You want some help? Laying him out? I did Daddy and Mummy and my sisters. Me and Matt."

"I'll manage."

Herb shrugged and went out.

What king?

Roselee touched his arm.

"Call your mother," David said, "and Dr. Elliott."

He sat for a few minutes in the chair beside Sir Richard's bed, then took the cool hand in his. He had never held it like this before. He turned it over gently, then drew up the sheet. In spite of everything else he had done over the months, the exercising, the bedpans and bottles, the shots, the spongings, he could not do this. Someone else would have to do it.

I loved you, good man, loved your good imperfections all my life. *It's the morbidity, d'you see, the morbidity of the unloved.* From a long way off he heard Ian's voice, saw Ian's sick hands over the blanket, knew now, acknowledged, that he too had not been loved. Long after a son's needs were past, his life had been spent upon winning, earning a father's love. Now, having failed, he had no father, only his own identity. A father's love? Ian knew it was never a father I sought. Darcy too? *There's no elixir of life, just water in that well.* My search was only a disguise, a cloak, for my desire to live in another. We own our own body, our time, no other. I see it now. While I look for another's place, my own dies for want of me. The future is not given to us by seed or plan or claim. Each seeks the future alone. Our own body, he repeated, our own time, our own life. *I chose this, get it?* With a crash it came. Darcy, I know now why you flung your manhood into the hemp-woman. You stole my sickness; wanted to live life through me. But at the last rejected it. You were right to die rather than live like that.

He climbed the stairs to his own room, took the sheet of paper with the words: *What king?* and turned it over. On the back he wrote: *I remember Darcy and I remember Ian. Both crippled with my sickness tried to make me straight. But most often I shall remember the night the old King died.*

He was looking at the words when Roselee came in, knelt on the floor and picked up the scattered papers, then sat leaning against the bed with her legs drawn up under her like a child.

"Is that Prince?"

He listened. "Yes."

"You were waiting for him to die."

I was waiting for him to claim me, yes. It is the same thing. When we claim a son we resign our portion of the future. But do not give it.

"I'll go with you," she said.

"Where?"

"Wherever you're going now. To England. Anywhere."

"Can you?"

He slid down beside her on the floor and touched her arms. She gripped his hands; her fingers were surprisingly strong, cutting in sudden fear.

"Can we really love and forget it all? I've never been loved by anyone."

It's the morbidity, d'you see . . . The echo brought a smile into his eyes.

"I do," he said. "And we will. How are your hands so strong?"

"Golf and driving Dad to the office now because he's so tired, and holding Mother when she cries and being empty for you. Can we make it right? All the hating and the—not being loved? The horror? Darcy?"

"We needn't." Their eyes met and she caught the sense of it. "I've a long way to go. It may take me ten years to get Mouse Bluffs and him out of myself."

She thought he meant Darcy, said, "I won't mind."

"I know you won't. And now shall we talk about it, about the long way and the things we'll do in it?"

"But first you'll make peace with him, David? Green?"

"The one man in my life who never wanted to live my life for me or blame me for anything and he wants me to forgive him for it."

"You will."

"Yes."

The hardest thing of all.

Soon I shall have to go downstairs to the office and find an envelope addressed to me. He saw himself very clearly with the letter, opening it to find his mother's words. The paper would be yellow, the ink old. And then . . .

What name would he find? No name at all? What man has a father?

He was still holding, he realized, the sheet of paper with the sketchy words: *What king?* Without looking at it he crumpled

315

it in his hand; calmly, knowingly, with the action, relinquished his long search.

Freed then to loss, the pain of the good man gone, his good imperfections vanished from the earth, "There's only," he said, "only one Gavin Ross in a man's life."

Roselee put her arms around him, for it was time to mourn and mourning in Mouse Bluffs must be done in private, spoken gently against the tender green of the valley, lest the wind, hearing, should tear it to tatters against the great sky.

A NOTE ON THE AUTHOR

Patricia Blondal, the former Patricia Jenkins, was born in Souris, Manitoba. She graduated from the University of Manitoba in 1946. She died tragically of cancer in November of 1959. She was married, the mother of two children and was living in Montreal at the time. *A Candle to Light the Sun* was accepted for publication just prior to her death and is her first published book.

A NOTE ON THE TYPE

The text of this book is set in a type face designed by John Baskerville, a writing-master of Birmingham in the mid-eighteenth century. During his career as writing-master and engraver of inscriptions he developed his ideas of letter design which are based on calligraphic forms. The type is wide and open, suggesting the vertical stress of the calligrapher. Baskerville type was used exclusively in Monotype until 1931 when the Linotype series was introduced as a facsimile cut direct from Baskerville's own matrices.